Praise for
MINDWALKER

'LOVED EVERYTHING ABOUT THIS BOOK!!
CANNOT WAIT FOR THE SEQUEL, MINDSTORMER!!!!!'

Jessica on Goodreads

'[It's] not only thought provoking, it's funny. As in, laugh out loud
in a crowded room funny.'

GC MacQuarie on Amazon

'If you love dystopian novels that somehow resonate profoundly
with the present, pick up this book today. I promise you won't
be disappointed.'

Megan Johnson on Goodreads

'A brilliant choice for a book club.'

Lynsey on Goodreads

'This book was surprisingly awesome. I enjoyed every minute of it.'

Haley on Goodreads

'This book IS JUST WONDERFUL. THE CHARACTERS MADE ME
LAUGH AND CRY … Definitely would recommend it to anyone!'

Kassidy on Goodreads

'It is one of the best books I've ever read.'

Bren on Goodreads

'The perfect book for someone who wants a heart-pounding and
thought-provoking thriller with a little romance on the side …
Best book I've read in a while.'

…ood on Amazon

MINDSTORMER

A. J. STEIGER

ROCK THE BOAT

A ROCK THE BOAT BOOK

First published in North America, Great Britain and Australia
by Rock the Boat, an imprint of Oneworld Publications, 2017

Copyright © A. J. Steiger 2017

The moral right of A. J. Steiger to be identified as the
Author of this work has been asserted by her in accordance
with the Copyright, Designs and Patents Act 1988

ISBN 978-1-78074-926-6
ISBN 978-1-78074-927-3 (ebook)

Printed and bound in Great Britain by Clays Ltd, St Ives plc

This book is a work of fiction. Names, characters, businesses,
organizations, places, and events are either the product of the author's
imagination or are used fictitiously. Any resemblance to actual
persons, living or dead, events, or locales is entirely coincidental.

Oneworld Publications
10 Bloomsbury Street
London
WC1B 3SR
England

Stay up to date with the latest books,
special offers, and exclusive content from
Rock the Boat with our monthly newsletter

Sign up on our website
www.rocktheboat.london

To Grandma,
for telling me stories when I was little and
thus igniting my love of fiction

PART I
REDUX

1

I wake slowly, with the sense that I'm floating.

The first physical sensation that registers is an ache pulsing between my temples. The next is thirst. I swallow, smacking my lips, and try to pry my eyes open, but they're glued shut. In the distant past, people would put coins on the eyelids of corpses to keep them closed. The detail comes to me at random, flickering through the inner haze.

Where am I?

Who am I?

My pulse quickens. Why can't I remember my own name?

Stop. Breathe. I walk through my identity affirmation exercises, and my name comes with a jolt. *I'm Lain Fisher. Mindwalker. Seventeen years old, student at Greenborough High. Brown hair, light brown eyes. I like chocolate and squirrels and the color pink.* The tightness in my chest eases. With a push of will, I break the seal of sleep-crust and open my eyes a crack.

I'm lying in a bed, in a room with soft eggshell-white walls. The light comes from tubes on the ceiling, bright but not glaring. I have the sense that I've just woken up from a long, complicated, and very stressful dream, but I can't recall what it was about. All that remains is a dim, grainy vision of someone's eyes—pale blue, like mercury and faded denim and clouds reflected in the ocean—but it's gone an instant later.

I rub my eyes, yawn, and stretch. There's a satisfying pop in my spine, like something shifting back into place. Then I frown, puzzled. Why aren't I in my bedroom?

My head feels oddly light. I touch my hair. It's shorter than usual. Did someone cut it while I was asleep?

On a table next to my bed stands a bouquet of daisies in a vase with a card propped against it. I pick up the card—which has a peaceful image of a garden on the front—and open it. *Get well soon, Lain. We miss you.* The card is signed, *Ian.* There are a few other names beneath it, names of my classmates from Greenborough High.

Was I in an accident? Gingerly, I touch my chest, my legs. I don't seem to be injured anywhere, and this doesn't look like a hospital room, or at least, not an ordinary one. Actually, it looks like IFEN headquarters. I recognize the style of the lighting fixtures, the off-white of the walls and floor, but there are no windows, nothing to help me orient myself.

Next to the card, there's a tray of food. Standard hospital fare: a bowl of soup, a blueberry muffin, and some red gelatin cubes. I'm not exactly hungry, but there's a hollowness in my midsection, a wobbliness in my limbs, that suggests I haven't eaten for some time. I should probably at least try to get something down, so I pick at the blueberry muffin. Once I've had a few bites, my appetite awakens, and I peel the cellophane cover off the bowl of soup. Steam billows out. With a plastic spoon, I scoop some of the yellowish broth into my mouth. It's bland but satisfyingly hot.

As I eat, I try to piece together how I got here. What's the last thing I remember, before waking up in this room?

Noodles float around in my bowl. They turn to yellow blobs as my eyes drift out of focus. I try to mentally retracing my steps, but there's a lot of fog. I remember going to school, sitting in the classroom at Greenborough High after a session with one of my clients, an old ex-soldier who wanted to forget the war. There's a vague recollection of receiving a text message from . . . someone. Probably Ian, since he's the only one who ever texts me.

And then nothing. It's like there's a wall in my head, blocking me.

My appetite has evaporated. I set aside the half-finished soup, push the sheets off, and climb out of bed. I'm wearing a hospital gown with a pair of pale blue cotton pants, and my feet are bare, the floor icy cold underneath them. I notice a set of blue slippers next to the bed, so I put them on and walk to the door. Beside it, there's a panel bearing the shape of a hand traced in green, but when I place my own hand inside, it doesn't respond to my touch. Unease prickles under my skin.

The door slides open, and I take a startled step backward. A woman in white stands in the doorway—I recognize her as Judith, one of the Immersion Lab technicians. She usually monitors my sessions. When her gaze meets mine, she freezes, and a deer-in-headlights expression flashes across her face. "Oh, you're awake!" She quickly pastes on a smile and steps into the room. The door whisks shut behind her. "How are you feeling?"

"I'm . . . fine, I guess." I squint at her face, as if it might reveal some clue about my situation. "What happened to me?"

She hesitates. Just for a heartbeat, but still. I'm immediately suspicious. "You needed a procedure, but you're fine now."

"What sort of procedure?"

She looks back and forth furtively. "I only came to check on you. Dr. Swan instructed me to inform him immediately when you regained consciousness."

So, I *am* in IFEN headquarters. I look her in the eye and switch to a tone I think of as my Mindwalker voice—level, calm, professional. "Tell me what happened."

She hesitates and glances over her shoulder, as if debating whether to make a run for it. Then she gives me an apologetic look.

"You've been through a very traumatic experience. You chose to have the memory erased. Dr. Swan performed the modification himself."

My jaw drops. It takes me a moment to find my voice, and when I do, it comes out small and unsteady. "What did I forget?"

"I'm not authorized to tell you." Her tone softens, turning apologetic. "You know how it is."

I do know. Clients who've just undergone neural modification are often confused and easily upset. Their recovery goes more smoothly if the people around them avoid talking about the procedure or the incident they erased and instead surround them with familiar, comforting things. It sometimes takes a few days or even weeks for them to get their mental bearings and start interacting normally with the world.

"Why don't you sit down?" Judith says. "You shouldn't strain yourself."

I shake my head, wincing as a small twinge of pain shoots between my ears. "I'm fine." Lightly, I touch my left temple with quivering fingertips.

So, I've chosen to have my memories modified. But why?

Statistically, sexual assault is the number one reason why females my age go to a Mindwalker. A cramp grips my stomach. That would explain why Judith is so visibly uncomfortable. No one wants to tell someone that she's been raped.

Yet something about this whole situation feels . . . off. For one thing, why am I in here, instead of the Immersion Lab? Or at home? Clients often don't remember the first hour or two after the modification; usually, they're taken straight home and looked after by their loved ones until the disorientation goes away. Of course, there's no one at home for me, except possibly my housekeeper. "I want to talk to Dr. Swan," I say.

"He said to wait until you were well-rested. He doesn't want to overstimulate you so soon after—"

"Judith. If you don't want me to get stressed out, then at the very least, let me see my guardian. Keeping a client alone and confined is absurd. I can't imagine that he'd approve."

She presses her lips together and looks away. After a few seconds, she lets out a small sigh of defeat. "Follow me."

She leads me out of the room and down a long, narrow hallway, softly lit with faintly bluish light. Though I've worked here for years, there are parts of IFEN headquarters I've never seen before, and this is—or was—one of them. An eerie silence pervades the air.

We get into an elevator, which takes us smoothly to the top floor of headquarters. She leads me to a door and knocks.

"Come in," Dr. Swan calls. His voice sounds deeper and hoarser than usual, as if he's getting over a cold.

Judith opens the door, revealing the familiar sight of Dr. Swan's office—the snow-white carpet, cool eggshell walls, and huge picture window. Dr. Swan stands near the window, his back to us. As we enter, he turns. His eyes widen. "Judith, what is the meaning of this?" His tone is sharp. Unusually so.

"I'm sorry, Director, but she insisted on seeing you. I didn't want to alarm her." She gives him a pointed look, and I sense there's another layer of meaning to her words. "Maybe you should just talk to her for a few minutes?"

He hesitates, his gaze flicking from Judith to me—then nods once.

"I'll just wait in the hall." She leaves, quietly shutting the door behind her.

Dr. Swan and I face each other across the room. For a long moment, he just studies me. There's a tension in his face, his posture, and he looks . . . old. He's lost weight, though I don't see how that's possible, since I saw him just the other day. Didn't I? Dark half-moons underscore his eyes, and the lines in his face look deeper, like grooves etched into wood.

I reach up to twist my left pigtail around my finger, an old habit, but my hand encounters only empty space. My arm flops awkwardly to my side. "Hello, Dr. Swan," I say, mostly to break the silence. I find myself adjusting my posture, straightening my back, as I always do in his presence. "Are you all right? You look a bit—tired."

The tension eases out of his shoulders. He closes his eyes and exhales a soft breath. Then he meets my gaze and smiles. "I'm fine, Lain. Thank you. I apologize for the . . . unorthodox nature of your situation. You must be confused."

"Very," I admit. Curiosity itches at the back of my mind, like the desire to pick at a scab.

"Sit down." He gestures to the chair across from his desk.

I sit, catch myself fidgeting, and stop.

He sits across from me and leans back in his black leather armchair. "How much did Judith tell you?"

"Not much. Just that I'd been through a traumatic experience. She wouldn't tell me what happened."

"That's just as well. Asking too many questions is counter-productive to the healing process, as you're well aware. It's better for you—for all of us—if you make a fresh start." He smiles, but there's a flash of pain in his eyes.

Whatever happened to me, it must have been horrible. I wonder if I really want to know. If I was desperate enough to erase my memories—if I wanted so badly to forget—I should probably trust that it was the right decision. Even so . . .

I bite my lower lip. "Can I go home tonight? I know it might be a few days before I can go back to school, but I'd like to sleep in my own bed."

He pauses. "Your case is a bit . . . unusual. Nothing to be alarmed about," he adds quickly. "But I'd like to keep you here for another week or so for observations. Just to be sure."

My head spins. "Another *week*? But I feel fine."

"Better to be safe."

I heave a sigh, raking a hand through my hair. I can't miss that much school. And what about my training? My clients? "Can I have my phone, at least? I'd like to thank Ian for the card he left me." If I can get a hold of Ian, maybe he can help get me out of here early. Dr. Swan is just being overprotective, I'm sure. It's because he cares, I know, but his constant hovering gets exhausting.

"I apologize, but your phone's been lost," he says. "We're still trying to locate it."

I don't buy that excuse for an instant. Obviously, he's afraid that I'll discover what happened to me and that it will trigger a relapse. An understandable concern, but he can't keep me locked up here forever. "At least let me stop at home tonight, then, so I can check my email and tell Ian I'm all right."

"I'll speak to Ian myself," Dr. Swan says. "I'll tell him you've regained consciousness and that you're feeling well. In the meantime, you need to rest. You're still in a fragile state."

I grit my teeth. I'm losing patience. "Dr. Swan, I know how memory modifications work. This is not how it's normally—"

"That's enough!"

I fall silent, mouth hanging open. I can't remember the last time Dr. Swan's snapped at me. He can be strict, but he never loses his cool. "Dr. Swan? Are you . . . okay?"

He closes his eyes briefly and rubs the lids. "I'm sorry. I've been under a lot of strain." He gives me a tight smile. "Please. For now, just trust me."

Goosebumps prickle on my arms. Something is very wrong.

He stands, places his hand on my shoulder, and squeezes briefly. "Judith will take you back to your room. She can bring you whatever you want—just nothing with a Net connection. We want to avoid overstimulation, after all. I know it's difficult, but try to get some rest. We'll talk more tomorrow."

I lower my gaze. A wave of helplessness and frustration washes over me, and a bitter knot forms in my throat. "It seems I don't have a choice."

"It's for your well-being, Lain." He stands, and so do I. I start to walk toward the door, but then—to my surprise—he hugs me.

My back goes rigid. Even though he's my guardian, there's always been a certain distance between Dr. Swan and I; he's not an affectionate person by nature. The smell of his cologne tickles my nose as he pulls me closer, trapping me against his chest. A stab of revulsion goes through me, and I have to fight back the urge to pull away. After a few seconds, he releases me, ducks his head, and wipes at the corner of one eye with his thumb, though I don't actually see any tears. "I apologize," he says. "It's been a difficult time for all of us, and it's a relief to see you like this. As your usual self."

"It's all right," I murmur, avoiding his gaze. My own reaction troubles me. I've known him for years. He's almost like an uncle. There's nothing strange about him hugging me, even if it *was* uncharacteristic. Why do I feel so repelled?

I leave the office, and Judith escorts me back to my room. "If you need anything, just push the call button on the armrest of your bed," she says. "And don't worry about a thing. You're safe now. You're on the road to recovery."

I nod uncertainly. She walks out, and the door swishes shut.

I try to open it again, but of course, it doesn't budge. With a sigh, I flop down in bed and stare at the ceiling. I *am* tired. Now that my initial burst of curiosity has faded, I can feel the ache of fatigue in my bones, like I've just come back from a long hike. My skull feels overstuffed and tender.

There's a remote control on the nightstand, so I pick it up and push ON. A holoscreen winks into existence, hovering near the foot of my bed. I scroll through the menu. Judging by the dates next to the title of each show, these are all prerecorded programs from months ago—mostly nature and history shows, a few news programs—nothing live or current. I flip randomly through the channels and pause when I encounter a public debate that I vaguely remember—a debate on the legal suicide drug, Somnazol. Dr. Swan sits across from a woman with dark, intense eyes. I recognize her as Susan Bleeker, head of an anti-Somnazol group called Do No Harm.

I select the program.

"If someone is suffering deeply and wants to die badly enough, he or she will find a way to make it happen," Dr. Swan says. "We can't prevent that. What we *can* do is offer them a safe and humane way to pass on. It's a choice that must be made by individuals, families and doctors. Certainly not one that should be made lightly, but our system has safeguards in place to prevent impulsive decisions. That's why we have waiting periods and evaluation processes. That's why Somnazol is only prescribed after other treatment options have been tried."

"You seem to have a lot of faith in those safeguards," the woman says. "If an unemployed Type Four comes in asking for a Somnazol prescription, do you really believe a doctor will respond to them the same way they would to a wealthy Type One asking for the same thing? Realistically, how many Fours do you think have the resources to explore all their treatment options? Can dying really be called a choice when people have been denied what they need to live? Instead of making death a more appealing option, we should be asking ourselves, as a society, why do so many people feel the need to die in the first place?"

"No one is denied access to treatment. Weren't you recently complaining, in one of your articles, that Conditioning is actually *over*used in our society?" His tone is weary and patient, as if he's humoring a child. "Memory modification therapy is still cost-prohibitive, it's true, but IFEN is working steadily toward making it more accessible to the public. What more should we be doing?"

"For one thing, you could stop limiting Fours' employment options. Give them equality. Allow them to vote and hold seats as elected representatives, take away the laws that keep them in poverty—"

He raises his eyebrows. "That is your solution? Undo all the progress we've made as a society and send us back to the past? There's a reason the Type system was implemented."

Fury flashes in her eyes, and she leans toward him, gripping the arms of her chair as if to hold herself back. "The system is designed to suppress—"

The picture suddenly breaks down into tiny colored squares, then vanishes, leaving the screen a dull green. I frown and switch to a nature program. Otter cubs are tumbling and playing in a riverbank. I switch back to the debate, but the screen is still green. Maybe the rest of the program failed to record. Or maybe someone decided it was too stimulating for me. The thought makes me bristle, but I have to admit, the interview has left me troubled. The topic of Somnazol always does.

It bothers me that even Dr. Swan, who has dedicated his life to helping others, supports the legal suicide pill. Most of those who take Somnazol are not terminally ill, but simply troubled individuals whose minds have been deemed irreparably broken. I've always believed that the system is supposed to *help* those who are suffering, not sell them poison. But then, who am I to make that decision for anyone else?

I shut off the TV, then toss and turn in bed for awhile. I must have dozed off, because I'm awakened by the squeak of a cart wheel. My eyes fly open. A woman wheels a cart toward my bed, but it's not Judith. A nurse? She's young, more handsome than pretty, with jaw-length, perfectly straight dark hair. "Dinner," she says, smiling.

"Thank you." Slowly, I sit up. "I don't suppose you can tell me anything about my situation here?"

"That depends. What do you want to know?"

"For one thing, what's today's date?"

"February 28th."

In my last clear memory, it was early October. At least, I'm pretty sure it was. My birthday is October 17th, which means I'm eighteen now. There's an uncomfortable sensation in my chest, like someone is pressing down on my sternum. Dr. Swan erased more than three months of time from my head. "Listen. I know you can't tell me anything specific, but I'm extremely confused. If you could just give me a general idea of what happened—"

"You'll know everything soon," she says. She might just be brushing me off, trying to keep me quiet. But when she speaks the words, she gives me a long, significant look. Her eyes are a clear, light gray, tinged with green. "Just be ready."

"For *what*?"

She smiles. "People are looking out for you."

I'm starting to feel like I'm trapped in a silly dream. "Well, yes. I suppose. But—"

"Enjoy your dinner. Finish it all. Proper nutrition is important." She turns and wheels the cart out of the room. I examine the contents of the tray. The nurse's behavior was so cryptic that I half expect to see a secret message written in gravy, but the food is all very ordinary: a bottle of milk, another muffin, and a chicken pot pie. Maybe I'm imagining things.

I take a bite of the chicken pot pie and feel something strange inside my mouth, something smooth and round. I pull it out. It's a pill—a white, glossy oval. Imprinted on one side are the words EAT ME. Like in *Alice in Wonderland*. Dizziness rolls over me, and I press a hand to the side of my head, overcome by the sudden sense that I've seen a pill like this somewhere before.

Footsteps echo down the hall toward me. Someone is coming. My fingers curl around the pill. I'm not supposed to have this, am I? I'm not about to take a drug without having any idea what it is or what it does, but I don't want to lose it, either. I keep my hand under the covers, hidden.

The door opens, and Judith peeks in. She blinks. "Oh. Someone already brought you your meal. Is the food okay?"

I force a smile. "It's fine, thank you."

"You're sweating. Is everything—"

"I just strained myself a little. I probably shouldn't watch TV in this condition." When she doesn't move, I say, "I'm going to eat now."

She shuts the door again. I pull out the pill and examine it, but it offers no clues about its nature or purpose. My plain cotton clothes don't have any pockets, so I dry the pill off with a napkin and tuck it into my slipper, under the arch of my foot. The slipper is tight enough that it will stay in place. I can decide what to do with this mystery drug later.

I eat a little more of the pot pie and pick at the muffin, but my appetite has shriveled. With nothing else to do, I pick up the card on the nightstand and study the innocuously pretty picture. It doesn't seem like the sort of card Ian would pick out. Usually, his are more witty. Everything about this experience feels . . . off. I keep remembering Dr. Swan's strange behavior, that stab of fear and disgust I felt when he hugged me.

I pull the covers over my head and close my eyes. I'm more tired than I thought, and I'm on the edge of drifting off when a dull boom shakes the room, like thunder. It's so strong that my bed vibrates. I sit bolt upright, heart pounding. A freak storm? Or . . .

I leap out of bed and press my ear against the door. Another boom shakes the floor, louder and closer.

It's not thunder.

2

I take a few steps back from the door. A cold, hollow space opens inside my chest. Someone set off an explosive. But who would do that? Why?

The answer comes at once: *Terrorists.* My heart hammers against my ribs.

No. Ridiculous. Terrorist attacks just don't *happen*, not anymore. That's the whole point of IFEN's existence, of the Type system—to identify potential threats to public safety before they can cause real harm. Of course there's still crime, because no government has ever been completely successful at eliminating wrongdoing. But shootings, bombings, mass killings—those things are unheard of, in this day and age.

Regardless, something is definitely wrong. My own ragged breathing fills my ears as I scan the room for an escape route.

I hear voices talking in the hallway, a man and a woman, but I can't make out the words. The voices are growing closer, closer. They're right outside the door. For a few seconds, they fall silent. Then a man calls out, "If anyone's in there, back away! This door is gonna explode in about ten seconds!"

There's no time to think. I dive behind the bed and huddle against the wall, covering my head.

The explosion seems to shatter the very air. The door bursts open. Fire unfurls like a blossoming flower, petals of bright light and smoke shooting off in every direction. Shards of metal and plaster rain to the ground, and the heat sears my skin. More smoke pours from the door, though the fire has died down.

I muffle a coughing fit against my fist and stumble to my feet. For a few seconds, I can't see anything through the billowing clouds of smoke. Then I hear footsteps, and a silhouette emerges through the haze. Smoke stings my eyes, making me squint as the figure slowly comes into focus: a tall, thin form with the head of a gray-feathered hawk.

A holomask. I've seen them before, though people mostly wear them at parties. Brilliant, copper-gold eyes stare at me from above the dagger-like beak.

"Stay away!" I shout, knowing it won't do any good.

He reaches up to touch his neck, and the bird head vanishes, revealing a young man with pale blond hair and a diagonal scar on his cheek. He's wearing a ragged black coat, boots, and equally ragged jeans, and he's wielding the biggest rifle I've ever seen.

He stares at me, eyes wide. For a few seconds, the very air seems to hold its breath. Then he smiles—a peculiar, crooked smile. "Sorry I'm late." Slowly, he walks toward me. I don't move. There's nowhere to go.

Sweat plasters my thin smock to my back. "What do you want with me?"

He lowers the gun as he walks closer, then reaches out, as if to touch my cheek. I flinch away. He freezes. "Lain," he says, very quietly, "it's me, Steven."

I look up into his face. His features are thin and sharp, his eyes a pale, penetrating blue. They search mine deeply, as if hunting for something. I can see the fear in his expression, but I don't understand it. He's the one holding the gun here.

Then he drops the weapon. It clanks to the floor as he takes my face between his hands. I'm too stunned to react. "Come on, Doc." His voice is low, husky, trembling. "It's your Steven. You know me. You have to. I know they did something to you, but they can't take those feelings away. Look at me. Look in my eyes."

My pulse drums in my throat, like a tiny heart trapped behind my mouth. He's delusional. He must be. His expression is so earnest, so desperate, I feel a tug of sympathy for him in spite of myself. Then I remember that he just blew up the doors. I grab his wrists and push his hands down. "I assure you," I say, struggling to hold my voice steady, "I've never seen you before in my life."

He takes a step back, as if I've slapped him. The color drains from his face.

"Look. I have no idea what this is about or what's going on in your head, but that—" I point to the still-smoldering doors with an unsteady hand "—that is unacceptable." My heart races, and sweat trickles down my back, but I keep talking, because if I don't say something, I'll probably start panicking. "You're obviously going through some issues right now, but breaking into a medical facility and setting off explosives is not going to solve anything."

He bows his head and lets out a choked laugh. His shoulders shake as his forehead drops into one hand. "Well," he whispers, his voice cracked, "you're as bossy as ever."

A voice inside whispers, *What if you do know him?* I shove it away. There's no way I'd get involved with someone this unstable. I'm too aware of the risks.

My gaze darts to the gun near his feet. I think about making a lunge for it, but before I can, he picks it up, and I have a feeling I've just lost my only chance to escape.

Another form appears in the doorway—a young woman with the head of a lynx, wielding a gun even bigger than Steven's and

23

wearing a black coat identical to his. Her jade eyes flick toward me, and her whiskers twitch. "We're too late," she says flatly. The mouth of her holomask moves along with her words, showing sharp white teeth. "She has no idea who we are. I doubt she'll come with us willingly."

"We're not leaving her here, Rhee," Steven snaps.

"I didn't say we should. I'm just saying, it won't be easy—"

"Excuse me," I say, raising my voice, "maybe you didn't hear me the first time. I *don't know you*. And you don't know me."

His jaw tightens. He looks me straight in the eye. "Your name is Lain Fisher. You have a stuffed squirrel named Nutter, and your holoavatar was a cat named Chloe. When you were thirteen, your father killed himself, and you blamed yourself for it. Since then, you've spent your life trying to save people. Whenever someone claims to be a lost cause, whenever they say there's no hope, you're the one there telling them they're wrong. You don't believe in lost causes."

A cold tendril curls around my heart. "Who are you?" I whisper.

"No time," the cat woman—Rhee—says. "We've got to get out of here."

"I'm not going anywhere until you tell me where we're going!"

"Canada," he replies.

"*Canada?*" The name conjures up a whirl of confusing emotions and jumbled images—verdant forests and concrete spattered with spray-paint and blood, soaring hawks and desolate towns overrun with bandits.

"We're taking you back to the Citadel."

My thoughts spin. Apparently, these people are somehow connected with the traumatic incident that has been wiped from my mind. Maybe they kidnapped me, and now they're trying to take me back. But something about that assessment doesn't feel right. I remember the way the man—Steven—looked at me when

I said I didn't recognize him. Like his soul was crumbling. I shake my head. "I—I can't—"

Rhee holds up a hand, forestalling my protests. "Here's all you need to know right now. A lot has changed for you in the past few months. We're your allies. IFEN is your enemy."

"That's absurd," I snap. But I'm shaken, all the same.

Steven reaches out to me, and I flinch back. A spasm of pain crosses his face, as though I just opened up his chest and punched him in the heart. "Lain . . . please."

I don't move.

In the hallway outside, I hear the thunder of approaching footsteps. Steven stretches out a hand. His gaze holds mine. "Trust me."

The world is breaking apart, shattering into a thousand jagged shards, and those shards are cutting me into pieces. My head hurts. Steven remains motionless, hand extended, his eyes filled with mute pleading. "I must be insane," I mutter, and take his hand. He drags me into a rough embrace, and I let out a squeak of surprise as he pins me against his chest. He's squeezing me so hard I can barely breathe.

A line of armed men in IFEN uniforms burst into the room, aiming handguns at us. The pistols look like toys compared to the assault rifles the two terrorists are holding. "Let her go," one of them says.

Steven spins around to face them, aiming his machine gun with one hand, the other arm still locked across my chest, pinning me in place, and I realize—I'm a hostage. Oh God. How could I have been so stupid?

"One last warning," the man barks. "Let her go, or we'll—"

Rhee raises her gun and sprays them with bullets. Two of the guards manage to scramble away in time. The other two go down. One of them twitches a few times, then they're both motionless. Blood spatters the walls and the floor.

I scream.

Steven curses under his breath and drags me out, down another hallway. I struggle, trying to free myself from his grip. "Calm down," he says.

"*Calm down? You killed them!*"

"They would have killed us," Rhee says.

I hear the stampede of footsteps and tense. A group rounds a bend in the hall, but they're not guards or police. They're dressed in black coats and carrying guns, and they're all wearing holo-masks that look like animal heads—a wolf, a snow leopard, some kind of short-eared, brown-furred rodent with a snout full of pointy teeth.

So many people. Whatever's happening, it wasn't engineered by a pair of psychopaths. This is organized. I take in their attire again, and my already rapid breathing speeds up. *Blackcoats.* They exist, after all. IFEN always insisted the last of them had been wiped out during the war.

"We found him," the rodent says in a sharp female voice. She pushes a man forward. He stumbles and falls to his knees, head bowed, wrists bound behind his back. His clothes and hair, both white, are stained with blood. "He was trying to escape in his private helicopter. Coward."

The man lifts his head, glaring at the rebels through the blood on his face. A cold jolt of shock runs through me. It's Dr. Swan.

The snow leopard steps forward and nudges Dr. Swan with the butt of his gun. "What should we do with him, Sparrowhawk?" he asks, looking at Steven. "You want us to kill him?"

"No!" I burst out. I struggle, trying to pull myself from Steven's grip, but he clings to me. My elbow cannons into his stomach, and he releases me with a grunt.

Rhee quickly grabs me and pins my arms behind my back.

"Let me go!" I shout.

The rodent woman casts a disdainful glance at me, teeth bared. "Why don't we just knock her out?"

"We're not doing that," Steven snaps at her. "If you lay a hand on her, I'll—"

"Fine, whatever. I won't touch your Pookie."

Pookie? I look at Steven. He flushes and looks away. Then he takes a deep breath and marches up to Dr. Swan. "Tell Lain—tell all of us—what you did to her."

"You already know." Dr. Swan squeezes the words between clenched teeth.

"I want to hear you say it."

Dr. Swan's gaze flicks to me, then away. "We performed a neural modification treatment. She's already aware of that."

"Does she know what you erased?"

I listen, holding my breath.

Dr. Swan smiles, a bitter twist of his lips. "Why don't you tell her? Tell her how you seduced and brainwashed her, how you indoctrinated her into this life of violence—"

Steven slams the butt of his gun into Dr. Swan's nose. Crunch. A choked cry escapes my throat.

Dr. Swan gasps, wheezes, then looks up, still smiling through the blood. "Those masks of yours are very fitting." His voice comes out thick and nasally. "You're animals, through and through."

"Tell her the whole truth," Steven says.

"And what truth would that be?"

"That you wiped her memories against her will because you wanted to mold her into your puppet. You wanted her to forget the fact that IFEN performed illegal experiments on children, on me and Rhee. On Lizzie." His voice cracks slightly over the name. "You wanted her to forget that you were responsible for her dad's suicide, because you pushed him into a corner. If he hadn't died, you'd have wiped his memories. She fled the country to get away from you. But you made her forget that, too."

I stare at Dr. Swan, mouth open. He doesn't deny it. His face is a tight mask of pain, though whether it's from his broken nose or something else, I don't know. I wait, holding my breath, and still he doesn't say anything. "That's not true." My voice wavers. "What they're saying. It's not true. Is it?"

He doesn't answer.

"Why are we wasting time?" the rodent asks. "Let's just shoot him."

"No!" I lurch forward, but Rhee just tightens her grip.

Steven stares at Dr. Swan for a long moment. His finger rests on the trigger of his rifle, and a muscle in his jaw flexes and clenches. Then he lowers his gun. "We're taking him back to the Citadel. We can decide what to do with him once we get there."

Rhee narrows her eyes, then gives a small nod.

Dr. Swan twists on the floor, his face contorted. His wrists are still bound, but he's managed to loosen the restraints. His fingers creep toward something at his hip. I glimpse the hilt of a neural disruptor—or is it a gun?—peeking out from under his jacket. "Look out!" I blurt.

Steven's eyes widen. He brings his rifle up. In the same instant, Dr. Swan's fingers close around his weapon. A sharp *crack* rings out, and Dr. Swan slumps to the floor. He twitches once, then goes still. Blood pools beneath his head. I hear someone screaming and realize that it's me. I thrash blindly, trying to pull free. Rhee's grip tightens. "Murderer!" I shout at Steven, my voice choked with tears. "*You killed him!*"

"No, he didn't," Rhee says quietly. "Dr. Swan shot himself."

My jaw drops. A cold shock hits me as I look at the inert form and realize she's right. Dr. Swan managed to angle the gun toward his own head. His finger is still on the trigger. I start to shake. "Why?" I whisper.

"Probably so we couldn't get any information out of him," she replies. "He had conviction, I'll give him that."

Steven is breathing hard, still clutching the rifle. His face has gone pale, his eyes glassy. He turns to face the others. "Why didn't you search him for weapons?"

28

They shift their weight and hang their heads, like children caught playing hooky. Silence hangs over the hallway.

"Oh well," the rodent woman says. "It's easier this way. Now we don't have to worry about bringing him back—"

Steven shoots a glare at her, and she falls silent. He looks down at the rifle in his trembling hands, sheathes it, and takes a deep, shaky breath. "Get him out of here."

"And take him where?" the snow leopard asks.

"I don't care."

The wolf and snow leopard grab Dr. Swan by his bound arms and drag him off, leaving a smear of blood.

"If I let you go, do you promise not to do anything crazy?" Rhee asks.

Numbly, I nod.

Rhee releases me, and I slump against the wall. She follows the others around a bend in the hall.

The rodent woman starts to follow, too, then stops, and turns to face me. I can't tell exactly what her mask is supposed to be. She looks like a cross between a rat and a skunk, with a dash of bear thrown in. "Let's get one thing straight," she says. "The only reason I'm here is because I owe you. Besides, if we left you behind, lover boy here—" she shoots a glare at Steven "—would probably spend the rest of his life moping and writing crappy, angsty poetry. And none of us want to see that." She points a gloved finger at me. "After this, we're even."

Nothing she says makes any sense to me. I can't even bother trying to work it out. "All right," I mutter.

She stomps down the hall and disappears around a corner, leaving me alone with Steven in the charred, blood-spattered hallway.

He looks into my eyes. The lines in his face deepen, and his shoulders slump. "I'm sorry," he whispers.

So much blood. It's on the walls, the floor. A chunk of something pinkish clings to the tiles nearby. A wave of lightheadedness passes over me.

Dr. Swan did this to me against my will—he didn't deny it. He didn't deny any of it, not even the part about being responsible for Father's suicide. The thought makes me sick. And now he's dead. I don't want to stay here, in IFEN headquarters, but I don't trust these people with the black coats and guns either. I don't trust anyone.

Steven reaches toward me. "Lain . . ."

"Leave me alone," I whisper.

Steven stands motionless. His fingers tighten on the grip of his gun, and his expression contorts, as if he's about to roar or scream. Then, all at once, the pain in his face vanishes, as if wiped away by an invisible hand. "We can't stick around. The police will show up any minute."

"And what then? Will you kill them?"

"If I have to. If someone points a gun at me with intent to kill, I shoot back."

I shouldn't be arguing with him now; not only are we in danger, but I have no idea what he'll do if provoked. Still, I look him in the eye and say, "You're the ones who broke in here and started setting off bombs."

"We broke in here to *rescue* you."

So I'm the reason that those guards are dead—that Dr. Swan is dead. A dull ache spreads through my chest. "I never asked to be rescued."

He doesn't reply.

I press my fists to my temples. If I stay here, what then? Will IFEN wipe this entire incident from my memory? I think about the guards' bloody bodies contorted on the floor, about the moment when Dr. Swan went still, and I wonder if forgetting would be so bad. Push the reset button and wash away this whole, confusing, horrible night.

But *it would be a lie*, a voice inside whispers. I'm breathing so hard and fast, my head starts to feel light, like it might drift away.

"I wish Ian were here," I whisper. The words slip out of me without my permission.

There's a long pause. Then Steven replies in an odd tone, "He is. He's on the roof, waiting."

My head jerks up. "That makes no sense. Why would he be on the roof?"

"He's one of us now."

Ian, a terrorist. The thought is so ridiculous, I would laugh if I wasn't so scared. "You're lying."

Steven smiles a tight, humorless smile. "He's there. Scout's honor. New haircut, same Ian. We'll go up there and he'll greet you like a big, overexcited puppy. Probably slobber on your face and everything."

"But he left a card—" I stop, feeling silly. Dr. Swan probably forged his signature. All part of the ruse.

Of course, there's no way to know whether Steven's telling the truth, but at this point, it's a chance I have to take. I need to know what happened to me during the missing months of my life. I search the inside of my head for some flicker of memory, but there's only a blank, like a paragraph in a book that's been neatly and completely inked out.

If Ian's really there, he will explain all this to me. He'll make sense of this chaos.

Steven's gaze drills into me. "So what'll it be?"

I breathe in slowly, meeting his eyes. *His* eyes. Pale blue mixed with silver. I've seen them before, I know I have. "Let's go."

Again, he extends his hand to me, and again, I take it. His skin is warm, his palm studded with small calluses, his fingers thin and strong. They tighten on mine until I squirm. "You're hurting me."

He loosens his grip. "Sorry."

The apology catches me off guard.

We take an elevator up to the top floor, to Dr. Swan's office. Steven doesn't let go of my hand, even when my palm starts to sweat. The picture window is broken, and a rope ladder hangs down, swinging. We climb up, into the cold, clear night. A few stars shine dim and faraway, pinpricks in the black dome of the sky, and all around us, the city of Aura twinkles—towering skyscrapers, gleaming high rises, toy cars moving through the grid of streets below. Wind whips through my hair. On the roof itself is a gray helicopter, its propeller whirring.

A figure steps out, black coat billowing behind him.

My heart leaps. His hair is longer, and he appears thinner, all sharp angles. But it's unmistakably him.

"Ian!" I release Steven's hand, rush forward, and tackle him in a hug. He wraps his arms around me and squeezes me tightly. I pull back to look into his eyes. Warm, deep, velvety brown—though they're a little darker than I remember. For a long moment, I just soak in the sight of him. Slowly, I reach up and run a finger over his stubble. "You need to shave."

He laughs, a small, choked sound. "God, I'm so glad to see you. You have no idea."

I swallow. There's a feeling of something sharp in my throat. "Ian . . . Dr. Swan is dead."

His expression turns serious. "I know. They told me. I'm sorry, Lain. This must be terrible for you."

I press a hand over my mouth. Tears blur my vision.

He frames my face between his hands. "It's gonna be okay."

"Somehow, I doubt that," I murmur.

Steven walks briskly past us. "Let's go. We don't have any time to waste."

We climb into the chopper, and Ian slides into the pilot's seat. "You can fly this thing?" I ask.

"I used to take lessons during the summer," he says. "Never thought they'd be so useful."

All right, I think, trying to arrange the chaos inside me into some semblance of order. So we're going to fly away in a helicopter.

To Canada—to someplace called the Citadel. Where I've apparently been before. And then we'll do . . . what?

Dr. Swan's corpse floats up behind my eyes again, and a wire starts to tighten around my throat. Did he really drive my father to suicide? Did IFEN truly do those horrible things? I don't want to believe it. I *can't* believe it.

Steven shuts the doors, and I buckle myself in.

Consciously, I slow my breathing. I walk through my compartmentalization exercises, shutting my emotions away in a big wooden box, closing the lid, and locking it tight. Dr. Swan's suicide, the revelation about my father, about IFEN . . . I'll deal with those things later. There's no space inside me for anything except the present.

The wail of sirens drifts toward me on the wind. In the streets below, police cars are pulling into the parking lot. It feels like a scene from a movie, or maybe a dream. Surely, any moment now, I'll wake up in my own bed.

Ian adjusts the controls, and the helicopter lifts into the sky. My stomach lurches, and the chicken pot pie I had earlier shifts uneasily inside me as the roof drops out from beneath us. We break through a screen of low-hanging clouds, and then we're skimming along through the open sky, surrounded by nothing but vertigo-inducing darkness. Through breaks in the clouds, I glimpse the city below, sailing past. I lean back. A dull pain pulses behind my left eye.

Steven's fingers drum rapidly on the seat as he stares out the window. "They're going to come after us. Stealing these choppers was a risky choice."

"It was the only possible way to get her out of IFEN headquarters," Ian says. "If we tried to escape by car, they'd just block off all the city exits."

I close my eyes and focus on the rumble of the engine, the faint vibration of the seat. My throat throbs with thirst, and I rub it absently.

"Here."

I open my eyes to see Steven holding out a bottle of water. I accept it, twist off the cap, and take a swig. "Thank you." I steal a glance at him from the corner of my eye. He sits motionless, staring straight ahead. He has an attractive profile. It's an absurd thing to notice, under the circumstances. Is this some sort of early onset Stockholm syndrome? I take another sip of water and ask, my voice faint and scratchy, "So, what is the Citadel?"

"The base of the rebellion against IFEN," Ian replies.

Oh. Apparently, I'm not just associating with terrorists; I'm part of a plot to overthrow the government. The world swims and wiggles like something seen through a foot of water, and darkness eats at the edges of my vision. My fingers clench on the half-empty bottle, nearly crumpling the thin plastic.

"Maybe you should just rest," Steven says.

"Fuck that," I snap. "I want answers." My own language surprises me—and apparently Steven, too. He looks at me like I just started speaking in Aramaic. "I want to know how, in the space of a few months, I went from being a Mindwalker-in-training and a good student to . . . this." I wave a hand, indicating the entire situation. "And I want to know who you are. I don't just mean what sort of political stuff you're mixed up in. I want to know who you are to *me*. That rodent woman called you 'lover boy.' She said I was your *Pookie*. What was that about? Were we actually . . ." I trail off, unable to finish the sentence. My ears burn.

Steven shifts in his seat. His face has gone pink. "We kissed. A few times."

It's surreal, to see him blushing like a schoolboy after how ruthlessly he behaved in IFEN headquarters. I've had my first kiss, and I don't even remember it. Maybe I should be relieved that it was just kissing.

What else have I lost?

Steven's shoulders droop, as if he's bearing a tremendous weight.

His eyes are hollow with exhaustion, the black circles around them as vivid as makeup. I didn't notice that before. "There's something else you should know," he says. "You got mixed up in this because you made a choice to help someone. Someone the rest of the world had given up on. Dr. Swan didn't want you to do it, but you wouldn't let him stop you. That's how IFEN became your enemy."

I chew my lower lip, wondering how much to believe. Ian glances back at us, but says nothing.

Below us, the clouds break, and I see forest sprawling for miles like a dark green blanket. In the distance, some huge body of water—Lake Michigan?—shines like steel.

Questions circle through my head and crowd my throat. But I wonder if I really want the answers. My mind has shifted a little to the left, and everything feels unreal—like I'm watching a documentary about myself. That sense of unreality is probably the only thing keeping me from a full-fledged mental breakdown. I'm sitting next to the man responsible for my guardian's death. I should want nothing to do with these people, but Ian's presence among them makes me question everything.

I sink into the seat. The steady hum of the engine blends with the whir of the propeller blades, the sound surrounding and enfolding me like a cocoon. Steven keeps stealing glances at me from the corner of his eye. I half expect him to reach over and touch me, brush his hand against my hair. For some reason, I almost want him to do it, but he doesn't. He sits with his hands balled into tight fists in his lap, staring out the window.

"They're tailing us," Ian says suddenly.

Steven jerks upright. "Shit."

I crane my neck, and sure enough, two white helicopters with IFEN's logo are behind us, gaining rapidly.

"Brace yourself. I'm gonna try to shake them off." Ian grabs the cyclic stick and pulls. The helicopter veers to one side, and I let out a shriek.

Gunfire explodes behind us. Ian yanks the cyclic again, and the helicopter plunges straight down, then bobs up again. My stomach roils, and the chicken pot pie tries to crawl up my throat. I clamp a hand over my mouth.

"We just have to make it across the border." Ian's breathing fast, fingers clenched tight around the steering bars. "They won't follow us into Canada. International treaties."

Below, I see nothing but a dark ocean of pines. Where is the border? How close are we? I want to ask, but I'm afraid if I open my mouth, I'll throw up.

"They're right behind us," Steven says.

"Hold on," Ian says. We're picking up speed. The hornet-like drone of the pursuing choppers fills my ears, growing louder and louder. The thunder of gunfire fills the air, and there's a sickening lurch.

Then we're falling, plummeting like a stone. Ian wrestles with the controls, trying to slow our descent. Smoke fills my lungs, choking me. This is it. I'm going to die here. Without thinking, I grab Steven's hand and clutch it tight as the helicopter spirals down and the ground races toward us. There's an impact, and I could swear that every bone in my body shatters in that instant.

Nothingness seizes me and drags me under.

3

Summer sun warms the back of my neck as I clutch Father's hand. I lick my apricot ice cream—it's cool and sweet, melting on my tongue—as I count the sidewalk cracks, skipping to avoid stepping on them. *Don't step on the cracks, or you'll break your mother's back.* That's the rhyme I've heard the other kids chanting. Except I don't have a mom. Father has explained to me that I came from one of his cells, and that I grew inside a tube instead of a lady's tummy. *I watched you grow,* he said. *Until you were big enough to come out.*

I see a chubby green caterpillar crawling over the sidewalk. "Look." I point, smiling.

Father slows. "He's a long way from home, isn't he?"

"Can we take him back with us?"

Ahead, I hear loud sobbing, and I freeze. A woman in ragged clothes and a collar is struggling as two men in IFEN uniforms grip her arms, pulling her toward a white car. "They took my baby!" she screams. "I just want to see my baby! Please let me go!"

One of the men says something quiet to her. She screams louder—bad words, now, words I've heard bigger kids saying at school. Then she jerks and goes limp, like a dead fish. The men push her into the car, and the car drives away.

Father puts a warm, steadying hand on my head, and I press closer to his side, clutching his shirt. "Was that lady sick?" I whisper.

"Maybe," he replies.

We stand on the sidewalk as people brush past us, talking and laughing on their phones. No one seems to care that a lady in a collar was just shoved into a car.

"Are they going to make her better?" I ask, looking up at him.

There's a funny look on his face. For a long time, he doesn't answer. Then he says quietly, "There is a lot of sickness in the world. A lot of suffering. But, Lainy . . . sometimes we call people 'sick' when they make us frightened or uncomfortable. Even if we don't really know them. It's possible that that lady never had a baby, or if she did, maybe it was taken away for a good reason. But it's also possible that her baby was taken for a wrong reason. Maybe she's just really angry and scared. And being angry or scared isn't sick. Do you understand?"

I bite my lip and nod, though I'm not sure I do. "So what should we do?"

He opens his mouth, then closes it. "I'll talk to someone at work. Maybe I can find out what's going on."

"But . . . what about the lady? If she's in trouble, doesn't she need help now?"

He crouches in front of me, looking me in the eye. "Sometimes, you can't help people right away. You have to change the way the system works."

I wonder why. Maybe if we tried to stop those men, we'd get in trouble too. Maybe they'd take us away in a car, and other people would watch it happen and say we were sick. My stomach hurts. Suddenly, I'm really confused. "Isn't IFEN good?" I whisper. "Don't you work for them?"

He breathes a little sigh and smiles, though he seems sad. "Yes, Lainy. They're good, mostly. They've made our country a much safer place, and they help people who need it. But they make mistakes."

My ice cream is melting, dripping to the sidewalk. Apricot is the best kind, but I don't want it right now.

*　　*　　*

I'm swimming up through a shining mist. Something hard pokes the small of my back, sending a tiny jab of pain through me, but it's nothing compared to the throbbing inferno in my skull. My thoughts are a tangled mess, but I remember falling. Falling through the air—and then an impact shattered the universe.

I was dreaming about something a moment ago, but now the images are fading, leaving only a dim impression, like the blurry outline of footprints in the sand, smoothed away by waves.

It takes an effort to pry my eyelids open, and when I do, I find myself staring into a pair of big brown eyes, just inches from mine. Ian. A moment's disorientation washes over me.

"Lain? Lain, can you hear me?"

I'm a little amazed that I'm still alive, much less conscious, but I manage to form the word *Yes*.

He lets out a quiet breath of relief and straightens.

Memories rush back. IFEN headquarters. A blur of explosions and terror. Dr. Swan's death. Escape. Then the helicopter crash which left us stranded here, wherever *here* is. Overhead, sunlight winks through the trees and clouds sail across a bright, innocent blue sky. The small, prickly object pokes my back again—a pinecone? I roll onto my side, wincing. A strand of loose hair tickles my cheek, and I brush it away.

"How do you feel?" Ian asks.

I do a mental scan of myself. The blood pounds in my skull, and my body is a collection of aches—I feel like one big bruise—but I can move all my limbs. Despite the bone-jarring impact of the crash, I don't think anything is broken. "Sore." I touch my hair, and my fingers come away sticky with blood. My vision wavers, and my stomach turns hollow.

Ian rests his fingertips on my cheeks, ten spots of warmth. "Count backward from ten."

I do it without a hitch. He asks me a few more questions to ascertain that I don't have a concussion, then straightens. "You're okay," he says.

If I was unconscious for any length of time, there's still a chance that I'm concussed, even if I feel relatively lucid, but there's not much I can do about that. Slowly—very slowly—I sit up, and my brains seem to slosh around in my skull. Ugh. I place a hand gingerly against my temple, as if that will help to steady my ravaged gray matter, and look around. We're in a forest, though I'd already deduced that much. Pines loom around us, interspersed with a few scrawny, leafless deciduous trees. The air is cold. The helicopter rests on its side about thirty feet away, smoking. Steven sits on a log nearby, his rifle propped next to him. He avoids looking directly at me.

"Where are we?" I ask.

"The good news is that we made it into Canada," Ian says.

I shiver.

For the first time in my life, I'm in another country. Here, on this ground, our Types mean nothing. Vertigo washes over me, as if the earth has shifted beneath me.

Back home, we were taught so little about the world outside the URA. They told us that Canada is wild and dangerous, a decayed civilization a few steps away from anarchy. I have no idea how much of that is reality and how much is propaganda, because I've never even met anyone who's traveled abroad. There *are* a few Americans that do, but they're mostly the wealthy elite, people who can afford bodyguards. Leaving the country requires all sorts of special permits and papers. Well, assuming you do it legally.

"So what's the bad news?" I ask.

"The bad news is that we're stuck in the middle of nowhere with no way to contact the others. The equipment's shorted out."

"You don't have cell phones?"

"Hell no," Steven says. "They're too easy to track."

Ian rocks back on his heels, chewing his thumbnail. "What's our weapon situation?"

"We've got our rifles," Steven says. "That's it."

"Well, let's hope we don't get attacked out here." Ian adjusts the straps of his pack. "We've got some food and water, at least. Though not a lot."

My gaze keeps straying to Steven's rifle. Before this, I've never even *seen* a gun, at least not in person. Most security guards and policy use NDs, these days. All things considered, I think, it's impressive that I'm not panicking. Ian's presence helps, but considering the recent turn of events, I wonder how well I really know him. How long has he been involved in this madness?

One thing at a time, I tell myself. "So what now?"

Steven rises to his feet. "We start walking. Hopefully, we'll come to a road."

I just want to lie here on the soft, mossy ground until my head stops pounding. But that's not an option. There are probably border patrols in Canada too, and the longer we stay, the greater our chance of getting caught.

Would that be so bad? a voice inside me whispers. I'd probably be sent back home. From all outward appearances, it would look like these people kidnapped me—which is pretty much what happened—so I wouldn't get in trouble. But then what?

If it's true that Dr. Swan erased my memories against my will, then I need to understand why. I need to know what happened to me. Which means staying with Ian and Steven, at least a little while longer.

I push myself to my feet and sway like a drunkard. Steven steadies me with an arm around my waist, and I tense. The way he touches me—so familiar—sends a shock through my nerves. "I'm fine," I mutter, pulling away.

41

I see the flash of hurt in his eyes, and for a second, I actually feel guilty. Like I've just kicked a puppy. A violent, scarred puppy with an assault rifle. Then his expression closes off, going stony again, and he turns away.

His scent lingers in my nose. Leather and gun smoke and the faint, coppery tang of blood . . . and beneath that, another, subtler smell that stirs an echo of memory. Neurons nudge each other, whispering like leaves in the wind as his scent ghosts through the corridors of my brain. An image flares, bright and sharp. I'm sitting across from him in the Underwater Café, and he's telling me . . . telling me . . .

It's gone.

Steven and Ian are watching me intently. "What is it?" Ian asks.

I give my head a shake and look away. "I don't know."

Ian puts a warm, gentle hand on my shoulder. "Don't force it. Your mind is still fragile."

I nod. My gaze catches briefly on Steven's, and he looks away.

"You're really not dressed for hiking," Ian remarks. He opens the pack and pulls out a heavy flannel shirt, a pair of sweatpants, and some sturdy brown hiking boots.

"You came prepared."

He smiles. "I'm always prepared." He tosses the clothes to me. "We'll keep our backs turned while you change."

"Thank you." I walk a little ways into the woods, just enough to give myself some privacy. Quickly, I shed my thin cotton hospital clothes and pull on the warmer clothes Ian brought. They're too big for me, so I have to roll up both the pant legs and sleeves. I sit down and tug off my slippers, and the pill tumbles out and lands on the ground. Slowly, I pick it up. In the rush of everything else that happened, I'd almost forgotten about it. I tuck the pill into my pocket and walk back. Steven and Ian are still standing with their backs turned. "You can look."

They face me.

I think about showing them the pill, asking them what it is. Instead, I ask, "Who was that nurse? Was she a Blackcoat, too? One of your contacts?"

"Nurse?" Ian sounds puzzled. "What nurse?"

If she *was* working with the Blackcoats, it seems like they should know about her. "There was this strange nurse who . . ." Something stops me. I find myself reluctant to tell them about the pill, not knowing what it is. What if they try to take it away from me? "Never mind. It's probably nothing."

Ian frowns, but doesn't reply.

We start to walk. The blood surges and ebbs behind my eyes, a tide of dull red. Every few minutes, I have to pause and lean against a tree to catch my breath. Steven walks ahead of us, keeping his rifle in his hands as we make our way through a maze of trees. Somehow, he seems to know exactly where we're going. The oversized pack bounces against Ian's back.

Orange light bleeds through the forest canopy, making me squint as the sun sinks lower, vanishing behind the horizon, leaving only a pink haze in the western sky. Branches form sharp black shadows against the light. Somewhere in the forest, a coyote howls, a long, high, mournful sound.

I stumble again, pausing to lean against a tree.

"What's wrong?" Ian asks.

The world wavers and blurs. Leaves lose focus, becoming soft green spots. "I just need to rest." I slide down and sit on the cold earth. The throbbing in my head hasn't quieted; if anything, it's gotten worse. Maybe I do have a concussion.

"We shouldn't stay in one place for long," Steven says. "Even if IFEN can't touch us in this country, there's still the Canadian authorities to worry about."

"Just give her a minute," Ian says. "I'll stand watch."

I lean back against the tree. Steven sits a few feet away from me while Ian paces the area, scanning the surrounding forest.

He's just out of earshot. Several times, Steven opens his mouth as if he's about to say something, then closes it. He draws his knees to his chest and wraps his arms around them. "You really don't remember anything," he says at last.

"No."

His throat muscles constrict. He rests his forehead against his knees, and for an awkward moment, I wonder if he's about to cry. I'm not sure how I would deal with that. My brain keeps replaying the clip of him slamming the butt of his rifle into Dr. Swan's face, the crunch of bone. But I remember, too, the look on his face when I pulled away from him. He doesn't *feel* like a cold-blooded killer.

Still, I can't bring myself to offer him any words of comfort. My chest aches, and I turn my head away, unable to look directly at him.

"I'm not going to hurt you," he says quietly.

I stare off into the woods. "I know." And I do—that's the odd thing.

His arms tighten around his knees. "I'm sorry," he says, "about . . . about what happened back there."

My chest aches. "You said Dr. Swan did horrible things to you. That he experimented on you."

He nods.

"If that's true, I guess you must be glad he's dead."

"I thought I would be."

In the woods, an animal rustles through the foliage. Even in my heavy flannel shirt, I'm cold, and I rub my arms, listening to Steven's quiet, unsteady breathing. I should despise him. Why don't I?

Steven told me I got mixed up in this because I chose to help someone. Was he talking about himself?

I remember that flicker of memory when I breathed in his scent. The olfactory bulb is tightly wired to the hippocampus—the part of the brain responsible for processing memory and emotion. That's why smells are a powerful memory trigger. Maybe . . .

I scoot closer to him.

Steven raises his head. His brows knit together. "Lain?"

He tenses as I grip his jacket in both hands and lean toward him. My heart is pounding. What I'm about to do will look ridiculous and possibly a little creepy, but it's worth a shot. "Hold still." I press my face against his neck and breathe in deeply. He makes a small, choked sound.

Leather. Smoke. Coffee. Beneath that, a distant whiff of rain and stone and dust and the ocean. I close my eyes, holding onto that scent, trying to follow it back to its source within myself. But whatever I glimpsed before, it's gone now. There's only that blankness, like a solid wall. When I pull back and look at Steven, he's a stranger once again. "I'm sorry," I say. "For a moment, I thought . . . but it's gone."

The hope in his eyes flickers and fades. He stops and inhales slowly, then rakes a hand through his hair. "If you remembered something, even if it was just for a second, that means it's still there." He says the words firmly, as if that will make them true.

Of course, that's not how memory modifications work. Even if a few bits of sensory data remain, floating around in the murk, they don't mean anything if they're disconnected from the larger context. It's like having a handful of fragments from a shattered stained-glass window. You might be able to see some things—a leaf, a flower, the curve of a cheek. But it's not enough to put together an image. Whatever was taken from me, it's gone for good. I don't have the heart to tell him that.

I push myself to my feet. "Let's keep moving."

* * *

By sundown, we still haven't found a road. We set up camp in a small clearing. Ian takes a small electric lantern out of his pack, along with a folded stack of blankets. He sets the lantern on the ground, where it casts a small circle of pale light.

"It's freezing," Steven says. He hasn't looked at me once since our brief conversation. "Do we have any matches?"

"Nope," Ian says. "If we want to start a fire, we'll have to do it the Boy Scout way. You know how, right?"

Steven snorts. "You think I was in Boy Scouts?" He flops to the ground and rests his folded arms on top of his knees.

Ian shrugs. "Probably shouldn't risk a campfire, anyway. Too much smoke and light. We don't want to attract anyone's attention out here."

I lean back against a tree, head pounding. The temperature is dropping rapidly; my teeth start to chatter. Ian sits down next to me and drapes a blanket around my shoulders like a cloak. A tiny smile tugs at my mouth, and I hold out one arm. "Here. We'll share body heat."

He hesitates briefly, then slides under the blanket with me.

I lean against his side. It's warm, and I close my eyes. There's so much I need to think about, but I don't want to think. I just want to exist here, tucked into the curve of Ian's body. He holds a water bottle to my lips. "Drink some. It'll help with your headache."

The water splashes down my throat, soothing the raw, parched flesh. He drips some of the water on his fingers and rubs them over my forehead, cooling my skin, which is fever-hot despite the cold air. "That's nice," I murmur. I glance up and see a pair of pale blue eyes staring back at me from across the clearing. They cut quickly away.

He seems so very alone. A part of me wants to reach out to him. But right now, I can't deal with the tangle of questions he represents. I'm too exhausted.

For awhile, I doze, anchored by the pressure of Ian's shoulder against mine. He smoothes my hair, fingers sliding over and through it. I like his hands. The thought appears randomly, but I've always liked them—how long they are, how graceful and dexterous. The hands of an artist, or a piano player. I breathe in his scent, so comforting and familiar, like a favorite book, and I find myself thinking of the first time I saw him in IFEN headquarters, wearing his white Mindwalker robe. He seemed so young, with his big puppy eyes and a pink glow in his cheeks, but there was an easy confidence about him that I envied. His hair was long back then, I recall, tied back into a loose ponytail. He was always changing his hair, but I think I liked it best at that length.

A sound catches my ears. It takes a moment for me to recognize it. Hoof beats.

Ian tenses. "What is that?"

Steven stands up, cocking his rifle. "Be ready."

Ian stands, and I rise with him, still leaning against his shoulder. The beats come closer and closer, *clop-clop, clop-clop*. The leaves rustle, and a huge, black shape emerges from the surrounding forest. The horse snorts and paws the ground with one hoof, ears twitching. A woman sits astride its back, holding the reigns—a woman in a short-sleeved black coat, dusty jeans and cowboy boots. An abstract design of intricate, spiraling black tattoos covers her arms from wrist to elbow, and she's wearing a holomask of . . . a wild dog, I think.

She smiles, her narrow muzzle opening to reveal rows of sharp teeth. I notice the pistol slung low on her hip. "Well," she says. "I finally found you."

4

I blink a few times, trying to adjust to the surreal image of a dog-headed woman sitting before us astride a black stallion.

Steven raises his rifle.

She drops the reigns and raises her hands, though she doesn't seem alarmed. "Relax. I'm not an enemy."

"What do you mean, you finally found us?" Steven asks, his voice low and cold. He keeps the gun trained on her. "What do you want?"

"Allow me to guess," she says. "You've just crossed the border, and you're on the run?"

He tenses. Ian leaps to his feet.

She laughs, showing rows of sharp teeth and a long pink tongue. "I told you—I'm a friend. You can call me Jackal. I was out riding when I saw your chopper crash. Followed the smoke to the wreckage and tracked you here. No offense, but you left a pretty obvious trail, and you were going in circles, so I figured you were lost."

"How do we know we can trust you?" I ask, trying to sound bolder than I feel.

"You don't," she replies. "It's up to you. I can lead you to a safe place, or I can turn around and leave you here in the woods."

Steven and Ian exchange glances, then Ian says, "How far is it?"

*   *   *

I don't know how long we trudge through bushes and brambles, picking leaves and bristles off of our clothes, following the woman on the horse. She keeps her holomask on the whole time; her pointed ears swivel back and forth like miniature satellite dishes. By the time we arrive in an open clearing, it's dawn. My feet are aching stumps, my clothes drenched with sweat despite the cold.

In front of us looms an ancient house, weathered and gray. It looks abandoned.

"Here it is," Jackal calls.

"So, um." I clear my throat. "Is this the Citadel?"

Ian smiles. "No, our base is a lot more impressive than this, I promise."

Jackal places a cigarette between the black lips of her mask, inhales, and breathes out a smoky cloud. "So, you're headed to the Citadel? You've got a long trip ahead of you."

"It might be smart to lie low for a few days," Ian remarks. "I mean . . . considering everything, it seems safer." He casts a glance at Steven, who nods.

I frown. I feel like there's a secret they're not letting me in on. "Why? Why is it safer?"

Ian tilts his head, as if weighing his words. "Things are a little chaotic in the Citadel right now. That's all."

"Well, you'll be safe here," Jackal says. "This place is totally off the grid. No electricity or anything."

The house's windows are dark and boarded up. If someone asked me to picture a haunted house, this is probably what I'd come up with.

Jackal dismounts from her horse and tethers it to a nearby tree. She pats the sleek neck—it's slick and foamy with sweat—then takes another drag off her cigarette and breathes the smoke out through her nose, like a dragon. The smell makes my eyes water.

She walks us up the half-collapsed steps to the front door, unlocks it with a tarnished key, and leads us through a dimly lit foyer, down a narrow hallway. The wooden floorboards squeak and groan in protest under our footsteps. She pauses to open a closet and rummage through its contents, then she fishes out two kerosene lamps and lights them with a long wooden match. "There's food in the kitchen," she says, waving a hand toward a doorway. "Mostly canned stuff. There's no way to heat it—well, I guess you could use the fireplace. But it'll fill you up, anyway."

I look around at the faded, grayish wood walls, the saggy floor and shaggy cobwebs in the corners. "Do you live here?"

She laughs. "God, no. I live on a farm a few miles from this place." She blows out the match and hands me one of the lamps. "I discovered this empty house here awhile back, and it seemed like a good place for people to hide. So I keep it stocked with food and supplies."

"That's . . . very kind of you." I'm not sure how to feel, actually. Can helping terrorists really be considered admirable, even if her motives are altruistic?

She shrugs. "When I first crossed the border, the Blackcoats got me a fake ID, helped me start a life here. I'm just paying it forward." She hands the second lamp to Steven. "Anyway, I'm going to head out."

"You're not staying?" Ian asks.

"Got a little girl back home. It's just me and her."

I wonder how someone with a child can take these kinds of risks. What if something happened to Jackal? What if she got caught?

Maybe she reads the thoughts on my face. She smiles, showing a flash of white teeth. "I came here so Sara could grow up without Types, without being watched all the time. I want a world where all children can have that freedom. I'd be a hypocrite if I didn't fight for it." She drops a house key into my hand. "The bedrooms are upstairs. There's an escape tunnel in the basement, in case the cops show up—it comes out in the forest about half a mile to the west. Oh, and here." She hands Ian a cell phone. "Prepaid. It's got my number on it. Use it to contact me, if you need to. But only if you need to."

The floorboards groan under her boots as she walks out and shuts the door behind her.

"So," Steven says, "guess we're staying here tonight."

"Guess so," Ian replies. The flickering light of the kerosene lamp reflects in his eyes. "I wish we had a way to contact the others. They probably don't even know we're alive. But given Lain's condition—" he glances at me "—it might be better to wait a few days before we have any more contact with them."

By my condition, I don't think he's just talking about the bump on my head. Without my memories of the past few months, how well would I manage being thrown in with a bunch of hardcore antigovernment types? The thought sends a twinge of panic through me. Then again, Jackal didn't seem that bad. Her words replay through my head, and I shift my weight, suddenly uncomfortable. "Do you really want to take down IFEN?" I blurt out.

Steven and Ian look at me in surprise.

"Do you think we'd be here now if we didn't?" Ian asks.

"Trust me," Steven says, "if you had your memories, you'd hate them, too."

"Well, I don't have my memories," I say, a little more sharply than I intended. "Am I supposed to just take your word for it? Am I supposed to believe that Dr. Swan was really involved in illegal human experimentation? That he was responsible for my father's suicide?"

"You were there when I said those things to him," Steven says. "He didn't deny it."

"He didn't confirm it, either. And even if it's all true, that doesn't mean IFEN itself is evil. You can't blame the entire system for the actions of one person."

"Lain . . ." Ian's voice is soft, almost apologetic. "There's a lot you don't know."

"Then explain it to me! Because frankly, I'm having trouble understanding why my best friend is suddenly a terrorist."

"We aren't terrorists," Steven says. "We're revolutionaries. And so are you. You just don't remember."

I struggle to keep my tone level. "All right, maybe I was. I don't know. But doesn't this all strike you as a bit extreme? I know the system isn't perfect, but it's not like we're living under some sort of totalitarian regime."

"Actually, yeah, that's exactly what it's like," Steven says, his tone hardening.

"That's absurd. We have elected representatives—"

"Who are basically puppets. And a fourth of the population can't vote, anyway. You lose the vote once your Type gets bad enough."

"Well, yes. That's not something I completely agree with, but still, I'm sure even you can understand the rationale . . ." I trail off. Steven's eyes are cold and flat.

"What the hell did Dr. Swan do to your brain?" he asks. "Because the Lain I know is smarter than this. Did he screw around with your personality, too?"

I flush. "Of course he didn't. That's not even possible." Still, the faintest hint of doubt flickers. The truth is, I have no idea what Dr. Swan did to me. And now I'll never have a chance to ask him.

Ian clears his throat. "Maybe now isn't the best time for this conversation." He places a warm hand on my back. "You should get some rest."

"Yeah," Steven mutters. He turns and trudges down the hallway, toward a set of stairs at the end, leading upward. We follow. I step gingerly, wincing at every deafening creak. I can't shake the feeling that, at any moment, the entire house might collapse around us.

Steven's voice, laced with scorn, echoes through my head. *The Lain I know is smarter than this.* I bite the inside of my cheek. Why should his opinion bother me, anyway? Why do I care?

At the top of the stairs is a long hallway. Water drips from a gap in the ceiling and into a tiny puddle on the floor. The lamp throws a circle of yellow light on the floorboards. A mouse scuttles away from the glow, vanishing into a crack in the wall. Steven opens the first door we come to, and the hinges squeal.

I peek inside. The room is little more than four bare walls with a narrow bed. The plaster on the walls has peeled away in places, revealing the brick beneath. Ian crosses the hallway and opens another door, then a third. "Two bedrooms and a bathroom," he announces. "Though I wouldn't bet on any of the appliances working. The shower in here looks like something out of a horror story."

I peer in. "Well, at least there's a skylight." I point to the hole in the ceiling. A thin, gray beam of sunlight shines through.

Ian lets out a small laugh. "I guess that helps."

"I'm gonna go look for some food," Steven says without looking at us. He descends the stairs.

I walk into the first bedroom and carefully sit on the edge of the bare mattress. It feels like a slab of rock, but it holds my weight, at least. There's a thin, ratty blanket folded up at the foot of the bed. "Well, it beats sleeping in the forest."

Ian cracks a tiny smile. "Yeah."

We sit in silence for a long moment, listening to the *drip-drip-drip* of water in the hall. Two bedrooms, I think, and three of us. Well, I suppose we can rotate. It would make sense for one person to stay awake and stand guard, anyway.

A tiny furrow appears between Ian's thick, dark brows as he studies my face. "How are you feeling?"

"All right, I guess." I pause. "Well, no. Not all right."

He nods, shoulders hunched beneath his long black coat. His long fingers are tangled together in his lap. "You want to talk?"

I rub my forehead. "My last memory, before all this, is going to class. Then I woke up in IFEN headquarters with one of the technicians telling me that I'd had a trauma erased from my mind. And then . . ." Tears sting my eyes, and I blink them away.

Dr. Swan practically raised me after my father's death. Just twenty-four hours ago, I believed that he was someone I could trust. Within the span of a few minutes, I found out that he'd lied to me about everything. And then I lost him. Steven's face swims into my head. "Has he killed a lot of people?"

"Who? Steven?"

I nod.

A brief pause. "I'm not completely sure, but I don't think he's ever killed someone with his own hands."

"That woman—Rhee—mowed down a row of guards in IFEN headquarters, and he didn't even flinch."

"Yeah, well. We've all had to get used to death, whether we wanted to or not." Pain tightens his expression. "Sometimes, you have to kill people if you want to survive."

"I don't accept that. There's always another way."

He smiles sadly. "I hope you're right."

I wonder how I'd feel about all this if I still had my memories. I don't even know who I am right now. I can't even begin to imagine the chain of events that might have led the other Lain to become a Blackcoat.

The other Lain. That's a strange way to think about it, but that's what it *feels* like. In a relatively short time, I somehow became a person with different values, a person who abandoned her dreams, her future, her entire life. And now I can never go back. There's a small, sharp pain in my throat, like a fragment of metal is caught there. "Ian . . ." I swallow. "I'm really scared."

"I know." He rests a hand on my back. He's touched me many

times before—we've hugged each other, comforted each other after bad sessions. But this time, something is different. His touch is more tentative, like he's not sure where we stand. It puzzles me. His hand lingers on my back for a moment, then slips away. "You don't have to take it all in at once. Just focus on getting through today. We'll have something to eat, then get some rest."

I want to tell him to put his hand on me again, but something stops me.

My fingertips wander across the mattress, tracing a gray stain. Faintly, I can hear Steven downstairs, rummaging through the kitchen. In my head, I see him sitting next to me, knees drawn up to his chest, looking so oddly young and vulnerable, despite the rifle on his back. "What sort of person is he?"

"You want my opinion?"

"I just want to know more about him, I guess. Apparently he and I were . . . close."

"Yeah. You were."

The endless drip of water echoes through the silence. I moisten my dry lips with the tip of my tongue. "How did I meet him? Do you know?"

"You took him on as a client, even though Dr. Swan ordered you not to. They said he was a hopeless case, but you wouldn't accept that. After that, you and he started spending a lot of time together."

"Wait," I say, alarmed. "He was my client? I kissed a client?"

A smile twitches at the corners of his mouth.

"There's nothing funny about it! That's a huge breach of professional ethics!"

"Sorry. You're right, it's not funny. It's just, considering everything else that's happened, the whole 'professional ethics' thing doesn't seem like a huge deal."

"Just because there are bigger things going on doesn't mean it's not important," I mutter. I look at Ian from the corner of my eye. "So, what is your opinion of him?"

55

Ian makes a slight face, mouth twisting to one side, as if he just bit into something funny-tasting. "Honestly? At first, I hated the guy. I was really worried about you. He seemed . . . unstable. Dangerous. And of course, he was a Type Four, and I'd grown up hearing that we were supposed to feel sorry for Type Fours but never get too close to them, because they might infect us with their paranoia."

I nod—not because I agree, but because I've heard the same thing. That line always bothered me, though. Father taught me that all people were to be accepted as equals, and that if someone is suffering, you shouldn't avoid that person, you should try to help him. Of course, you can't argue with the data. Studies have consistently shown that humans tend to mirror each other's emotions. Spend enough time around people who are depressed or angry or afraid, and you'll start feeling the same way. Was that what happened to me?

"You said 'at first.' Does that mean your mind changed?"

He shrugs. "A lot of things changed. Including my Type. To make a long story short, I couldn't handle the psychological strain of being a Mindwalker. I got depressed. And suddenly I was one of those people I'd always looked down on and pitied. I started to understand why so many of them hate IFEN. When the system is set up to control you and keep you powerless, being angry and paranoid makes sense. It becomes a survival strategy. But the more we fight back, the more IFEN tightens the leash, and the more freedoms we lose, the harder we fight. It's a big self-reinforcing loop." He gives me a tiny, wry smile. "Sorry. Didn't mean to start lecturing there. That's not even what you asked me about. You wanted to know about Steven."

"That helps, actually." I want to ask what Ian's Type is now, but that would be rude and invasive. I study his face. "Your eyes have changed. They're darker."

He rubs the back of his neck; his long lashes flick down, hiding the objects of my scrutiny. "I think it's just the lighting."

"No. I noticed it earlier, too, in the sunlight. I don't mind, though. I kind of like it. They're . . . intense."

He lets out a small laugh, more exhalation than sound. "Intense, huh?" His smile fades, and his eyes lift, meeting mine. For a long moment, we just look at each other.

He's still Ian and I'm still Lain, and yet everything is different. Over the past few months, he's seen a side of me that I've never seen myself, and now I'm seeing a side of him I never knew about. I wonder how many of those other selves are locked away inside us.

"I'm the same person as before, you know," he says, as if reading my thoughts. We've known each other so long, we can do that sometimes.

"Well, you look strangely comfortable in that black coat."

"I've gotten used to it."

I hesitate, half afraid to ask the question hovering in my thoughts. "What did Steven want me to erase from his mind, anyway?"

"Um. That's kind of personal, so I should probably let him tell you. But he ended up keeping the memories, anyway. And there was this whole thing where you two left Aura together and went looking for this place from his memories . . . it's complicated."

I breathe a small sigh. "I wish I could remember."

There's another pause. "Do you want that?" he asks quietly. "Really? If there was a way to bring your memories back, would you do it?"

It strikes me as an odd question. Of course I would want that. Why wouldn't I? And yet, when I open my mouth to say yes, something stops me. I think about the pill in my pocket, then dismiss the idea. "It's a moot point. Once memories are erased, they can't be recovered."

"Yeah. You're right." He brushes a few loose strands of hair from my face, the touch ghost-light. "I've missed you, you know."

A flush creeps into my cheeks. "I wasn't gone *that* long, was I?"

"I guess not, but. I dunno. It feels like a long time. I'm just glad you're back."

I hesitate, then lean my head against his shoulder. His breath catches, and his muscles tense briefly. Then he relaxes and slowly puts an arm around me.

We've done this before, too. Once, after a day of training at IFEN, I'd been sobbing over a client—a quiet, terribly sad young woman who wanted to forget the parents who'd told her over and over that she was worthless, who'd starved her as punishment for the slightest offenses. Ian hugged me and wiped my puffy eyes with a cool, damp cloth, then said, "Come with me."

He took me to the planetarium. "I know it's nerdy," he said, "but in a weird way it can help, remembering how small all our human problems are."

We sat together in the dark amphitheater, watching the lights of stars and galaxies glide across the black dome overhead. And it did help, a little. The narrator's deep voice was hypnotically calming, and I found myself dozing a little, resting my head on Ian's shoulder. After a few minutes, he put an arm around me. He leant closer and whispered, "No matter how bad things are here on Earth, there's still thousands of other worlds out there. Millions."

"Do you think there are people on them?" I murmured drowsily. "Like us?"

"They probably don't look much like us. But I think—I hope, anyway—that they feel some of the same stuff we do."

"Like kindness?"

"Yeah. And loneliness, even. And love."

At the time, I didn't think much of it. Ian and I understood each other; we both knew the pain of being Mindwalkers. Of course we comforted each other, held onto each other for strength. Like castaways in a stormy ocean, we buoyed each other up. It didn't imply anything romantic—even if, to the rest of the world, we probably looked like a couple.

We were always so busy anyway, between school and training, there was no time for anything more than friendship, and I assumed he felt the same. But now, looking back, it seems strange, that I never wondered.

I'm not sure what alerts me to the fact that someone is watching us. Maybe it's a sound, maybe just a sense of eyes on me. But when I look up, Steven is there in the doorway, his expression unreadable. Warmth creeps into my cheeks, and I quickly pull away from Ian, like a child caught playing with something she's been told not to touch. Steven doesn't react.

"What's that?" Ian asks, and I notice Steven's carrying an arm-load of boxes and jars.

"Crackers, peanut butter, and beef stew," he says. "I couldn't find any spoons, but there was a can opener in one of the drawers. Dig in."

My stomach wakes up with a gurgle. Until now, I've been too overwhelmed to focus much on my hunger, but now it opens up inside me like a yawning cavern. How long has it been since that unsatisfying meal in IFEN headquarters?

Steven sits on the foot of the bed and opens the jar of peanut butter. I scoop up a glob, using a cracker as a makeshift spoon. We pass the food around, dipping the thin, salty crackers or just eating with our fingers. Within half an hour, we've finished everything. I suck the last traces of beef stew from my fingertips and let out a small, satisfied sigh. It's amazing how much better I feel, now that I've got something in my stomach.

"There's some bottled water," Steven says. "And it looks like there's a pump behind the house, too." He studies his feet. "Dunno if it still works, but we could give it a try."

"Okay." I'm not sure what else to say. "That sounds good."

He stands and walks out, leaving me with a strange emptiness in my chest, though I should be glad for the distance between us.

Ian sits in silence. I pick at the edge of my thumbnail, searching for words.

A muscle in his jaw flexes. "Can I tell you something I shouldn't?"

My brows draw together. "What?"

"I don't want you to get your memories back. Because if you do, I'll lose you."

The words send a thin chill sliding down my spine. "Why would you lose me?"

His eyes hide from mine. "It's just . . . people's feelings change. That's all."

I take his hand. His skin is warm and smooth. I meet his gaze— so soft and dark, so different from Steven's penetrating, icy-blue stare. "Ian. You're my best friend. You're more important to me than anyone else in the world." His eyes widen slightly. I've never actually told him that before—maybe I never even consciously realized it until now—but it's the simple truth. Since Father's death, Ian's the one who's always been there for me, the only one I truly trust. "Nothing will ever change that."

"Yeah. Maybe you're right." He blinks a few times, and I see the glint of moisture at the corners of his eyes. But it disappears so quickly, I can't be sure. "We should probably get some sleep. Unless . . . do you want me to stay? To talk, I mean."

I hesitate. A part of me wants that, the comfort of his close- ness, his smile. But I shake my head. "I'm all right." I need space to process everything I've learnt. I need to think, and when he's around, it's too easy to sink into the feeling of safety he offers, too easy to shut off the questions circling in my head.

"Okay." He leans in and very softly kisses my forehead. My breath catches in surprise. Before I can respond, he slips quietly out of the room.

I sink into bed. My body is heavy with exhaustion, but my mind spins like a top.

He's in love with you. The words rise out of the depths inside me, out of the void where memories once lived. Ian, my best friend, is in love with me? Maybe I'm in love with him too. I don't know;

my emotions are a mass of tangled threads, and I can't begin to sort them out. He thinks that if I recover the past few months, he'll lose his chance, because then I'll be in love with Steven again. Which means that I *was* in love with Steven. It wasn't just some little crush. Of course, that makes sense—I wouldn't have kissed a client unless my own feelings were strong enough to override my conscience and training. The question is, do I *want* those feelings to come back? Do I want to be in love with a man who's so comfortable with death and killing? A man who loathes IFEN and wants to destroy it?

For awhile, I lie awake, watching the patterns of moonlight on the walls and floor. When the wind sighs through the trees, making the branches sway, the patterns dance and flicker. Near the door, the kerosene lamp glows softly, a steady yellow flame. The house is like a living thing, sighing and crackling all around me. In the walls, I can hear the claws of tiny animals scratching. The pain in my head has died to a faint ebb and flow behind my eyes, like waves on the shore. I think about the pill, still tucked into my pocket.

After an hour of tossing and turning, I take it out. I roll it between my thumb and forefinger, studying it in the dim light.

What if I *could* recover my lost memories? And why does that thought frighten me?

It's not just that I'm afraid of what I'll learn, though that's part of it. It goes deeper. I'm afraid of her—of the other Lain. I feel like there's a stranger locked inside my body, waiting to seize control.

I set the pill carefully on the rickety table next to the bed and close my eyes.

5

I wake with a start, gasping. Sweat trickles down my temples. Slowly, I sit up. I can't remember what I was dreaming about. There's only a hazy tangle of impressions. But the image of Dr. Swan's blank, empty eyes—the bullet hole in his head—lingers.

At first, I don't know where I am. The walls around me are wood, weathered to a dull gray. Dawn light creeps in through the window. I'm alone. I raise a trembling hand to my forehead—and then the memories of the past day come rushing back.

The pill still rests on the rickety table next to my bed. I turn it over. The words—EAT ME—are a mockery and an invitation.

The details of the dream are already fading, but the sense of terror remains, and I know I won't be getting back to sleep.

The light outside has a misty green quality, eerie and deep, like something from the dawn of time. A bird lets out a cackling cry—a wild sound. There were never so many birds in Aura.

I get up and peer through the dingy glass of the window. The pink dawn sky shows in bright patches through the trees. There's a figure outside, working the ancient, rusted pump, filling a pail of water. Steven.

He's not doing anything remarkable, but still, I can't look

away. It's a strange feeling, watching someone and knowing he's unaware of my eyes on him. Maybe that's the only time you truly see people with their masks off. His back is to me, so I can't see his expression. He pauses to wipe his forehead with one sleeve. For a few seconds, he just stands there, staring off into the woods. Then, abruptly, he falls to his knees and buries his face in his hands.

I pull myself away from the window and press my back to the wall. My heart is pounding. When I finally dare to sneak another look through the glass, Steven is gone.

Just what *am* I to him? What were we to each other?

I search the dark space inside me for an echo of what I felt for him, but there's nothing. I've gotten pieces of the puzzle, bits of information, but information alone can't tell you who a person is. Only memories can.

Memories. They form the basis of all human relationships, all love and hate. They're more than our past; they're our present, the fabric of the living souls within us. They're the foundation of our emotions, our understanding of the world, our choices. A true Mindwalker understands that. And I find myself wondering, not for the first time, if that's a power that anyone should have—the power to rewrite a person's being.

My gaze falls on the pill, still sitting on the nightstand. I curl my fingers around it, feeling it press into my palm.

By now, Ian's probably awake too. I need to tell them about this. I can't deal with it alone. Secrets are a heavy burden to bear.

I pick up the kerosene lantern from the floor and creep down the hallway. Voices echo from downstairs, and I freeze, listening. Holding my breath, I tiptoe down the stairs. The door to the kitchen is shut, and inside, I hear Steven and Ian talking.

"Look," Ian says in the calm, reasonable voice he uses on diffi-cult clients. "I know it's tough, but you've really got to get a grip. We're in the middle of nowhere, here. We need each other to survive. I understand why you want to leave, but—"

"Don't tell me you understand," Steven snaps. "You don't fucking understand."

"Okay, fine. Explain it to me."

Leave? Holding my breath, I press my ear to the door.

I hear pacing. Then the footsteps stop, and Steven takes a deep, shaky breath. "Because it would be better for her. You calm her down. I scare her."

"She just needs to get used to you."

"Don't you get it?" His voice cracks. "I've been screwing up her life ever since she met me. I dragged her into this hell, but even when things started going wrong, when she realized she'd made a mistake, she couldn't leave me. Because she knew I'd fall apart. She can't stop herself from helping people, even when it hurts her. That's what I am—I'm a bad habit she couldn't break. Maybe now, she's just seeing me clearly for the first time."

A quiet sigh. "She's not seeing anything clearly right now. She doesn't even know who she is."

I don't move. A bead of sweat carves its way down my neck.

"As far as she's concerned," Ian continues, "the first time she saw you is when you barged into IFEN headquarters with a gun on your back. Of course she's not going to immediately trust you. If you'd get your head out of your ass and take off your self-hatred goggles for two seconds, you'd see that you're actually not that bad a guy."

Steven snorts. "Right. I'm only a terrorist and a former drug addict with about a dozen psychiatric disorders and a brain full of holes and scars. I'm a real catch. Why are you trying to talk me out of this, anyway? You want to be with her, right? Why not just let me leave and have your little happily-ever-after?"

There's a long pause. Ian lets out a flat, bitter chuckle. "Good question."

I try to breathe quietly, shallowly. My feet are rooted to the floor, my ear glued to the rough boards.

"Maybe . . . maybe because I know it would be a lie. If she chooses me because she doesn't remember you, and if I just go along with that, then I'm no better than Dr. Swan, trying to hide the truth for my own benefit. Sooner or later, I'd start to hate myself." His voice has grown quiet, almost inaudible. Now it rises again. "But this isn't about what either of us wants. There are bigger things going on. The Blackcoats are in serious trouble. They can't afford to lose any more members. Besides, there are still things we could try. If we showed her our memories of the past few months through the Gate, maybe it would help her regain some sense of herself. And her bond with you."

"It doesn't matter." Steven's voice is empty, quiet. "She'd already made her choice, even before she lost her memories. She chose you."

"I'm not sure about that."

"You didn't see—"

I push the door open. They lapse into silence and stare at me, still as statues. I walk over to the table and sit down. They remain standing. "You know," I say, "if you're going to talk about me, it would be polite to include me in the discussion."

Suddenly, neither one of them can look at me. They shuffle their feet. "I thought you were asleep," Ian murmurs.

I turn to Steven. "What's this about you leaving?"

He shifts his weight. "I thought—"

"That it would be better for me?" Anger creeps into my voice. "It's not your place to decide that."

He doesn't look at me. "You said it yourself. You didn't ask to be rescued. If I were a less selfish person, I would've just left you there."

"I know what I said, but I was suffering from more than a bit of shock, at the time. I had no idea what was going on. I still don't, but I know that I don't want to go back there. I was a prisoner in that place."

"At least you were *safe*."

"I don't want to be safe. I want answers. Dr. Swan tried to steal the truth from me. And I intend to find out why." I pause, heart drumming. "I want to know who you are, too."

His eyes snap toward me, sharp and bright. A muscle twitches in his jaw.

"What's that you've got?" Ian asks.

I glance down at my curled fist, hesitate, and open my fingers, revealing the tiny white circle nestled in the center of my sweat-damp palm.

Steven blinks, mouth opening. "Is that Lucid?"

"I don't know what it is," I say. "It was given to me by a nurse back in IFEN headquarters. Why? What makes you think it's Lucid?"

"It looks like the kind I took before," Steven says.

Ian frowns. "Can I see it?"

I hand him the pill, and he holds it up to the fluttering light from the kerosene lamp. For a long time, none of us speaks. "Well?" I ask.

"A nurse gave this to you?" he asks. "Really?"

"Yes, but . . . I don't think she really worked for IFEN."

Ian and Steven exchange startled, puzzled looks.

"I don't know what it is," I say. "But . . . somehow, I have the feeling that it will help me recover my memories." Still, I know that's not rational. Memory modifications aren't reversible. That's the first thing they teach us in our training. Ever since Mindwalking was invented, there've been people who regretted having their past erased, and a few have tried experimental methods of getting it back. It never works. Sometimes, the attempts have had disastrous consequences.

"That's silly of me, isn't it?" I prompt, looking at Ian. "Once you destroy a cluster of neurons, you can't un-destroy it."

Ian studies my face, his eyes moving in tiny flicks. The pill still rests in his palm. "Neural modification doesn't destroy *all* the cells responsible for those memories, because episodic memories aren't stored in a single location in the brain. The hippocampus integrates them, but that's only one part of the process—they're formed and given meaning by different neural networks working together."

He's right. And that means some of that data is still there. I just can't access it.

I feel a tickle of excitement and curiosity, mingled with a pang of dread. "So you're saying, if you could stimulate the growth of new connections between the neurons—"

"Exactly. It might be possible to recover some of your memories."

"But if information in the brain isn't connected to a larger context, it tends to decay very quickly," I point out. "The only reason we remember events from long ago is because our brains are continually recalling them and touching up the faded parts, like repairing an old painting. You're actually recalling the last recall, rather than the memory itself."

"Right. It takes the brain about forty-eight hours to heal after a memory modification procedure. During that time, everything gets shuffled around and reintegrated. But after that, the loose bits of sensory data from the old memories start to decay. And once that's gone, it's gone."

"Wait, wait," Steven says. "That's not how it worked with me. I mean, when we recovered my memories."

"Recovered your memories?" I ask.

"Long story," Ian says. "It was different for him, though." He turns to Steven. "Your early childhood was erased during the neural modification procedure at St. Mary's—those memories are gone for good—but your memories of St. Mary's itself weren't actually deleted. Instead, they Conditioned you to tweak the details. It was less like neural modification and more like a strong subliminal suggestion. You see the difference?"

He frowns. "I guess so. I still don't really get it."

"My point is, if this actually is a memory-recovery pill, she'll have to take it soon." He meets my gaze. "The longer you wait, the smaller the chance of it working."

Steven stands stiffly, hands shoved into his pockets.

I hold out a hand, and Ian gives the pill back to me. I turn it over in my fingers, roll it along the pad of my thumb. It's smooth, almost slippery. Somehow, just holding onto it feels dangerous, like it might seep through my skin.

I remember reading about clinical trials for high-dose Lucid and its effects on Alzheimer's patients. The patients did remember things, but they weren't always able to connect the pieces into a coherent whole. It just made them confused and agitated. One of them jumped out a window. If there was a way to integrate the new information more smoothly into my consciousness, maybe . . .

An idea sparks, and the scientist in me leaps on it like a puppy on a ball. A tingle of electricity travels down my spine. "Ian. You said something about using a Gate to show me your memories?"

He hesitates. "Well, yeah. We could do that, but—"

"Memory isn't just raw data, after all," I say, interrupting him in my eagerness. "Memory is a *narrative*, a story about who you are. Right now, you and Steven know me better than anyone else. You both have memories of me during the months I lost. If I take the pill and you both share your memories with me—using a three-way loop—it could be enough to tie the sensory data together into a coherent whole."

Ian's mouth opens in surprise, then closes.

"Three-way loop?" Steven asks.

"They're used when young Mindwalkers are in training," Ian says. "It's a way for superiors to observe their progress. Usually, that's *all* it is. This . . ." He glances at me, uncertain. "You're talking about some kind of three-way mind meld? Has that ever been attempted?"

"Well, no." I swallow. If we try this, we'll be the guinea pigs. "The only problem is, I'm not sure where we'd get a Gate."

"I have one."

"Here?" I ask, startled.

"I brought yours. From the Citadel." He offers a small, sheepish smile. "Sorry I didn't tell you earlier, but, well, with everything else that was going on . . ." He shrugs. "I thought maybe it would help you believe us, if you could see our memories of the past few months."

"And what if it doesn't work?" Steven asks sharply. "What if it goes wrong?"

"Well . . ."

"We don't even know what that drug is. It could be something even more dangerous than Lucid."

My heart hammers against my sternum. "I'm willing to take that chance."

His pale eyes drill into mine, but I don't look away. Steven is the one who finally breaks eye contact.

"Are you sure you don't want to do the Gate thing on its own? Without the pill?" Ian asks quietly. "It would be safer."

I shake my head. "There are certain things that you and Steven can't tell me about the past few months—like what was going on in my head that whole time. I need to understand myself. If there's a chance I can get those memories back, I want to take it, no matter the risk."

"It's your decision," Ian says. He doesn't exactly look happy about this. "If this is what you want, I'll do it."

"Well, I won't," Steven snaps. "It's too risky."

I remember the sight of him kneeling in the yard, face buried in his hands. It kills him, what we've lost. And still, he's not willing to risk my safety.

Slowly, I reach out and take his hand, and his fingers twitch in surprise. They're thin and fever-hot. "I have to try." My heart is beating hard and fast, knocking like a fist against my sternum. "Please. We need your help for this."

The muscles of his throat constrict as he swallows. "I can't—" His voice breaks. "I've hurt you too much already."

My fingers squeeze tighter around his. I don't know what he means, when he says that he hurt me, and for a moment, I wonder if I really want to find out. "Even if that's true, it's my pain. And I want it back. I want it all back."

I can feel his heartbeat drumming beneath the skin. At last he nods, once. His face is drawn and pale.

I release his hand, trembling. I feel like I'm about to step off the edge of a chasm. Fear tingles at the base of my spine.

"Shouldn't we at least wait till we get back to the Citadel?" Steven asks.

"We don't have that sort of time," Ian says. "Memories decay quickly, remember? She's got maybe a forty-eight-hour window."

Suddenly, my chest is small and tight. It's a struggle to fill my lungs. "I—I think I need to get some air." I leave the pill on the table and walk out into the yard, into the crisp late-autumn coolness. The pines are still green, but most of the leaves have turned brown. They litter the ground, crunching under my feet as I walk deeper into the forest.

A spike of pain shoots suddenly through my left eye and sinks into my head like a long, burning fang, and I cry out, clapping a hand to my eye. My vision swims, shimmering around the edges. I stop to lean against a tree, my shirt sticking to my skin with cold sweat. The world wobbles like Jell-O. I press my cheek to the rough bark and close my eyes, waiting for it to pass. The pain fades to a manageable pulse, but my head feels like it's made of glass, like a sudden movement might shatter it.

I hear movement behind me and whirl around to see Ian. Another wave of pain slams into me, and I wince.

"Sorry," he says. He hangs back awkwardly. "Didn't mean to scare you. I just wanted to make sure you didn't go too far from the house. It's not safe."

"I know." My breath plumes in the air. I stand with my feet close together, hugging myself, wanting to curl into a tiny ball and disappear.

He approaches and gently touches my temple. "Are you okay?"

"Sort of." I grimace. "Actually, it feels like someone has a pair of pliers clamped around my optic nerve."

He touches my face, careful, gentle. "Close your eyes. The light can make it worse."

I do. Almost immediately, the pain recedes. "How did you know that?"

"Because I've gone through neural modification before. You really have to take it easy for a few days if you want to avoid those headaches. But then, I guess that's not really an option now."

I open my eyes in surprise. "You've had your memories modified? When?"

"That's another long story." He gives me a strained smile. "Keep those eyes closed."

My eyelids slip shut again. And then I feel his lips against the left one, and my heart jumps. The pressure is an explosion of light and color in my head. It doesn't hurt, but it leaves me breathless and shaky. "Ian . . ."

"I'm sorry." He rests his forehead against mine, breathing in small, unsteady hitches. "I know it's selfish. But I have to say it. I—"

"I know," I whisper. I open my eyes and tangle my fingers in his shirt, pulling him closer, and I crush my lips to his. They're full and soft, like sinking into a warm bed. His stubble scratches my chin as I move my lips against his. I wind my arms around his waist, and his arms slip around me, and our chests are pressed together. When I pull back, I can barely breathe, and the world is spinning around me like an out-of-control carousel. My knees start to buckle, and he catches me.

His eyes are wide. "Lain . . . are you . . ."

"Too much stimulation," I whisper. Then I let out a breathless laugh. "God. I'm seventeen, and I just had my first kiss."

"Eighteen."

"Right," I murmur. "Eighteen."

A shadow slips across his face. "And that wasn't your first."

"Well, I don't remember my first. So I guess now I've had two firsts."

He touches a thumb to the corner of my mouth, a light, cautious touch, as if he's not quite sure I'm real—like I'm an illusion that might dissolve at any second. In the shadows of the forest, his eyes are almost black, and his long, messy hair stirs in the breeze.

Ian. My Ian. Why did I never see him like this until now?

"I don't want this to end," he says. "I want to stay here, in this moment."

"It doesn't have to end," I say.

He smiles at me, pain in his eyes. His fingers graze the curve of my neck, tuck a few strands of hair behind my ear. "You're in love with him, Lain. You just don't remember it yet. And you're a Blackcoat. But I'm not—not deep down. I can't be. When I went on that mission . . . you don't even know what I'm talking about now. But I realized then that I couldn't do it, that I couldn't fight the way you and Steven could." He drops his gaze. "In a little while, you'll know who you really are. This is only a dream."

I draw in a shaky breath and let it out slowly. The other Lain, apparently, was pretty hardcore. I wonder again if I really want to be her, if I want to become someone that ruthless. "Why don't you let me decide what's a dream and what's real?"

"Fair enough."

I chew my lower lip. The sunlight fills his eyes, highlighting the small hints of brown in the blackness. "Have I ever killed anyone?" I'm afraid of the answer, but I need to know.

A brief pause. "I don't think so," he replies. "I mean, if you did, you never told me."

That's not the most reassuring answer I could have hoped for.

I've already made up my mind. If we don't act now, we'll lose the chance forever. I just wish I had more time.

The sunlight ripples through the leaves, dancing like water shadows at the bottom of a pool. It's disorienting. I wince, and Ian covers my eyes with one hand. "You don't have to look. Just follow me."

I nod. His fingers slide between mine, and I keep my eyes shut against the light as he leads me back to the house.

Without warning, a blinding agony explodes from the center of my head. Fireworks burst behind my eyes. I thrash, gasping, unable to catch my breath.

"Lain? Lain!" Ian grips my shoulders. "What's going on?"

I open my mouth, but I can't speak. I can't even breathe. The world vanishes in a wash of silver sparkles.

6

"Lain? Lain! Can you hear me?"

I moisten dry lips with the tip of my tongue and focus on his face. I'm flat on my back, on the ground. Cool grass tickles my neck. "What happened?"

"I was about to ask you that." He helps me to my feet. His eyes are wide, the whites visible all around. "You just . . . collapsed."

I try to remember exactly what I was feeling before that moment, but I can't recall anything triggering it. One second I was walking along, the next, my whole world was incinerated by the fire in my head. The pain is still there, but it's dimmed to a manageable level. It seems like I've had a more or less continuous headache ever since I left IFEN headquarters.

Of course, I've just had a neural modification. There's a glossy pamphlet we hand out to clients and their families after every procedure, filled with recommendations about what to do after returning home, and number one is the word REST! In large, bright red font, just in case the exclamation point wasn't enough. Too much stimulation can worsen their condition and cause long-term side effects, similar to a traumatic brain injury.

What I should do, medically speaking, is rest for the next few days and try to avoid any form of stimulation. But that's not an option.

I close my eyes. The lids feel like sandpaper, and there's a pressure at my temples, like huge hands squeezing my head. Trails of tiny rainbows dance in the darkness.

"Hey . . . everything okay?"

I open my eyes, breathing raggedly. Steven is standing in the doorway. The image blurs, pulses, then steadies.

"I'm fine," I say, though my voice sounds thin and watery. "I just need to lie down. Ian, help me upstairs." I don't want Steven to see how bad my condition is.

Ian helps me up to the bedroom and eases me into bed. He starts to pull back, and I catch his arm. "The Gate," I say, "where is it?"

A pause. "In my pack."

"We should get it set up. We have no time to waste."

Ian carefully touches my face and leans in, examining my undoubtedly bloodshot and dilated eyes. "Lain . . ." His teeth catch on his lower lip. "Maybe Steven is right. Maybe we should reconsider this."

"I've made up my mind."

"This could damage you beyond repair," he says flatly. "It could kill you."

Fear swoops through my stomach, though the words don't surprise me. He's right, of course. Is it stupid to risk my safety—my life—just to recover my memories?

My mouth is painfully dry, and I swallow, wincing at the twinge in my throat. "You said before that it isn't safe in the Citadel right now," I whisper. "What did you mean?"

He breathes in. "You've already got a lot on your mind. Trying to explain everything would just—"

"Ian."

He rubs his face with one palm. "Right now, we don't know who we can trust."

My hands clench. "You're saying there's someone there who might be working for the other side."

"Yeah. That's the situation."

"And what if I know who it is? What if that information is in my memories?"

He shakes his head, looking bewildered. "Why would you know that? Lain, this is—everything about this is dangerous. I can't—"

My fingers dig into his arm. "I need to know who I am."

He presses his lips together into a thin line. His gaze meets mine, and I see the worry in his eyes. The fear. But he nods. "I'll get the Gate ready."

Ian walks out of the room, and I sink back into bed. Icy sweat beads on my forehead as a rainbow of patterns forms behind my eyelids—matrices and grids of bright lines. Visual distortions are another side effect of neural modifications. When I open my eyes, everything appears different—dreamlike and yet somehow more *real*, more three-dimensional, and weirdly shiny around the edges. It might be fascinating, if I weren't so terrified and worn out. As it is, I wish it would all just stop so I can get some rest. I want to turn off, to stop thinking and sleep for three days. But I've denied myself that option.

I'm playing Russian roulette with my own brain. I shudder.

* * *

"This is it?" Steven asks.

"This is it," Ian replies.

There are three wooden chairs arranged in a triangle, all facing each other. Three helmets rest on the seats. In the center of the triangle stands the Gate's slim black hard drive.

I hang back in the doorway, examining the concrete-walled room. We're in the basement of the house—a bare, damp place filled with exposed pipes and water stains. A few kerosene lamps sit on the floor, flickering and filling the room with eerie shadows.

The ambiance is more fitting for a seance than a medical procedure, but Ian thought it would be safest to do this down here. While we're all strapped in and tripping out on Lucid—if, indeed, that's what the mysterious pill is—we'll be unaware of our surroundings. Vulnerable. But even if the police come searching for us and discover the house, they probably won't think to look down here.

I meet Ian's gaze, then Steven's. His expression is flat and unreadable as ever—at least on the surface. But there's something beneath, something roiling and wild, like a storm. "You ready?" he asks me quietly.

I open my mouth, but my voice is frozen. The cold, strong hand of panic squeezes my lungs. Once the other Lain is freed from her prison inside me, what will happen? Will she swallow me whole, or will we both exist simultaneously inside the same skull, an uneasy mishmash of different ideals and perspectives? Maybe that won't be so different from the way I feel now. "Yes." Trying to ignore the tremor in my legs, I approach the chair and sit down. "So . . . how will this work?"

"I'll activate the Gate," Ian says. "And you take the pill. You'll be guiding the session. That is, you'll be in the role of the Mindwalker, and you'll be receiving signals from Steven and I. If it all works the way it's supposed to, your mind will integrate those signals, and when it's over, you'll be more like the person you were before Dr. Swan erased your memories."

My fingers are slick with sweat as I pull the helmet on. Ian approaches and hands me the Lucid pill, then sits down in his chair and puts on his own helmet, buckling the strap beneath his chin. Steven remains standing. The amber kerosene glow casts shadows beneath his eyes, in the hollows of his cheeks.

My gaze meets his, and a small shiver races through me. Right now, he still feels almost like a stranger to me. Like a mystery. If this works, that mystery will unravel. I'll know not just Steven, but myself—I'll know about the Citadel, about the people I met in IFEN headquarters. And if this *doesn't* work—

Quite possibly, we'll all go running into the woods screaming like lunatics and get eaten by a bear or something. Or maybe my brain will disintegrate into a lump of catatonic oatmeal, and I'll spend the rest of my life drooling and wearing diapers. Maybe we all will. I picture the three of us all sitting around in a treatment facility, our eyes like dead screens filled with static, our bodies withering away in silence, tended by indifferent people in white uniforms.

No. That won't happen. I won't let it.

Slowly, Steven lowers himself into the chair and straps on his helmet. We all look at each other, and the empty space in the center of our triangle feels alive with tension.

"Ready?" Ian says. I nod. After a moment, Steven does, too.

He switches on the Gate. A faint hum fills the air, and my scalp begins to tingle. The tingling spreads slowly down my spine, throughout my body. I close my eyes and feel my heart beating. Then I can feel another beat, a second pulse beating within mine, like one image superimposed over another. I somehow know that it's Ian's. His pulse is steadier than mine. A third joins in—*Steven*—filling my chest with a cacophony of beats—and then, all at once, our heartbeats synch up. *Ba-dum. Ba-dum.*

"I'd almost forgotten how freaky this is," Steven mutters.

Ian utters a short laugh. "No kidding."

He rubs his chest absently. "Aren't you used to it by now? You've done this a lot."

"That was different. You know. Clinical. This is more like—"

"Like some kind of psychedelic *ménage à trois?*"

"Well, I wasn't going to put it like that. Thanks for making it extra weird."

I don't say anything—I'm too preoccupied by the steady thrum of their heartbeats inside my chest. It's oddly soothing. Or would be, if I wasn't so terrified.

"Hey." Steven squints at Ian. "You're not going to be able to read my thoughts, are you?"

"Honestly," Ian says, "I don't really know how this is going to work. There's a chance we'll get some mental feedback from each other."

"Great," Steven mutters. He's rigid with tension, fingers digging into the arms of the chair. "You get to wade through my angst. Welcome to the funhouse."

My mouth has gone dry, and my whole body feels strangely heavy. I keep my sweat-slick fist balled tightly around the Lucid pill, as if it might try to wriggle free.

"Lain?" Ian says, his voice softening.

I force a smile. "Just give me a moment."

I can feel a steady hum of tension from both of them, though they're both making an effort to keep their thoughts quiet. They're probably just as scared as I am. They're about to open themselves to me—we're opening to each other, all three of us—and once it begins, none of us will have any control over where we end up.

My hands tremble slightly as I stare at the tiny pill in the center of my palm. Before I have time to lose my nerve, I drop it into my mouth and swallow it dry. I lean back in the chair and close my eyes, focusing on the sound of my own breathing. Waiting.

At first, nothing happens. I start to wonder if maybe the drug's not going to work at all. Maybe my memories are hopelessly, irretrievably lost, and we should just forget about this whole thing and go have dinner or something. I open my mouth to ask Ian how long it usually takes for Lucid to kick in, but I realize that, strangely, I can't remember how to speak. Steven says something, but the words are meaningless sounds—ruh ruh-uh-ruhh—dancing fuzzily through my head. I try to stand up, but vertigo slams into my brain like a fist, and I'm hurtling out of my body, up through the ceiling, into the sky. It feels like I'm strapped into a rollercoaster and the car suddenly veered off the track and into empty space.

Stars wheel past my vision. A void opens in front of me, swallowing the world, and I careen into it. Then up and down lose all meaning, and there's just darkness.

Flash. I'm running along a beach in slow motion. The world is strangely luminous; a bright, hazy aura glows around everything. Glass-green waves lap the sand and break against sharp, black rocks, sending clouds of sparkling droplets and cream-colored foam into the air. I'm running after a tall, slender boy with red hair, a boy of about twelve.

He waves to me, grinning, and then wades out into the ocean. "Wait!" I call, hanging back. "We're not supposed to go too deep!"

He laughs and wades deeper. "Come on, *Eeeeee*-yan." He draws out my name, making it into a joke, and splashes me. "It's just water."

The waves are getting bigger, frothing and angry, rising up and crashing down. The boy swims out, unafraid.

"*Malcolm!*" I scream.

He's getting farther and farther away. A wave covers him and swallows him up, and then, very suddenly, he's gone.

Sobbing, panting, I fling myself into the water, then shrink back as a wave lashes me. The water is freezing, and my teeth chatter. I stand on the shore, toes buried in wet sand. My brother is nowhere to be seen.

My body doesn't want to move. Fear tries to glue me to the shore, but I pull free, throw myself into the water and paddle out after him. The waves grow larger and larger, rearing over me, then slapping me down like huge hands. I gulp in air, paddling frantically to keep my head above the salty foam. I no longer know which way the shore is. There's just water stretching in every direction toward a misty horizon. Then a current grabs me and yanks me under, and I'm surrounded by cold darkness. It presses against my eyes and into my nose, thick and smothering, pulling me down and down. The light dwindles above me into nothingness, and there's only the still, dark ocean. I can't hold my breath anymore. My mouth opens, air escapes in a cloud of bubbles, and water rushes in. I gasp . . .

And suddenly, inexplicably, I'm breathing, pushing water in and out of my lungs like it's air. The crushing pressure in my chest vanishes. I open my eyes, but it's no longer dark. The water has changed—or maybe my eyes have. I'm in a dim, glass-like, sleepy green world. I can see the ripples of sand a few yards beneath my feet—can see, ahead, the place where the continental shelf drops off into the deep and endless valley of the ocean floor. But Malcolm is nowhere to be seen. Panic lashes through me.

Then a voice echoes in my ears, muffled and distorted by the water. *Come on, Doc. Focus.*

I start to swim, my body cutting like a knife through the water. There's something buried in the ocean floor ahead—the curve of a huge black orb, nearly ten feet across, protruding a few feet above the sandy bottom. I swim deeper, toward it, breathing in the water, until I'm hovering directly over the orb. I can see my fuzzy reflection in its surface, the pale lines of my body. Somewhere along the way, I must have lost my swim trunks. Then I swim closer.

I'm not Ian anymore. I'm Lain.

I place my hands against the cool, smooth surface of the orb. My reflection stares out at me, wide-eyed, and I realize suddenly that it's not a reflection, but another girl, one who looks just like me. She's trapped in there, pounding her fist against the inside and shouting, mouthing words, but I can't make them out; her voice is swallowed up in the silence of the ocean. I push sand away from the orb, trying to uncover it. I press my hands against the glossy smoothness . . . and then my hands sink through it, into the orb. The girl grabs my wrist and yanks me in, and the blackness engulfs me.

A dizzying terror grips me. My heartbeat is racing out of control. Oh God. I'm not ready for this. Help me. Someone help me.

But it's too late to turn back. I'm flying through a tunnel of fragmented images, a thousand voices and faces, and there's nothing I can do but ride the wave.

A girl lies dead at my feet, her hair stained with blood. The sky erupts above me, filled with fire and smoke.

A man in a wheelchair sits across from me, staring at me with cool gray eyes, slender fingers touching my cheek. *Remember this, Lain,* he whispers urgently. *You have to remember. The soul of humankind is at stake.*

PART II
CITADEL

Three months earlier

7

Birdsong filters through the layer of fog in my head, pulling me toward a distant light. The drone of a car's engine vibrates in my bones.

The car hits a bump, jolting me from my half-doze. I sit up, pushing loose strands of hair from my face, and wipe a bit of drool from my lower lip.

Outside the window, the sun's hazy golden glow seeps through the pine branches. It's late afternoon, approaching evening. Steven's fingers are locked in their usual death-grip on the steering wheel, knuckles bone-white, pale blue eyes focused on the road ahead. "You were dreaming, weren't you?"

"Sort of." A dry, stale taste fills my mouth. I grimace and take a swig from the bottle of water in the cup holder. "You could tell?"

"You were sleep-talking. Wasn't sure if I should wake you. You seemed to need the rest."

I've managed to grab a few meager handfuls of sleep since we left the safe house, but I'm too tense for more than that. My head aches, and my eyes are filled with sand. I feel like we've been driving for eons, though it's been less than two days.

Two days since we started fleeing for the border. Two days since I officially became a traitor to my country. Or am I a hero? I don't know. I told the truth—that's all I'm sure of. Anxiety flutters inside me, and I walk through my identity affirmation exercises. *My name is Lain Fisher. I'm eighteen years old. I'm a Mindwalker. Former Mindwalker.*

Does "wanted criminal" qualify as an occupation?

The car bumps and jolts over potholes in the narrow road. Ahead, a bright orange sign glares at us: IT IS UNLAWFUL AND DANGEROUS TO PASS BEYOND THIS POINT. I sit up straighter. "We're almost there."

The road won't take us all the way to the Canadian border, but it should bring us close enough that we can hike the rest of the way. The real problem will be getting past the fence.

His eyes move back and forth, scanning our surroundings. "Is it just me, or does this seem way too easy? I mean, shouldn't IFEN have a search party on our tail by now?"

I chew on the mouth of the plastic water bottle. "Well, we don't have a GPS or cell phones, so they have no way to track us. And even if they're searching for us by satellite camera, they don't know what sort of car we're driving."

"Yeah. Well. They've got ways of finding people."

He's right. This is too easy, and it makes me nervous. I feel like a trap is about to spring shut at any moment. But there's nothing we can do except keep moving forward.

The road dwindles to little more than a dirt path, overgrown with patches of weeds. Gravel crunches under our tires. Trees tower over us, blocking out most of the sky.

Steven stops the car. I unfasten my seat belt and open the door. Ahead, the road ends; a rusted iron chain hangs between two cement poles, blocking the way. Beyond lies more forest. The pine trees are thin here, standing a respectful distance apart. Not much cover. "Well," he says, "I guess we're walking from here."

We get out. A breeze ruffles my hair, and my hand drifts up to touch the loose strands. I cut it short after it was singed by the blast from the explosion back in IFEN headquarters. My head still feels strangely light and naked without the extra weight.

I knew that we'd have to leave our vehicle behind. There are only a few roads running across the border, and those are heavily guarded, so there's no chance of getting through by car. We'll be less conspicuous on foot, anyway. There's still a risk of being caught by a patrol, but they can't monitor the entire border twenty-four hours a day, so we'll just have to hope they don't catch us.

I don't like relying on luck. I feel like I've already used up my supply. But we don't have much choice.

"Let's get the stuff," Steven says.

There are two packs in the backseat, and inside, a few days' worth of bottled water, trail mix, and protein bars, along with a first-aid kit and even a small box of toiletries. I sling one pack onto my back and tighten the straps, then freeze as a thought flashes through my head. "My Gate." The slender hard drive is now sitting in the trunk of the car, wrapped in a blanket, along with the two helmets. It could conceivably fit in a backpack, but it would be extra weight for us to carry. It would slow us down. "Maybe I should leave it here."

"Take it," Steven says.

"But—"

"It's yours," he says. "I can carry the food and water. Take it."

I hesitate.

That Gate belonged to Father, then fell to me after his death. It's the only tangible connection I have to him now. Everything else—the house, my possessions, even my holoavatar, Chloe— are gone, taken from me by Dr. Swan. Not to mention, it seems ungrateful to leave the Gate behind, since Ian went to the trouble of finding it for me. But at this point, what would I use it for? I'm not a Mindwalker anymore. "It's really not necessary."

"I know you, Doc." His voice softens on the old nickname. "If we leave it behind, you'll regret it."

"If you say so." Secretly relieved, I open the trunk, take out the blanket-wrapped bundle, and wrestle it into my backpack. The straps dig into my shoulders; I can feel the Gate's weight pulling on them. The helmets are too bulky to fit in my pack, so I knot the chinstraps together and then tie them to the loop at the top. "You're really okay with carrying all the supplies? It's not too much?"

"Give me some credit. I know I'm scrawny, but my arms aren't gonna fall off."

A smile tugs at my lips. "You aren't scrawny. You're svelte."

He snorts, though he's smiling, too.

We start walking. Dead leaves rustle under our feet. Overhead, late-afternoon sunlight filters through the pine branches and drenches the forest in sepia tones. "So," I say, "once we reach the fence, someone named Lynx is supposed to find us." We've already gone over this, but I feel the need to keep talking. The silence and stillness is oppressive. "And this person will help us across the border and take us to a safe place."

"That's the plan." He squints against the sunlight. "Though I don't like relying on some random stranger to get us across. I mean, what if she doesn't show up?"

"She will. Ian said he'd arrange it all. He wouldn't let us down."

Steven makes a noncommittal sound.

A squirrel perches on a branch overhead, shaking its tail and scolding us. Chk-chk-chk. I think of Nutter, the plush squirrel back in my bedroom, and suddenly wish I'd brought him with me. Silly. I adjust the straps of my pack. The dangling helmets bounce lightly with each step. My shoulders are already starting to get sore.

"Are you okay with this?" Steven asks suddenly.

"With what?"

"This. Everything." His expression is unreadable. "Once we cross that fence, we can't go back."

There's an invisible rope around my throat, pulling tight, making it hard to swallow. I keep walking, planting one foot ahead of the other. "It's already too late to go back. I made my choice when I uploaded my memories to the Net. I knew what the consequences would be. What's the point of second-guessing ourselves now?"

"No point. Just curious, I guess. If you could rewind your life, do everything over, would you make the same choices?"

For a few seconds, I look away and focus on breathing. If my decision plunges our country into a new civil war, will it still be worth it?

Father chose to entrust me with the dark truth about the St. Mary's experiments and the origins of Mindwalking. He must have believed that I would make the right choice, which—in some odd, roundabout way—probably means that I did. At least I hope so. Or maybe, sometimes, there is no right choice. Just different shades of gray.

Steven's expression is carefully blank, but I can see a faint shadow of uncertainty lurking in his eyes.

"I've already made my decision, and that decision is part of who I am now," I say. "There's no going back."

"Yeah." He doesn't sound reassured.

"Steven . . ." I stop and place a hand on his shoulder. He tenses, caught off guard. "I'm not going to leave you. Not ever. Okay?"

He looks up, his gaze meeting mine. His eyes turn different colors depending on the lighting. In shadow, they're a murky blue-gray. Now, in direct sunlight, they're a clear, pure blue— almost luminous, like stained glass lit from behind. "Promise?" He smiles, like it's a joke, but his voice catches a little, like cloth snagging on a thorn.

I hold up the little finger of my right hand, put on a solemn expression, and say, "Pinkie-swear."

He bursts out laughing. "You're such a dork." But he hooks his pinkie through mine, and a subtle tension eases out of his shoulders. His gaze flits over my face again, focusing briefly on my lips, then shifts away.

He hasn't kissed me since we left the safe house. I think he's waiting for me to make a move. He knows that I've been through a lot in the past week. I've lost the future I planned for myself, and Dr. Swan—my legal guardian, a man I trusted—turned out to be a cold-blooded monster who experimented on children and tried to mindwipe Steven. Romance hasn't exactly been my biggest priority. But now, I find myself remembering the warmth of his lips, the smell and taste of him.

If I start kissing him now, I don't think I'll be able to stop, and it would be pretty ridiculous to get shot by a border patrol because we were too busy lip-locking to hear them coming. So I link my arms around him and settle for giving him a long kiss on the cheek. His ears turn pink. On impulse, I put my lips against one and whisper, "I can't wait till we're in Canada."

He draws in a slow, unsteady breath and closes his eyes, as if struggling for control. "Yeah." His voice is low and huskier than usual. I can see his pulse beating in his throat. When he opens his eyes again, his pupils are dilated under his pale eyelashes, two dark pools ringed with blue. We start to lean toward each other.

Abruptly, his muscles go rigid against me. His head snaps to one side, and he stares into the forest.

I blink, disoriented. "What—"

"Shh."

I hold my breath, listening, but I can't hear anything.

Behind us, a twig snaps. I give a start, and we both spin around to face the forest. A few heartbeats of silence pass. Then a plump raccoon waddles out from behind a tree. It stops to peer at us, its eyes shining coins of reflected light, and scuttles away, vanishing into the underbrush. We exhale as one, and I smile, feeling a little silly. "They're funny little creatures, aren't they? They look like they're wearing party masks."

"I was just thinking they look like insomniacs."

"You could say that." God knows Steven and I are both sporting those dark circles lately. Just give us a pair of stripy tails and we'd fit right in with the other forest dwellers.

The moment has passed; it's as if the universe has given us a nudge, reminding us that we're not safe until we're outside the country. And probably, we won't even be safe then. We can't let down our guard. We keep walking.

After a few minutes, he takes off his pack and rummages through it. "Hungry?"

"Very."

He tosses a protein bar to me, then unwraps one for himself. The bar is dry and dissolves into tasteless, pulpy grit when I chew it, but it takes the edge off my hunger.

Steven grimaces and swallows. "Man, what I wouldn't give for a chili cheese dog and some black coffee."

"The way you eat, I'm amazed your heart hasn't stopped yet." I immediately regret the words; I've come too close to losing him too many times.

But he just glances at me from the corner of his eye and says, "Me too." He takes off his shoe and shakes out a rock. Then he freezes, looking over his shoulder.

"What's wrong?"

Steven slides his shoe back on and keeps walking, head down, shoulders stiff. His hands are shoved deep into the pockets of his long black coat. "I keep getting the feeling that someone's watching us."

"Another raccoon?"

"Maybe."

The sun sinks toward the horizon, and the light turns red, bleeding through the crosshatch of branches above us. A dull ache takes root in my calves and spreads up the backs of my thighs. "I'm starting to think it'll be night before we—" I stop. "Wait. Is that it?"

Ahead, something huge and gray looms through the trees. I quicken my pace, and there's the fence—twenty feet of solid concrete topped with snarls of barbed wire. It stretches in both directions as far as I can see. "Well," I say, "there's no way we can climb this on our own."

"So what now? We just wait?"

"I guess so." I lean against a tree. My legs hurt, so I slide down. The mossy ground is cool and slightly damp beneath me.

Steven doesn't sit. He paces, shielding his eyes from the glare of sunset with one hand. Then he stops. "Shit," he mutters.

My pulse quickens.

A flock of crows bursts from a tree and into the purple-blue sky, cawing. The dull thunder of their wings doesn't quite drown out the drone of machinery, growing louder and louder, closer and closer. I leap to my feet.

A helicopter.

8

A bead of sweat trickles down the center of my back, cold against fever-hot skin. In the distance, I can see the helicopter moving toward us, following the line of the wall—a sleek white shape against the dusky purple sky. The border patrol.

"We need to hide," I say, breathless. But where? The trees around us are too scrawny to offer any shelter. My gaze darts frantically around, searching for something, anything that can conceal us.

Steven grabs my arm. "Run."

"Where?"

"Just run!"

We charge ahead, plunging blindly through the woods. Branches whip my face. Roots and rocks leap up to trip me, and I stumble.

The droning hum becomes a roar, then a hurricane. The trees sway and rustle as the helicopter appears overhead like a white dragon, huge and terrible. A woman's voice rings out, amplified to a godlike boom: "You are in violation of the law. Stop where you are. Do not resist arrest. I repeat, do not resist. If you cooperate, you will not be harmed."

Like we'd believe that.

We keep running. The helicopter follows, skimming low over the treetops. I see someone leaning out of the window, aiming a weapon.

Crack!

Steven lurches forward. There's something embedded in his shoulder—a dart, long and thick as a pencil.

"Steven!"

Gritting his teeth, he grabs the dart and yanks it out. The barbed end drips with blood. He tosses it away, then sways and falls to his knees. "Drugged," he gasps.

The helicopter hovers in the air. A door on its underbelly slides open, and a ladder drops out. Two people in combat gear descend.

Steven is on his hands and knees, chest heaving. "Lain," he whispers hoarsely. "Keep running."

"I'm not leaving you!" Panting, I hook an arm around Steven's waist and haul him to his feet. He slides back down, limbs loose and rubbery. I grip his wrist, pulling. "Come on!"

His eyes roll beneath the lids, whites flashing, lids quivering as he struggles to hold them open.

The two people let go of the ladder and land in a crouch on the ground, one by one. They straighten and stride toward us, their steps purposeful but unhurried, as if they've done this a hundred times before. In a single smooth movement, they both draw their NDs from the holsters at their belts. I haul Steven upright again and break into a run, or try to, but his weight drags me down. He's a rag doll in my arms. His legs move weakly, this way and that, as if he can't find the ground. "Gun," he murmurs. "Take it."

I look down at the pistol butt jutting from the waist of Steven's pants. Can I really shoot someone? This isn't an ND. If I pull the trigger, it will seriously wound or kill the person at the other end. I tug it out and click off the safety, mouth dry.

The footsteps grow closer and closer. I start to turn, raising the gun, but I'm not fast enough.

Something slams into the back of my head, and a loud *bzzzzt* fills my ears. Stars burst inside my skull, and I'm on the forest floor, my cheek pressed against the cold earth. I will my body to move, but it won't obey me. The world fades in and out.

In some distant corner of my mind, I'm aware that I've been shocked by a neural disruptor. It's happened to me once before, but this is the first time I've been conscious enough to feel the effects. My fingers twitch, and my legs shake with convulsions. Warm drool slides down my chin. At the edge of my mind, I hear voices, but I can't make out what they're saying; the words are meaningless sounds, like dogs barking. I catch my name swimming through the sea of nonsense. A weak groan escapes my throat.

A pair of black boots appears in front of my face, and a flashlight shines in my eyes, momentarily blinding me. Gold sparks burst like fireworks against my retinas, then melt into a weird swirl of green and brown. *Move*, I order my legs. *Stand up.* They ignore me and continue to spasm.

The flashlight beam disappears, and my vision returns in bits and pieces, interspersed with swaths of black fog. When I strain my eyes upward, I see two figures—a man with a stubble-covered jaw and black shades, and a woman with military-short hair. The helicopter hovers overhead, buzzing like a giant hornet.

"Well," the woman says, smiling. The words echo faintly in my skull, and I have to struggle to make sense of them. "Look what we've caught." She holds my gun between her thumb and forefinger, like it's a soiled dishrag. Disdainfully, she hands it to her partner, who clicks on the safety and tucks it into his pocket.

The fog is clearing. I can feel my body again; every nerve tingles with fire and ice, but my muscles aren't responding properly. My arms flop on the ground, useless. I feel like an infant learning to crawl. Quivering, I try to push myself off the ground. A spasm seizes my lower back, and pain radiates outward. For a few seconds, I'm certain I'm either dying or paralyzed from the waist down.

The barrel of an ND presses against the base of my skull. "I wouldn't move, if I were you," the woman says. "I've got this on the highest setting. If I pull the trigger, it will deliver a shock to your medulla, stopping your heart for a few seconds. Maybe it'll start up again, maybe not. A lot of 'accidental' deaths happen that way."

I don't move. I'm shaking, nauseous. It hurts to think, hurts to breathe. This is horrible. Aren't NDs supposed to be humane?

Steven. Where is Steven?

"Cuff her," the woman says.

Rough hands grab my arms and wrench them behind my back, and a pair of restraints snaps shut over my wrists. I manage to lift my head a few inches, enough to peer over my shoulder. My hands are engulfed in what looks like a pair of metal oven mitts, held together with a powerful magnetic force. I can't budge them. I try to call Steven's name, but all that comes out is a mangled, "Nnngh." Where is he?

There. He lies on the ground nearby, motionless, already wearing a similar pair of restraints. His eyes are closed. "Steven," I manage to croak, though it comes out more like *Teee-yan.*

No response.

The woman removes the ND from my head, circles around to my front, and crouches so we're at eye level. Her eyes are a dull, washed out blue-gray, like water-worn stones. "Did you really think you could just hop across the fence? Just waltz on over to Canada?"

I grit my teeth.

"Dr. Swan sent a message to all the patrols telling us to keep an eye out for you," she says. "We've been doing satellite sweeps of the fence all day. They even doubled the usual number of agents on the task. I must confess, I thought it was a waste of time. I didn't think you'd actually be stupid enough to make a run for the border."

I gulp. It takes an effort to form words. "Let us go. Please." It sounds more like *Less go peas*.

Her partner chuckles. She just narrows her eyes. "Why would we do that?"

Pleading with her is futile to the point of absurdity—I realize that—but I don't know what else to try. "Nod hudding any-un." The words are mushy, slurred. Even through the terror, my head burns with humiliation. This is what the ND does—turns you into an infant, crawling and drooling and struggling to speak.

The woman's expression hardens. "You're not hurting anyone? Is that what you think?" She leans closer. "You leaked classified information on the Net. You were involved in a terrorist bombing that killed two people. You're officially a Type Five now, which means you've been designated a serious threat to society. You're looking at a whole lot of involuntary treatment. Conditioning, memory modification . . . maybe even a total mindwipe."

My breathing quickens.

Steven groans, stirring. The man presses the heel of one boot down on his back, pinning him in place.

"We've been ordered to bring you back to Dr. Swan alive," the woman says. "You, that is. But your friend—he's not necessary. If you give me any excuse to kill him, I won't hesitate. I'll just write up a report saying he was violent and we were forced to defend ourselves. So why don't you save us all a lot of trouble and behave?"

A sickening knot of anger burns in my chest and rises into my throat, choking me. I struggle, pulling at the restraints. When I try to gather my legs beneath me, the woman kicks me in the side with bruising force.

"I'll notify the Director," the man says. He pulls a cell phone from his pocket.

She places a hand on his arm and says, "Wait." Frowning, she stares into the forest. For the space of a few seconds, there's just the drone of the helicopter—still hovering over the treetops a short distance away—and the rapid thud of my own heartbeat.

A gunshot cracks through the stillness. The helicopter lurches, then spins around crazily in midair. The two border guards watch, mouths open, as the vehicle plummets, roaring like a wounded beast. It seems to be falling in slow motion as it crashes to the forest floor. The ground vibrates under the impact. Black smoke pours from the wreck.

The male border guard whips out his ND. Crack. A bullet hole appears in his forehead, directly above and between his eyes. He lands on his back, limbs splayed.

The woman holds out her ND and turns in a circle, screaming, "Who's there? Show yours—"

Another shot rings out, and she goes down. Her limp body flops down on top of me, knocking the wind from my lungs. For a few seconds, I lie beneath her, mouth open, lungs empty. I'm too stunned to move, to think. Her body is a warm weight atop mine; hot blood oozes from a wound in her chest and drips onto my face. Then the air rushes back into my lungs, and horror crawls over me like a wave of squirming maggots. I wriggle out from under her, gasping.

There's blood on the ground, on my clothes and skin. Something warm, thicker than blood, slides down my cheek.

The forest is suddenly, unnaturally silent. Smoke stings my nostrils and burns my throat.

Steven blinks, eyes cloudy. The drugs, it seems, are starting to wear off. "Hey." His voice comes out thick and cracked. "What the hell just happened?"

"I don't know," I hear myself respond. None of this feels quite real. I half expect the man and woman to get up and dust themselves off, but they remain motionless on the ground. The man's eyes are open, empty and staring. The woman is curled into a fetal position, blood soaking through her shirt. It looks too bright, too red. Like paint. Like this is a movie, or a dream.

In the nearby forest, leaves rustle. A tall, slender figure jumps down from a tree, lands lightly in a crouch, and walks into the clearing.

She's wearing ragged, dusty jeans and a long black coat, and she carries a black assault rifle which looks far too large and bulky for her slim hands. She has the head of a wild cat, with silky gray fur and brilliant green eyes. A holomask. In the moonlight, she resembles something out of a legend, unearthly and wild.

I swallow, mouth dry. "You're . . . Lynx?"

She turns to face us. Her gaze locks onto me, and for a few seconds, she just stares. Her pointed ears angle backward. "Obviously," she replies.

The helicopter lies on its side about a hundred feet away, a beached whale, still trailing smoke. Even from this distance, I can see the bullet hole in the window, the spiderweb of cracks spreading across the blood-flecked glass.

She shot the pilot through that tiny window. From the ground. Is anyone's aim actually that good?

Lynx glances down at the bodies in the clearing. One of them stirs—the woman—a single breath breaks the silence, wet and raspy. Her eyes crack open, glazed with pain.

Lynx walks over and calmly presses the rifle against the woman's temple. The woman whimpers. She starts to raise a hand, weakly, as if to push the gun away. "Please." Her voice is faint and thin. "Don't—"

Lynx pulls the trigger. I flinch. The woman twitches and then goes still. A deep hush hangs over the forest; even the birds have stopped singing.

"Did you have to do that?" The words sound oddly flat, disconnected, like I'm listening to a recording of myself.

"She was already dying. I just sped things up." Lynx walks over to me and pulls something out of her pocket. I tense and start to pull away. "Hold still." There's a loud hiss, a brief, searing heat against my hands, and my restraints fall off. I rub my wrists and watch as she slices through Steven's cuffs using a small laser knife. It glows white-blue, like a gas flame.

I help Steven to his feet, and he leans against me.

Lynx glances at him. "Is he wounded?"

"Tranquilizer dart," I say.

"Can he walk?"

Slowly, he straightens. "I can walk." His voice is still weak, but there's an underlying firmness.

She nods. "Follow me." She strides forward, into the woods.

My head is spinning.

"Well?" Lynx calls. "Are you coming?"

I breathe in, trying to focus my thoughts. There are other helicopters patrolling the border, and they probably communicate with each other. It won't be long before they realize that this particular unit isn't responding and come to see what the problem is. Then they'll see the wreckage, the dead bodies. We shouldn't be around when that happens. Ian sent this woman to help us, I remind myself. We're supposed to trust her.

I meet Steven's gaze, and he gives a small nod.

We follow Lynx into the dark woods, leaving the corpses in the clearing behind us.

9

Lynx walks with the brisk, measured stride of an experienced hiker. A glossy brown braid trails down to the center of her back, swaying lightly with each step. As we walk, my mind slowly surfaces from its shock-haze, and I notice the tiny scar, white and puckered, on the back of her neck. She had a collar, like Steven. She hasn't even made an attempt to hide it.

"You look different than you do on TV," she says.

I assume she's talking to me. By now, I'm sure I've been on the news, but the photos they've shown of me are probably from before the explosion at IFEN headquarters. In a short time, I've transformed completely. The fresh-faced, hopeful, pigtail-wearing girl has become a pale, hollow-cheeked creature with haunted eyes.

"I thought your hair was stupid," she says. "It looks better now."

"Thank you. I think." I'm sinking back into the haze, thinking about myself in the third person. *Subject is entering a disassociative state, likely brought on by acute emotional trauma. Symptoms include numbness, disorientation, and a sense of detachment from reality.*

I place a hand against my temple, as if that will help steady my brain somehow.

Steven's arm is still bleeding where he ripped the dart out of his shoulder. Blood soaks through his sleeve in a dark, wet patch. "Shouldn't we do something about that?"

"Here." Lynx hands Steven a small blue bottle. "Use this."

Steven rolls up his bloody sleeve, exposing the ragged puncture. He pulls the cap off of the bottle with his teeth and squeezes the transparent blue gel onto the wound. It comes out in loops and coils, like toothpaste. "What is this stuff?"

"Blue goo," she replies.

"Well, yeah, but what *is* it?"

"That's the brand name. BlueGoo. Painkiller and antibacterial agent. It hardens to form a seal over the rupture. It'll wash off in a few days, once the wound has closed."

"Oh." He pokes at the goop, which has already turned firm. "That's handy. It's already stopped hurting."

"I use it a lot."

The conversation is so mundane, it's surreal. There are dead bodies behind us, and they're discussing a medical disinfectant. I suddenly feel like we're in a commercial for BlueGoo, and the absurd urge to laugh flutters in my chest again. I press a hand over my mouth.

Steven leans closer to me. "Hey . . . you all right?"

I lower my hand and watch as it trembles. "I'm perfectly fine. Why wouldn't I be?"

He frowns but says nothing.

Lynx stops, examining a nearby tree. I notice a green zigzag painted onto the trunk—the sort of thing you could easily mistake for a splotch of moss, if you weren't looking for it. She raises one boot and stomps on the ground three times. Then she moves a few feet forward and does it again. This time, there's a hollow thump, as if she's struck wooden planks. She crouches and brushes dead leaves from the edges of a trapdoor, cleverly disguised with a shaggy carpet of fake grass and moss. With a grunt, she yanks the door open, revealing a rough circular hole lined with stones—a deep well descending into blackness. A set of rusted iron bars juts from one side of the curved wall, like rungs of a ladder. Lynx slings her rifle onto her back, tightens the straps of the leather holster, and says, "You first."

I stand motionless, staring down into the darkness.

The whiskers of her lynx mask twitch. "There are no monsters down there. I promise."

My palms are slick with sweat. I dry them on my shirt, though that doesn't help much, because my shirt is sweat-drenched, too. Slowly, gingerly, I descend. My shoes are slippery with mud, but I manage not to lose my footing. Steven follows.

My feet touch the bottom, and he jumps down beside me, landing lightly, like he's done this a thousand times. Lynx climbs a few rungs down and closes the trapdoor, blotting out the moonlight. Darkness engulfs us, thick and heavy. A few seconds later, I hear Lynx's boots on the ground. There's a hiss, and a bright orange glow pierces the shadows. Lynx holds up a flare, illuminating our surroundings.

We're in a tunnel, about six feet wide and ten feet tall. The walls and floor are rough stone blocks, supported by broad wooden beams.

Steven lets out a low whistle. "This goes under the fence?"

Lynx nods. "It's not the only tunnel, either. This is how most refugees get into Canada. The border patrols fill the holes in when they find them, but we just dig more." She's already striding ahead, flare held aloft. We follow, and for awhile, there's no sound except the rhythmic thunk-thunk of shoes on stone, echoing through the stillness. The flare casts dramatic black shadows that leap and dance on the walls like demons. Lynx's holomask doesn't cast a shadow; the fuzzy outline of her actual profile glides along the wall like a ghost.

In my head, I see her walk over to the wounded woman, place the gun against her temple, and fire. Those few seconds keep replaying, an infinite loop behind my eyes.

Those border guards threatened to kill us if we gave them trouble, I remind myself. Lynx saved our lives. She's not the enemy. Yet the unease in my bones won't go away—a feeling like seeing the black smear of an approaching storm on the horizon. What bothers me is not that she killed them, per se, but that she barely even glanced at the bodies once the deed was done. As if, for her, killing is a chore as mundane as folding the laundry.

My own breathing sounds very loud in the confines of the tunnel.

"Here we are," Lynx says.

The tunnel ends in a set of narrow stone steps leading upward, bracketed by rough, pebbly earthen walls. I start to ascend, then stop. Once we come out on the other side, there'll be no going back.

But then, it's already too late to turn back.

We emerge through another trapdoor, into the cold night air. For a few seconds, I stand there, breathing it in. The woods don't look any different on this side of the border. Same trees, same ground, same starry sky.

Lynx paces, scanning the surrounding forest. Her tufted ears turn back and forth like satellite dishes. "Coast looks clear."

"Hey," Steven says, "can we see your face?"

She turns toward him, ears laid back. "Why?"

"Just curious. We're on the same side now, right? Plus I feel a little weird talking to a giant humanoid cat."

She hesitates. Then, slowly, she reaches up, fingers sliding through the thick fur on her neck. She tilts her head to one side and fiddles with something under the fur, and the mask vanishes. Her face is small and oval-shaped, her skin the color of coffee with a bit of cream, her eyes a pale glass-green, ringed by dark lashes. Her expression is blank and impassive. There's a small, bright spot of blood on her cheek.

"Um—you've got a little—" I tap my own cheek.

She wipes at the blood with gloved fingers, but only succeeds in smearing it across her skin, like war paint.

"Thanks, by the way," Steven says. "For saving us."

"Yes. Thank you," I add.

A tiny furrow appears between her eyebrows. "You don't have to thank me. It was a mission." She resumes walking. "Keep moving. We're not safe yet."

The moon hangs overhead, a huge yellow Cheshire cat smile, as Lynx leads us through the trees, to a battered pickup parked on the shoulder of a gravel road. She slides into the driver's seat and shoves a key into the ignition. It starts up with a groan. "Get in."

"Wait," I call, still trudging toward the road. "Where are you taking us?"

"Toronto."

I bite the inside of my cheek. "Isn't that kind of risky? I mean, being around so many people?"

"We'll only need to blend into the crowd for a few minutes. Then we'll go underground. There are places in the city that don't officially exist. We can move through them undetected."

"And after that? What then?"

Her eyes snap toward me. They're uncanny, with bright flecks of bronze in the green and dark rings around the outer edge of the irises. Animal eyes. "Then you become one of us," she says. "You join the Blackcoats. That's what you came here for. Isn't it?"

My legs tremble.

Steven nudges me with an elbow.

"I—yes," I say. "That's right." Though, to be honest, I hadn't actually thought that far ahead. Our goal was simply to get across the border in one piece. Once we arrived, I thought, we would figure out what to do. Well, here we are. Of course we're going to go with her. What other options do we have?

Lynx opens the back door to the truck, and we slide in. The seats are hard, cracked faux-leather, and a musty, dusty smell tickles my nose. Lynx presses down on the gas. The headlights slice through the darkness as the truck bumps and jolts down the narrow, unpaved road.

"Will anyone be able to track us by GPS?" Steven asks.

"This truck's been modified. I took the computer out. No GPS, no AI features. It's a good idea to stay off the grid, whenever possible."

"My kind of car." Steven pats the seat. "Never liked those damn AIs."

"Never trust to a computer what you can do yourself," she says.

"Amen."

I shift in my seat, and a loose spring pokes my bottom. The dryness in my mouth is starting to feel like a chronic condition.

The narrow road takes us to a highway, which stretches out toward the horizon, a ribbon of faded tarmac running between rows of towering pines. The forest gives way to open fields dusted with a light coating of snow, and I start to see signs of human civilization—a truck stop with a decrepit-looking diner, a pub with lit-up beer signs in the windows. We pass through areas with small clusters of houses and stores, towns and suburbs, the kind of places that don't exist back in the URA. It seems . . . inefficient. Too spread out. Oddly, I don't see any people.

"Does anyone actually live in these towns?" Steven asks, echoing my thoughts.

"Not many. A few decades ago, there was a recession in Canada. A lot of other countries, too. It hit the towns and rural areas pretty hard, and they never really recovered."

We learnt about that in school. The civil war with the Blackcoats caused an economic collapse in the URA—which was, back then, still the United States—which in turn triggered a global recession. A rash of small wars broke out on every continent, unleashing horror after horror. Chemical weapons, engineered viruses and neurotoxins wiped out entire cities. The misery finally came to an end when the most powerful nations of the world joined together to enforce a strict ban on all weapons of mass warfare, with the promise of swift retaliation to any who violated the agreement. The treaty has held, tenuously, ever since.

After that, the URA adopted an isolationist policy and shut down most communication with the outside world. Even back then, refugees were starting to flee across the border—mostly terrorists looking for a place to hide, or so they told us in school. Canada didn't want to get involved in our troubles, so they started tightening border security and eventually built the wall—a massive, outrageously costly construction stretching across the continent, creating a barrier between our two societies. Of course, refugees still make it across. We're living proof of that.

We pass a dilapidated barn next to a dead, bone-white tree with twisting branches, like tentacles. The branches are filled with crows, and they watch us as we glide past, their heads turning slowly to track our movement. I'm not the sort of person who believes in omens, good or bad. Still, the sight sends a chill wriggling down my spine.

Then suddenly the crows are cawing, flapping away. Two men on motorcycles veer out from behind a barn, engines snarling. They're wearing bulky coats and hats with earflaps. One of them draws a pistol. Three flat cracks ring out, and I give a start. "They're shooting at us!"

"Hold on," Lynx says. She cranks down the window and leans out, taking her hands momentarily off the wheel. With her body twisted around, she fires twice, managing to make it look graceful despite the awkward angle. The motorcycles spin across the road, front tires blown out. The men yell and jump off their bikes, sprawling across the grass. One of them stands up and waves to us. It's an odd gesture—as if he's saying, no hard feelings.

"What the hell was that?" Steven asks.

"Just bandits. Probably wanted the truck." She says it as if being attacked by men on motorcycles is an everyday occurrence.

Maybe for her, it is. She made that shot from a moving vehicle—while driving, no less—as casually as someone might take a sip from a cup of coffee. Is she even human?

For the rest of the drive, I'm tense, nails biting into the imitation leather seats. I keep watching through the window, expecting more thugs to come after us, but it never happens.

It's late afternoon when the road takes us over a low bridge, and beyond the trees I spot a huge body of water—Lake Ontario, I assume. Beyond that, skyscrapers cut clean silhouettes against the pinkish-violet pre-dawn sky.

Toronto.

Even from a distance, it looks so different from Aura, the city where I spent most of my life. Aura has a stately, pristine dignity; its skyscrapers are mostly silver and white, so when the sun strikes it, it glows like an illustration of Heaven. It's a subdued radiance, all cool serenity. Toronto is awash with a rainbow of candy-colored lights. The buildings glow pink and neon-green, their reflections in the water like smears of luminous paint. Spotlights shine from the tops of skyscrapers, spinning through the sky in a wild dance.

We pass a video billboard with an image of an attractive woman. She holds up a small black pistol, then tucks it into her purse with a knowing smile and a wink. DISCREET PROTECTION, the tagline reads. I realize my jaw is hanging open and snap it shut.

Steven raises his eyebrows. "People can buy weapons here? Like, in stores?"

"Of course," Lynx replies.

"Seems like an invitation for disaster," I mutter.

"Canada is still a free country," Lynx says. "Things are different here. You'd better get used to it, and fast."

I think of the men on motorcycles snarling toward us. Is this what people do when they're free? Shoot at each other?

Lynx's gaze flashes toward me in the rearview mirror. A cool, strange light burns in those jade eyes, and I have the uncomfortable feeling that she knows exactly what I'm thinking. "Freedom isn't the easy choice," she says. "It's not something handed to you on a platter. It's a contract signed in blood. You have to be willing to accept the sacrifices—to fight for it, die for it, and kill for it, if necessary. If you don't cling to it with all your strength, it won't be long before someone tries to take it from you, and they'll have a seductive, reasonable-sounding argument for why you should submit. If you're not certain of your convictions, you'll waver. And then, suddenly, it will be too late."

Pain shoots through me, and I realize my nails are digging into my thigh. I force myself to relax my grip.

Steven clears his throat. "So how 'bout we celebrate our freedom with some burgers and fries? Maybe some coffee? I'm in serious need of a caffeine fix."

"We need to keep moving. We'll eat once we arrive at our destination."

Outside the window, lights go by in a blur as we draw closer to the city. A slender tower rises high above the other buildings, like a needle with a series of rings near its top. I recognize it from pictures—the CN Tower.

We pass another billboard, and my stomach drops into my feet. I press a hand to my mouth.

WANTED: LAIN FISHER. Beneath the words is a photo of me, short hair in disarray, staring straight ahead with haunted eyes and a blank expression. I look psychotic. And I wonder, distantly, where they got the photo. It must have been taken from a security camera. Beneath it is a number to call and a cash reward. The amount makes my head spin.

I scrunch myself down in the car seat, sweating.

"Man," Steven says. "That's almost as bad as my yearbook picture." His voice is light, but I can see the tension in the muscles of his neck.

The billboard changes to an ad for some kind of virtual reality helmet, but the feeling of terror and exposure remains.

Steven places a hand against my back. "Breathe," he reminds me.

I manage a faint smile, though it probably doesn't look very convincing. "Maybe I should find some way to hide my face."

"That reminds me." Lynx hands a circle of black plastic to me and another to Steven. "These are yours."

Steven turns his over in his hands. "This is a holomask?"

She nods. "Slip that around your neck and push the button on the side."

I slide the black ring over my head, and it tightens until it's snug against my skin. I push a tiny button. When I glance in the rearview mirror, a white canary stares back at me with round black eyes.

Steven hesitates, studying the black ring in his hands. It's about the size and shape of the collar he used to wear.

Lynx reactivates her own mask. "Put it on," she says.

He takes a deep breath, slips it on, and pushes the button. His mask is a bird, too, but much fiercer-looking, with sleek gray feathers, a short, dagger-sharp beak, and yellow eyes. He examines himself in the rearview mirror. "What am I supposed to be?"

"A sparrowhawk," Lynx replies. "From now on, that's your codename."

He raises his hands, as if to touch his new face. His fingers pass through the mask as if it's made of smoke. "Sparrowhawk," he repeats. His beak moves along with his voice.

We drive over the bridge, and suddenly, we're surrounded by buildings—a maze of stores, high rises, and blinding lights. People are everywhere. Some are ordinary-looking; others have lavish tattoos or brightly dyed hair, gel-sculpted into abstract shapes.

I spot one woman in a shiny, crinkly outfit, like a spacesuit made from tinfoil. Another wears nothing but leopard body paint. Once again, I find my mouth hanging stupidly open, and I shut it.

Lynx slides into a parking space and gets out of the car. "Stay close to me."

I don't move. I'm almost afraid to step out of the truck. "Lynx—" I pause. "I feel strange calling you that."

"Call me Rhee. That's my name. You might as well know it."

"Rhee, then. Are you sure this is safe?"

"If you want safe," she replies, "you're in the wrong place."

10

We climb out of the truck and make our way down the sidewalk. A few people glance in our direction, but for the most part, no one pays attention to us. Considering how everyone else here is dressed, I suppose three people in animal masks aren't particularly noteworthy.

All around, the skyscrapers are clothed in glittering, moving ads. Logos glow in the sky, beamed onto the very clouds by huge projectors atop the highest buildings. Music pulses from night clubs; the heavy, grinding thump of the bass beat vibrates in my teeth, in my bones. I'm starting to get dizzy.

Steven takes my hand, and I clutch it, a lifeline in a sea of chaos. Rhee walks briskly, her rifle still slung over her back. No one seems to notice.

Overhead, a red dragon the size of a house sails across the sky, spewing flames. I gasp. It's just a holo, of course, but startlingly real, every scale rendered in exquisite detail. The people around me hoot and applaud as the dragon flies in a circle, wings spread wide, then erupts into a burst of red and silver fireworks. I glimpse a small black drone, almost hidden in the spray of color; a compartment slides open on its underside, and tiny objects rain down from the sky, pattering on the pavement. Pills. The words DRAGONFIRE—FREE SAMPLES! burn across the sky.

People fall to their hands and knees and start grabbing up the pills like candy. One man shoves another aside, and they fall to the pavement, wrestling.

We give them a wide berth. Behind us, I can still hear their shouts. My heart pounds as I walk close to Steven's side.

A window-screen displays a black-and-white image of a woman chained to a bed, staring out the window. An orange capsule appears in the window like the rising sun, spreading light and color. The chains vanish, and the woman smiles and gets up. REVITALIZE—SAMPLES AVAILABLE INSIDE!

Another ad shows a man in a cubicle, staring into space with a bored expression. The man injects something into his elbow. Then he gets a wide grin, transforms into a huge, hairy ape, tears off his business suit, and pounds on his chest. GORILLA—PUMP UP YOUR LIFE! CASH ONLY.

"This place is crazy," I mutter. "They're just handing out these mind-altering drugs to anyone who wants them."

"There are plenty of drug ads back home, too," Steven says.

"Yes, but . . . you know. That's different. There are procedures you have to follow—"

"Hey! Hey, birdy!" someone shouts. I tense, realizing that he's talking to me. "Polly want a cracker? I got one for you."

Steven stiffens and moves closer to me, shielding me with his body.

A group of teenaged boys stands on the street corner, smirking. One of them has a bottle in his hand.

Steven lifts his head. Under his mask, I can't see his expression, but I can feel the tension in his body. He starts to move toward them, but Rhee catches his arm. "Just keep walking." Her voice is low, almost inaudible. "They don't matter."

We hurry past, their laughter ringing in our ears.

We pass a store with holographic windows, three-dimensional images floating inside. A silver neural disruptor rotates, words flashing next to it as a soothing baritone emanates from unseen speakers: "Non-lethal, effective, easy to use, and small enough to fit in your pocket, Blue Lightning is the perfect travel companion and the compassionate choice for self-defense."

Below the glistening ad, tiny letters appear next to an asterisk: *May cause temporary paralysis, short-term memory problems, and nerve damage. Use only for self-defense.*

A pair of laughing women walk out of the store, carrying NDs and waving them around like sparklers. Instinctively, I flinch away.

We keep walking. Rhee leads us away from the bright, glittering, store-lined streets, down narrower and darker roads lined with drab gray and brown buildings.

"Here we are," she says.

We're standing in front of a narrow brick building sandwiched between a shuttered restaurant and a grimy-looking store called VR-SEXXX. Bits of broken glass litter the sidewalk.

The building is featureless except for a door and a single window. If I didn't know better, I'd say it had been abandoned for years. The window is covered with taped-up newspapers, and the steps leading to the front door look like they might collapse at any moment. "This is it?" I ask.

"This is a safe house," Rhee replies. "But we won't be staying here. It's a gateway to the Underground." The way she says it seems to imply a proper noun.

The wooden stairs sag and groan beneath our feet as we ascend. Next to the front door, a spray of red paint wanders across the bricks. It might be a random zigzag. It might also be a Z. Gracie, one of the rebels back home, told us that all the safe houses in Canada are marked this way.

Rhee knocks on the door in a complicated rhythm. There's a pause, followed by the slow *clomp-clomp* of approaching footsteps. The door opens a crack, and I find myself staring into the mouth of a double-barreled shotgun. Instinctively, I put up my hands. A dark, bloodshot eye stares at us from inside. "Password?" asks a deep voice.

"Sovereign," Rhee replies.

The door opens, revealing a dark, musty-smelling foyer and a man, small and hunched, with the head of a beaver. His huge, yellowish incisors look like they could bite through bone. His nose twitches as he peers at us through beady, bloodshot eyes. "You coming in or not?"

I hesitate, then step through the door.

"This way." The man leads us down a narrow, dimly lit hallway and down a set of stairs, into a boxlike cement basement. He flicks on a light. There's a huge, circular metal disc sitting in the center of the floor, like an oversized manhole cover. The beaver-man crouches, grabs the iron ring on top, and heaves the disc aside with a grunt. It slides slowly, metal grinding against cement, exposing a circular hole leading straight down.

Another tunnel?

The man holds out a hand clad in a dirty, fingerless glove, and Rhee hands him some pastel-colored paper which I assume is money. We haven't had cash in the URA for decades. "Safe passage," the man says, inclining his head toward her. The words have the ring of a formal saying, or maybe a blessing.

There are rungs on the side of the hole. We descend. The manhole cover slides back into place overhead, blocking out the light.

I have no idea what we'll find down here. I should probably be more scared, but I feel like my brain is wrapped in gauze. I'm overloading. I can't make sense of it all, and there's nothing to do except keep moving.

Below, I glimpse a dim light. We climb toward it. Finally, my feet touch cement.

We're standing in what appears to be a subway tunnel, but one that hasn't been used for years—at least, not for its original purpose. Graffiti covers the walls, and bits of trash—broken bottles, cans, used needles—glint on the cement floor. The tracks are hidden beneath a layer of dark, grimy-looking water, sluggishly flowing.

The light comes from a small fire a short distance away. A group of people huddle around it, warming their hands, talking and laughing. As we approach, they fall silent, their expressions going blank. Several pairs of wary, alert eyes follow us as we pass. All around us are crude lean-tos, tents, shelters pieced together from scrap metal and wood. A man roasts a spitted rat over a grill, whistling a cheerful tune. A shaggy dog sits near his feet, watching attentively.

So, this is the Underground.

"Who are these people?" I whisper.

"Some refugees. Some homeless." Rhee steps over a sleeping man bundled in blankets.

Two dirty children chase each other around, laughing. Someone has strung up a clothesline with pairs of long underwear and shirts hanging out to dry—though how anything *can* dry in this damp air, I'm not sure.

I see a teenager sitting outside a tent made of blankets and poles, eating hash from a can with her fingers. When we pass, she hugs the can to her chest and curls around it protectively. A woman sits next to her, sharpening a knife, watching us with a guarded expression. Nearby, a small girl is huddled against the wall, clutching a stained, floppy toy monkey. She's painfully thin, her arms and legs little more than sticks.

The girl smiles at us, showing several missing teeth. If she's at all frightened by our strange animal masks, she doesn't show it. "Hi." She sticks a dirty palm out. "You got any money?"

"Lacy," the woman hisses. "What did I tell you about begging?"

"Not to do it." The girl chews on her toy monkey's foot. "But—"

"You just hush now, you hear?" She casts a nervous glance in our direction.

I stop. We may not have money, but we have food bars and water bottles. I cast a glance at Steven. I don't even have to speak; he understands. Rhee waits as he takes off his pack.

The woman stands up, fingers clenched tight around the hilt of her knife. "Leave us alone." Her voice is firm and clear.

"Wait," I say. "I just want to give her some food."

"She already had her supper. We don't need your help. Or your pity."

I hesitate. "Are you her mother?"

The woman looks away. "Her mother's dead. I look after her now."

The older girl with the can of hash stares at us, mouth slightly open, a lump of half-chewed food still inside.

"Becca, what have I told you?" the woman growls. "Eat like a goddamn lady." The girl snaps her jaw shut, swallows, and licks her fingers.

"Please," I say. "You need this food more than we do."

The little girl sucks on her toy monkey's foot and casts a hopeful glance in the woman's direction.

The woman sighs, tense shoulders loosening. The lines in her weathered face deepen, and she waves a hand at me. "Fine. Do what you want."

I rummage through the pack and pull out a handful of food bars. When I extend them to the girl, she flinches. "Here," I say quietly. "It's all right. They're protein bars. A little dry, but they'll fill you up." I smile and unwrap one, showing her.

The girl grabs the bars from me and starts ripping off pieces with her fingers, stuffing them into her mouth.

"Make them last, okay?" Steven says.

The girl nods, cheeks bulging.

As we keep walking, a dull ache fills my chest. How do all these people survive down here? How can they possibly have enough? "Do *all* refugees end up here?" I ask. "I mean, aren't there any opportunities for them?"

"Not many have the resources to become Canadian citizens. If they don't come here, they usually end up in Area 9." At our puzzled silence, she adds, "Refugee shelter. That's what they call it, anyway. It's actually more like an internment camp." Our footsteps echo through the tunnel. Water drips somewhere in the darkness.

The ache in my chest deepens. If people knew it was like this, would they even try to cross the border?

A rat scurries away from my feet. A few yards ahead, a boy lunges forward and impales it with a sharpened stick. The rat flails, squealing, then goes still. He holds up his catch, smiling, and another boy whoops in excitement.

"It's not an easy life, in the Underground," Rhee remarks. "But it could be worse. I lived here for two years before Zebra found me."

"Zebra?" I repeat.

"Our leader. Your leader, soon."

"Who is he? I mean, what sort of person is he? What's his real name?"

"He's Zebra. That's the only name he needs."

I frown. "So you don't know his real identity. And yet you trust him?"

"With my life," she replies calmly. "I owe him everything. If not for Zebra, I'd have been rounded up and sent to Area 9 a long time ago. Or maybe shipped back to the lab for IFEN scientists to dissect my brain."

My pulse speeds. Next to me, Steven stops walking. I can't see his face under the mask, and its avian features aren't very mobile or expressive, but his hands are suddenly balled into white-knuckled fists. "What do you mean?" he asks.

She faces him. "Did you think that you and the other children at St. Mary's were the only victims of IFEN's experiments?"

"I don't know," Steven whispers. "I—I guess I did."

"What happened?" I ask. "What did they do to you?" She doesn't answer. And only then does it occur to me that I just asked a very personal, very intrusive question. "I'm sorry. I shouldn't have—"

"Let's keep moving." She turns away. Tense silence fills the air between us as we follow her through more abandoned subway tunnels.

"You can deactivate your masks now, if you want," Rhee says. "It's safe."

I push the tiny button on the side of my collar. Steven does the same. He's pale, his gaze unfocused and glassy.

I lean toward him. "Steven?"

He doesn't answer, and I know he's thinking about St. Mary's. His eyes jerk back and forth in tiny, involuntary movements. He's drifting into the past, falling into a hole inside himself. I lay a hand on his arm; he gives a start. He's shaking.

"Stay with me." I squeeze his arm.

He nods. Beads of sweat glisten on his forehead. I start telling him some random story about a time I tried to bake brownies from scratch and ended up nearly setting the kitchen on fire. The words don't matter; I'm just trying to keep him anchored in the present. I know from experience how easy it is to slip into memories. They can rise up and drag you down like quicksand, if you're not careful. So I keep talking, even knowing that I must sound like a complete airhead to Rhee. My hand slides down his arm until my fingers interlock with his. He gives my hand a light, grateful squeeze. Gradually, his rapid breathing slows.

She's watching us over her shoulder—looking at our intertwined hands, I realize. Her eyes aren't quite blank. There's something in them, beneath the surface, something I can't quite read.

We keep walking for a long time. Rhee seems to know exactly where she's going; she makes turns without hesitation, taking us down branching tunnels, and I quickly lose track of how to get back to the point of entry. We're at her mercy.

She fishes a flashlight out of her jacket and flicks it on, then leads us down another, narrower tunnel of brick. She sweeps the flashlight beam over the wall until she finds a small alcove. "Stay here. I'll be right back."

"You're leaving?"

"I won't go far. There's something I need to take care of." She tosses us the flashlight and takes another one out of her pack. Then she hands me the rifle.

"Wait," I say. "I don't—"

She turns and jogs down the tunnel, back the way we just came from. The shadows reach out and engulf her.

Steven and I sit huddled in the tiny alcove, shivering. The air down here is damp and foul. Gingerly, I grip the rifle and rest the butt on the ground, keeping it pointed at the ceiling. It's cold and heavy. Water drips in the darkness—a steady plip-plip-plip.

"So," Steven says, "what do you think of her?"

"She's very . . ." I trail off, fumbling for a polite word. "Intense."

He gives a short laugh. "Yeah, that's for sure. I mean, wow. I don't think I've ever seen someone kick so much ass in a single day. If all the Blackcoats are like her, IFEN's going to have its hands full."

For the hundredth time, I see Rhee walk up to the wounded border patrol woman and put a bullet through her head. A shudder runs through me. Rhee said freedom is a contract signed in blood. Apparently, she meant other people's blood.

What's wrong with me? She saved our lives. If not for her, Steven and I would be sitting in white-walled cells, waiting for a Mindwalker to erase our identities. So what if she's a little cold, a little harsh? So what if she carries a huge gun and probably has a massive body count to her name? Are those reasons to be afraid of her?

Well, all right, those do seem like sensible reasons. Then again, what was I expecting? She's a Blackcoat. Maybe I'm just being prissy.

Steven frowns. "Hey. You all right?"

"Yes." I can't meet his gaze. "Well, no. I'm just . . . overwhelmed, I guess." I chew my lower lip. I've been doing that so much lately, it's starting to feel raw. "Are you sure that joining up with these people is a good idea?" The words slip out of me before I can stop them.

"That's the whole reason we came here. Isn't it?"

He's right. More to the point, what other options do we have? Seeing my face on that WANTED billboard made it clear that wandering around above ground isn't safe. I hug my knees to my chest and lower my voice to a whisper. "I was thinking . . . maybe we could find somewhere to hide out while we decide what to do? Like a safe house. There are lots of them up here, right? There's got to be some other way, even if we can't see it right now."

His expression hardens. "I didn't come here to hide. I want to fight back."

"So we start blowing up buildings, then? Or shooting people? How will that help?" I keep my voice low. I don't want to risk being overheard.

"When did you start having second thoughts? I thought you were on our side."

"This isn't about taking sides."

"Oh, I think it is." His voice is cold, but there's something else there, too. Hurt. Betrayal.

We shouldn't be arguing about this now. I don't want to alienate Steven. He's my friend. More than that. I need him; we need each other. If we start fighting, there'll be no solid ground to stand on, and we'll fall into a deep abyss where nothing means anything. "I just . . . the way she talks and acts . . . it's like she accepts violence and killing as natural. Ian told me that this movement is supposed to be about hope, not fear, but maybe he's wrong. Maybe they *are* just terrorists. And if that's the case, then I can't see anything good coming out of this."

"Jesus, I can't believe—after all we've been through—"

"I told you before that I don't agree with the Blackcoats' methods," I reply, a little more sharply than I intended. "Why are you surprised?"

"You know what I think?" he says quietly. "I think you're afraid."

I try to ignore the thick knot in my throat. "Yes, I'm afraid. And you ought to be, too. Sometimes fear can stop you from making mistakes."

He stares straight ahead, silent. A rat sits a few yards away, nibbling on a crust of moldy bread.

Where is Rhee? Has she abandoned us? No—she wouldn't have left her gun, if that was her intention. What if something happened to her? My breathing quickens, and my fingers tighten on the rifle.

Scuffles and grunts echo down the tunnel. "What's going on?" I whisper.

Steven leans forward. "Dunno. Sounds like a fight." His jaw tightens. "Get ready."

A loud thud reverberates through the cement, then another. Then silence descends. Steven mutters a curse under his breath. "I'm gonna go see if she's okay." He stands. "You keep the gun."

"Steven, wait!" But he's already jogging off into the shadows, leaving me huddled in the alcove. I sit, fingers clamped around the grip of a rifle I'm not even sure how to use, wondering what will happen to me if they never come back. My heart jerks in my chest, sharp staccato beats. I try counting them for awhile, but that just makes me aware of how fast my pulse is.

After what feels like an hour of waiting—though it's probably closer to a few minutes—Rhee and Steven reappear in the entrance to the tunnel, Rhee holding her flashlight in one hand. As they approach, I stand. "What happened?"

"Some men were following us, carrying baseball bats and clubs. Probably hoping to sneak up on us, knock us out and steal our food."

"She'd already taken care of them by the time I got there," Steven says with a half-smile. "She didn't need my help."

With her sleeve, she wipes blood off the flashlight.

"Did you kill them?" I blurt out.

"Of course not. They weren't much of a threat." After a moment, she adds, "Though one of them is going to be eating meals without his front teeth from now on."

I exhale, the tension running out of me. Maybe I'm judging her too hastily, after all. Still, the back of my neck tingles as she brushes past.

11

We keep walking. There's a thin layer of water over the ground, and it seeps into my shoes, soaking my socks and numbing my feet. The air smells like garbage and other, fouler things. I want to ask where we're going and how much longer we'll have to walk, but there doesn't seem to be much point. We'll get there whenever we get there.

The narrow corridor opens up into another, wider tunnel with curved cement walls, which ends in a pair of towering, rusted metal doors. Rhee takes off her glove and presses her thumb to a biometric scanner on the wall. A green light blinks. The doors open with a low, grinding whir.

Beyond lies a cavernous room. The walls are constructed from sheets of metal, bolted together and rusted to a dull, coppery red. Electric panel-lights hum on the ceiling, and rows of doorways lead off into hallways. On the wall facing us is a huge silver plaque engraved with words: MY MIND IS MY ONLY SOVEREIGN. REASON IS MY ONLY COMPASS. EVEN IF FETTERS BIND ME, IN MY THOUGHTS I AM FREE.

We step into the room, and the doors clang shut behind us.

I stare, dazed. "Where are we?"

"The Citadel," Rhee replies in that matter-of-fact way of hers, as if it should be self-evident. She keeps walking, down the center of the room and through one of the doorways. The hallway is constructed in the same way, from bolted-together sheets of metal.

Steven cranes his neck. He seems to be trying to look in every direction at once. "Did you guys build this place?"

"No. It was built a long time ago, by the Canadian government, as a bomb and chemical weapons shelter. After the war ended, it was abandoned. The Blackcoats discovered it and modified it for their needs. There are about four hundred of us here. Of course, we aren't the only Blackcoats living in Canada. But we are the largest single group anywhere in either country." She stops suddenly and cocks her head, as if listening to something. I notice the tiny silver earpiece glinting in her ear. She nods and says, "Yes, they're here." A pause. "All right. I'll bring them."

Her gaze snaps back into focus, and she resumes walking.

"Bring us where?" Steven asks.

"The Assembly starts in a few minutes. Attendance is manda-tory." At our blank stares, Rhee adds, "The daily Assembly is when we're given updates about the situation in the URA. Once it's over, I'll show you to your rooms."

Right now, the last thing I want is to stand in a crowded room filled with armed Blackcoats. What I want is to eat something, take a hot shower, and collapse into bed, in that order. But we might as well get this over with.

My backpack is still on the floor. I slide it on and tighten the straps. "Let's go, then."

Rhee leads us down another hallway. The echoes of our foot-steps bounce off the metal walls. Beneath the floor, there's another sound, harder to define—a low rumble, like distant machinery, combined with a steady, deep thunk. Thunk. Thunk. It's faint—you can't even hear it unless you focus—but it sends a cold tremor through my nerves. Like we're in the intestines of some gigantic metal monster, listening to its heartbeat.

Rhee stops in front of a towering set of doors. She pushes, and they swing ponderously open.

Beyond lies a vast, dimly lit room resembling a concert hall. The floor is packed with people. Dozens of heads turn toward us. At the front of the room stands a massive wooden stage, and behind that, a huge screen—currently blank—takes up most of the wall.

The blood beats in my throat as we enter. I grip Steven's hand tightly, not wanting to be separated from him. As we make our way deeper into the crowd, murmurs spread outward from us like ripples in a pond. Eyes widen, and lips frame my name.

My gaze flits from face to face. Most of these people are teenagers. They would look perfectly at home walking through the hallways of Greenborough High—well, if not for the rifles strapped to their backs. Those that don't have guns are armed with knives in sheaths at their hips or strapped to their arms. "So many children," I whisper.

Rhee glances at me. "The average age here is eighteen. Same as yours."

A good point. Still, it makes me uncomfortable that most of the people involved in this rebellion aren't even technically old enough to drink in the URA.

A man steps up onto the stage, followed by a spotlight. He's tall and thin, wearing a long black coat—which, logically enough, seems to be the standard attire here. He appears to be in his twenties, but despite that, his hair is a shock of pure snowy white. His features have an androgynous, classical beauty; they might have been sculpted by an artist. He faces the crowd and spreads his arms, and all at once, the murmurs fall silent. Every pair of eyes latches onto him.

Steven leans toward Rhee and asks quietly, "Is that Zebra?"

"No," she replies. "It's Nicholas Claybird, his right-hand man. Zebra himself rarely attends the Assembly in person. But he's watching and listening."

A leader who observes everything from the shadows but doesn't like to show his face. Already, I don't trust him.

"Brothers and sisters." Nicholas' voice is deep and silky-smooth, amplified by the microphone pinned to his coat collar. "We are on the brink of war. The time draws ever nearer—the time when we will come out of hiding and show the world that we will no longer stand for these injustices." He gestures to the screen with a sweep of his arm. "What you are about to see is IFEN propaganda, tainted and twisted by their lies . . . but it is progress, nonetheless, because they've finally acknowledged to the public that we exist. They can no longer pretend otherwise. We've grown too strong."

An image appears on the screen behind him—a news program, judging by the banners scrolling along the bottom of the screen. An aerial shot pans over IFEN headquarters, which is visibly damaged. The doors have been blown out, and rubble is strewn across the parking lot. There are police and construction crews all around. "The nation is still reeling from the unexpected terrorist attacks which occurred last week," an announcer says, her voice low and solemn. "Four IFEN employees were injured in the explosions, and two more were killed. Their families and communities are devastated."

The screen displays a pair of closed caskets decorated with sprays of white roses and lilies. I taste blood and realize I'm biting the inside of my cheek.

Ian and his friends set off those bombs, to help Steven and I escape.

The camera cuts to a woman, her face pale and streaked with tears. Her eyes are hollow and distant. I recognize that look, because I felt it myself after Father's death—that numbness, the mind's unwillingness to accept the reality of loss. Beside her, a tiny blond toddler clutches her hand and looks around with wide, uncertain eyes. A child too young to understand the concept of death. How long, I wonder, before it sinks in? How many days before she stops asking, *When is Daddy coming home?*

Beside me, Steven squirms, and I realize I'm clutching his hand too hard. I force myself to relax my grip.

The announcer continues: "In the wake of this national tragedy, a public memorial service will be held tomorrow to honor the dead. Those responsible for the attack have not yet been identified. This means another attack could happen at any time, in any place. IFEN's Board of Directors has discussed temporarily strengthening certain security measures until the terrorists are apprehended. Lain Fisher, former Mindwalker-in-training, is among those still missing from the blast. There is speculation of her involvement in the incident, but to date that remains only hearsay."

My stomach hurts. I press a hand against it.

The image on the screen cuts back to the caskets, surrounded by weeping mourners, then freezes. Nicholas stands in the center of the stage, silhouetted against the screen's glow. "Two IFEN employees die in an explosion, and they're treated as heroes. Their deaths are held up as a national tragedy." His voice is calm and cold. "I ask you now—how many Fours died by Somnazol in the past year? Does anyone know?"

Silence.

"What about the political dissidents who have been mindwiped behind closed doors? How many? Do you suppose their families will ever be given a national ceremony to honor their loss?" He smiles, showing a sliver of white teeth. "Of course not. Their loss will never even be mentioned. Why? Because to IFEN and the government, not all human lives are equal. While the whole country sheds crocodile tears over those two dead guards, doctors will quietly write out prescriptions for another few hundred suicide pills, and it will be viewed as an act of mercy. Of compassion. Because they think we're lost causes, better off dead than alive." He flings his arms open wide. "I ask you now, brothers and sisters—are you a lost cause?"

"No!" the crowd thunders back.

"Will you be swayed by this propaganda? Will you allow them to bring down the hammer of shame on your heads and beat you into submission?"

"No!"

His smile widens. "No, of course you won't. There can be no compromise when it comes to freedom. Freedom is life—it is the blood in our veins, the air in our lungs. It is the basic right of every man, woman and child who walks this Earth, and we will not let them take it! Will you fight with me?"

"We will fight!"

There's a dark energy in the room, like fire and shadow. Nicholas has them all by the throat. Every pair of eyes is locked onto him, even Steven's.

"Oh, but there's more," Nicholas says. "Watch."

The image on the screen unfreezes, and the announcer continues: "We take you now to Dr. Swan, Director of IFEN, for comments."

And suddenly, there he is—Dr. Swan sitting in an armchair, his expression professional and neutral. At the sight of him, the hollowness in my gut becomes a cold weight. The camera angle widens to show him sitting across from a woman in a suit. "Thank you for taking this time to speak with me, Director," the woman says. "I'm hoping you can clear some things up for us."

"Certainly," he replies in his smooth baritone.

"First of all, you've mentioned an upcoming trip with your new protégé, isn't that right?"

New protégé? Already? He didn't waste much time replacing me. The thought stings unexpectedly.

"That's correct," Dr. Swan replies. "Mr. Freed and I are visiting Toronto."

I hear the soft hiss of breath from between Steven's teeth, and his hand twitches against mine. Dr. Swan will soon be in the same city as us. It's not a comforting idea.

"And what is the purpose of this visit?" the woman asks.

"Simply to foster better relations with Canada and open the door for future trade and cooperation. The URA's isolationist policy cannot last forever, after all. Canada is our neighbor. It's necessary to maintain tight border control for the sake of our national security, but that doesn't mean we can never talk to each other."

"He's got something up his sleeve," Steven mutters, and I nod in agreement. Swan's words sound innocuous enough, but I don't believe that's all there is to it. Why would he be visiting Canada now, after ignoring its existence for years? It can't be coincidence that he's chosen to do this so soon after I exposed the truth about St. Mary's.

The interviewer speaks up again, pulling me out of my thoughts: "On a more serious note, Dr. Swan, there are a lot of rumors floating around about Lain Fisher, the young Mindwalker who recently leaked some of her own memories onto the Net. What can you tell us about the incident?"

"First of all," he says, "I should mention that memories are inherently subjective and flawed—particularly in individuals with higher Types—so they shouldn't be taken as fact."

The woman purses her lips and leans forward. "Are you saying, then, that what appeared on the Net was a fabrication? A hoax?"

"Not a hoax in the ordinary sense of the word, but they are indeed fabrications. Lain is in a delusional state. Before her disappearance, she'd been behaving oddly. She'd become secretive and distrustful, very unlike her usual self. She was seen frequently in the company of a Type Four, and though her own Type had already started to slip, she repeatedly refused treatment. It's a pattern I've seen many times over the years . . . and it can happen to anyone.

Sick individuals slowly lose touch with reality, and their illness prevents them from seeing how desperately they need help. They become infected with a sort of paranoid narcissism, which leads to feelings of persecution, which—in turn—lead to violent behavior and criminal activity. Lain herself probably believes that the misinformation she spread about IFEN and myself, which is what makes this case so tragic."

I hear an odd sound, like rocks scraping together, and realize I'm grinding my teeth.

The interviewer presses a pen to her lower lip. "You're saying, then, that IFEN never actually experimented on children?"

"Of course not."

He says it with such surety, firm and direct. If I hadn't seen the truth with my own eyes, I might believe him.

Now Steven's the one squeezing my hand too hard. "That piece of shit," he mutters. "He's still denying it."

Dr. Swan continues in that quiet, calm, poisonously reasonable-sounding voice: "I must stress, this is not Lain's fault. She's an impressionable teenager infected by conspiracy theories. But unfortunately, her sickness poses a danger to the stability of our society, so we must treat her as a threat. Too many people are willing to believe the worst about IFEN, the very organization designed to keep them safe from the real dangers. Fear is an easy trap to fall into." His expression tightens—the first sign of emotion he's shown, though I don't doubt it's as calculated as everything else. "I consider this my own failing. I was her legal guardian, after all. I should have taken action sooner."

"What about Lain? Do you have a message for her?"

"Yes." He looks straight at the camera. "My message is this. Come home. It's not too late to do the right thing. Let me—let us—help you."

The screen freezes again, Dr. Swan's face still staring out at us. I stand in a bubble of silence and stillness, my breathing filling my ears. My chest is hot, and there's a dull burn behind my forehead. I'm shaking. Not with fear. With anger.

How can he do it? How can he sit there and lie so easily, so smoothly, to the entire country?

Nicholas' gaze locks onto me, then he reaches out and curls a finger in beckoning. "Lain Fisher, will you step forward, please?"

A lightning bolt of terror goes through me. Rhee didn't say anything about this. Does he want me to make a speech?

Nicholas nods to the stairs leading up to the stage. I give Steven a panicked look, and he squeezes my arm in encouragement. Bracing myself, I push forward, through the crowd. My legs wobble as I ascend the steps and stand in the center of the stage, facing everyone. The stage lights dazzle my eyes, blinding me so I can't see their faces. Maybe that's a mercy. I'm already so nervous, I'm starting to feel nauseous. It's a good thing there's nothing in my stomach; the protein bar I ate feels like eons ago.

Nicholas places a hand on my shoulder. His long, bony fingers clamp down like a bird's talons, making me flinch. "This girl needs no introduction. She risked her life to expose the truth about IFEN. And now, she is one of us."

Sweat trickles down to the small of my back as I stand on the stage, pinned in place by a burning spotlight, my legs like jelly.

Nicholas smiles at me. His teeth are large and very white. "Dr. Swan wants you to come home." He leans closer. His blue eyes drill into mine. "What do you say to that?"

Panic flutters in my chest. My mind is a white blank.

Nicholas reaches up and brushes back a lock of his hair, discreetly switching off his microphone in the process. He hisses into my ear, "Swear allegiance to the Blackcoats. Tell them you intend to take down IFEN, no matter the cost."

My pulse thunders in my head, and more sweat worms its way down my back. I want to get off the stage, away from the pain of his fingers biting into me, the heat of his breath against the side of my neck.

Nicholas squeezes my shoulder, making me flinch. "Say it."

Deep within me, there's a small, steel-blue flash of defiance.

Nicholas switches his microphone back on. "Well, Lain? You've just heard Dr. Swan call you a delusional, frightened little girl. You must have *something* you want to tell everyone."

My gaze locks with Steven's. What would he say, in my place? I brace myself, take a deep breath, and raise my voice: "Dr. Swan can—can go fuck himself." My voice cracks a little over the word fuck. "With a red-hot cactus."

Silence fills the Assembly Hall.

I interlace my hands behind my back. "That's all I have to say." I give a small, awkward bow. "Thank you."

Another heartbeat of silence passes. Then, all at once, the crowd bursts into laughter. The dark, focused energy dissolves. Cheers break out, applause punctuated by whoops and whistles. A few people raise their voices:

"Yeah, Dr. Swan! Go fuck yourself!"

"Fuck yourself with a rabid porcupine!"

"Fuck yourself with a chainsaw!"

Nicholas smiles tightly at me, lips framing bared teeth. He releases me, and I quickly descend from the stage, dizzy with relief. My shoulder throbs from his grip. I rub it, wondering if it will leave a bruise.

12

The Assembly is over. People filter out of the Hall. They sound like normal teenagers, talking and laughing, giving each other high fives. A girl jumps up onto a boy's back and wraps her legs around his waist, and he carries her through the open doors.

Rhee leads Steven and I into a long, empty hallway. The quiet is deafening.

"Nice speech, Doc," Steven says, grinning. "I was inspired."

"Thanks." I blush. Then I think about Nicholas' icy smile. He doesn't strike me as the sort of person who likes being defied. Already, I'm treading in dangerous waters.

"Hey." Steven's voice softens. "You okay?"

I don't trust Nicholas. I don't trust any of this. That's what I want to say. But Rhee is standing right there. "I'm fine. Just . . . over-whelmed."

Rhee points to two doors, side by side. "Your rooms are here. Just press your thumbs against the scanners and they'll log your biodata, so only you'll have access."

I place the pad of my thumb against the small, black square next to my door, and Steven does the same with his. The scanners flash green.

"There are rations inside," Rhee says. "Get some rest. Tomorrow, you'll start your simulation training."

"Simulation . . .?"

"Pretty much what it sounds like," she says. "If you're going to stay here, you'll participate in missions."

"What sort of missions?" I ask, uneasy.

"Currently, most of them involve helping refugees across the border."

"Oh." I relax a little. Helping people. That's something I can do, surely. Then again, even rescue missions can result in casualties. I saw that for myself.

Rhee watches me in that unsettling way of hers, as if all my thoughts are laid bare. "It's not easy," she says. "You have to be ready to fight. To use a gun. The simulations will prepare you for that. After training sessions, we have lunch in the mess hall. You can eat alone in your room if you want, but you're encouraged to eat with the others. It facilitates bonding with your fellow soldiers."

I must be exhausted, because this all strikes me as sort of funny. It's like being at a summer camp for killers-in-training. "What next? Will we make bombs out of macaroni and glitter?"

Steven snorts a small laugh. Rhee stares at me blankly.

"Never mind."

She turns away. "Wake-up call is at seven. Be ready." She walks away, leaving Steven and I standing together in the hallway.

"Well," Steven says, "here we are."

"I guess so." I lower my gaze. I'm so tired; I feel like there are a lot of important things we need to talk about, but the whole day is a chaotic mishmash inside my head. I can barely make sense of it all.

His fingertips brush over my cheek, the barest ghost of a touch. "Are you okay?"

How am I supposed to answer that? I study my shoes, which are still damp and caked with mud from trudging through the sewers. "I'll be a lot better once we get some food and sleep." I offer a weak smile, then press my thumb to the scanner again. The door opens with a faint whir, revealing a rather plain room, its walls and floors constructed from the same metal sheeting as everything else. "I'm going to get cleaned up. See you in a few minutes?"

"Sure."

I step inside my room, and the door slides automatically shut behind me. As a test, I touch the panel on the wall, and the door opens. So we're not locked in our rooms. Nice to know. It *does* seem odd that they're placing so much trust in us. I suppose if you're building a rebel guerrilla army, you can't afford to be too picky about who you let in, but still . . . I spent years working for IFEN before defecting. How do they know I won't change my mind about all this?

I brush the questions aside, take off my backpack and set it in the corner. Then I pull open a drawer, revealing piles of neatly stacked pants and shirts. I choose a simple white blouse and a pair of dark blue jeans. In the closet-sized adjoining bathroom, I strip off my bloody, filthy clothes and chuck them into a slide-out compartment on the wall marked LAUNDRY. To my relief, there's a shower, though it's cramped. I quickly wash off, then start looking around for the rations Rhee promised. In a small steel freezer, I find a pile of frozen meals; there's a microwave sitting on the counter nearby, alongside a small stack of dishes and cheap tin cutlery.

Well, my diet here won't be much different from back home.

I heat up a meal of frozen beef cubes and potatoes. Then I step out into the hallway and knock on Steven's door. "It's Lain," I call.

The door slides open, and I step inside. "I thought we could eat together."

Steven has changed into fresh jeans and a clean T-shirt, though he's still wearing his mud-stained coat over it. He seems to sense that I don't want to talk, so he doesn't ask questions. Instead, he heats up a tray of chicken and green beans, and we sit next to each other on the edge of his bed.

With my fork, I poke at the potatoes, little wheels decorated with bits of rehydrated herbs. The utensil has an unpleasant metallic taste, so I pick up a beef cube with my fingers and pop it in my mouth. The meat is tough and salty. "Once we go through training, do you think we'll be like Rhee?" I ask, half joking. "I mean, will we be able to leap tall buildings and beat up a dozen armed thugs while playing the fiddle?"

He half smiles. "She's a special case."

"What do you mean?"

Steven's smile vanishes. "Um. Well, it's kind of personal."

"Personal," I repeat.

He opens and then closes his mouth. "I probably shouldn't have mentioned it. I mean, I guess it's not a secret, really, but she told me—"

"When did you even have a chance to talk to her in private?"

"In the Underground. You know, when she went back to take care of those thugs and I ran off to see if she needed help. While we were walking back to you, I told her about St. Mary's. And she told me some things about her past. You know how she mentioned being part of an experiment?" He toys with the frayed sleeve of his coat. "Basically, IFEN was trying to create perfect soldiers. People who wouldn't freeze up during a battle or get PTSD and need lots of expensive therapy later. So they started messing with people's brains to make them less sensitive to fear and guilt, even physical pain. They used orphaned kids from state homes. Just like the St. Mary's experiments."

"That's horrible." But the sad truth is, I'm not shocked or even particularly surprised that IFEN would do something like that. A month ago, I would have denied it fiercely. No more.

"Yeah. Anyway, the project was scrapped. Maybe it got too twisted even for IFEN's tastes. The kids involved—the few that survived—were kept locked up in treatment facilities. Most of them went crazy. Rhee's the only one who escaped. That was years ago."

"So . . . she doesn't feel fear? At all?"

"That's what she said. You'd think that would be a good thing. But when she lost fear, she lost other things, too. She said it's like being underwater all the time. Everything muffled." His jaw tightens. "Guess that's what happens when you fry part of someone's brain with a laser."

I think of Rhee—her blank expression, the cool, merciless way she took down the border patrol. It wasn't the Blackcoats who made her that way, after all. It was IFEN. It surprises me that she told Steven; she doesn't seem like the type to self-disclose, particularly to someone she's just met.

But then, both she and Steven have been hurt in the same way. They both carry scars in their brains, marks of IFEN's abuse. I've seen Steven's memories—experienced them even—but still, I didn't *live* through them. She can understand him in a way that I can't. The few inches of bedding between Steven and I suddenly feel like an uncrossable ocean. "Is she . . . okay? I mean—" I'm not sure *what* I mean, really.

"She's okay. Sort of. She's got a purpose now. A purpose helps you stay alive."

"Yes. It does." For a long time, Mindwalking was my purpose, the thing that held me together. Now . . .

Now, I don't know.

"I'm sorry," I say quietly. "About what I said earlier, in the tunnels."

"I'm sorry, too." He stares down at his feet. "I know you don't like killing. That doesn't make you weak or scared. It just means you aren't numb." His fingers tighten on his fork. "I think I could have done what Rhee did. I could have shot those border guards and not felt the slightest bit guilty about it. But maybe that's not something to be proud of. Maybe there's something wrong with me, after all."

"No," I reply quietly. "You were right. I knew what joining the resistance would mean. I just didn't want to think about it." My throat is suddenly tight. I try to swallow, but the lump inside it swells, making it hard to draw breath. "I don't want to kill anyone. Not even in self-defense. I hope I never have to."

"You won't," he says.

"What makes you so sure of that?"

"Because I'll protect you."

I look into his eyes. They're ringed by dark circles, and the whites are bloodshot, but his gaze is clear and determined.

He means it. I can see that. But I don't want him to kill for me, either. I don't want anyone to take on that burden for my sake. My vision blurs, and I turn my face away, trying to wipe my eyes discreetly, but it's too late. He sees.

"Did I make you cry?" He sounds a little nervous. "I was kind of trying to do the opposite." He sighs and rakes a hand through his hair. "Guess I'm not very good at this."

"It's not you." I lay a hand over his and give it a squeeze. "I'll be all right once I get some sleep."

He nods, gaze downcast.

I push my empty tray into a slot on the wall labeled DISHES, retreat to my room, and slip into the plain white nightgown hanging on the wall. Then I slide beneath the covers and turn out the lights. But sleep won't come. A slideshow of death keeps flashing through my head. Over and over, I see Rhee pull the trigger, snuffing out the woman's life. I see the guards at IFEN headquarters, too—watch them dissolve into the blinding light of the explosion.

I press my hands against my temples, as if I can squeeze the images out by force.

Finally, sheer exhaustion weighs me down, blotting out the day's events, and I start to drift off.

A knock on the door jerks me awake. I sit up, pawing sleep from my eyes.

The door slides open. A tall, thin figure stands, silhouetted in the light of the hall, features lost in shadow.

I clutch the edge of my blanket. "Steven?"

"Get dressed and come with me," says a deep voice. It's not Steven. Nicholas?

"Why? What—"

"I'll give you two minutes." The door slides shut.

Apparently, Nicholas can unlock any door in the Citadel, regardless of whose biodata it's keyed to. So much for privacy.

Slowly, I climb out of bed, ignoring the way my heart is suddenly trying to smash through my ribs. Once I'm dressed, I step out into the hall. Without a word, Nicholas turns and starts walking, his long black coat flapping behind him.

I follow, still half asleep and rubbing at my eyes. "Where are you taking me?"

No response.

"Say something, already."

He turns and studies me with a bland, unrevealing expression. I keep my face as blank as his, putting on the same calm, professional façade I always showed to my clients, but my heart is pounding.

He seems to be weighing me with his eyes. They're blue, but not like Steven's. Nicholas' are like sapphires; unnaturally blue, oversaturated with color. They don't look real, but I don't see the telltale rings of contact lenses around the irises. "Frankly, this is the first time we've allowed a Mindwalker into our ranks," he says. "Until very recently, you were with the enemy, and your refusal to swear allegiance to us does not inspire trust. We need to take certain precautions. Zebra has decided that you will undergo a test."

Somehow, I have the feeling it's not multiple choice. "What kind of test?"

"I'm not permitted to tell you anything else. It wouldn't matter if I did, anyway. There's no way for you to prepare." He keeps moving ahead with his rapid yet seemingly effortless stride.

This place, I think, is like a giant metal anthill. So many twisting corridors, and they all look the same. If I lose him in this maze of passageways, I'm not sure I'll be able to find my way back again. Our footsteps follow us through a hush overlaid by the low, constant rumble of machinery.

"Who is Zebra, anyway?" I ask.

"Our leader."

"I mean, aside from that. If he's the one who outfitted this place as a base for the Blackcoats, he must have a lot of resources."

No response.

I sigh. After a moment, I try one more question. "Why does he call himself Zebra?"

"Because he looks good in stripes," Nicholas replies snippily. He spins to face me. "You ask far too many questions. You have already tried my patience considerably. Try it any more, and you'll find yourself in the timeout room."

"What is that?"

"Do you want to find out?" he asks pleasantly. "Because I can certainly arrange that."

I bite my tongue. Rebellion, it seems, is not tolerated among the rebels.

We reach another door—a small, ordinary door, gray and rust-flecked. He opens it, revealing a plain, boxlike room lit by a single dim bulb. In the center of the room stands a reclining, leather-padded black chair. On the chair's headrest, at the end of a short black wire, is a white helmet.

It's a Gate.

13

"What is this?" My voice shakes.

"Just what it looks like. You're familiar with this machine and what it does, I'm sure."

My stomach is sinking through the floor. If I get into that chair, whoever's on the other side will have access to my thoughts, my memories. Not only that, but they might be able to alter them. I'll be placing my mind in the hands of a stranger. "And if I refuse? What then?"

"Then you'll have to leave the Citadel. If you choose to leave, we'll give you a drug that will blur your memories of the past twenty-four hours. Not enough that you'll completely forget what happened, but enough that you won't know how to get back here. It's your choice."

Anger fills my chest, heating me from the inside. "We don't have anywhere else to go."

"That's not my concern."

I can feel the rope around my throat again, tightening like a hangman's noose.

If I left the Citadel, Steven would go with me. I'm pretty sure of that, anyway. But then he and I would be on our own in this strange, hostile country. How long would we last before being caught and locked up in Area 9 . . . or hunted down by IFEN and shipped back to Dr. Swan?

Steven was right. We came here to fight back against IFEN, and for better or worse, these people are the ones who can help us. That means playing by their rules, at least for now.

I look at the Gate and take a deep breath. My knees have turned to water. If they wanted to harm me, I reason, they've had plenty of chances to do it. I'm already at their mercy. "Fine."

"One word of advice," he says. "Whatever happens, don't fight it. You'll just make it harder on yourself." He nods toward the Gate room. "Go on. You know what to do."

I step forward, through the doorway. The door slides shut behind me, and I'm alone.

Electric lights hum overhead as I approach, slowly. I reach out and run my hand over the helmet's familiar, smooth contours.

This Gate is the same model as mine—first-generation, older technology, no longer made. But there's only one helmet. The other one can't be far away. A Gate's range isn't very large. There must be someone in another room close by.

A small silver box sits on a plain wooden stand next to the chair. I flip the box open. Inside gleams a slender hypodermic filled with a clear, yellowish fluid. A sedative, maybe? Something that will make me too disoriented to resist whatever is about to happen? There's a tiny, packaged sanitary wipe, as well. The implication is obvious. I'm supposed to inject myself with this unknown substance, then put the helmet on and open my mind to a complete stranger. I wonder if I've gone insane.

Well, here goes nothing.

I slide into the chair, place the helmet on my head and buckle the strap under my chin. Then I tear open the package, swab the inside of my elbow, and pick up the hypodermic. I hold my breath as I insert the tip of the needle under my skin and depress the plunger. There's a brief sting. I watch the yellow liquid disappear from the tube as I push it into my vein.

The empty hypodermic slips from my fingers and hits the floor with a click. My vision blurs. My breathing echoes in my ears as if it's coming from the end of a long tunnel. When I look down at my own arm, there's a golden aura shimmering around it. I close my eyes for a few seconds, dizzy.

The room warps and bends as a familiar tingling spreads over my skin. My instincts are clanging like alarm bells. But of course, it's too late to back out. I'm not even sure I could stand up if I tried.

Whatever happens, don't fight it, Nicholas told me. I close my eyes and follow his advice, surrendering. As soon as I make the decision not to fight, the fear dissolves. There's a sense of floating in empty space. The chair, the room, the helmet all fade into oblivion. I can no longer feel my own body.

I'm alone. Yet suddenly, I have the clear sense that someone is nearby. With my mind, I reach into the darkness, casting tendrils of my being outward, searching.

Hello? I think.

"Open your eyes," says a soft male voice. It's inside my head, but I hear it as if he were standing next to me.

I try to do what he says, but that's difficult when I can't feel my body. I can't even tell if my eyes are open or closed.

"Not your physical eyes. Open them on the inside."

I imagine myself opening my eyes. And suddenly, I'm standing in the living room of my old house. Sunlight filters in through the windows, illuminating the warm wood floors. A tall, broad-shouldered man stands near one of the windows, staring out. His hands are interlaced behind his back. I recognize those hands. I know them like my own.

Father turns toward me. He looks the way he did before his mind started to deteriorate—eyes bright, face unlined, hair and beard neatly trimmed. "Hello, Lainy," he says.

At the sound of the familiar nickname, my eyes fill with tears. I press a hand to my mouth and take a step back.

He smiles, a sad, complicated smile. "Can you ever forgive me?"

I squeeze my eyes shut. Whatever was in that hypo is causing me to hallucinate. My mind is creating this. That's the only rational explanation. Even knowing that, I want to run across the room and hug him tight, to feel the solid warmth of his arms, the slight roughness of his tweed jacket against my cheek.

"You've grown so much," he says. I open my eyes, and he's walking toward me. "Let me look at you." Slowly, he raises his hands to frame my face. His palms are warm. I can smell the faint whiff of coffee and old books that always seemed to follow him around when he was alive. A smell of comfort, of home.

I shake my head, take an unsteady breath and force myself to step backward. "You're dead."

"That's not true. I may no longer have physical form, but I still exist here. You might say, in some ways, I'm even more real now."

"I—I don't—"

"It's all right. You don't have to understand. Just accept what's in front of you."

The world blurs. The walls tilt, and I squeeze my eyes shut. Think. I have to think.

"I am so very proud of you, Lainy." His voice is warm, soft. "You made the right choice. Just like I knew you would."

I take a slow, deep breath. This doesn't feel like a dream or an illusion—it's too crisp, too clear. My rational mind tells me it can't be real, and yet, what if it is? What if, somehow, in some way, he's still alive, still conscious within this dreamspace?

He holds out his arms. "It's all right," he says, very quietly. "You don't have to be afraid anymore. I'm here now."

Almost against my will, I take a small, shaky step forward. Then I stop. I squeeze my hands into fists, focusing on the pain of my nails digging into my skin. "That woman," I say. "The one you fell in love with. The one who died. The one you never wanted to talk about. What was her name?"

His brows draw together. "Why do you want to know that?"

"Just tell me."

He hesitates, and his frown deepens. Of course. He doesn't know, because I don't know it either. "You aren't Father," I say.

He's silent, his expression inscrutable. "I'm exactly as you remember, aren't I? Isn't that enough?"

A dull burn of anger pulses inside me, spreading through my chest. "My real father was more than my memories of him. He was a person with his own thoughts and feelings. He had a whole life before I existed. And he's dead. The dead don't come back."

"Lainy, I told you. Death is only an illusion—"

I slap him, hard. He blinks a few times. There's a pink mark on his cheek where my hand connected. "Stop it." My voice shakes.

He rubs the mark. His eyes narrow. "You wanted to see him, didn't you? That's what you've been wishing for, all this time."

"Not like this!"

The corners of his mouth curve in a tiny smile. His eyes have changed from brown to a cool, light gray. "Well," he says in a voice that's not my father's. "I expected no less of you."

"Who are you?" And then realization clicks. "Zebra. You're Zebra."

His smile widens, just a little.

I back away. "Let me out of this—this simulation, or whatever it is."

"Not yet." He takes a step toward me, hands interlaced behind his back. "We aren't finished."

I keep retreating until my back is pressed against the wall. The room warps and bends. Somehow, he's influencing what I see and hear. Gates don't normally work this way. "Let me out." I can't keep playing this game. Seeing Father's face, hearing his voice, was like having a half-healed wound ripped open and nettles rubbed into the raw, bloody flesh. "*Let me out!*"

He pauses, head cocked. And then his body contorts and bends, limbs thickening, face stretching as he transforms into an animal, a huge dark beast out of nightmares, a thing of claws and fangs and red, glowing eyes. He runs at me, snapping and snarling. Before I can move or react, he's upon me. Teeth sink into my shoulder. I open my mouth to scream—

Then the living room vanishes. I'm strapped to a table in a white room, and the air is frigid against my bare skin. A glaring white light fills my eyes, blinding me. Dr. Swan looms over me, a surgical mask over the lower half of his face. "Such a bad girl." He holds a rusty saw in one hand. "Something must have gone wrong on the assembly line. A missing part, perhaps? Or one too many? We'll have to open you up and see what the problem is."

I struggle, panting. Panic whites out the inside of my head. *Not real*, I think.

The saw bites into my flesh, slicing through the smooth skin of my stomach, sinking into me. I freeze in surprise. There's no pain, no blood, only an uncomfortable pressure. He pulls the saw out, leaving a neat slit, like I'm a doll and my skin is made of rubber.

No. This isn't. I'm not. This—

And suddenly it's not Dr. Swan standing over me. It's Steven. "How about it, Doc?" he says in that throaty voice I know so well. "You've seen my insides. How about showing me yours?" He slides his hand into the cut in my stomach, disappearing up to the wrist. It doesn't hurt, but I can feel his hand moving inside me. His fingertips press against the inside of my stomach; I see their shape under my skin, moving. Caressing. A shiver runs through me.

Not real not real not—

His arm slides deeper, vanishing almost up to the elbow. "You want to tell me, don't you?" he whispers against my ear.

My shuddering breaths echo through the room. I'm not cold anymore; I'm warm. My head has gone soft and fuzzy, and suddenly I'm having trouble remembering why I'm here or what's going on, but I don't really care. "About what?" I murmur drowsily.

"Your secret." His hand moves deeper still. Up, into my ribcage. "It's okay. You can let me in."

My breath hitches. "I can't."

"Why not?"

"Because you'll hate me, if I tell you." What am I talking about? Tell him *what*?

"I could never hate you, Lain." His voice lowers. "Just whisper it to yourself, in the darkness of your mind. Whisper it."

My eyes slip shut. *Don't be afraid.* Is the voice mine or his? I can't even tell. I exhale softly, and something clenched inside me loosens. His fingers touch my beating heart. He wraps his hand around it, squeezing lightly. "Oh . . . there you are." He laughs, low and husky. "Interesting."

A chill ripples through me. That's not Steven's voice. "Zebra."

"Had you going for a minute there. Didn't I?" He smiles, cold and thin. "Of course, I pushed you harder this time. All you have to do is suppress the activity in the medial prefrontal cortex, and people will accept whatever's in front of them as truth. Though you put up an admirable fight." There's a teasing note in his voice. "So feisty."

"Get your hand out of my chest," I say through gritted teeth.

His hand slides out, covered not with blood, but with a silvery, translucent fluid. He shakes it off. "I apologize for the intrusion, but it was necessary." He smiles, his pale gray eyes alien and chilling in Steven's face. "Let's move on, shall we?"

Blackness sweeps over me. And then I'm standing in a huge outdoor arena under a hot, cloudless blue sky, surrounded by the blur of a crowd and the roar of cheering. Rhee stands across from me in a gold and red gladiator's outfit, holding a huge axe. She tosses me a broadsword. I fumble and nearly drop it. The sunlight half-blinds me, making me squint. "Where are we?"

148

She charges at me with a roar, swinging her axe. I let out a startled cry and lunge to the side, and the axe buries itself in the ground. She wrenches it out and faces me, chest heaving. "If you want to live, then fight me."

"Rhee!" I gasp. "What are you doing?"

She charges at me again, swinging. I thrust the sword out, and the axe clangs off of it. "Stop this!" I shout.

"I'm going to kill you if you don't fight back." Tendrils of brown hair have slipped from her braid, and cling to her sweat-damp face. She glares at me with her tigress eyes. "Do you understand?" She comes at me again, swinging.

Again, the axe bounces off my sword, and I feel the impact down to my bones. "This is ridiculous! I don't even know why we're fighting!"

Her eyes narrow. "It doesn't matter." Her boot cannons into my stomach. I collapse, wheezing. She towers over me, drowning me in her shadow, and raises the axe high above her head. "So, what will you do, Lain?" Her heel presses into my sternum, pinning me like an insect to a board. "Will you die or live? The choice is yours. It makes no difference to me, either way." Her expression is flat, impassive. "Personally, though? I think you'll let me kill you."

The thunder of the crowd fills my ears. Red pennants snap in the wind, and the world tastes like dust and metal. "Rhee." I gasp for breath. "Listen to me. Please. We don't have to do this. Just put down your weapon."

She stares at me, her eyes utterly empty. "Sometimes," she says, "there are only two paths. And they're both ugly." She raises her axe high above her head with both hands.

There's no time to react. I thrust my sword out with a ragged cry. The blade punctures her throat, and blood bubbles out of her mouth. Her eyes glaze over. Horrified, I yank the sword free and take a few steps back. The hilt slips from my numb fingers as Rhee crumples to the ground. Blood pools beneath her, shockingly red.

I just killed her.

It's not real. It's not real. But it feels real. I can't look away.

Then Rhee vanishes, along with the crowd, the sky and ground. The world dissolves, and I'm floating in emptiness. My own irregular breathing echoes in my ears, the only sound.

"Hello?" I call out. My voice falls into the void. There's no echo, no nothing. The blackness is perfect and endless. I can't even feel my body. I'm nothing but a mind, a voice. An icy, primal terror spreads its tentacles through my brain. I force it down.

"I know you're there, Zebra. Where are you?"

Silence.

The fear is fading, smothered by anger. It feels surprisingly good—something solid to grab onto. "Do you enjoy this? Do you like rummaging around in people's heads, controlling what they think and feel?"

No response. But he's there. I feel him.

"Rhee told me about you. She said that you hide in the shadows, that you don't even tell people your real name. If you can't even look me in the eye—if you can't even give me that much—then I want nothing to do with you or your rebellion. Do you hear me?"

An echoing male voice replies, from nowhere and everywhere: "And where will you go? What will you do, once you've left the Citadel?"

"I don't know." I don't care.

He doesn't respond, but I sense him weighing me, examining me.

"*Show me your face!*" I scream. "*Stand in front of me!*"

Another long pause. "Stand in front of you, you say." He chuckles, as if at a private joke. "I must confess, I am intrigued by you, Lain Fisher. Perhaps a meeting could be . . . advantageous."

I feel myself sinking, slowly, as if through layers of quicksand. Then something breaks, and I plummet into nothingness.

14

I come to, blinking, in the Gate room. I pull the helmet off, and cool air washes over my feverish head. My hair clings to me in loose strands. Everything looks a little fuzzy and spinny, and a sharp ache pulses behind and between my eyes. When I lick my lips, they feel like sandpaper.

A low, grinding rumble fills the air. I stand and turn around to see the back wall open inward like a huge door, revealing another room.

"Come in," calls a man's voice. It's the same voice I heard in the Gate, but smaller, less imposing.

Slowly, I stand. My legs almost give out, and I clutch the arm of the chair, waiting for the vertigo and weakness to pass.

"Don't be shy."

My heartbeat is far too loud. Cautiously, like I'm stepping into the den of a wild beast, I enter.

The floor is dark, lacquered wood, decorated with gold-tasseled rugs. The walls are paneled with creamy-white marble. A fire crackles in a stone hearth; I can't tell if the flames are holographic or real. Behind me, there's a low groan, and I spin around in time to see the door swing shut. It's actually an enormous bookshelf, filled with leather-bound volumes, the authors' names shining in gold letters on the spines—Thomas Paine, Friedrich Nietzsche, Ayn Rand, Edgar Allan Poe, Jean-Paul Sartre, and countless others.

"I'm over here."

I turn. In front of me, a small man sits in a sleek black chair. He nods toward an empty chair. "Sit."

I'd prefer to stand, but I'm still weak and shaky, and my legs are in danger of giving out. Slowly, I make my way over to a red-leather-upholstered chair and lower myself into it. I look at him. He's short and thin, with fine, mouse-brown hair—it's starting to gray at the temples, though he only appears to be in his forties—and thick-framed glasses perched on his long, narrow nose. His face is forgettable in a pleasant, mild-mannered way. "So," I say. "You're Zebra."

"You were expecting someone a bit more impressive-looking, I suppose." He gives me a wry smile. "But yes. I'm Zebra." He extends one gloved hand. "Pleased to meet you."

I don't take the hand. After a moment, he withdraws and lowers his head slightly. "Fair enough," he says. "I just put you through something rather unsettling."

"Unsettling? That's how you describe it?"

"I wouldn't have done it if you weren't strong enough to handle it. And I knew you were. After all, you chose to reveal the truth to your country, even knowing the considerable risk. 'In a time of universal deceit, telling the truth is a revolutionary act.'"

The words sound familiar. I frown, trying to place them.

"George Orwell," Zebra supplies. He tilts his head. "You've read his work, haven't you?"

"My father had copies of everything he wrote. He collected old books." I look away. "Of course, you already know that. Don't you?"

"I, too, am a collector. As you may have noticed." He stares at me through those cool, unnerving gray eyes. They seem both flat and unfathomably deep. Empty and not empty. "We lost something, as a society, when we stopped producing paper books. But then, we also lost something when we transitioned from handwritten books to printed ones, and when we first gave up clay tablets and parchment for flimsy pulp paper. Something is always lost. But something is always gained."

"I'm really not in the mood for a philosophical conversation about books." Pain pulses behind my eyes. An after-effect of the drug or just stress, I'm not sure. "You had no right to look through my mind."

"An interesting perspective, from a former Mindwalker."

I try to rekindle my anger, but I feel tired and deflated, like I've used it all up. "I'm still a Mindwalker. But I would never snoop through someone's memories without their permission."

"I had to make sure you weren't a spy. I'm placing a considerable amount of trust in you simply by allowing you into the Citadel."

I remember Zebra's cold gray eyes in Father's face, Steven's hand working its way into my chest. I shudder. "Even so, you didn't have to deceive me. You didn't need to use the faces of people I care about. What was the point of all that? Nicholas called it a test, but I don't see what it was supposed to prove."

"When I faced you as your father, you chose to reject a comforting lie in favor of an uncomfortable reality. And when I confronted you as Rhee, you chose to fight me, to save yourself, proving that you are willing to do what's necessary even when it means getting your hands dirty."

I'll probably be seeing that moment in my nightmares for weeks to come. "And when you pretended to be Steven . . . what was that? You kept asking me about a secret. I don't have any secrets."

"Don't you? Sometimes the biggest secrets are the ones we keep from ourselves."

"What do you mean?"

"We are not always who we believe ourselves to be. As someone who has studied psychology, you should be aware of that. You

153

might say I had a glimpse of your true self . . . of what drives you, at your core."

I grit my teeth. Is he trying to make me question my own motivations, to doubt myself, so I'll be more vulnerable to his manipulation? If that's his game, I'm not going to play it. "I've been through plenty of psychoanalysis. I don't need yours. Whatever you think you saw, you're not the one who decides what drives me. I am."

He raises his eyebrows slightly, then smiles. If he's at all annoyed with me, he hides it well. If anything, he seems pleased. "In that case, let's get down to business. I must say, despite my initial misgivings, I'm glad to have you here. You're a bit of a celebrity, you know. If word gets out that you're on our side, it could be very good for the Blackcoats. Though I realize, of course, that you have your qualms about our methods."

"Well, I don't approve of terrorism, if that's what you're asking." And yet I'm here.

"One could easily call IFEN a terrorist organization," he replies. "They use fear to manipulate public sentiment and achieve their goals. We must fight terror with terror. This is a war. Everything we do, we do out of necessity."

"Sacrifices for the greater good?" I ask, bitterness creeping into my tone. Dr. Swan said the same thing.

His lips tighten. He leans forward, looking straight into my eyes, and lowers his voice until he's almost whispering. "You have no idea what sort of danger the world is in."

I hesitate.

I have no reason to take him at his word. But I remember the holographic message Father left for me after his death, telling me about IFEN's sordid history. *Secrets within secrets.* "What do you mean?"

He averts his gaze. "Simply that IFEN will not be content to rule over the URA. Sooner or later, they'll reach for more. Their influence will spread to every country, every corner of the world . . . unless we do something to stop them."

He's being vague, which makes me wonder if he knows as much as he claims. I feel a twinge of frustration. "So what can I do?"

"You've already made quite an impact on people, you know. Watch." He waves a hand, and a holoscreen appears in the air between us.

In spite of myself, I'm curious. I lean forward.

The screen displays a street in Aura, crammed with people. They surge forward, shouting. A wall of police officers blocks their path, brandishing neural disruptors. I'm looking at a protest.

Quickly, I realize that this isn't an ordinary recording. Certain details are in sharp focus, while others are blurry. Most of the buildings are just fuzzy shapes, vague impressions, but the protestors are crystal clear. "What is this?" I already know, but I want to hear him confirm it.

"It's a memory. One of the protestors uploaded this to the Net."

"Where did they even get a Gate? Those are closely monitored."

"IFEN can't control everything. You saw for yourself, the rebellion has its own Gates. Ever since you shared your memories of St. Mary's, others have followed your example. I downloaded this one before it was deleted by the censors."

The people are shouting and waving signs. I glimpse the words painted in red on white poster board: WE'RE NOT SICK. SOCIETY IS SICK. Another sign: SWAN KILLED KIDS. WHERE'S HIS COLLAR?

And then something clicks into place. "They're *all* wearing collars."

"That's right." The screen reflects in Zebra's glasses as he watches the action. "A group of Fours decided to march in front of IFEN headquarters, but the police tried to stop them. The protest was supposed to be non-violent. But, as you can see, things quickly got ugly."

A policeman jams a neural disruptor against a woman's temple, and she falls to the street, convulsing and foaming at the mouth. A few gunshots ring out, short and sharp. A collared man goes down. And still, the people keep pushing forward. The crowd is enormous—hundreds of protestors, all yelling and waving signs. The line of police can't contain them.

And then, all at once, the crowd falls. They collapse to the ground in a wave, like tiny toy figures knocked over by a gigantic hand. A chill washes over me. Somewhere, at that very moment, an unseen IFEN official was sitting in a control room, pressing a series of buttons to activate the collar of every person within range.

That's all it takes to crush a movement. The push of a few buttons.

The image goes fuzzy, melts into a blur of colors, and vanishes. The screen winks out. "Since you revealed the truth about St. Mary's, there've been several of these mass protests," Zebra says. "In all of them, dozens of protestors have been injured by neural disruptors. A few have been killed outright. IFEN has been trying to keep it quiet, to suppress it as best they can. They don't want the people to know that there's a revolution in the works. Make no mistake—it is happening. And you helped make it possible."

"How?" My nails dig into the meat of my palms. "I leaked some information, that's all. And then I ran away. I didn't even face the consequences of my actions. How can anyone be inspired by that?"

He tilts his head. "That's what you think? That your escape into Canada makes you appear weak? Had you stayed and 'faced the consequences,' as you put it, you would be sitting in a treatment facility, broken and molded by Conditioning. Instead, you're still fighting them. You've proven that it's *possible* to defy them and remain free. And because of that, you have become a hero."

I don't feel heroic or inspiring. I feel small and scared.

"I want to show you something else." He waves a hand, and the screen reappears, displaying a photograph of a brick wall and the words I BELIEVE LAIN FISHER spray-painted in neon blue. The image changes. More photographs, more graffiti, on benches and sidewalks, scrawled across the faces of ad posters and billboards.

IFEN LIES.

NO MORE TYPES.

TAKE BACK OUR LIVES.

THE REVOLUTION IS HERE.

And over and over again, my name, and the words I BELIEVE.

Zebra stares intently into my eyes. "You see," he says quietly, "what you have done?"

I don't answer. There's a small stab in my throat, like a hook catching, and tears prick the corners of my eyes. I don't understand why my name means so much to these people. I've never met them, and likely never will. Yet they've chosen to place their faith in me.

"They're crying out for your help." His voice is soft. Seductive. "All those people. They need you."

"I'm not much of a fighter," I mutter.

"You don't have to be. There are other ways to help the cause." Zebra steeples his gloved fingers, pressing the tips together. "I realize that we have certain ideological differences. But if you agree to work with me, I think you'll find that I'm not an unreasonable man."

I almost laugh. This is the man who put me into a hallucinatory state, sliced me open and rummaged through my guts. And yet, if I want to do anything except hide from the authorities for the rest of my life, I need his help.

Still, I hesitate. His words sound familiar, and after a moment, I realize—Dr. Swan once said something similar to me.

His eyes are sharp, intent. "Do we have a deal?"

My heart rattles in my chest, and my shirt sticks to my back, glued there with icy sweat. I have the sense that I'm about to step off the edge of a cliff. "I have a condition. This initiation of yours, this test, or whatever it is—I don't want you to put Steven through it."

He raises an eyebrow. "And why is that?"

"You know what happened to him. He's already been tested more than enough. I don't want you sticking your grubby fingers into his brain and using his past against him." I don't want him to have to face Lizzie's ghost. "He's off limits. Understand?"

He tilts his head to one side, like an inquisitive terrier, then nods. "Very well." With a subtle movement of his hand, his chair glides forward. Until that point, I hadn't even noticed the wheels, or the fact that he hasn't moved his legs once since I arrived.

He pinches the first finger of the glove on his left hand and pulls it off. I blink. His hand is translucent plastic, filled with countless tiny wires of gold, silver and red, all wrapped around a silver skeleton. He flexes the fingers, then extends the artificial hand to me. There's a slight tension in his shoulders, as if he expects me to flinch away.

I shake his hand. The plastic is warm, like skin. I release it, trying not to stare.

"It's all right. You can look." He curls his robotic fingers into a fist.

"It's just ... I've never seen ..."

"Artificial limb technology is more advanced in this country. While IFEN was learning how to rewire brains, we were discovering how to augment our bodies."

My gaze strays to the chair.

He shrugs. "Spinal columns are more complex than arms or legs. Besides ..." A hint of teasing creeps back into his voice. "Unlike your Dr. Swan, I don't believe that everything broken needs to be fixed." He pulls a small remote from his pocket and pushes a button. The bookshelf-slash-wall-slash-door swings ponderously outward, revealing the Gate room. I wonder how many people know that that room is directly connected to Zebra's study. "You're free to go," he says.

"Thank you." I start to stand up.

"Oh. One more thing." He slides his glove back into place. "Don't tell anyone about the test, or about our little meeting. It's rare for me to speak face-to-face with one of my followers. If word gets out, the others will be jealous. And that could be bad." After a half-beat, he adds, "For you." He snaps the glove and curls his fingers. "Just a friendly warning."

I glare at him.

He winks. "Welcome to the resistance."

*　　*　　*

As I leave Zebra's study, the bookshelf swings slowly shut behind me. When it closes, it's a wall once again, and I'm alone in the Gate room.

Now that it's over, the whole experience—even the conversation with Zebra—has a fuzzy, dreamlike quality. I wonder if the drugs are still wearing off.

I stand, legs wobbly. The door slides open, and I step out into the hall, where Nicholas is waiting. Without a word, he leads me back to the dorm wing and leaves me outside the door to my room. I stand alone in the hallway, staring into space. The whole nightmarish session in the Gate replays through my head. What does it all mean?

Instead of returning to my own room, I knock on the door to Steven's. After a few seconds, it slides open. "Lain?" he calls softly. He's sitting up in bed, his eyes cloudy with sleep.

Silently, I climb into bed with him. His breath catches, and his muscles tense against me. I can feel his warmth, his breathing. "I just need to be close to you," I whisper. "Can I stay?"

There's a click in his throat as he swallows. "Yeah."

I lean my forehead against his skinny shoulder and slip my arms around his waist. For a few heartbeats, he doesn't move. Then, slowly, he wraps his arms around me and pulls me closer. His slender, callused fingers slide under my shirt and brush against the small of my back, and my heart jumps. But his hand just rests there, against my skin.

We're pressed close together under the thin blanket. His breathing is a little husky, a little unsteady. I can feel his heart racing.

I don't want to think about anything that happened. I just want to be here, with him. In the darkness, the space between us shrinks to nothing. There's no impending war, no Blackcoats, no right or wrong, just Steven. I lean forward. Our lips touch, and he draws in his breath sharply.

It's the first time we've kissed since that night we spent in Gracie's cellar. His lips are slightly tight, and I move my own lips against them, trying to make them soften, like they did before. I'm still not sure I've gotten the hang of kissing—I feel clumsy, unsure of myself—but maybe it doesn't matter. His hand moves a little further up my back, his skin hot against mine. I feel the flick of his tongue, shy and unexpected, like wet velvet, but it retreats a moment later. I pull back, breathless, and lick my lips. My blood buzzes with electricity.

Right now, exploring these feelings should probably be the last thing on my mind. But I need to touch him, to smell and taste him, to remind myself that we're both still alive. Even if I'm terrified, even if I have no idea what the future will bring, this is real—the rapid thump-thump of his heart under my palm, the warmth of his skin seeping through his thin shirt.

Cautiously, experimentally, I slip my hand beneath his shirt and along his side. My fingertips skate over the hollows between his ribs, feeling them expand with each breath. I find his collarbone and run one fingertip over it, a small, careful touch. This is Steven. His body, his skin, his muscles and bones—the frame that holds his being.

I can feel other things. Scars, thin lines, like roads forming a map on his body. He tenses as I trace one with my thumb, and

I wonder where they come from, but I don't ask. Words will only get in the way.

He plants a small, careful kiss on my neck, just below my ear, and the shock of sensation is so strong that my body arches like a cat's. A tiny sound escapes me, more air than voice. His hand rests against the curve of my waist. His thumb brushes against my stomach, and I freeze. In a flash, I remember Steven's hand—no, Zebra's—working its way into me.

"What's wrong?"

I don't answer.

Zebra's voice snakes through my head. *Your secret. Tell me. Whisper it . . .*

For an instant, I glimpse something under the surface of my mind, like a dark shape swimming through murky water. My consciousness flinches back from it, and I'm left shaken and cold. "Can you just hold me?" I whisper.

Without a word, he pulls his hand out from under my shirt and folds his arms around me, pulling me closer.

I close my eyes.

All Mindwalkers receive training to help them cope with the horrors they see in their clients' minds. We learn to compartmentalize our emotions, to seal off the memories so we can function. Now, I walk through my usual set of visualization exercises.

I'm deep inside a stone labyrinth. I descend a set of steps to a room with a wooden treasure chest. With a heavy gold key, I unlock the chest and tuck the memories inside—the test, the hungry children in the Underground, the dead bodies in the forest. Then I close the lid, which is thick and solid. It shuts with a satisfying thud. I turn the key in the lock, sealing the memories away, out of sight.

But they're still there. They're always there.

15

Someone is knocking on my door. I grimace, hiding my face against the pillow. It must be Greta, my housekeeper, bugging me to get up. Is it time for school already? "Coming," I murmur. I roll over, away from the door, and find myself pressed up against something warm and solid. I freeze.

Someone is in bed with me, breathing softly. *Steven*. The memories rush back, slamming into me like a sledgehammer.

I'm not in my house anymore. I'm not even in my country. I'm in an underground rebel base with Steven.

The knock comes again—an echo of last night. My heartbeat quickens. But it's probably just Rhee. She said we'd have training today.

Steven stirs beside me, groaning. His hair is mussed, and there's a faint pink crease on his cheek, an impression from the pillowcase. His arms are still locked around my waist. A flush rises into my cheeks. It occurs to me that this is the first time I've woken up in another person's arms. I wish I had time to savor the feeling, but whoever's on the other side of the door won't stop. *Rap-rap-rap.* Like a giant woodpecker.

"If they ask for me, tell them I'm dead," Steven mutters, and folds a pillow around his head.

I slide out of bed. "Hold on! Just hold on." I open the door. Instead of Rhee, I find myself confronting a gaunt man with military-short hair, a jagged scar running from the corner of his left eye to his jaw, and a severe expression. He appears to be in his late twenties, which makes him one of the oldest people I've seen here, aside from Zebra and Nicholas.

Heat rises into my cheeks as I realize how this must look. Me and Steven in the same room, with a single bed, still in the process of waking up. "Um . . ."

"Just so you know, I'm not going to wake you up every morning," the man says gruffly. "I'm not your mother, and this isn't school. You're expected to report to the training room at seven o'clock sharp, of your own accord, and if you do not, there will be consequences."

Steven sits on the edge of the bed, his hair still messy, and yawns, not bothering to cover his mouth. "Just so you know," he says, "I'm not a morning person." He scratches the back of his head. "Any coffee in this place?"

The man wrinkles his nose, as if he just stepped in a pile of dog doo. "Eat some breakfast, then meet me out in the hall. Both of you."

"All right, but—who are you?"

"Burk. I'm one of the training instructors." There's a pause. "As an FYI, you might want to talk to one of the medics about getting a birth control chip."

"We weren't—"

The door slides shut, cutting off my words. My face is still burning. Why do I care what he thinks, anyway? "I guess we should eat," I mutter.

"Go ahead. 'M gonna sleep some more." He burrows under the covers.

I look at the lump under the blanket that is Steven and wonder briefly if I should tell him about what happened to me last night, then reject the idea. Later, maybe. The whole incident is already starting to scab over in my mind—it feels more like a bad dream than anything—and I'm not ready to rip the wound open again.

I open the freezer and select a plastic tray containing a section of hash browns and a spongy yellow rectangle which I think is supposed to be scrambled eggs. I heat it in the microwave and quickly wolf it down, then nudge Steven awake.

Outside, the gaunt man waits. Rhee is there too, leaning against a wall with her arms over her chest. "Lain, you'll come with me," Rhee says. "Steven, you go with Burk."

"I hope you're prepared to work hard," Burk says.

"Sure." Steven muffles a yawn against one hand and eyes the rifle strapped to Burk's back. "Say, when do we get guns?"

"Once you've earned them," Rhee replies shortly. "This way, Lain."

And before I can ask anything else, she turns and starts walking. Her stride is so brisk that I have to nearly jog to keep up. I look over my shoulder just in time to catch Steven's gaze, then we turn a corner.

"The main purpose of the simulations," she says without slowing her pace, "is to get you accustomed to fighting. People in the URA—in most developed countries—are raised to have a strong resistance to violence, even when it's justified. The system conditions them to trust and obey authority figures. Of course, in practice, that doesn't always work out so well, especially if you happen to be fighting the system. In training, you'll develop your reflexes until fighting become automatic. Using a weapon will start to feel instinctive and natural. Any questions?"

An image flashes through my head: Rhee's axe swooping down toward my head. I shudder. "No. No questions."

We approach a towering gray door which looks as solid and impenetrable as the side of a mountain. Well, we *are* in a decommissioned bomb shelter, after all. I wonder what this room's original purpose was. There's a rust-flecked metal wheel in the center of the door, like the steering helm on an old-fashioned sailboat.

From beyond the thick metal, I can hear muffled voices, mixed with the occasional giggle. Rhee grips the wheel and turns it, throwing her whole weight into the motion. Unseen gears creak and groan. The bulky hinges squeal as the door swings inward, revealing a group of three teenagers, all female.

The girls fall silent and turn toward us, their expressions alert and wary. There's a willowy blonde with a long, skinny neck. Next to her stands a small, chubby girl, her dark hair a mass of braids with colored plastic beads on the ends. She looks all of fourteen years old, and she bounces lightly up and down on her heels, vibrating with barely contained energy.

Off to the side stands a short girl in a black tank top, her green hair done up in spikes. She's digging in her ear with one pinkie. "Well," she says, "look who finally decided to show up."

The training room is enormous. Cement walls soar to a distant ceiling. Stacks of wooden crates stand here and there, forming a haphazard maze. Rhee and I step inside, and the door bangs shut behind us.

"Everyone, this is Lain," Rhee says. "She'll be training with our group today."

I give them an uncertain smile. "Hello."

The girl with the braids gives me a wide, gap-toothed smile. "Hi. I'm Joy."

The blonde shyly averts her gaze and murmurs, "Noelle."

"I know who you are," Joy says. "I've seen you on the news."

The one with the spiky green hair squints at me. She sports a faceful of piercings. They're in her ears, in her nose and lower lip, and running in a diagonal line across her cheek. It seems impractical, like all that metal would get caught on things.

Joy elbows her. The girl glances briefly at me and says, "Shana." She tongues the ring in her lower lip. "So, you're the famous leaker."

Leaker. It means whistleblower, but there's something con-temptuous about the term—like I'm a puppy who piddled on the carpet. "I'm the one who told the public about St. Mary's, if that's what you're referring to."

"That was very brave of you," Noelle says in her whispery little voice.

Shana turns her face to one side and rolls her eyes. She's not obvious about it, but she doesn't seem to care if I see it, either.

"Is something wrong?" I can't help asking.

"Oh, nothing," she says. "It's just that people have been telling the truth about IFEN for years. But no one listens to Fours and Fives, because we're all paranoid wingnuts, right? You're not the first person to come forward, or the first one to put her ass on the line. You're just the first one the public's taken seriously, because you were IFEN's golden girl and the daughter of some hotshot scientist. So, no offense, but I get a little sick of people calling you a hero."

"Shana," Noelle whispers.

"What? It's just the truth."

She has a point. Still, I feel attacked. And I don't like the way she referred to Father. "I'm not asking for any special treatment," I say, keeping my tone carefully neutral.

She gives me an unpleasant smile. "Let's see what you're made of, then."

"Enough talk," Rhee says. She hands me a helmet with an eye shield of transparent plastic. "You'll all wear one of these during the training session. It has an earpiece and a microphone inside, so you can communicate with each other. And you'll get one of these, as well." She holds up a pistol. "It's not real—it shoots beams of light—but it'll get you accustomed to using a gun, and it'll keep a record of your progress, hits versus misses."

"So what will we be shooting?" I ask.

"Holos. This room can generate holographic environments and enemies, like a VR game. The goal is simple. You run through the course—" she indicates the stacked boxes with a wave of her hand "—until you reach the red X at the end. You'll have three minutes, and if even one of you doesn't make it in time, the session fails and you have to start over again. Any holos get in your way, shoot them. Make sense?"

"I think so." I slide the helmet on. The visor, as it turns out, is a screen. A map appears in the upper right corner of my vision, showing the maze of hallways and our positions. The other trainees and I are blinking blue dots, standing at the entrance to the maze.

Rhee steps back and pushes a button on the wall. Suddenly, we're standing in a narrow hallway with white walls. It looks like an IFEN treatment facility. My pulse trips in my throat. I don't feel prepared for this at all. I'm like a small child being thrown into water for the first time and told to swim.

Rhee gives the signal to start, and we take off running, veering down different hallways. In the map, the blinking blue dots diverge. I follow mine, watching it move through the maze. Then I see a red dot coming toward me. An enemy.

Just like a videogame, I tell myself. Not real.

A man in a white IFEN uniform appears around the corner and runs toward me. Holo or not, he looks frighteningly solid. He raises an ND, pointing it at my face. "Freeze!" he barks. I brace myself, raise the pistol, and fire.

I expect him to simply vanish. I'm not prepared for the spray of blood as the bullet hits his throat. He falls to his knees, gurgling and choking, eyes glazing over. More blood bubbles from his lips and dribbles to the floor, pooling beneath him in a dark red puddle. The ND slips from his fingers as he slumps against the wall.

For a few seconds, I can't move. I just stare, watching as the life fades from his eyes.

"What the hell are you doing?" Shana's voice hisses in my ear, making me wince. "Hurry up!"

I keep running. There are two more red dots coming toward me, converging. A man and woman burst into the hall. "Freeze!" the woman shouts, ND aimed.

I fire again, then again. They go down. Another spray of blood decorates the walls, but this time, I force myself not to look, to keep running. But the woman isn't dead, just wounded, and I can hear her strangled screams behind me, fading slowly into silence.

Just a game.

I give my head a shake. *Focus*.

But I don't notice the red dot coming up behind me on the map until it's too late. I whirl around to find myself facing a tall, bulky man in white, aiming a pistol at my head. There's a loud buzz, then the hologram vanishes, and I'm standing between stacks of boxes in the vast cement room. I look around, blinking, dazed.

Rhee approaches. "You're dead," she says. "Try again."

We do the course a second time. I get killed when the goal is within sight. On the third round, we run out of time before I reach the target location. By round six, I'm exhausted, gasping for breath. Sweat plasters my shirt to my back.

Shana flings her VR helmet to the floor, points at me, and says, "I'm not working with her anymore."

I tense. "I just got here," I say, unable to keep the defensiveness out of my voice. "Give me a chance."

Noelle studies her feet. Joy toys with one of her braids.

"Hit the showers," Rhee says, speaking to the entire group. Noelle and Joy leave their guns on a table by the wall, then retreat, disappearing behind a free-standing concrete wall near the back of the room.

Shana remains where she is, glaring at me. "You aren't taking this seriously. Is this a game to you?"

I frown. "What's your problem with me, anyway?"

"My problem? My problem is that if I get stuck with you on a mission and you screw up, we both end up dead."

"Shana, Lain," Rhee says. "Knock it off."

Shana doesn't move. Neither do I. I've been through hell in the past forty-eight hours, and my patience is running dangerously low. "Well, your insults definitely aren't going to improve my performance, so why don't you just mind your own business?"

"This is my business! I'm not here to play babysitter to some spoiled newvie."

For a moment, I feel like I've been punched in the chest.

Maybe I misheard. Maybe she said "newbie." But no; I know that word too well. A rush of memories sweeps through me—children whispering together in the hallways of my old school, shooting cold glances at me as I walk past. The blood pounds behind my eyes.

"Shana." Rhee's voice is cold. "That's enough."

"Come on!" Shana whirls to face her. "I can't be the only person thinking this! If we put her on the field, she'll freeze up. Some rich, pampered bottle brat's got no place—"

"If I hear one more word out of you, I'll demote you to permanent cleaning duties, and you can spend the rest of your time here mucking other people's filth out of the toilets."

Shana narrows her eyes, her upper lip peeling back from her teeth in a snarl. She storms out of the room, slamming the door behind her.

I stand, struggling to control my breathing.

Rhee's gaze flicks toward me. "You all right?"

"Fine." I force a smile. Newvie, tubie, bottle brat—by age six, I'd already heard them all. By now, I should be used to it.

Rhee's still watching me, so I keep my face schooled into a neutral expression. I don't want her to know how much Shana's words affected me. I don't want her to think I'm soft, too. But the knot in my throat won't go away. "What does it mean?" she asks. "That word."

The question surprises me. I thought everyone knew. "It's short for New Vitro," I say, keeping my tone casual. "The cloning procedure." I'm not sure how Shana knows what I am, but I suppose it's not a secret. I've always been fairly well-known, as the daughter of the eminent Dr. Lain Fisher, and now I'm famous—or infamous, rather. When you're in the media's spotlight, the private details of your life soon become common knowledge.

"Anyway, it's not a big deal," I continue, though the casual note in my voice sounds forced. "Nothing I haven't heard a million times before."

She's staring at me intently, as if I'm a puzzle she's trying to take apart. "Where else have you heard it?"

I shrug. "School. You know how kids are."

"You went to public school?"

I wonder why she's suddenly so curious about me. "Yes, I did." Usually, clone children are sent to special schools where they'll be among their own kind—not just accepted, but embraced as part of the elite. As the children of wealthy Type Ones, they're groomed for cushy, high-paying jobs as future leaders of society. Scientists, politicians, IFEN officials. But Father didn't want me to grow up in a sheltered, artificial environment where I'd be indoctrinated into a self-serving upper class. He wanted me to know what the real world was like.

There are times when I'm grateful for that. Other times, I resent him. Sometimes I wish that, for once, he'd just made my life easy instead of trying to do the right thing.

"Go on," she says, nodding toward the back of the room. "Get cleaned up. You'll find fresh clothes on the rack."

A doorway on the back wall leads into a large bathroom with rows of stalls and showers. Noelle and Joy have already finished showering and are slipping into fresh clothes. "Bye," Joy pipes up. "See you next session."

I force a smile. "See you." Once they're gone, I get undressed and wash off, soaping away the sweat of training.

Shana's face flashes through my head, her teeth bared. *Newvie*, she hisses. *Bottle brat.*

I push her out of my thoughts. It shouldn't matter. I shouldn't care.

The water circles the drain near my feet, carrying suds, whirling around and around and then disappearing into the circle of darkness.

There are still those who believe that clones don't have souls, that only naturally conceived children go to Heaven—a quaint belief associated with the lower class, to be sure, but it has a certain sticking power.

Father never had much use for organized religion, but I remember him talking about the soul, telling me that it was the most precious thing in the world, that part of you that made you yourself. It made me wonder where the soul lived. Was it inside your body? At school, we read about ancient revolutions, about guillotines, and we learnt that people are still conscious for a few seconds after you cut their heads off. They're still themselves, in that tiny space before the light fades. So I thought the soul must be somewhere in your head, squeezed into one of the little curling furrows of the brain. When I asked, though, Father said that it wasn't anywhere in particular.

"But sometimes," he added, "you can see people's souls in their eyes." As a small child, I took that literally. I used to stand in front of the bathroom mirror, peering into my own eyes, thinking that if I looked long and deep enough, I might see my soul peeking out at me like a tiny person. But all I ever saw was blackness.

When I return to the training room, Rhee is still there. "We have a little time before lunch," she says, handing me my gun. "Let's practice."

I hesitate, looking at the gun in my hand, my fingers curled around the cold metal grip. "I know how to shoot," I say. "I mean, the basics. I'm just—not used to actually firing at people. Even if they're holograms."

"Then you'll keep doing it until you get used to it." She fiddles with a control panel on the wall. A holo materializes in front of me. This time, it's not a simulated environment, but a single person—a guard in a white IFEN uniform. He shifts his weight, glances around as if he can't see us, yawns, and rubs the back of his neck. His mannerisms are so lifelike, it would be easy to forget that he's a holo, if not for the slight, occasional blurring and flickering around the edges of his figure. "I've adjusted the settings to make it easier," she says. "He won't run or attack you. He won't respond to us at all." Rhee wraps my fingers more firmly around the gun, positioning my fingers. "Like this. Now aim."

I swallow, pulse tripping in my throat, and raise the gun. The holo stands just twenty feet away. Easy to hit, even for a beginner like me. But I have the feeling that that's not the point of this exercise.

Though holos aren't self-aware, they have a limited form of intelligence. Chloe, my computer avatar back home, could carry on simple conversations; she could tell when I was in a bad or a good mood by analyzing my facial expressions. These holos are probably much less complex than her, and they don't actually *die*, of course, just reset. Still, something about this feels cruel. Like shooting a kitten.

I grit my teeth, take a deep breath, and squeeze the trigger. The gun jerks to the side, missing by several inches. Even though there are no real bullets, a loud bang splits the silence, making me flinch. I exhale a frustrated breath. "Sorry. Let me try again." I start to aim, but Rhee grips my wrist.

"If you can't even shoot a projected image, how are you going to defend yourself if you're attacked?"

The blood burns in my ears. "My hand slipped."

"Your aim can't possibly be that bad." Rhee stands with her arms crossed over her chest, her face a cool mask. "Shana was right about one thing. You're not taking this seriously."

My shoulders stiffen. "I left my entire life behind me. I risked everything to come here. Do you think I see this as a lark?"

"No. But your heart is wavering, all the same. And the others can sense it."

I stare straight ahead.

"Are you a Blackcoat, or not?" she asks.

"What is that supposed to mean?"

Those catlike green eyes drill into mine. "Just answer."

"I'm here, aren't I?" I'm dodging, and I know it. But if I answer no, what then? "I just don't understand the point of these shooting spree simulations. All right, I understand that rescue missions are dangerous and that we have to be prepared to defend ourselves, but you're training us to go in with guns blazing. What are we planning to do? Storm IFEN headquarters and start massacring people?"

"A war is coming. Zebra will tell us the plan when the time is right."

"So you don't even know what you're training for?"

"We don't need to know," she replies, maddeningly calm. "We've put our trust in him."

"Well, maybe you should think twice about that." I'm going too far, and I know it, but I can't stop. "Look at what he's done. He's gathered up a bunch of desperate, homeless teenagers and molded them into soldiers because he has some personal vendetta against IFEN. You're fooling yourself if you think that anyone here had a choice. You can't call it a choice when the alternative is starving in the streets. Zebra's no better than the people we're fighting. He's exploiting all of us—"

Her eyes flash like steel. She moves so quickly, I don't even see it happen; suddenly, I'm on the floor, my arm twisted behind my back, and her boot is planted against my spine, digging in. I try to wriggle free, and she presses down harder. "Say whatever you want about me. But don't ever let me hear you insult him again."

Breathing hard, I glare at her over one shoulder. "Is this how things work here? Someone steps out of line, and you kick them down?"

She narrows her eyes.

My heart thunders in my chest, so hard I think it might burst. I'm quivering with pain. My arm is bent at an unnatural angle, and the longer she holds it in place, the worse it gets; if she exerts even a little more pressure, the bone will crack. "Go ahead." I squeeze the words through clenched teeth. "Break it. It won't change how I feel."

There's a pause, as if she's considering it. Then, slowly, she releases me and steps back. I climb to my feet, dizzy with relief. My whole body feels shivery and weak, like a newborn foal's.

"Come at me," she says.

I blink. "What?"

She beckons. "Attack me."

"With my bare hands? I'm not—"

"Do it."

My own ragged breathing fills my ears. I charge and swing my fist. It's clumsy, and she dodges easily. "Again," she says.

I swing my fists. She blocks the blows with her arms, almost lazily, then sweeps my feet out from under me with a kick. I land with a bone-jarring impact. "Again," she says.

I push myself to my feet and launch myself at her. She delivers a whirling kick to my abdomen that sends me stumbling back. Her braid swings behind her like a cat's tail. I grab it and yank, hard. It catches her off guard; enough that I manage to land a blow in her stomach before she can stop me, but it's like punching rock. She grabs my wrist and spins me around, twisting my arm behind my back. "Not bad, for a first try." She releases me. "You see? You *can* fight, when you're given sufficient motivation."

I stumble away, lungs burning as I gulp in air. My whole body is bruised and tender, and my stomach hurts like I've swallowed something rotten. "You manipulated me into that. You deliberately provoked me."

"If you hate me, then use that. Channel it." She picks up the gun again and extends it to me. "Go on."

The holo-man is still standing there, oblivious to us.

Fine. What does it matter, anyway? I'm sick of this game.

I grab the gun, aim it, and pull the trigger. A hole appears in the man's cheek. His eyes widen, and he slaps a hand to his face, as if suddenly remembering something he'd forgotten. For an instant, I could swear his gaze focuses on me, and his expression registers wounded surprise. Then he drops to the floor. Blood soaks through his hair where the make-believe bullet exited the back of his skull. His form wavers and vanishes.

I toss the gun aside.

Rhee gives a small nod. "Better. At this rate, you might actually be able to save your own life if someone comes after you with intent to kill."

The sick feeling in my stomach burns. The anger has evaporated, leaving me weary and cold and very, very tired. My limbs feel like sandbags. I look at Rhee from the corner of my eye. "Can I ask you a personal question?"

"Ask. Though I won't promise to answer."

"How many people have you killed?"

She turns her face away. "I don't know. I stopped counting a long time ago."

I chew my lower lip.

"You want to ask if it bothers me," she says. "If I feel any guilt."

"I guess . . . yes."

"Steven told you? About what happened to me?"

I hesitate. "He said that IFEN experimented on you. That . . . that they did something to your brain, to reduce your capacity for fear and remorse. They were trying to create perfect soldiers."

"Did he tell you that I volunteered for it?"

175

"No," I answer, surprised.

"Of course, I was only seven. I was desperate to escape the state home, and they made the procedure sound like some sort of magical medicine that would wipe away all the pain. They said it would make me strong. Back then, all I wanted was to be stronger.

"By that point, I'd already been classified as a Type Four. I don't even remember why it happened. I think another kid tried to steal my food and we got into a fight. That's all it takes, really, when you're living in that sort of place. Maybe it's different if you have a family—people to advocate for you, to protect you. But I never knew my parents." She keeps her arms crossed, fingers pressing into her biceps. Though her voice betrays no emotion, the skin around her nails is white. "When IFEN came to me, I saw it as a chance to escape that hell. I bear the responsibility for my choice." She raises her right hand, examining it in the dim light of the hallway. Her nails are short and blunt, the fingers calloused. "They forced me to kill, as part of the experiments. Animals, then people. I started to think about it as just turning off machines, because that's what a living thing is—a machine of flesh." Her lips are set into a thin, pale line. "So, to answer your question, no. I don't feel guilty. I don't remember how."

Seven years old, I think. Even younger than Steven was when he was kidnapped and taken to St. Mary's. While I was playing with dolls and going to the park with Father, Rhee was being molded into a killer. I feel like I should say something—anything—but no words come.

She turns away. "Turn left when you leave the training room. Keep walking until you see an arched doorway. That's the mess hall. In case I don't see you again today, report here tomorrow at the same time for training."

Without looking back, she walks away.

16

I find the mess hall with no difficulty. The room is huge and round, filled with people sitting at rows of long tables. Despite its size, it has a cozy air. The lighting is dim, the metal walls painted brown to simulate wood. As soon as I enter, my nose fills with the rich scent of cheese and grease and cooked meat and fried, sugary things—a carnival smell. The food is laid out on a huge table in the center of the room.

Mounds of roast beef sandwiches and burgers glisten with juice. There are pizzas—you can take as many slices as you want, apparently—and gigantic silver bins of ice cream next to a platter of powdered jelly donuts, piled high. All my doubts, questions, and hurt disappear in a sudden, roaring wave of hunger. Eagerly, I grab a tray and start heaping food on, a little bit of everything, because I'm too famished to decide.

As I take a donut, I think suddenly of the people in the tunnels, huddled around their tiny fires. How many of them will eat tonight?

I don't know where Zebra gets the money for all this food, but he must be someone of considerable wealth and power. The Blackcoats have this huge facility with holo-equipped training rooms, smack dab in the center of the poverty-stricken Underground. I look at my heaping plate and feel a tug of guilt.

On the other hand, denying myself won't fill their bellies.

I wander the lunchroom, scanning the tables, until I spot a flash of pale blond hair. Steven. There's another boy, too—a boy with curly auburn hair and ruddy cheeks. Steven and the new boy are laughing, and for a moment, I hang back, feeling like an outsider. I clear my throat. "May I join you?"

They look up. Steven smiles brightly. "Sure."

I take a seat next to him and glance at his plate. He's got four slices of pizza, a cheeseburger, and a stack of donuts, along with a dish of chocolate ice cream.

"I'm pretty sure you can go back for seconds," I say.

"Oh, I will."

He must have the metabolism of a hummingbird, to stay so thin. Then again, for most of his life, he's been subsisting on government rations, which are barely enough to keep someone alive. I remember the first time I ate in front of him, in the Underwater Café—the longing in his eyes as he stared at my meal. I can hardly blame him for a little overindulgence.

"The food here is amazing," Steven says through a mouthful of jelly donut.

The curly-haired boy grins. "It would be easy to get fat, if they didn't run us ragged with so many drills."

As he turns his head, I glimpse the back of his neck. No scar. No collar. He catches me staring and laughs. "If you want to ask, go ahead. Questions don't bother me."

I hesitate. "It's just . . . I was starting to think everyone here was a Type Four. Are you—"

"I'm Canadian. Eh?" He winks. "I don't *have* a Type."

"I see." It's odd, hearing someone say that. Most of the world doesn't have a system like IFEN's, yet I've always thought of Type as something universal and objective. It can be measured by neural scanners, it responds predictably to certain treatments, and it runs in families. Even if it can change over the course of a person's life, patterns inevitably emerge. Someone who has been a Three for many years probably won't become a One; an individual who reaches adulthood as a One rarely becomes a Four. And yet, step over the border, and none of it exists. "So how did you end up here?"

"I won't bore you with my sob story." He takes a swig from his cup. "Short version: shitty home life, I ran away, ended up in the Underground, and joined these folks because being part of a revolution seemed more exciting than picking my meals out of dumpsters." He pushes a glass toward me. It's filled with a clear, amber liquid. "Try some of this."

I pick up the cup and sniff at it cautiously. It has a sharp smell, almost like medicine. "What is it?"

"Rum. There's more over there." He points to a table near the center of the room, covered in cups and bottles.

"They have alcohol? But half the people here are minors. Aren't there any rules, or—"

The boy bursts out laughing.

My cheeks grow warm as the absurdity of my statement sinks in. We've joined a secret antigovernment movement; we're being trained to kill. Of course they're not going to quibble about things like underage drinking.

"They've got soda too," Steven says. "But the rum's pretty good. Just be careful. It's strong."

I take a tiny, cautious sip. My tongue tingles oddly, and the liquid burns a thin trail of fire down my throat. I cough, eyes watering, and push the cup away. The curly-haired boy shrugs and swigs some more. "Suit yourself. Name's Brian, by the way. Steven and I are training under Burk."

"You mean Captain Constipation," Steven says.

Brian snorts laughter. "Don't ever let him hear you say that. He'll have you doing laps until you pass out."

"Eh, he's just a loud dog," Steven says. "Always barking. He doesn't scare me."

The back of my neck prickles. I turn to see Shana sitting at a nearby table, talking to a small group of girls. She glances at me and whispers something to them, and they burst out laughing. My ears burn. Cliques, gossip and bullies. This feels remarkably like high school. I've never been Miss Popularity, but back at Greenborough High I was never actively targeted, just ignored.

I take a bite of pizza, but it feels like wet dirt in my mouth, gluey and tasteless. A dull heat pulses behind my forehead. I refuse to let her get to me.

"Hey," Steven says, "you okay?"

"Hmm? Oh, yes. Just thinking about the training session."

He gives me a lopsided smile. "It's kinda fun, huh?"

A lump of pizza sticks in my throat, and I force it down. I half think I misheard. "Fun?"

"Well, yeah. Stress relief, kind of. I mean, they're just holos. It's like, I dunno. Punching a pillow."

"Pillows don't bleed," I say. "Or scream."

"Come on," Steven says. "It's not real."

"Well, it's not like it's just a fantasy either." My voice comes out sharper than I intended. "They're preparing us for actual missions. Where we'll have to shoot actual people."

"Duh," Brian says. "What did you expect?"

I look away. What did I expect? This is exactly what I signed up for. "Have you been on any missions?" I ask him.

"Three," he says through a mouthful of donuts. "Border runs. Helping people across. You met Joy? She's one of the girls I helped across. You should have seen her back then. Such a sad little thing. She'd been Conditioned four times and it didn't put a dent in her depression. This place brought her back to life."

I think of Joy's bright smile. Amazing, what a powerful tonic purpose can be. I underwent a lot of Conditioning myself after

Father's suicide, but sometimes I think it was my training—my drive to become a Mindwalker—that really pulled me through.

"So where's Rhee?" Steven asks.

"How should I know?"

He blinks. "She's your training instructor, right?"

I exhale. "Right." Maybe I'm just tense. I look around the room until I spot her sleek brown hair. "There." I point.

She's perched at the far end of a table, alone, staring straight ahead and chewing her burger mechanically.

Steven's brows knit together. "Doesn't she have any friends?"

"Doubt it," Brian says. "I never see her with anyone else."

"Maybe she prefers being on her own," I remark.

Steven's expression hardens. "Yeah, well. That's probably what people thought about me."

An awkward silence hangs over the table.

"I'm going to invite her to sit with us," Steven says. He glances at me. "You okay with that?"

I remember the pain of Rhee's boot digging into my back, her iron grip as she twisted my arm behind me. Then I imagine her as a child in IFEN's brutal training program, her eyes flat and empty as she aims a pistol with her tiny hands. A small dart of pain shoots through my mouth, and I realize I'm biting the inside of my cheek.

The truth is, I don't really want Steven to invite her over, because she makes me uncomfortable. I don't know what that says about me, but it probably isn't good. Maybe I'm no better than those people who shunned him back in Greenborough High. "Go ahead," I tell him.

Brian snorts. "I wouldn't bother, man. Trying to start a conversation with that one is like talking to a log."

Steven ignores him, gets up, and walks across the room. Rhee looks up at his approach. He says something, and she replies. I strain to read their lips, but I can't make out what they're saying.

Rhee lowers her head, looking pensive. Finally, she nods, but they don't come over to our table. Instead, Rhee stays where she is, and he sits across from her. He glances over at us, waves, and shrugs.

"Well, looks like we lost him." Brian smirks. "He's got a thing for her, huh? Poor bastard."

My shoulders stiffen. "It's not like that. He's just being nice."

Brian frowns. "Oh. Sorry. Are you guys . . .?"

I don't know how to answer that. "It's complicated." I try to savor the food. It's been awhile since I had such a good meal. But I keep watching Steven and Rhee from the corner of my eye.

"Excuse me," I murmur, standing. "I've got to go." I deposit my tray in a slot marked DISHES and leave the mess hall.

17

The speakers crackle, and Nicholas' voice booms out: "Attention, brothers and sisters. Today's Assembly will begin in five minutes."

I sigh. Great. After a morning of massacring holos, I get to listen to more Blackcoat propaganda about the goodness and necessity of violence.

When I reach the Assembly Hall, it's already mostly filled. I scan the sea of heads for Steven's pale blond hair, but I don't see it.

Nicholas ascends to the stage. "We have a special show for you today." A sly, impish smile creeps across his face. He looks like a little boy with his hand in a forbidden cookie jar. That worries me. "Dr. Swan recently gave another interview. He wanted to discuss some recent events."

Nicholas steps aside, and the lights dim. The screen lights up.

Dr. Swan sits at a desk in a white room, hands folded in front of him. His expression is grim, his face drawn and pale. The calm, professional man I remember is gone. He looks older, wearier, his eyes sunken. "This morning," he begins, his voice uncharacteristically subdued, "a homemade bomb went off in the city of Aura, heavily damaging a treatment center."

The camera cuts away, displaying what must be footage from a security camera—footage of a large white building. The explosion is a volcanic roar. Fireballs blossom like orange pompons, flame shooting off in every direction, and clouds of black smoke fill the sky. Windows erupt outward in showers of glittering glass fragments.

The camera cuts back to Dr. Swan. "Four people were killed. Six more were injured by flying debris. But this was not the only incident. Several other bombs have gone off in other major cities across the country. All have resulted in at least one death."

As the message goes on, a creeping sense of dread fills my stomach like liquid cement.

"At first glance," Dr. Swan continues, "these appear to be isolated, unrelated incidents. The individuals who set off these bombs did not know each other. They were not working in tandem. Yet these crimes are indeed connected. They are the beginnings of a tide of radical violence which, if not stopped, could destroy our nation. I've spoken before about how anger and paranoia can sweep like a contagious virus through populations. Now, we are looking at a potential outbreak of massive proportions. I've just finished an emergency meeting with the other members of IFEN's Board, and we've all agreed what needs to be done. We must begin treating troubled individuals *before* the problem becomes severe enough that they might engage in violent behavior. Therefore, we are introducing proactive measures. All citizens who are Type Twos and above must report to the nearest treatment center. I urge you all to cooperate with this effort. If you are law-abiding, there's nothing to fear. In addition, I want to issue a caution to all citizens. Do not believe everything you hear. Avoid any anti-IFEN websites recklessly spreading rumors."

What rumors? What's going on in the URA that has Dr. Swan so on edge?

"These sites," he continues, "pose a direct threat to the population's mental health. They are designed to inflame fear and anger. As such, spreading and repeating these malicious lies will be regarded as an act of aggression. Anyone discovered to be responsible will be immediately categorized as a Type Five." He stops, as if to allow this to sink in. It's a shocking revelation. Type Fives—those people deemed to be threats to public safety—are very rare. And now, apparently, anyone with a penchant for gossip is eligible.

"Rest assured," he says, "we are doing everything in our power to guarantee that these tragic events are not repeated. Together, we will weather this storm, and the United Republic of America will emerge stronger than ever."

I expect the broadcast to end there. But it doesn't. He pauses, staring straight ahead, a strange look on his face.

"Lain?" His voice is very quiet. "If you are watching this . . . please, listen to me. I don't know where you are or who you're with, but I know that you must be frightened and confused. I know that, even if your actions inadvertently led to this violence, you don't condone what the terrorists are doing. You can help end this. It's not too late. Come home."

The screen fades to black.

A sickly knot of anger burns in my stomach. But beneath that, shame digs into me like a knife. *Even if your actions inadvertently led to this violence . . .*

Even if those words come from Dr. Swan, I can't help but feel there's a grain of truth in them. If I'd never uploaded my memories to the Net, would things have gotten this bad so quickly?

Nicholas faces the crowd. "We didn't engineer those attacks. We didn't *need* to. Across the United Republic of America, more and more people are taking up the cause of their own accord, fighting back against the forces of oppression. The war is shifting in our favor. We will not hide in the shadows any longer. Make no mistake—Dr. Swan's announcement was not a plea for peace. This is an order for us to surrender. Will we surrender, or fight?"

The crowd howls back, "*We will fight!*"

"Then be ready," Nicholas says. "Soon, now, we're going on the offensive. We must train and prepare. And once Zebra gives the order—" a smile spreads across Nicholas' face "the fireworks will be spectacular."

Cheers fill the Hall.

Suddenly, it's all too much. I turn and push my way toward the exit. The Assembly's probably not over yet, but I don't care. I stumble into the hall and lean my forehead against a cool metal wall.

"Lain?"

I turn to see Steven standing in the hallway, looking baffled. "Where'd you go? You disappeared during lunch."

I shut my eyes. "Steven, I don't think I can be a part of this."

His shoulders stiffen. "What are you talking about?"

"The Blackcoats! This isn't *right*. All those attacks back in the URA, all those innocent people dead—doesn't this bother you?"

"What makes you think they were innocent?"

"Okay, maybe some of them weren't. Maybe some worked for IFEN. So what? What about the patients? What about the janitors and security guards? Who even cares whether the victims were IFEN employees or not? I was an IFEN employee, remember? Not everyone working there is evil. And now the Blackcoats are talking about setting off *more* bombs, about going on the offensive. That means more people will die."

Steven breathes a heavy sigh and rakes a hand through his hair. "We have to take some risks if we're going to change things." His voice is low and gentle, like I'm a panicky little girl who needs soothing. "There are casualties in every war. If we don't fight, things will just keep getting worse, and so far, these people are the only ones I've found who are willing to fucking *do* something about it."

I lower my gaze. There's a catch in my throat, and I swallow, but it doesn't go down. "What if I decided to leave the Citadel?" I blurt out. "Would you come with me?"

"What?" His brows draw together. He shakes his head, alarm growing in his expression. "You're not actually thinking of leaving, are you? It would be suicide. What would we do? Spend the rest of our lives in the Underground, burning garbage and eating rat burgers?"

"Answer the question."

"What is this, some kind of mind game?"

"Steven. Just answer."

"I don't know, okay? I don't know."

Silence hangs between us.

This shouldn't surprise me. It shouldn't hurt so much. But with those three words, I feel like some intangible thread between us has snapped. I had assumed, on some level, that no matter what happened, no matter what I chose, Steven and I would be together.

I push the feeling aside and take a deep breath. "I really believe there's another way. If enough people rally together and try to change things, they can overcome IFEN's influence. What if we tried talking to the National Ethical Committee?"

Judging by the look he gives me, I might have just suggested solving the problem by painting ourselves with chicken's blood and doing a rain dance. "Are you serious?"

"Of course I'm serious. Why is that such a strange idea?"

"Because they don't bargain with terrorists. To them, we're lower than dung beetles. Nothing is going to change unless we take down IFEN first. Haven't you figured that out yet?"

I squeeze my hands into fists. There's an arrogant edge to his voice that I've never heard there before, and I don't like it. "That isn't true. We can organize and ally ourselves with citizens in the URA who share our ideals. We can educate people—"

"How? How are we going to do that, when IFEN silences anyone who speaks up?"

"We'll find a way."

He turns his back to me. "Sorry, but I'm not going to wait around another twenty years hoping that people's minds will change." His tone is flat and bitter, but there's a hint of sadness, too. "While you're handing out pamphlets or making speeches, another thousand Fours will self-euthanize because IFEN has made their lives a living hell. We need change now. And I'm going to make it happen, with or without your approval." He turns his back to me. "If you need me, I'll be in the training room. I'm going to practice on my own for awhile." He marches around the corner, his black coat flowing behind him.

Alone in the hall, I clench my fists, trying to choke down the lump in my throat. I hate this. I hate fighting with the one person I actually trust. But I can't just sit quietly by while people are dying. I can't pretend I'm okay with everything that's happening here.

I hear footsteps and turn to see Rhee approaching. She stops a few paces away. "You missed the end of the Assembly."

"I know. Sorry." With my thumb, I quickly wipe the moisture from the corners of my eyes. "To be honest, I'm really not in the mood to be lectured right now."

"I didn't come to lecture you. I wanted to ask you something." She pulls a wallet-sized tablet computer from her pocket and, with a few taps, brings up a photo. "Do you know this boy?"

My mouth falls open. A young man stands on a street corner, wearing a dark coat which nearly blends in with the night. His shoulders are hunched, and he's in the process of turning, so only his profile is visible, but I'd recognize him anywhere. It's Ian. "Yes, I know him. He's my friend. We trained as Mindwalkers together. Why?"

"He's been spotted in Toronto."

18

"He's here?" I ask, breathless. "Are you sure?"

"That photo was taken here in the city," she replies. "So yes, we're sure. We have a network of informants throughout the city. Apparently he's been asking people about the Blackcoats and the Citadel. Not very smart of him." She tucks the tablet computer back into her pocket. "At this rate, he'll be snatched up by the police in no time."

I already knew that Ian was secretly involved with the rebel movement, but on the surface at least, he was still a good student and a law-abiding citizen. If he's here now, it means his cover has been blown. Something must have gone terribly wrong. "Where is he, exactly?"

"He was last seen outside a club called The Cube. I know one of the bouncers there. I'm going to go back up there, talk to a few people, hopefully get some answers. I just wanted to confirm his identity with you first."

"I want to go with you."

"That would not be wise," she says. "There's a bounty on your head, remember."

"I'll wear my mask. Besides, Ian knows me. He'll be more likely to trust you and come with you willingly if I'm there."

Rhee crosses her arms over her chest. She's frowning, but I can see the gears in her head turning, weighing the benefits and drawbacks of my proposal. "Normally, we don't take new recruits to the surface so soon after their arrival. You've only just started training."

"I can't just sit around while Ian might be in trouble." I soften my voice. "Please. Let me help."

There's a brief pause. "I need to talk to Zebra. Meet me back here in ten minutes. And be ready to leave immediately. The sooner we can locate him, the better. With luck, we'll only be up there a few hours."

I let out a breath, and a knot between my shoulders loosens. "What about Steven?"

"What about him?"

"Is he coming with us?"

She shakes her head. "I have someone else in mind, and three is all we need. More than that will just attract attention."

Once she's gone, I'm left standing alone in the hall, listening to the omnipresent, rhythmic thump-thump of machinery behind the walls. Sudden uncertainty itches at the back of my brain. I need to tell Steven where I'm going, at least. I make my way to the training room and stand outside the door. The rattle of artificial gunfire is audible, even through the thick metal—Steven killing holos.

I raise one hand to knock, then stop. What if he's opposed to the idea of me accompanying Rhee? Going to the surface is risky, even if we won't be doing any fighting. What if Steven tries to talk me out of it? I don't want to deal with that right now. More to the point, I don't have that sort of time to waste.

His retreating back flashes through my head, along with his parting words: *I'm going to make it happen, with or without your approval.* Something inside me hardens. Why do I need his permission, anyway? Rhee said it wouldn't take long. I'll be back before he even knows I'm gone. Still, an ache of guilt pulses through me as I walk away. I tell myself that it'll be better for him not to know, that he'll just worry needlessly, if he does.

I make a brief stop in my room to grab a coat. When I return to the spot where Rhee and I agreed to meet, she's already waiting. "This way," she says.

She leads me to a small but very solid-looking metal door, keys in a code on a number pad, peers into a retinal scanner, and presses her thumb to a white square, which blinks green. A recorded voice intones, "State your name."

"Rhee Skylark."

The door swings open with a ponderous creak, and the lights snap on. My jaw drops. It's an armory—not quite as vast as the Assembly Hall, but close—and it's completely filled with weaponry. Hundreds of rifles hang on the walls. Rows of pistols glint on shelves. Grenades dangle from hooks like bunches of green fruit waiting to be picked. There are bags of fertilizer, too, stacked up in one corner. I don't want to think about their purpose, but somehow, I doubt they're for trees.

Rhee removes a small pistol from a table, loads it, thumbs the safety on, and tosses it to me. I fumble, nearly dropping it. "Just hang onto this for now. You probably won't have to fire it, but be prepared, just in case." She hands me a holster, too.

I buckle the holster around my waist and shove the pistol into it. It takes me a minute; my fingers feel thick and clumsy.

We leave the armory, and she leads me to the room where we first entered the Citadel. My stomach gives an unpleasant lurch. Shana's standing there, arms crossed over her chest. "Good," Rhee says. "You got my message."

My back stiffens. "She's coming with us?"

"I need backup, just in case anything happens," Rhee says to me. "And Shana is a good soldier. She's been on over a dozen missions."

Shana scowls. "So why is she here?"

"She's here because she knows the person we're looking for. If you don't like it, you're welcome to stay behind. I'll pick someone else."

Shana shoves her hands into her pockets and turns her back to me. "Just try to stay out of the way and don't do anything stupid."

I ignore the sting of indignation. "I won't."

"Ready?" Rhee asks.

This is all happening so fast. But then, every minute we wait around here is another chance for Ian to get caught. "Ready."

"Activate your holomasks," Rhee says.

The black hoop is still around my neck; I'd forgotten it was there. I turn it on. Shana reaches up to her throat, and a furry head snaps into place over her own. It's vaguely skunk-like, but the muzzle is different. Some type of bear or rodent, I'm not sure.

The main door opens, groaning laboriously, and we step out into the cool, damp air of the Underground. The door creaks shut behind us as we move forward, single file, with Rhee in the lead and Shana behind her. Lights sputter here and there in the shadows as my feet splash through puddles.

We turn down a low-ceilinged stone tunnel. Dark, sluggish water runs down the center; we creep along one of the narrow ledges to the side. Rhee and Shana are shadows flowing through the darkness, graceful as foxes.

"Slow down," I pant.

"How 'bout you speed up?" Shana calls over one shoulder. "You could stand to lose a few pounds anyway, princess."

She's trying to needle me. I clench my teeth, determined not to rise to the bait.

We stop. "Wait here," Rhee says. She shimmies up a set of metal rungs on the wall and vanishes into the darkness. From above, I hear the scrape of wood on metal, and a shaft of faint light falls in. She climbs down a few rungs and beckons us with one hand.

I grip the first rung. The metal is slimy with algae and other things I don't want to think about. I slip several times as I make my way up.

We emerge into a vast, empty warehouse with dim light filtering through a hole in the ceiling. Overhead, the rafters echo with the coos and rustles of pigeons. The white splatters of bird droppings cover the floor. At one end of the shadowy room is a huge, rusted iron door. Rhee shoves her shoulder against it. The hinges groan and resist, but she manages to prop it open a bit with her rifle, and we squeeze out through the gap, into the hazy gray afternoon. The cold city air fills my lungs. It's tinged with the smell of smoke and oil, but after the stale, recycled air of the Citadel and the sewery stink of the Underground, it's surprisingly refreshing.

A thick fog hangs over the city, and a cold, steady drizzle covers the streets with a reflective shine. Overhead, a holographic phoenix sails through the air, burning with brilliant sapphire flames. The words BE REBORN WITH PHOENIX ENERGY CRYSTALS trail after it, glowing pale blue, like a gas flame. People flow around us.

A small, inconspicuous gray car waits near the curb. Rhee pulls a key from her pocket and opens the door.

"Shotgun," Shana calls.

I slide into the backseat. Beads of rain trickle down the windows and gaudy, multicolored buildings roll past outside as we drive. We park alongside a narrow street and get out. The drizzle has become a full-fledged rain sheeting down from the sky, plastering our coats to our skin. Rhee leans her rifle against one shoulder as she walks. How does she carry that huge thing around and make it look so effortless? Doesn't she ever get tired?

She stops in front of a building—a perfect cube, large enough to fit several small houses inside, with glass walls. Or maybe Plexiglas. Rain runs down the sides like waterfalls, blurring the interior. A grinding bass beat pulses from within, vibrating in my bones, and ruby spotlights spin through the air and across the stage, where a group of men and women—wearing nothing but dinosaur holomasks—belts out something that seems to be more screaming than music. People gyrate on the dance floor, a sea of black leather, fishnet, and gleaming, sweaty skin. The whole club is totally transparent, save for the doors, which are lacquered bright red.

A man stands in front of the door, beefy arms crossed over his chest, eyes hidden behind mirrored shades. He looks like a bear who's been shaved and squeezed into an expensive suit. Rhee exchanges a few quiet words with him, showing him the picture of Ian. He squints at it, then points up the street and says something which I can't quite make out under the deafening beat. We keep walking.

"He can't have gone far," Rhee says. "We need to do a sweep of this area. We'll cover more ground if we split up. You and Shana, check the rest of this street and meet me back here in twenty minutes." She hands me a small black earpiece with an attached microphone, and I slip it in. "Contact me if you find anything."

Shana touches her own earpiece and nods.

I'm not crazy about the idea of separating from Rhee, but I'm not about to argue with her, either. Rhee heads in one direction, Shana and I move in the other. A sleek black police car rolls past, and I tense, but the driver doesn't slow. I remind myself that in Toronto, we don't particularly stand out, even with our masks and guns. People move through the rain like phantoms, and I watch each face, scanning for a flash of red hair, a glimpse of familiar features. Each time I see a tall, thin figure, hope leaps in my chest, but each time, I'm disappointed.

Ahead lies an expanse of cracked pavement, illuminated by a single flickering streetlight. Forms huddle in sleeping bags and makeshift tents; some of them sit warming their hands over fires in metal bins. "What is this?" I whisper.

"Homeless camp. Obviously. Not all bums live in the Underground."

"Calling them 'bums' is a little disrespectful, don't you think?"

"I used to be one. I'll call them whatever I damn well please."

We pick our way slowly through the mass. At the sight of our guns, people draw away, as if we're surrounded by a poisonous miasma. I smile, trying to reassure them, but I'm not sure they can even see it behind my mask. The masks do react to their wearers' facial expressions, but beaks don't mimic human smiles very well.

"Hey," Shana calls, raising her voice, "anyone seen a skinny red-haired guy around here? 'Bout eighteen years old?"

Most of the people shake their heads, barely glancing up. One girl squints at us, hugging her knees to her chest. Then, without a word, she points to a dark, narrow alley. Suddenly, it's difficult to swallow. My heart is caught in my throat. "Thanks," I say. We make our way toward the alley, and I hear a low ripple of male laughter from within.

"Be ready," Shana whispers.

"For what?" I ask.

"Anything." She cocks her pistol.

The alley is smothered in oily shadow; the streetlight's weak glow can't quite penetrate it. Then the clouds shift, allowing a hint of moonlight to peek through. A figure lies sprawled, motionless, eyes closed, face pale, blood leaking from one temple. He's disheveled, his skin smudged with black dirt, but it's unmistakably him. Three other figures crouch around him, rummaging through his pockets and the backpack beside him.

The cry leaps out of me before I can stop it: "Ian!"

The figures turn toward us. Shana raises her pistol. "Get the hell out of here."

They scramble away like startled mice, hopping over the fence at the end of the alley.

"Check him for injuries," Shana says.

I crouch beside Ian and stroke his cheek, smoothing his blood-stained hair away from his face. His eyes twitch beneath the lids, as if he's trying to open them. "You're okay," I whisper. "You're safe now." I check him over quickly. Aside from the bump on his head, he doesn't seem to be hurt. I raise my head. "Just a concussion, I think."

"Come on," Shana says. "Let's get him out of here before—"

"Step away from him and put your guns down. Now."

At the voice, a web of cold spreads under my skin, and I look up. A young man in a dark police uniform stands in the mouth of the alley, pointing a gun at us. His eyes are wide, his breathing ragged. A flash of panic goes through me.

"Now," he says.

My mind races, trying to make sense of the situation. Is he alone? Was he on patrol when he happened to see us walk into the alley, carrying pistols? Maybe to him, it looks like we're the ones who hurt Ian. "He's our friend," I say, speaking slowly and softly. "He was mugged. We came here looking for him. We're not trying to harm anyone, I swear."

"I said step away," he says through clenched teeth.

Shana whips up her pistol and fires, blowing the gun from his hand. The weapon spins through the air and lands a few yards away. Before he can react, she lunges, shoves him up against the wall, and presses the gun to the underside of his chin, tipping his head back.

The man's face floods with terror. His eyes are wide, whites brilliant in the darkness, and I'm suddenly aware of how young he is. Early twenties. "Please. Please, d—"

"Shut up." Shana's finger starts to squeeze the trigger.

In an instant, the deaths of the IFEN guards and the border patrol woman flash through my head, and I realize that I'm about to watch another person die in front of me—a man who's just trying to do his job. I'll see him along with the others every time I close my eyes. "Wait!" I blurt out.

She shoots a glare in my direction.

"We don't have to kill him. Can't you just . . . knock him out, or something?"

"I'm not taking any chances. Cover your eyes if you're squeamish."

There's no time to think, no time to hesitate. Breathing hard, I raise my own gun and point it at her. My fingers are clenched tight on the grip, my finger on the trigger, my chest heaving.

She looks down the barrel of the gun and snorts. "Give me a break."

I keep the gun trained on her chest. My hands tremble, but only slightly. "Let him go."

"You're not fooling anyone," she says, her voice thick with disgust. "You won't pull that trigger."

"I will. I swear." I try to make my voice sound deep and intimidating, but it comes out a strangled bleat, cracking on the last word.

Shana rolls her eyes. For a moment, she just stares into the man's frightened face. Snot leaks from his nose, and tears streak his smooth cheeks. She sighs and pistol-whips him. His head snaps to one side with a sharp crack, and he drops to the pavement. It happens so quickly, I'm left blinking in a daze. "Get him." She jerks her chin toward Ian. For a second, I don't move. "Hey!" she snaps. "You hear me?"

With a gulp, I holster my gun and hurry to his side. "Ian?" I whisper. He stirs and groans. His eyelids flicker.

"Help him up," Shana says. "The sooner we get him back to the Citadel, the better."

I glance at the unconscious policeman, choke back the bile in my throat, and try not to look at the glistening puddle of blood beneath his head as I slide an arm around Ian and help him up. He stumbles slightly. His eyelashes flutter again, revealing a hint of brown. "Lain?" he murmurs. "Where am I? What—what's happening?"

"It's all right. You're safe now."

We make our way back through the camp and reach the edge just in time to see Rhee approaching us through the gray curtains of rain.

"We found him," Shana says. "I knocked a cop out, so we'd better get out of here before anyone finds him."

Rhee nods shortly. "I'll get the vehicle." She runs off, and a moment later, the car pulls up, headlights slicing through the dimness.

Ian's slipped into a foggy, half-conscious state. Every so often, he mumbles something incoherent under his breath. The blood on his temple has dried to a thick, tacky consistency. Cold rain slides under my shirt collar and down my back as I stumble up to the car, pulling him. Ian sprawls across the backseat like a broken marionette. I prop him upright and fasten his seat belt, then get in.

Rhee drives in silence.

Shana deactivates her mask and glances over her shoulder. "Have to admit, he is hot, even all bruised and drugged. Then again, I kinda like 'em that way."

"I'm not in the mood for this," I mutter.

"Cut the angst. We're alive, we rescued your little boyfriend, and no one died. This should be like Christmas morning for you."

Maybe she's right. Ian is safe, his body a warm weight against my side. I stare at the back of Shana's head. Rain slicks down her lime green hair. "You weren't afraid when I aimed that gun at you."

She sniffs. "I knew you wouldn't shoot me."

"But you didn't kill him, either."

"Yeah, well. I decided he wasn't worth it. But that had nothing to do with you. If I wanted to, I would have blown him away. And you wouldn't have done anything about it, because the truth is, you don't belong in the Citadel. You're a sheep, not a wolf."

"Shana," Rhee says, a warning in her tone.

"It's just the truth," Shana says.

I ball my hands into fists. My face burns. I hate that she can make me feel this way. Even more than that, I hate the sense that she's somehow right—that this whole incident just proved her preconceptions about me.

Shana looks over her shoulder and smiles without mirth. "Consider this a free lesson. A gun is just a hunk of metal if you're not willing to pull the trigger."

19

I've been pacing outside the med wing for almost an hour now. I've practically worn a path into the floor. The medic took one glance at the gash on Ian's head and said he'd need stitches. But Ian is still inside.

"You know, you could've at least told me where you were going."

I look up at the sound of Steven's voice. He stands in the hallway, his expression unreadable. I lower my gaze.

"God, Lain. I can't believe you ran off on your own to save him."

"I wasn't on my own. Rhee and Shana were with me."

"You know what I mean."

I study my shoes, still splattered with mud and blood. "It all happened so suddenly. Once I heard he was in Toronto, I had to do something."

"And it didn't even occur to you that, I don't know, maybe I might have had a right to know what was going on?"

I grit my teeth. Guilt tugs at me, but it's accompanied by the dull burn of anger. Does he think he can speak to me like I'm a child? I raise my chin. "You told me earlier that you don't need my approval to do what's necessary. Well, I don't need yours either."

His back stiffens. Hurt flashes across his face, then his expression slams shut, going blank again. "Fine," he mutters. His receding footsteps echo in my ears.

I lean back against the wall and close my eyes. A dull pain drums between my temples. Maybe I should have apologized. If our positions had been reversed, if Steven had gone off on his own, I would have been upset too. Maybe tonight, when things have cooled down a little, I can talk to him.

The door creaks open. My heart jumps, and I spin around. "Ian!"

He smiles, though his face is drawn and pale. The blood has been cleaned from his temple, a small bandage taped over the injury. "Hey." Stubble roughens his jaw. His reddish hair is shaggy and unkempt, and falls over his right eyebrow. It's only been a few days since I last saw him, but it feels like an eternity. The truth is, I wasn't sure I'd ever see him again.

He clears his throat. "Lain, I—"

I tackle him in a hug and squeeze him around the waist, and he lets out a startled *oof!* His familiar scent envelops me, though it's mixed now with the sour smell of the Underground, of dirt and blood. I lean back, just enough to reach up and frame his face between my hands. "Are you all right?"

"Fine, mostly. I barely even remember what happened, thanks to this bump on my head. I was in that camp, then someone jumped me, and *bam*. I woke up here."

I hug him again. "I've missed you," I murmur against his shoulder.

He exhales a quiet breath, and his arms slip around me, returning the hug. "Missed you too." The hug lingers longer than usual.

When we finally separate, he looks around. "So this is the Citadel, huh? I knew it existed, but I had no idea how to get here. Lucky you found me." He studies my face. "We've got a lot to talk about, don't we?"

For the first time, I notice the faint lines etched around his eyes and mouth, lines that weren't there before. "We do. Let's not do it here, though." I take his hand and lead him to the dormitory wing. His palm is broad and warm against mine.

Once we're alone in my room, we sit on the edge of my bed, side by side. "Sorry I caused you so much trouble," he says quietly. "I heard you and Steven arguing outside. That's probably my fault."

"No. That had nothing to do with you." A hint of bitterness creeps into my voice. I clear my throat. "Don't get me wrong, I'm really happy to see you, but—what in the world are you doing here? How did you get across the border? Did you use one of the tunnels?"

"Actually, I came over on a plane." He gives me a small, embarrassed smile. "One of my mom's friends owns a private jet, so he flew me over. I made up some story about how I was writing an article on American versus Canadian methods of dealing with crime and how I needed some firsthand observation. I paid him off, so he didn't ask too many questions. It helps to have connections. Of course, once I arrived here I was kind of on my own, with nothing to my name but a backpack of clothes, a wad of Canadian cash, and a tip-off from one of my contacts that the Citadel was somewhere under Toronto."

Connections or no, it was a risky move, especially in the current political climate. Even with a passport, an American citizen needs specific approval from the government to leave the country, and they have to be a Type One. Ian still is, at least officially, since he bought a black market device to fool the neural scanners. He showed me the implant in his mouth once before. Still, this trip was undoubtedly illegal. "Ian . . . you can't ever go back. You know that, right?"

His smile fades. "I know."

"You gave up everything."

"I didn't have a choice. After you left, IFEN watched me everywhere—at school, on the mono. When I went for a walk, a black car tailed me. They didn't even try to hide the fact that I was being monitored. It felt like a threat, like they were looking for an excuse to take me in. I had to get out of there. If I hadn't, I'd probably be in a collar by now. Or worse."

A dull ache spreads through my heart. It's because he helped me. I don't know how much they suspect, but the mere fact that he was my friend has probably made him an object of suspicion. "But . . . what about your future? Your friends?"

He laughs flatly. "You think I care about that anymore? You're my only real friend, anyway."

"And your mother? Does she know you're here?"

He averts his gaze, and I suddenly realize how that must have sounded—like I'm scolding a kid for staying out after curfew. "I didn't mean it like that," I add quickly. "It's just—"

"She's gone."

I freeze. Dread settles into my stomach. "You mean—"

"Not dead. At least, I hope to God she's not. But she disappeared. She left a note telling me that she'd be gone for awhile, and she didn't know when she'd be back. She told me I should get out of the country while it was still possible. She's in some kind of trouble. I thought—" His voice breaks a little. "I thought maybe the rebels up here would know something about how to find her. I guess she's not here though, huh?"

"No," I whisper. "I'm sorry." I clutch my knees, so tightly it hurts. "I'm so sorry."

"Don't be. I just want you to understand, this isn't a game to me. I came here because I didn't know what else to do. And—" The muscles of his throat work as he swallows. "And I needed to see you again. I couldn't stop thinking about you, wondering if you were okay."

A strange feeling washes over me. I look down at my hands, suddenly not sure what to do with them. I tangle my fingers together, then pull them apart and clear my throat. "What are things like back in the URA, right now?"

The tension eases out of his shoulders. "Everyone's talking

about what you did. Some think you're a traitor, or that you're crazy, but others see you as a hero. People are starting to question the amount of power that IFEN has. There's this bill floating around called the Cognitive Rights Act. It started out as a petition, collecting signatures on the Net, but it's gained a lot of momentum in a short time. They're saying it might go all the way to the National Ethical Committee."

I sit up straighter. "What would it do, exactly?"

"For one thing, it would slash IFEN's funding to a fraction of what it is now. There'd be legal limits on the amount and types of data they could collect, and they wouldn't be able to reclassify or collar people based on psychological data alone. We'd go back to the old system of trial by jury, which means people could only be collared *after* they'd committed a violent crime, and only if they were convicted by their peers. The psychologists at IFEN would be totally removed from the legal process." He pauses. "Basically, it would destroy the Type system."

My heartbeat quickens. I feel a tiny flicker of hope. "What about all the refugees here in Canada? Would they be able to return home?"

"The law would grant them amnesty if they returned, so yeah. I think most of them would be able to go back to the URA. If this gets passed, it'll change everything."

I know it's a long shot. Still, I want to believe it has a chance. "IFEN's going to fight this every step of the way."

His expression turns grim. "Oh, they already are. They're cracking down hard on political dissidents. There's a secret police. At night, they raid people's houses and take them to this facility where Mindwalkers sift through their memories to see if they're involved with the Blackcoats. Afterward, of course, they make them forget."

I wish I could deny the idea that Mindwalkers would agree to participate in something so sinister, but by now, I know better.

A distant ache flares deep inside me; a sense of loss. I've become so jaded so quickly. "But if they forget, how does anyone know about this?"

"Sometimes people retain fragments of memories, and by sharing their stories, they've been able to piece together what's happening. There are too many accounts for it to be just coincidence or an overactive imagination. There are places on the Deep Net where you can read about this stuff—places hidden from the censors. Ever since you uploaded your memories, others have been coming forward with what they know." His gaze connects with mine, then flicks away, and his cheeks turn faintly pink. "You give people courage. That's why Dr. Swan has made finding you a top priority."

Cold trickles through my veins. I think about my face on that billboard and wonder how many people are searching for me right now.

I don't doubt that Dr. Swan is obsessed with finding me, but I don't think it's because I give people courage. It's because I made IFEN look foolish. I can imagine the jeers from the public: *If they can't even catch one runaway teenage girl, how can they stop the Blackcoats?* As long as I'm free, I'm a walking threat to their credibility.

I swallow, throat tight. Just a month ago, I was training to be a Mindwalker. Now I'm a thousand miles from home, a wanted criminal working for a terrorist organization. "I never planned on any of this," I whisper. "I never thought it would go this far."

Ian hesitates, then reaches out and takes my hand. His fingers are smooth and warm, his touch reassuring. Until now, I didn't realize how much I missed him. Sitting with him here, now, makes me feel like we're back in the cafeteria at Greenborough High, eating lunch together.

My thumb rests lightly against his wrist. I can feel his pulse beating. He takes a slow, deep breath and lets it out through his nose. Then he smiles at me, though I can still see the pain in his eyes, the ghost of what he's been through. "There's someone else who wants to see you." He reaches inside his coat and pulls out a brown, furry lump.

I nearly squeal. "You brought Nutter! How did you get him?"

"He must have followed me here," Ian says, a spark of teasing in his brown eyes. "Guess he missed you." He places the stuffed squirrel on the bed next to me.

I pick him up and hug him tight against my chest, burying my face in his fur.

Years of wear have dulled the shine from his eyes and dimmed his color from brownish-red to a muted gray. Some of his whiskers are bent or missing. But he smells the same as the day Father first gave him to me. It's the scent of childhood, of a time when I knew who I was. "Thank you."

A flush rises into his cheeks. "You're welcome."

Gently, I set Nutter on my pillow. He makes the room feel a little less sterile, a little more like home. Already, I feel better. "Come on. I'll show you around."

* * *

I spend a few hours walking the halls of the Citadel with Ian, giving him the grand tour. We talk easily, effortlessly, as if the past few weeks never happened.

That evening, after Ian's found his own room and gone to bed, I knock on Steven's door. "Steven?" No response. I knock again and wait, the silence stretching on. Maybe he's not in his room at all. Or maybe he doesn't want to talk to me. But I can't go to bed without at least trying to patch things up between us.

"Look, I'm sorry about earlier. You're right, I should have told you where I was going. The truth is, I was angry. When I asked you whether you'd pick me or the Blackcoats, if it came down to it, I wanted you to say you'd choose me. And when you didn't, I felt . . . betrayed." My throat hurts. Tears prickle in my sinuses, but I hold them back. "I mean, we've only just gotten here, and already . . ."

I trail off. Why am I bothering to say these things to the door? I'm not even sure if he's there. "Steven. Please, say something."

The door slides open, revealing Steven's pale, weary face. For a moment, we just stare at each other.

He sighs. "Look. I know how you feel about . . . all this. And I get it. It sucks. I don't want people to die either. But what else can we do? The Blackcoats might not be perfect, but they're our only chance of ever changing things back in the URA."

"That's not true. Ian told me about a law they're trying to pass. It's called the Cognitive Rights Act. It could make a difference."

His eyes go blank, like he's drawn shutters over them. "It won't pass."

"You don't know that. Do you even know what it is?"

"It doesn't matter. If IFEN doesn't want it to pass, it won't."

"The ethical committees are taking it seriously. If it goes all the way to the NEC . . ."

"Lain." His tone is weary. "It's all for show—to fool people into thinking that the URA is a functioning democracy. The National Ethical Committee reps don't have any real power over anything that matters. IFEN is running things, and they don't answer to voters. They don't answer to anyone. Either we keep living under their thumb or we crush them. There's no middle ground."

"What's happening to you?" I whisper.

His expression tightens. "Nothing's happening. This is who I am, Lain. This is who I've always been." He smiles a thin, hard smile. "Maybe you're finally figuring out that you don't like who I am."

I take a step backward. I feel like he's reached inside me and slapped my heart. "How can you say that? After everything we've been through, everything I've given up—"

"I never asked you to give up anything."

"You came to me for help." I can hear the anger creeping into my voice, despite my efforts to control it. "You asked me to erase your memories. You knew what that would mean for me."

"Yeah. I did." A muscle in his jaw twitches. "Maybe I was wrong. Maybe I should have taken that pill after all."

"Don't. Don't you *ever* joke about that."

He smiles again, but there's a terrible deadness in his eyes. "Who says I'm joking? If I'd died then, you wouldn't be here now. You and Ian would be on your way to a bright future, helping people in need. Instead, we're all here getting ready to risk our lives in a war. That's a pretty strong case for Somnazol, right there."

"That's not true, and you know it. Why are you talking like this?"

He looks into my eyes, and his expression crumbles. He lowers his head. When he speaks again, his voice is soft and cracked. "I'm not feeling so good right now. I—I think I should spend some time alone. Just forget everything I said, okay? I'll see you tomorrow."

"Steven—"

The door slides shut. I feel like my chest is caving in.

How did this happen? Where did we go wrong? When we had the argument in the Underground? Or when he left me at lunch to sit with Rhee? Or when I went to save Ian without telling him?

Or maybe Steven's right, and we never knew each other very well to begin with.

"Lain?"

I turn to see Ian standing in the hall behind me, his forehead wrinkled with concern.

A tear escapes my eye and slides down my cheek. I wipe it away, but not quickly enough.

"Hey . . ." Ian steps closer and encircles me with one arm.

I lean into the embrace. "Sorry," I whisper.

He pulls me closer, wrapping me in his arms. "Don't apologize." I close my eyes, aware suddenly of how safe I've always felt with him. I've been running for so long. I'm too tired to do anything but lean in.

20

My body moves on autopilot as I run through a maze of holographic gray halls. A guard lurches in front of me. My hand comes up automatically, and my finger squeezes the trigger. *Bang*. His eyes widen. He utters a choked sound, blood dribbling from his lips. I run right past as he falls.

We've been in the Citadel for over a month now. Killing holos doesn't bother me the way it used to. It's become like Steven said—a form of stress relief. Like popping bubble wrap.

Another guard runs toward me. *Pop*.

My body feels oddly weightless, like I'm floating.

When I reach the end of the course, I'm surprised; it went so quickly. I feel like I sleepwalked through the whole thing. Rhee deactivates the holo environment, and I stand, hands on my knees, panting as she approaches. "Very good." She checks a stopwatch. "Under four minutes. And your kill-count was a perfect forty out of forty. I'm impressed, Lain."

It's the first time I can remember Rhee ever praising me. "Thank you." I guess I'm not so hopeless at this, after all. But then, once you get over the emotional hurdle of being a killer-in-training, all you really need is spatial reasoning and a basic level of physical fitness. The only reason I failed so spectacularly before was because I hesitated.

Shana shoots a glare in my direction. The contempt in her expression could curdle milk, but I ignore her; I've given up trying to analyze why she despises me so much.

"All right, everyone!" Rhee calls. "Hit the showers."

In the bathroom, I wipe my forehead with a towel and take a swig from a plastic water bottle. I'm still drenched with sweat. A few other trainees are taking a hot shower in the stalls nearby, and steam billows out, filling the large, communal bathroom in the back of the training room. All around me, I hear girls' voices, laughter, slamming lockers—gym class sounds. I can almost pretend I'm back in high school.

I shower briefly, letting the hot water beat down on my head, sluicing away the salt and aches. I've started to gain a bit of muscle. Parts that were once soft have turned firm . . . though I've also lost weight. Despite the abundance of food in the mess hall, I've been taking most of my meals alone in my room, rather than face the sight of Steven chatting it up with Rhee. The two of them have been spending a lot of time together lately. They sit together regularly at lunch now, and more than once, I've caught sight of them sparring in the training room with boxing gloves, flushed and sweating.

It shouldn't bother me. Steven has made a friend, that's all. I should be happy for him. But ever since our fight, things have been different between us. A few times, I've tried to talk to him and lost my courage, but I don't even know what I'm afraid of.

I shut off the water, grab one of the white terrycloth robes hanging from the wall, and glance at my reflection in the foggy mirror. My face has grown narrow and pale, and my eyes seem to have sunk into the sockets. Damp tendrils of hair stick to my face and neck.

A row of blue lockers stands next to the showers, a place to store fresh clothes we can change into after our training. I start to open mine, then stop, gagging on the smell that wafts out. An invisible hand squeezes my stomach, and the reheated pancakes I had for breakfast surge up my throat. I clamp down on my gag reflex and pinch my nose shut, breathing through my mouth. Suppressing my dread, I force myself to open the locker.

A dead rat stares at me through one glassy eye, yellow incisors bared in a frozen grimace, neck twisted at an unnatural angle. Blood seeps from a slit in its belly, soaking through my clothes; pink intestines poke out through the wound. I back away, shaking.

The nape of my neck prickles. Slowly, I turn around. Shana is washing her hands in the sink.

"What is this?" I point.

She glances at the contents of my locker. "It's a dead rat. Not too bright, are you?"

"Did you do this?" I ask, struggling to keep my tone level.

She smirks. "If I had, it would be pretty stupid of me to admit it."

I want to grab the rat and hurl it at her face. Did she kill it herself? Is she such a sociopath that she'd take the life of a living creature just to get under my skin? "I'm going to tell Rhee about this."

"Whatever." She shrugs. "It actually wasn't me . . . and I've got an alibi. I was with my friends this morning. And that thing is fresh."

"So maybe you got someone else to put it there."

"Or maybe someone else put it there on their own. I'm not the only person here who doesn't like you, you know." She plants her hands on her hips. "Go ahead. Squeal. Your kind are always the teacher's pets, aren't you?" She slams her locker and walks away.

Anger seethes inside me, hot and suffocating. I ram my fists against the wall. "Damn it," I whisper. I should tell Rhee. But she's the last person I want to talk to right now. I'll deal with this on my own.

*　　*　　*

At lunch, I pile my plate with food I know I won't be able to eat, then take my seat across from Ian. Steven isn't there; he's sitting with Rhee. Again. At the sight, something dark and ugly stirs inside me. Today, Brian is with them too. Steven's got a cup of coffee in one hand. His lips are moving, and his companions nod along, but I can't tell what they're talking about, but they all seem to be getting along swimmingly.

"Hey," Ian says. "You okay?"

"Yes." I give him a distracted smile. "Just a little worn out."

"I know the feeling."

Come to think of it, Ian's looking a little pale and ragged too. His hair keeps getting longer. It hangs in his eyes now, like a curtain, and he's always brushing it aside. "Ian . . . when you first came here, did you have to . . ."

"What?"

I look away. "Never mind."

There's a pause. "You want to ask if Zebra put me through that test," he says quietly.

My breath catches. I meet his gaze. He's pale, his face drawn, his lips a thin line. "What did you see?" I whisper.

"I saw my brother."

I frown, puzzled. "I didn't even know you *have* a brother."

"Had. He died. A long time ago, when we were kids."

"Ian, I—" For a few seconds, I can't find words. "Why didn't you ever tell me?"

He gives a one-shouldered shrug. "Never came up, I guess."

He was always the one who comforted me. Maybe it never occurred to me that he might have wounds, too.

His eyes go fuzzy. "I knew it wouldn't be easy, getting into this place. But I never thought I'd have to go through something like that."

Anger flashes inside me, hard and bright. "What he did to us, shoving our faces in our past trauma . . . it's sick. And we're probably the only ones here who had to go through it."

"Well, we did work for IFEN. It's understandable that he wasn't too eager to trust us."

"He could have just read our minds. I think he wanted to scare us, to break us. It's a form of mental terrorism."

"It doesn't matter. It's over now." His fingers tighten on his plastic spoon. "I don't really want to talk about it."

I nod, lowering my gaze. A forkful of macaroni and cheese hovers halfway between the plate and my mouth. I'd forgotten about it. The cheesy smell makes me nauseous, so I set it down. "Have you heard anything about the Cognitive Rights Act lately?" I ask. "I've been trying to find information about it, but it's hard when there's no Net down here."

Instantly, his demeanor changes. He sits up straighter and leans toward me, a spark of excitement in his eyes. "I've been asking around. I found this." He pulls a folded printout from his pocket, unfolds it, and smoothes out the creases on the table.

I lean forward to study it. It's an excerpt from an article, with a quote from Dr. Swan:

Many people have asked for my opinion of the Cognitive Rights Act. And, considering its growing popularity, I feel the need to make my stance clear. If passed, the Act would be a disaster. The Type system exists because it is necessary. And it works. For every attack against us that occurs, dozens more are stopped because we take proactive measures to find and treat troubled individuals before they act. Yes, there are problems. No system is perfect. But we can work to address our problems without compromising the safety of our nation. To weaken or remove the Type system now would be to invite back the chaos and misery that tore our country apart. I ask you, the American people, to let IFEN do its job in this time of need. Do not support any measures which would tie our hands.

"He's on the defensive," I remark.

"Exactly. People are pushing hard for change. And if Dr. Swan feels the need to address it directly, it must be gaining a lot of momentum. He's nervous. And he should be. If this passes, it will be a game changer."

Hope stirs inside me. Ian is right. Despite the renewed fear caused by the terrorist attacks, a growing number of people want a better world. They're sick of this caste system masquerading as psychiatry.

Of course, there's also plenty of renewed prejudice and hatred toward Type Fours. Nicholas read us some statistics (never revealed on the news, of course) about the escalating number of hate crimes, most of which IFEN has chosen to overlook. But judging from the news clips I've seen, the number of protestors is growing, too. There's change in the air.

I glance over at the table where Steven and Rhee sit. I watch them get up, push their dirty trays into the wall slot, and leave together.

"You know, you've barely touched your food."

I glance down at my burger—a grease-soaked bun, a glistening gray chunk of meat smeared with ketchup resembling red paint. It makes me think of the dead rat in my locker, oozing blood. Mostly, I've been picking the bun apart, tearing it into tiny pieces. "Maybe I'm coming down with a bug."

Ian doesn't respond, and I know he doesn't buy it. When I first started spending time with Steven, I recall, Ian tried to warn me away from him, and I didn't listen. Now that Steven has apparently abandoned me, I wouldn't begrudge him an I told you so, but he hasn't said a word. "I know you're going through a rough time," he says at last. "I won't force you to talk about it. I just want you to know, if you do want to talk, I'm here."

The concern in his voice almost undoes me. A lump fills my throat, and tears fill my eyes, threatening to spill. And suddenly, it's all too much. All the things I haven't talked about are building up inside my chest, straining against my ribcage, threatening to burst out. "Shana put a dead rat in my locker," I blurt out. "I found it this morning."

His mouth falls open. "Shana? The green-haired girl?"

"She hates me, for some reason. It's stupid. It wasn't a threat or anything—at least, I don't think so."

Slowly, Ian puts his silverware down. There's a strange, intent look in his eyes. He stands up and walks across the room, toward the table where Shana's sitting with her friends.

Oh God.

"Ian, wait!" I leap to my feet and follow him.

As he approaches, Shana looks up and narrows her eyes. "What do you want?"

"I want you to leave Lain alone." His voice is firm and clear. It carries throughout the room. People stop eating and turn their heads.

"Ian, it's all right," I whisper, a hand on his arm. "You don't have to do this."

"Yeah, I do," he says. "You shouldn't have to put up with her bullshit."

I expect Shana to deny everything, to say she doesn't know what he's talking about. But she rises to her feet and faces him, hands on her hips. "You've got no proof that I did anything. So why don't you and the bottle brat just go hug and cry about it?"

A flush creeps into Ian's cheeks, into his ears. But the look in his eyes isn't embarrassment. It's fury. "Apologize to her," he says, his voice dangerously soft. "Or I'll—"

"What? You wanna hit me?" She shoves his chest. "Take your best shot! I never back down from a fight."

The flush in his face darkens. "I'm not going to fight you."

"Oh, so you thought you'd waltz over here and start telling me what to do, and I'd just take it?" Shana snorts. "You're as bad as she is."

"What is that supposed to mean?" I ask.

She curls her lip. "Don't play dumb."

By now, most of the people in the mess hall are watching us intently. A small crowd had gathered, forming a circle around us, like scavengers around a carcass.

"Seriously," I say. "Tell me. Why are you so angry at me? What did I ever do to you?"

She lets out a flat laugh. "You really don't get it, do you? In case you didn't notice, your people are the ones we're fighting. You might've switched sides, but you worked for those butchers for years."

My back stiffens. It's not a fair accusation—I wasn't aware of all the atrocities IFEN had committed while I was with them—but still, the words wriggle through the cracks in my mental armor. "Well, I'm not one of them anymore," I say. "I'm not even a Type One anymore. Neither is Ian. We lost all that when we chose to defy IFEN."

"At least you had a choice. At least you had something to lose in the first place."

Ian glares at Shana and opens his mouth, but I place a hand on his arm, a silent caution. A muscle twitches in his cheek.

Shana narrows her eyes. "As far as I'm concerned, you're still Type Ones. And I spent most of my life being kicked around by people like you."

"So you hate us because of the situation we were born into? How is that fair?"

"I don't give a flying fuck if it's fair," she snaps. "Do you think anything about this sick world is fair? I was collared because I tried to stop IFEN's thugs from dragging away my mom to be mindwiped. I grabbed a pan and swung it at one of them. It left a bruise. Just a bruise. I couldn't even stop them from taking my mother, but because I stood up to them, I was suddenly a danger that needed to be controlled. I spent four years with

216

a piece of metal wired into my spine. At school, I was anyone's meat. Boys felt me up whenever they wanted, because they knew that if I tried to defend myself, the collar would knock me out, and when I tried to tell people what was happening, no one ever believed me because I was a Four. Or maybe they just didn't give a shit, because they thought I was getting what I deserved. Is that fair?"

For a moment, I can't respond. I stare into her burning dark eyes. "I'm sorry," I say quietly. "I didn't—"

"I don't want your sympathy." She spits out the words. "I don't want to be your friend. What I want is for you to get out. This is our revolution. We don't need your help."

Silence fills the space between us. The crowd seems to hold its breath.

I grit my teeth. Fine. If that's how she wants it, so be it. "Too bad. You don't own this revolution, and you don't get to decide who's worthy of joining. You're not the only person who's been hurt by IFEN. I have as much stake in this as you, and you're just going to have to accept that, whether you like it or not."

She rolls her eyes. "I don't have to take that from some posh, uppity bitch who was grown in a petri dish. You're barely even human." She says it almost casually, tossing the insult lazily in my direction before turning away. As if it doesn't matter. As if the words don't rip me open.

And suddenly Ian's in her face, looming over her. "Take that back," he says, his voice dangerously soft.

"Back off," she says, "or that pretty-boy face of yours is going to be all bloody."

"*Take it back!*"

She laughs. "Well, don't say I didn't warn you." Her fist whips out. Blood flies through the air, and he staggers backward. I scream Ian's name and lunge forward, but the crowd is closing around them, blocking my path.

Ian swings. His fist clips her on the cheek, and she hoots in excitement. "That's more like it!" She widens her stance and beckons him with both hands. "Let's see what you got."

He grabs her arm, and then they're wrestling in a blur of limbs as the crowd hoots and roars all around us. She tackles him, pinning him between her knees, and slams his head against the floor. Her friends go wild, jumping up and down and cheering her name.

This is insane. I have to get her away from Ian. I think she might actually kill him.

I shove my way through the crowd, lunge at Shana and grab a fistful of her hair, yanking her head back. She cries out. I seize both her arms and haul her off Ian as she struggles. There's blood on her face, blood in her hair. Ian's on the floor, gasping, bleeding from a split lower lip. His eyes are wide and dazed. "Holy shit," he mutters.

Shana breaks free from me and charges at Ian, howling. Two burly young men grab her arms, dragging her backward. She thrashes like a cat in a bag until one man presses a gun to the back of her head. She freezes. "I think you need a few hours in the timeout room," he says.

Her breathing quickens. Panic flashes in her eyes. "Let me go, you prick!"

The other man presses a small hypo to her neck. She jerks, shudders, and goes limp. They carry her away. For a second or two, I almost feel sorry for her.

I crouch beside Ian, who's still on his back. One side of his face is rapidly swelling. When I touch his cheek, he flinches. Carefully, I brush his hair back, examining his eyes. "We need to find a medic."

He averts his gaze. "I'm fine."

"Now."

21

Within minutes, I find one of the medics, marked by a white sash tied around her arm. She's maybe nineteen; she has pink streaks dyed into her hair and huge, gold hoop earrings, and the sleeves of her black shirt look like they've been chewed up by rats. She takes us to a room in the med wing and tells Ian to follow a light with his eyes, then asks him his name and age and has him count backward from ten. "Any dizziness? Nausea?"

"No. Just a headache. A small one."

She nods. "Lie down for awhile and don't do anything too strenuous for the rest of the day. You should be fine."

She leaves, closing the door. Ian is stretched out on the cot, staring at the ceiling through his good eye. The other is a puffy slit.

"How are you feeling?"

He tries to smile, then winces. "Could be worse." He turns his face toward the wall. "Embarrassed, mostly."

"Why?"

"Do you really need to ask? You just watched me get beaten up by a girl."

"By Shana," I correct. "She's more like a cross between a shark and a psychotic baboon."

One corner of his mouth lifts, then falls.

I pull up a chair and sit. "Thank you, by the way. For standing up for me."

"I just made things worse. She probably hates you even more now."

"I'm not sure that's possible. But even if it is, I don't care. It helps, knowing that someone is on my side."

A light flush creeps into his cheeks. "I'm sorry she said those things to you."

A lump fills my throat, and I push it down. "Maybe she had a point."

"Lain." His voice is firm. "Don't let her get under your skin. She's the one with the problem here, not you. If she gives you any more trouble, tell someone. Okay?"

I nod, studying my feet. I know what he's saying is true, but even so, Shana's words have lodged themselves somewhere inside me, and I can't shake them loose. I can't hate her, either—not now. I see her in my head, a tiny, fierce-eyed girl wielding a frying pan, trying to protect someone she loved. And for that simple, understandable gesture, the system squashed her like a bug.

The Blackcoats are bound together by their pain. I've suffered too, but not in the same way, not for the same reasons. Here, Ian and I are the outsiders. "Lately," I whisper, "I've been wondering if I made the right choice, coming here."

"I know the feeling." He hesitates. "Is everything okay? I mean . . . between you and Steven. I don't see you two together very often."

I swallow, throat tight. "What Steven does is his own business."

"You don't have to pretend, Lain."

I meet his gaze—those clear, earnest eyes.

They're beautiful. It's just a fact. My mind flashes to an incident back in Greenborough High. I was in the bathroom, washing my hands, and overheard two girls talking and giggling. I caught

Ian's name and honed in on their conversation. "I know," one of them cooed. "He's soooo yummy. His eyes are like melted chocolate."

"Eyes? I was looking at another part."

More giggling. I bristled. Ian and I were never more than friends, but it bothered me to hear them talking about him like that, like he was candy and they wanted to eat him up. Ian was always popular, but it always seemed to me that most people just wanted to talk about the surface of him—the crazy parties he threw, or his wild clothes and hairstyles. No one knew how honest and gentle and kind he was, how giving. Even I never fully understood that, until recently.

"He drowned," Ian says suddenly.

The words jerk me back to the present. "Who?"

"My brother. He drowned. When I was ten." He closes his eyes. "My mom never got over it. He was her favorite. I mean, she'd never admit that, obviously. But if you'd ever met him, you'd understand. I think . . . ever since he died, maybe, I've just been trying to be him. To fill the space he left behind."

There's a dull throb in the center of my chest. I reach out and take his hand, sliding my fingers between his. The gesture is instinctive, natural.

"I should have done something," he says. "I should have swum out and tried to save him. But I just stood there on the beach, screaming for him to come back. I was afraid of the ocean. I never waded in more than a few feet."

"It wasn't your fault," I say. "You were just a child."

"Believe me, I've been over all this. After it happened, my mom sent me to a lot of therapists, and they told me the same thing, all of them. But the fact is that I stood there and did nothing, and my brother died. I spent the rest of my life trying to be perfect, to make up for it. But I didn't dare let anyone in. And then, suddenly, you were there."

I'm aware of my pulse beating away in the hollow of my wrist, and I wonder if he can feel it.

"When I met you," he says, "it was like you saw through all that. You saw me. Not the big, loud, fake me, but the one on the inside." He smiles. It looks like it hurts. "Sorry. I barely know what I'm saying. Maybe that knock on the head scrambled my brains a little, after all."

"It's all right." I swallow. And suddenly, I can't stop staring at his lips. They're a shade between pink and beige, fuller than Steven's, softer-looking, and I wonder suddenly what they'd feel like—if it would be different.

What's wrong with me? He just told me about his brother's death, and I'm fantasizing about kissing him. How sick am I?

"Lain?"

His voice makes me jump, and I quickly stand up. "I—I'm sorry. I should—"

"It's okay." His fingers dig into the cot, knuckles white. "Go on. Steven is probably worried about you."

I'm not sure Steven even knows what happened; he left the mess hall with Rhee before the fight. But that's not really the point. Ian is giving me an opening, a chance to leave before I weaken and do something I might regret. That's the sort of person he is. He'll never pressure me, never accept anything I'm not fully prepared to give. "But your head . . ."

"Is fine. I'm bruised, but that's all."

A part of me wants to stay. To keep holding his hand and looking into his eyes—to be with someone I understand, who understands me. But I can't. I'm already so confused; I need space to breathe, to think.

Quietly, I leave the room and walk down the hall. I stop, lean against the wall, and squeeze my eyes shut.

Ian has been my friend for so long. Even if he hasn't always been in the foreground of my consciousness, he's always there. Like the sun. You hardly ever think about its existence—it's just in the sky, shining away, but if it ever disappeared, the whole world would go dark. I wonder if the sun ever feels unappreciated.

I look down at my hand, flexing and curling the fingers, remembering the sensation of his fingers interlocking with mine like puzzle pieces.

"Hey . . ."

I open my eyes to see Steven standing in the hallway, looking baffled. "The medic told me that you and Ian were here. What happened?"

I look away. "He had a fight with Shana. He's not injured, though."

"A fight?" he repeats. "Like, a fight-fight?"

"He was defending me. It's complicated. But everything's fine now." I know that's not much of an answer, but it's all I can muster.

Steven nods uncertainly. There's a rifle strapped to his back, I notice. That's new. Does he just carry it with him all the time, now?

Lately, it's so awkward to be alone with him. Though, come to think of it, this is the first time in several days that that's actually happened. We both hang in the hallway for a few seconds, and I feel like I should say something, but I have no idea what. I've studied psychology. You'd think that would make me better at human relationships. Apparently not. "How have you been?" I ask at last. My voice comes out stiff, like I'm talking to an acquaintance at a party.

"I'm all right, thanks."

He does look healthier, I realize. He's gained weight—which he desperately needed—and his arms are corded with muscle. He's blossoming here. He's found his place, his people. Maybe I should be happy for him.

But I wanted his place to be with me, not with a band of anti-government radicals.

He exhales a gust of breath. There's an uncertain look on his face, and I have the sense that the barrier between us has cracked open, just a little. "Listen, Lain, I . . . I know things have been kind of weird lately, but . . ." He rubs his face. "Damn it. I suck at this stuff."

"Well, you could start by explaining why you've been ignoring me." The words come out a little more tart than I intended.

He tenses. "You haven't exactly been friendly with me, either."

"I *wanted* to talk to you. But you were never around." And every time I saw him, he was with Rhee.

He shrugs, gaze averted. "I've been going through some stuff, okay? I needed to clear my head."

"Well? Is your head clear now?"

"Pretty much." He meets my eyes. "I've decided that I'm going to go on the next mission. Whatever comes up. I've been training long enough. I want to start doing something."

So, he's still committed to staying with the Blackcoats. Not that I'm really surprised.

There are so many other things I want to say. I want to tell him that I miss him, that I just want things to be the way they were between us. But when I open my mouth, the words won't come out. "Be careful," I say instead.

"Sure. I will." A pause. "You could come with me, you know."

I shake my head. "I'm useless with a gun. You know that."

His expression goes blank. The opening is closing off, and we're back to acting like strangers. "Suit yourself." He turns and walks away, down the hall.

There's a stiffness in my chest, like the inside has been turned to wood. Steven doesn't need me anymore. He's going his own way. And when we're together, all we seem to do is cause each other pain.

And suddenly the voice of my Psych-Ethics professor is back in my head, nattering away: *What did you expect? You chose to become* intimate with a client, even knowing the risks. You abused your position of power over him. Why are you surprised that it went wrong?

But he wanted it as much as I did. He wanted me. He loves me, he—

It's called codependence. Clients often develop strong feelings for their Mindwalkers. But to pursue such a relationship always ends in disaster. You knew that, didn't you?

Yes, I knew. I was arrogant enough to think that we could beat the statistics, that our love was stronger than society's rules.

Even with the evidence in front of me, I don't want to believe that our relationship was based on something as flimsy as need. Yet, from an outside, objective viewpoint, it seems undeniable. When we met, he was suicidal, and I was his last thread of hope. His survival was dependent on my willingness to help him. I should have recognized what was happening, but like any stupid child with a crush, I blinded myself. And now, I feel like he's slipping away, like I'm losing him forever.

Maybe I've already lost him.

I feel a hand on my shoulder, give a start, and whirl around. It's Nicholas—the last person I want to see right now.

"Zebra requests your presence," he says.

There's something odd about his eyes—I've always thought so. The whites are too white. Even the red threads of capillaries at the corners look too perfect, somehow. "For what?"

"You'll see." He starts to walk, his long black coat swishing around his legs.

"Wait," I blurt out. "Can't I tell Ian where I'm going? He's in the med wing."

He pauses to look over his shoulder. "This is top secret. Tell no one. If you disobey me, I will be very displeased." He resumes walking.

I follow, teeth gritted.

Nicholas stops in front of what appears to be a blank wall, runs his fingertips over the metal, and prizes open a hidden panel. He presses a thumb to the screen, which blinks. A section of the wall swings inward, revealing a long, narrow corridor lit by bluish lights. We walk to the end of the corridor, and he opens another door, revealing Zebra's study. Apparently, the Gate room isn't the only way in.

Cautiously, I step forward. Nicholas stays behind as the door rumbles shut, leaving me alone once again with the leader of the Blackcoats.

22

Zebra sits behind his desk, reading a book bound in wine-colored leather. "Ah. Lain." He sets the book on the desk. "Good to see you again."

I glance at the book's title. *Paradise Lost.*

"John Milton," he remarks, running his finger over the gold-embossed title on the leather cover. "Have you read his work?"

"A long time ago," I say. Father had *Paradise Lost* in his collection too.

"'The mind is its own place, and in itself can make a Heav'n of Hell, a Hell of Heav'n,'" he quotes. "A fascinating insight, don't you think? Milton was quite the psychologist."

I make a noncommittal sound. "I suppose Lucifer is your favorite character? Being the leader of the rebellion and all."

"Eve, actually. I always thought she was misunderstood."

My gaze wanders. So many books. Has he read them all? I wonder, suddenly, if he ever leaves this room. Why does he so rarely show himself to the Blackcoats? Why is Nicholas the one who hosts the Assemblies, the one who relays his orders? True, Nicholas is young, handsome, able-bodied, and good at giving dramatic speeches. Superficially, at least, he's a more appealing figurehead. But Zebra is the one whose name they revere. They use his initial as their symbol. Is there some other reason he hides himself away?

"Tell me," he says, "do you think it was worth it?"

My brow furrows. "What?"

"The Fall. Was gaining free will worth the loss of Eden?"

I can't quite suppress the urge to roll my eyes. "Did you call me here for a mission or a book club discussion?"

A smile tugs at one corner of his mouth. "Well, since you're so eager . . ." He turns his chair and glides toward the bookshelf on the back wall. He slides out a book and keys in the code on the hidden panel behind it, and the shelf opens with a grinding rumble, revealing the Gate room. A gasp flies from my mouth.

Inside, strapped to the chair—shoulders slumped, head bowed—is a young, dark-haired man in a bloodied, light gray suit and jacket. The Gate's sleek white helmet covers his hair. Raspy, pained breathing echoes through the room. He stirs, but he doesn't seem to have the strength even to look up.

So much blood. It drips from his face, staining the front of his shirt. A small puddle of it shines on the floor. He doesn't appear to be seriously injured, but he's obviously been beaten. "Who is this?" I whisper.

"His name is Aaron Freed. He's a Mindwalker, and Dr. Swan's new protégé. Since you and Ian fled the nest, I suppose Swan needed some other young thing to use as his puppet."

So, what Dr. Swan said in that interview is true. I've been replaced. Maybe he'd been secretly grooming replacement Mindwalkers all along, just in case Ian and I didn't work out. The thought leaves a bitter taste on my tongue.

Slowly, Aaron raises his head. He's wearing glasses, the lenses cracked and smeared. His left eye is swollen shut, engulfed in black and purple flesh; his right is the startlingly bright green of a leaf in summer, peering out through a maze of cracks.

"We captured him a few days ago," Zebra continues. "He accompanied Dr. Swan to Toronto and was foolish enough to wander off on his own without a bodyguard."

"Dr. Swan is in Canada now?"

"Yes. Though for what purpose, we aren't sure. Of course he claims it's just a goodwill visit, but we have reason to believe that he met secretly with a Canadian government official. So far, the prisoner's refused to talk." Zebra's clear gray eyes lock with mine. "That's where you come in."

Cold washes over me. This is what I'll be doing for the Blackcoats? Using my Mindwalking skills to extract information from prisoners?

Aaron coughs. Blood flecks his lips. Suddenly, my lunch isn't sitting well, and I cover my mouth with one hand.

"I must confess, I didn't expect you to be so squeamish," Zebra said. "You've seen worse than this in the minds of your clients, haven't you?"

"That's different," I mutter against my palm. Immersing myself in my clients' traumas wasn't easy, but it was a necessary part of the healing process. This . . . this isn't about healing. "Why do you even need me? You obviously know how to use a Gate. Why not just do it yourself?"

"I've already attempted it and failed. As you know, examining a person's memories usually requires some degree of cooperation on the part of the subject. My Gate is capable of influencing a person's thoughts and emotions, but still, it's not foolproof. The subject can fight back, if his will is strong enough—and this boy has been trained by IFEN to resist mind control techniques. Drugging him has proved ineffective, as well. If we work together, we'll have a better chance of overpowering him and prying out the memories by force."

"A three-way loop?"

He nods. "Besides . . . I need to know if you're capable of doing what's necessary for the sake of the movement."

So, this is another test. He wants to see how much I can handle. Just like Dr. Swan. "And after we get the information, what will happen to the prisoner?" I can't quite bring myself to call him by his name.

"We'll execute him, of course. He knows too much. We can't risk leaving him alive."

Aaron's skin gleams with sweat and blood. My pulse hammers through my body, in my wrists and fingertips.

"And if I refuse to help you," I say, "then what?"

"I'll ask your friend Ian. I'm sure he wouldn't mind shouldering the burden for you."

So, he's playing dirty. My hands squeeze into fists, uncurl, then squeeze again. Zebra waits. At last, I look him in the eye. "I'll help you, but only on the condition that you don't kill him. Let me alter his memories, instead."

Zebra raises an eyebrow. "You want to save him. Why?"

"A friend once told me that this rebellion isn't about fear, it's about hope. If that's really true, then spare him. Unnecessary death won't help your cause."

He presses the tips of his slender, gloved fingers together and runs the tip of his tongue slowly over his lower lip. "An ordinary memory modification isn't foolproof. I'll settle for giving him a total mindwipe."

"No," I reply firmly. "A mindwipe is no better than death. The person has to relearn the most basic of skills—how to tie their shoes, how to speak. There's no reason to destroy his entire identity."

Zebra narrows his eyes. "You know, merely allowing him to live is a considerable risk. This boy is being groomed to replace Dr. Swan. He's an asset to the enemy."

"Killing him wouldn't make any difference, in the long run. Dr. Swan would just replace him with another pawn."

It might be my imagination, but I think I see Aaron flinch.

Zebra tilts his head. "Very well. After the interrogation, you will erase his memories of this entire encounter, under my supervision. But if the prisoner gives us too much trouble, I'll rescind the offer."

I've never modified someone's memories against his will. My principles squirm in protest at the thought, but it's better than letting him be killed or mindwiped. "Fine." I take a breath. "One more thing."

"My, you are full of conditions, aren't you?"

My mind flashes back to my conversation with Ian, and his words replay: *You're a symbol. You represent everything they can't control.* Images flicker through my head—the graffiti on the walls, the words I *believe in Lain Fisher.* I have a power I don't fully understand, the power to influence others, people I've never even met. If I learn how to harness that, maybe I can accomplish something. "If I record a message to the people of the URA, is there a way you can get it onto the Net?"

"Of course. Any other conditions?" There's a note of mockery in his voice.

"No. That's all." I close my eyes, fighting for composure. "May I speak to the prisoner?"

He lets out a little sigh. "Go ahead."

I enter the Gate room. Zebra lingers in the doorway. Aaron sits motionless, breathing raggedly. I take a tentative step forward, and he tenses. "I'm not going to hurt you."

His fingers twitch. Unexpectedly, he smiles—a nervous, wry smile. "Under the circumstances, I'm sure you can understand why I'm a little skeptical about that." His voice is soft and hoarse.

"Do you know who I am?"

"Yes. I know."

"And did you understand what we were talking about?"

He licks blood from his upper lip. "Well, the beating they gave me hasn't interfered with my hearing."

"Then you know that if you cooperate, there's a chance you'll get out of this alive, with your memories modified. I'm sure you'd prefer that."

For a few heartbeats, he doesn't respond. Then he draws in a shaky breath. "Lain, listen to me," he murmurs, his voice low and urgent. "I don't know why you're working with these people, but they aren't what you think. They don't want a better world. They want to rip everything apart, to send us all back to the Dark Ages. Look at what they've done to me." His fingers clench on the chair's arms. "I've never harmed anyone in my life. My only crime is working for IFEN."

"That's crime enough," Zebra replies.

Aaron's breathing quickens. His gaze flicks nervously toward Zebra, as if he were a coiled viper, then locks with mine again. His expression is filled with terrified pleading, his visible eye so wide the white shows all around. "You worked for IFEN yourself. So did your father. If I've committed a crime, so have you."

I swallow, hard.

Even if I wanted to help him, setting him free wouldn't do any good. We're buried underground. This whole place is locked up, and attempting to break him out would be suicidal. Still, his words awaken a flicker of doubt. Once I do this, I'll have crossed some invisible line. In my head, I hear Rhee's voice, the words she spoke to me in my initiation fever-dream: *Sometimes there are only two paths. And they're both ugly.*

Slowly, I lean toward him. "IFEN conducted experiments on its own citizens. On children. I'm sure Dr. Swan has done his best to convince you that was a lie, but it's not."

"I know," he says. "And I think you did the right thing by telling people."

That catches me off guard. "Then why are you still working for them?"

"Because the best way to change a system is from within. Do you really want the Blackcoats controlling our country? Whatever they set up in place of our government will be just as bad, maybe even worse."

It's a strange and confusing thing, to realize that I agree with him.

"Please, Lain," he whispers.

In the end, it doesn't matter. I'm stuck. "I can't help you." The words emerge quiet and bitter. I don't feel good about this. But if I intend to stay here, I have to walk the line, to help the Blackcoats when necessary without giving myself over to their ideology.

Aaron's shoulders sag. His breaths wheeze through his damaged nose. "You won't get anything out of my head," he says through clenched teeth.

"Oh," Zebra says lightly, "I think we will."

23

Two helmets sit in the corner of the room atop a wooden chair. Zebra dons one; I take the other, buckling the strap snugly beneath my chin. I pull up a chair. Zebra and I sit a few feet apart, facing Aaron, so we form a triangle. I'm breathing too fast.

It's just an immersion session, I tell myself. I've done this plenty of times. I'm practically a professional. Though this is about as far from the Immersion Lab at IFEN headquarters as it's possible to get.

"I'll activate the connection," Zebra says.

I nod.

The Gate snaps on. A familiar tingling spreads over my scalp and down my spine, like electricity dancing under my skin. Aaron's pain hits me like a bucket of boiling water, and the air hisses between my teeth. Every breath brings searing agony, as if my lungs are filled with needles. One side of my face throbs, a dull, hot pulse. His heart is racing. He's hidden it well, until now, but he's utterly terrified.

Breathe. Not my feelings. I walk through my identity affirmation exercises. *I am Lain Fisher, eighteen years old, brown hair. Mindwalker. I am—*

What am I? A traitor? A hero? A rebel? A scared, confused girl?

I shake off the questions and focus on breathing. As the connection deepens, the fear and pain become less overwhelming, and I can sense the emotions beneath. First and foremost is shame, a dull burn that consumes his entire being, but I can't sense the source. Is he ashamed about being captured, or about working for a man like Dr. Swan? Or maybe it's something else entirely—something deeper, older.

It occurs to me that I can't feel Zebra's mind at all. He said this was a three-way connection, but his thoughts are an utter blank. No—there's *something*—a cool, dry sensation that reminds me of wind on stone.

"We're going to review some of your memories now," Zebra says. "Why don't we start with your arrival in Canada?"

A spark of defiance leaps in his green eye. *Why don't you go to hell?* He shoots the words in Zebra's direction.

Zebra places a hand over his chest and widens his eyes theatrically. "Truly, I'm wounded. Such a cunning barb." He pulls a small box from his pocket and opens it, revealing a glittering hypodermic. "This should help. If it doesn't work, we can use harsher methods."

"You'll torture me, you mean."

"I don't want it to come to that," Zebra says. "I find such methods barbaric. My associate Nicholas, however, enjoys it. The drug will make you *want* to cooperate. If you still refuse, I'll give Nicholas five minutes with you, and I can assure you, they will be the worst five minutes you've ever endured."

A fine sheen of sweat gleams on Aaron's brow. I wait while Zebra injects him. I lower my visor, blocking out my own vision, and focus on the signals from Aaron.

Don't let me break. His voice is a whisper inside my head. *Give me the strength to resist. Please.*

I dig my nails into my palm, anchoring myself in my own body. But I can still hear him praying silently. I'm surprised at the strength of his conviction. He's not begging to be spared suffering; he's more worried that he'll betray his government by spilling sensitive information. His worst fear is that he'll fail, that he won't be strong enough, and now it's happening.

"Going soft on me already?" Zebra asks me.

"No."

Aaron's head falls forward, and his breathing slows and evens. His lassitude drifts over me like a gray fog. "Now," I say. "There was a reason you came here to Canada, wasn't there?"

Sleepily, he murmurs, "Yes."

"What was it?"

His eyes roll and twitch beneath the lids. "Meeting."

"What kind of meeting?"

He murmurs something unintelligible. I close my eyes, exchanging one darkness for another, and focus. Small flickers break through the blackness behind my eyelids. A tiny, fuzzy spot of light appears, and I focus, zooming in.

Then a curtain of darkness sweeps down, like a wall. Even now, he's resisting. I push at the darkness. It's almost tangible; a spongy barrier, pushing back against me. A deep voice booms all around me, reciting words: *There's a certain slant of light, winter afternoons, that oppresses like the heft of cathedral tunes. Heavenly Hurt, it gives us. We can find no scar—*

I recognize the words. Emily Dickinson. He's reciting poetry.

"A resistance technique," Zebra says. "Try again. Push, with your mind. Envision the wall dissolving."

The darkness surrounds me, heavy and thick. "Aaron," I say. "Go back to the meeting." *Push.*

I feel him shudder and flinch. Still, the wall of shadows in his head won't budge.

A faint tension hums beneath the surface of Zebra's consciousness; it's all I can sense from him. He must be very good at shielding his thoughts. "Now," he says. "With me. Push."

A bullet of sweat slides down my neck. A vein flutters in the hollow of my temple as I pour all my will into the mental thrust. Aaron tenses up. Then the wall breaks into a thousand black fragments and disintegrates, and he goes limp, the resistance draining out of him. I moisten my lips with the tip of my tongue. "We're in," I whisper.

Soft breathing echoes in my ears. Aaron's heart beats slowly.

"All right, Aaron," Zebra says. "Let's try one more time. Go back to the meeting."

A hazy vision swims into my head: a large room, mostly dark, with a round table in the center, spotlit from above. A gray-haired woman sits at the head of the table, her face stern and devoid of makeup. She wears a charcoal-colored suit and a pair of small, gold-rimmed spectacles. Dr. Swan sits to her right, dressed in white, as always.

The woman squints at me, and I feel an urge to straighten my posture, though my back is already ramrod-stiff. "And who is this?"

"My protégé," Dr. Swan replies smoothly. "He'll be sitting in to observe."

She frowns. "Is this standard procedure?"

"If all goes according to plan, young Mr. Freed here will be my successor." He smiles, but a pressure constricts around my throat and chest. In a flash, I remember his fingers biting into my shoulder, his whisper in my ear: *Do not leave my sight.* "He needs to understand exactly what this role entails. A form of job-shadowing, if you will. There is no need to worry; he'll be as quiet as a mouse."

I incline my head forward in a tiny nod. My heart is beating too fast.

The woman purses her lips, scrutinizing me. I sit very still, keeping my face smooth and calm, remembering Dr. Swan's advice. *Conceal your emotions. Become a piece of furniture, easily forgotten, and quietly absorb everything.*

At last, the woman lets out a small sigh. "Very well, then." She turns back to Dr. Swan. "Regarding the alliance we discussed earlier, I see no reason not to make an agreement with IFEN. Canada's Bureau of Psychological Welfare may be new, but our goals are similar to yours. If we could share our technological advances with each other instead of acting like we're on opposing sides, we could accomplish so much more."

"I'm glad you agree," Dr. Swan says.

She keeps her hands folded on the table. One manicured finger absently strokes another. "The United Republic has some amazing technology in the field of mental modification. And I'm not just talking about the Gates. You're developing a weapon, aren't you? Something called Project Mindstormer?"

I cast an uncertain glance in Dr. Swan's direction. His shoulders stiffen. "Let me assure you, those rumors are nonsense."

She taps a neatly filed, unpolished nail on the tabletop. "Of course, if such a thing existed, we would be very interested. Though we would have to proceed with utmost caution. If the UN found out—"

"They won't, because it does not exist," he replies firmly. "I don't know where you heard such nonsense, but I would advise you not to believe everything you read on the Net. Those conspiracy websites breed like rabbits, despite our efforts to control them, and they are nothing but fear-mongering and rampant idiocy. IFEN is a medical organization. We do not make *weapons*. Is that clear?"

She shrugs. "As you say." But a smile tugs at her lips, as if they're sharing an inside joke. It makes me uneasy. All of this feels wrong—sneaking around in the shadows, making deals.

I remind myself, again, that it's all necessary. If I want to make a difference, if I want to save my country from being ripped apart by war, I have to play the game. At least for now.

"We would be happy to share our existing technology with you," Dr. Swan continues, "but first, we would need to be certain that it won't be misused. In other words, we'd want to know that you share our values and goals. Admittedly, I have some concerns in that area."

The woman frowns, her brows pinching together. "Oh?"

Dr. Swan waves a hand, bringing up a holoscreen filled with bullet points, and clears his throat. He pauses, as if to make sure we're both paying attention, then continues: "Ever since the war and the resulting recession, Canada's penal system has been ranked the harshest and most brutal of any developed nation." He scrolls down with a finger. "In addition to having high rates of capital punishment, you incarcerate large numbers of people in appalling conditions and sensationalize their plight. Three years ago, your prison industry created a reality show titled *Nothing to Lose* where prisoners on death row volunteered to fight each other in a massive battle royale, with the promise that the winner would receive a full pardon. As I recall, it was hugely profitable, but it got canceled after a few years because of complaints from human rights groups. Then there was that scandal last year, in which—"

"You've made your point, Doctor." The gray-haired woman presses her lips together. "Our system is . . . problematic. I won't deny that. But we are striving to push the country in a more progressive direction. That's why we're asking for your help."

"Glad to hear it," Dr. Swan says. "You've already begun collecting psychological data on your citizens, correct?"

"That's right. We've been doing it for some time, actually. But there's so much data, it's difficult to know where to begin. A computer can't decide whether or not someone represents a potential threat—or at least, our technology isn't that advanced yet. Hiring people to sift through all that information is time-consuming and expensive, as I'm sure you'll appreciate."

Dr. Swan nods. "That's where we come in. We'll send in some of our people to upgrade your computers and help you implement a system like ours."

"There will be concerns, you understand, about the legality."

He waves a hand. "Modern laws are flexible. They adapt to the changing times. The important thing is to do what's best for your country."

"Indeed."

"Where, if I may ask, is your central database?"

With a flick of her fingers, she brings up a holoscreen displaying an overhead view of the city and enlarges it, zooming in on a large, warehouse-like building. The address glows in green numbers.

Dr. Swan makes a thoughtful sound. "That's close to a residential area, isn't it?"

She nods. "Hidden in plain sight, so to speak. If we ever want to implement a system like your collars, it makes sense to have the databases close to highly populated areas."

"Excellent," Dr. Swan says. "Then we'll begin immediately."

Their voices echo in my ears. The memory is fading, growing soft and blurry around the edges, and I'm slipping backward. Gradually, I become aware of physical sensations—the chair beneath my bottom, the cool air against my skin, my own breathing sliding through my nostrils and down into my lungs.

I open my eyes, dazed, and I'm Lain Fisher again. Aaron remains slumped in his chair, head bowed, his shirt translucent with sweat.

"He fell asleep," Zebra remarks. "Must have given him too strong a dose. Still, we learnt what we needed to know."

My throat prickles with thirst, and I swallow, wondering how long I was in his mind. It didn't *feel* like more than a few minutes, but time can slip by in chunks during immersion sessions. "Who was that woman?"

"Canada's Minister of Psychological Welfare."

Zebra was right. IFEN isn't content to rule over the URA. They're trying to expand their influence into other countries. "Do Canadians know about this?"

He snorts. "Of course not. No government *announces* that it's planning to strip away its citizens' liberties. The Bureau of

Psychological Welfare is supposed to be a research institution. At this point, they don't have much legal power. But that will quickly change, once the infrastructure for their system is in place." His eyes turn distant, inward-focused. "I'll review the recording from the Gate later, but I believe we have everything we need. You may as well do it now."

My stomach sinks. "Erase his memories, you mean."

"Yes. I'll observe, using the link, but I don't think I need to give you any instructions. Clean him out as quickly as possible. Any memories related to the Blackcoats or the Citadel must be completely removed. Beyond that, you may erase as much or as little of his personality as you wish. Use your discretion."

Why is he giving me the choice? Is he curious to see how I'll handle this?

It doesn't matter, though, because I'm not going to destroy any more of his mind than is absolutely necessary. Zebra ought to know that. "All right. Let's get this over with. Aaron?"

He makes a faint sound.

"We're going back to the day you arrived in Toronto."

The modification proceeds quickly and smoothly. Older memories require more work and preparation to remove, but Aaron's experiences with the Blackcoats are all very recent. I review his arrival in Toronto with Dr. Swan, his brief stay in the hotel, the night he slipped away into the streets, against Dr. Swan's orders. He was desperate for some air, for some time alone—the sense of being constantly watched by his mentor was like a rope around his neck.

He was only planning to stay out a few minutes, but then he was kidnapped—grabbed from behind, a chloroform-soaked rag shoved against his nose, a black bag pulled over his head. His next memory is of waking up in a small, dark room with a couple of Blackcoat thugs looming over him. They asked him questions, and when he refused to answer, rock-hard knuckles slammed into his left eye, setting off a flashbulb of pain in his head. The memory of the beating goes on and on. It's sickeningly detailed. Every blow, every kick, is encoded with crystal clarity. One of the Blackcoat thugs pulls a cigarette from his mouth, holds the burning end in front of Aaron's good eye, and threatens to shove it in if Aaron doesn't talk. I feel his terror as he sits, breath whistling through his smashed nose, blinking rapidly as the cigarette singes the ends of his eyelashes.

Finally, the other thug laughs and says, "Why waste a cig? Whatever Zebra does to him will be worse than that."

They chloroform him again, and he wakes up in the Gate room. I see myself, briefly, through his eyes. I look young and nervous, my eyes wide, my short, unkempt hair sticking out in every direction. There's an odd, shimmering glow around me, like an aura—it fades in and out, and I wonder if it's the result of the drugs or a minor concussion.

At last, I reach the present. I've constructed a mental map within my own head: a grid of bright blue lines linking the glowing nodes of memory.

This should be a very straightforward modification, a simple matter of wiping out the past few days. No need to dig any deeper. And yet . . . I can feel something else beneath the surface of his mind, some very deep, very old wound. His identity has grown around it, shaped by it. I can't see the details—I'd have to probe around a little more. For an instant, I find myself considering it. I could slip into the depths of his mind, find the pain at the center of his being, and quietly wipe it away. He'd never even know. He'd awaken clean and new, unburdened—

Why am I even considering this? I shake off the thoughts, troubled. I sense Zebra watching me, silent, observing and analyzing everything. When I glance over at him, there's a knowing smile on his lips. "What?"

"Nothing," he says. "Continue."

I make my way slowly through the chain of memories, starting with his kidnapping, and wash them away. I watch it all fade into nothing—the terror and pain of the beating, the long hours spent strapped into a chair, body aching, throat raw and burning with thirst.

When it's over, the lines of tension have smoothed out of his face. He sits, slumped in the chair, breathing softly.

Zebra removes his helmet. "That will do." He looks at me from the corner of his eye. "This boy owes you his life, you know."

I'm just glad it's over. My whole body is weak and shaky with exhaustion. "What's going to happen to him now?"

"I'll have one of my followers leave him in the streets of Toronto, close to a hospital or a police station, somewhere he'll be found. You have my word that he won't be harmed."

"Thank you." I take off my helmet and set it on the floor. Sweat drenches my hair and neck.

Zebra rolls out of the room. I follow him out, and the bookshelf swings shut, sealing Aaron in the Gate room, alone. I have the clear sense that I'll never see him again, but his very existence awakens all sorts of uncomfortable, conflicted feelings in me. He's the face of the enemy, the people we're supposed to crush, yet he doesn't seem all that bad. Maybe that shouldn't come as a revelation to me, given that I myself was the enemy not long ago. Yet, unlike me, he knows the truth about St. Mary's, and he still thinks IFEN can be reformed. If he were to take Dr. Swan's place as Director, perhaps it could be.

"You may return to your room, if you wish," Zebra says.

"Wait," I say. "You promised you'd help me get a message onto the Net."

He pauses, then turns toward me. "So I did. You wish to record it now?"

A small, hot point of pain throbs behind my left eye. I don't want to think; I want to lie down and let sleep wrap me in oblivion.

But I'm not about to let this chance slip away. I have no idea when I'll see Zebra again. "Yes."

He waves a hand, and a holoavatar appears, hovering in the air in front of me—a purple bat with bright yellow eyes.

"Delilah," he says, "Lain wishes to record a message."

"With pleasure, my master," the bat replies in a purring, throaty female voice. She flaps down to perch on his wrist, then turns to me and smiles, showing tiny fangs. "You may begin whenever you're ready."

I thought I knew what I wanted to say, but now my brain is empty. And I probably look as exhausted and wrung out as I feel. I shut my eyes for a moment, gathering my strength, then open them. "My name is Lain Fisher," I say. "And I'm addressing this message to you—to all of you, the people of the United Republic of America."

Delilah's eyes glow a steady yellow. They're fixed on me, recording silently.

"Dr. Swan recently gave an interview in which he called me delusional, paranoid and frightened. These are words that IFEN hurls at anyone who dares to ask questions. I urge you, now—do not let them bully you into submission. It is not just your right, but your moral duty to continue asking questions. It's the obligation of every citizen of every nation to question and scrutinize those in power. We are all born with the right to freedom, but that right doesn't come automatically. It must be defended, and the moment we stop fighting for it is the moment we begin to lose it. It's not an easy choice, and never has been. It's a contract signed in blood."

Why am I using her words?

I push on: "But I urge you all to remember that there is more than one way of fighting. You can be a soldier of freedom without picking up a gun. When you tell others the truth, when you refuse to be silenced, when you stand up and demand that your rights be respected, you're fighting the system. Words are the most powerful weapon we have. As I speak, a bill called the Cognitive Rights Act is making its way toward the National Ethical Committee. It is our job, as a nation, to make sure that it gets there. We must not succumb to the temptation to use tactics of fear and violence. That's what IFEN does. Fear is our enemy . . . and truth is the only power great enough to overcome it." I stop and swallow, mouth dry.

Delilah the bat remains crouched on Zebra's wrist, eyes unblinking.

"That's all I have to say."

Zebra nods. "You may go, Delilah. Thank you."

She bows. "It is, as always, my greatest honor to serve." She vanishes in a flurry of purple sparkles.

"Well, Lain Fisher," Zebra says, rolling my name over his tongue. "You enjoy testing the limits, don't you? You join my organization, then send your entire country a message condemning our methods."

"You promised me you would upload it to the Net."

He inclines his head forward. "I will make sure the people of the URA hear your words. That's a promise. And I always keep my promises."

"Good." There's no way to know for sure that he's telling the truth. I have no choice but to trust him.

I glance toward the bookshelf. Toward Aaron. For the first time, I've erased someone's memories against his will. Even if it was just a few days, even if I saved his life in the process, I feel disgusted with myself—like I just stomped around inside his soul with my muddy boots, leaving tracks everywhere. This is not the sort of work that Mindwalkers were meant to do. Using my skills for Zebra—for the Blackcoats—is a betrayal of everything I believe in. Yet in spite of all that, a part of me almost enjoyed the familiar process of wiping away someone's pain, soothing the ache of trauma.

Suddenly, it hurts to breathe. My chest is knotted with razor wire. "Zebra? I don't want to do this ever again."

"You will, though," he says. "Because otherwise, the task will fall to Ian, and you want to protect him. Isn't that right? Your gentle friend, who's already endured so much suffering on your behalf—"

"Shut up."

"I could tell you a lot of things about Ian. You might be surprised how much darkness lurks behind those brown eyes."

He's playing another game, and I won't let him. I won't betray Ian or violate his privacy by asking questions I shouldn't. "That's for Ian to tell me about, if he wants to."

"Still, you're curious. Aren't you?"

I turn away. "You're no better than Dr. Swan. We're all tools to you."

A long silence stretches between us. "You're right," he says at last, his voice flat and empty. "I intend to use you and control you for my own purposes. Because, you see, I am a desperate man." I look at him, and he smiles, just a tightening of the muscles in his face. "I see what's happening to the world. If things continue along this path, we will find ourselves in a hell worse than all the wars and atrocities of the past, and there will be no hope of escape. The very concept of freedom will vanish. We have only a short while to make a difference, to turn back before it's too late. And our chances are slim. Probably, this is a futile endeavor. But until that last bit of hope is gone, I will continue to fight, and I will be as ruthless as necessary." He leans toward me. "We are fighting for something more important than life itself."

"And what is that?"

"Our souls."

His nails dig into the arms of his chair. His pulse flutters in his throat, and a thin chill slides through me. Zebra is afraid. And suddenly, I think about the words the woman spoke in Aaron's memory. On impulse, I ask, "What is Project Mindstormer? Is it even real?"

"I've seen only bits and pieces of information floating around on the Deep Net. But if it's even half as powerful as the rumors suggest, then once it's complete, no one will be able to stand against IFEN. Unless we stop them first."

I bite the inside of my cheek. "Is it some type of chemical weapon? An airborne neurotoxin? What?"

"I told you. I don't know."

"But you must have *some* ideas, if you've heard about it."

He stares into space. "I saw a statement from a former scientist at IFEN, a woman who resigned several years ago—a matter of conscience, she said. The statement quickly vanished from the Net, and soon afterward, the woman had her memories modified as a form of 'emergency therapy.' Allegedly the treatment was consensual, but . . ." He shrugs. His gaze flicks toward me. "She spoke of a device which, once perfected, could bring an entire country to its knees in a matter of hours. She said that no one, nowhere, would be safe from its reach."

Goosebumps crawl over my skin. "She might have been exaggerating."

"Let's hope she was." He waves a hand toward the door. "You're free to go. I'll summon Nicholas to escort you back to your room."

"I can find my own way."

He shrugs. "As you wish."

As I walk away, I cast a glance over my shoulder. Zebra sits facing away from me, thin shoulders hunched. He looks suddenly very old, very tired.

24

I don't know how long I spend wandering the hallways, turning left and then right and then left again. Eventually, I find my way to the spacious entrance room. The towering entrance doors are closed tight. Next to them, a row of biometric scanners lines the wall: handprint, retinal scan, a few others I don't even recognize. I think about trying them just to see what would happen, but I'm worried about triggering some sort of alarm. And anyway, I know the doors won't open. Even if they did, it wouldn't matter, because as soon as I set foot above ground I'd be recognized and captured.

I turn around, and for a few minutes, I just stand there staring at the words engraved on the wall. MY MIND IS MY ONLY SOVEREIGN. REASON IS MY ONLY COMPASS. EVEN IF FETTERS BIND ME, IN MY THOUGHTS, I AM FREE.

What a joke. We've stumbled from one cage to another.

I lean back against the wall and let my legs give out beneath me, and I slide to the floor, where I sit huddled, hugging my knees. Aaron's memories replay in my head. The rough hands grabbing him from behind, the blows thudding into his body, over and over. I bow my head, shut my eyes, and walk through my compartmentalization exercises. Soon, he'll wake up in some hospital room, and he won't remember any of that. He'll have no idea why he's bruised and bloodied or where he's been over the past few days. Maybe that's a blessing. Or maybe not knowing will be even worse.

A noisy crackle fills the air, and Nicholas' voice emanates from unseen speakers somewhere above me: "Attention, everyone. Please report to the Assembly Hall."

I curl into a tighter ball. I'm not going.

Time goes by in a fog. Footsteps echo, coming toward me, and I raise my head to see Burk—the man with the scar, the one Steven called Captain Constipation—step into the room. He frowns at me, his face pinched and dour, and I can see where he got his nickname. "You're supposed to be at the Assembly. Attendance is mandatory, as I'm sure you're aware."

"I have a headache."

"That's irrelevant."

I'm really not in the mood for this. I push myself to my feet and walk across the room. "I'm going to lie down somewhere." As I brush past him, he grabs my wrist, fingers digging in.

His gaze drills into me. "Perhaps you'd like me to escort you."

"Let me go." When he doesn't, I stomp on his foot. He grunts and tightens his grip. I ram an elbow into his gut, and he doubles over. His grip loosens just long enough for me to twist free. I'm rather impressed with myself. Apparently, the training session with Rhee paid off, after all.

I march forward, down the hall. An arm wraps around my throat, dragging me back, and I gasp. I didn't even hear him coming up behind me. I start to struggle—then freeze as the cold muzzle of a gun presses against my temple.

"Attendance is mandatory," he repeats. "Unless you're at death's door. I have no patience for people who don't take our cause seriously. Do you understand?"

"I understand." I squeeze the word through gritted teeth. He releases me.

"Follow me." He walks briskly down the hall.

I follow, head down, heart pounding. I can still feel the impression of his fingers on my wrist.

*   *   *

The Assembly Hall is packed. I hang in the back of the crowd as Nicholas ascends onto the stage. I spot Ian in the crowd and sidle up next to him. His face is still mottled with bruises, but the swelling has gone down. He gives me a quick smile. I can't bring myself to return it. His smile fades. "Lain, are you—"

"Brothers and sisters!" Nicholas' voice rings through the room. He spreads his arms. "During our last Assembly, I assured you that we would soon be called upon to fight. I realize that you are all impatient. And why not? You have endured injustice and cruelty for far too long. You have submitted to indignity after indignity at the hands of the system, and you want a chance to strike back. Of course. IFEN claims that violence is sickness. Our perspective is that violence is the only natural response to oppression. We do not destroy without meaning. But if someone pushes us, we push back. Hard."

A few whoops of agreement greet this.

"Are you ready to push?"

More shouts of excitement.

Nicholas' smile widens. "Then look, brothers and sisters, upon our next target." An image appears on the screen—a gray, unremarkable-looking warehouse on a city street. The familiar shape of the CN Tower looms in the distance. A brief, puzzled silence falls over the crowd.

"That's right," Nicholas says. "IFEN is stretching its tentacles into this country, now, as well. We've received recent intelligence that IFEN has set up a database to help Canada collect information on its own citizens. What this means, my friends, is that IFEN now has an eye in Toronto . . . and it's only a matter of time before that eye falls upon us. So we will attack first. We will hit them so hard that Dr. Swan himself feels it in the core of his cold, iron heart!"

The crowd erupts in cheering once more. My mouth is dry, my stomach clenched so hard it's starting to cramp. *My fault. My fault.* The words sound inside my skull like a drumbeat. I made it possible for Zebra to break into Aaron's mind. And now, using the information I got from him, the Blackcoats are going to set off more bombs in Toronto. The attack could plunge both Canada or the United Republic, or maybe both, into all-out war with the rebels.

Well, what did you expect? a voice inside me whispers.

"Only a small handful of soldiers will be chosen for this mission," Nicholas continues. "But we will all be there in spirit. And so I ask—are you prepared to give everything, to stain your hands with the blood of our enemies? Are you ready—"

Another voice suddenly fills the Hall, emanating from unseen speakers. "Nicholas? If you don't mind, I'll host the rest of the Assembly today."

Shocked whispers spread like ripples in a pond.

Zebra.

Nicholas stands, frozen. Of course, the *if you don't mind* was just a formality. Zebra has delivered an order—but Nicholas seems reluctant to move. At last, he gives a small bow. "As you wish, my leader." He retreats from the stage.

Zebra's voice booms out, surrounding us: "I'm sure you all recognize my voice. I wish to address you personally today, because I have an important message." He pauses. The silence swells, so deep and thick you could knead it like dough. "Recently, a certain video appeared on the Net. It was quickly removed by government censors, but we were able to download it first. I warn you, these images are disturbing. But they serve as indisputable proof that IFEN is not the civilized, humane organization it claims to be. You're either with them, or you're their enemy. And this is what they do to those they consider enemies."

The screen lights up again, flickering dimly. I realize immediately that I'm looking at a recording of someone's memory; I recognize the fuzzy edges, the shifting center of focus. It's so dark that I have to struggle to make out the image—a room with bare wood walls. A small group of people is huddled in a corner, breathing fast. A loud pounding reverberates through the silence. "Open up," says a low, cold voice. "This is your last warning. If you refuse to cooperate, we will use deadly force."

A girl whimpers. The viewpoint swings to the left, focusing on her face. She clamps a hand over her mouth. Her face is sheet-white, eyes huge with terror. She's no older than sixteen.

The door cracks open. A thin, faint ray of light falls in across the floorboards. An instant later, silhouetted forms burst into the room. I catch a glint off the face shield of a helmet, but it's too dark to make out any details. The thunder of footsteps fills the air. Gunfire rattles. A scream pierces the din as people scramble for cover. A man flops to the floor as an attacker riddles him with bullets. Blood flies through the air and splatters the walls, black in the dimness.

A woman stands and whips out a pistol. Her face is pale and grim, her hair bright red threaded with gray, and in the beam of light falling from the open doorway, I recognize her with a cold shock. It's Ian's mother. Next to me, Ian makes a strangled sound.

She manages to shoot once before the intruders open fire. She falls against the wall, eyes wide and empty, blood staining her chest and hair. Another body falls on top of hers, but I can still see a lock of her hair shining. It's almost the same color as Ian's.

Then the viewpoint swings away, and someone is running down a hall, breathing in ragged sobs. A deep voice shouts, "After him!" More gunfire. More shouts and chaos.

The screen goes dark.

"What you just witnessed," Zebra says, "was a raid. A group of would-be refugees in the URA were hiding out in a safe house on their way to the border. They weren't Blackcoats or terrorists, simply people trying to escape into Canada. But to IFEN, that doesn't matter. To them, all those who try to leave the country are traitors."

I'm shaking. Ian's face is deathly white, his mouth open. I touch his arm and whisper his name. He doesn't respond.

Zebra continues: "Of course, no one in the URA will learn about that incident. It won't be shown on the news. But IFEN's intentions are clear. They are prepared to massacre anyone who defies them or speaks out against them. As Nicholas said, they are now reaching into Canada, trying to establish centers of power here so they can wipe us out. But we will not relent. This—my fellow Blackcoats—is our chance to seize back the land that is our birthright, to claim our place as free and equal citizens of America."

There's a brief silence. Then the crowd erupts in roaring cheers, pumping their fists into the air. They're chanting his name: "*Zebra! Zebra! Zebra!*"

Nicholas stands at the foot of the stage, his expression dark and sullen. I turn to Ian, but he's not there. I didn't even see him leave.

The Assembly Hall suddenly feels hot and stuffy; the air is thick and suffocating. I can't breathe. I turn and push my way through the crowd, into the hallway. Cool air washes over me, and still, I have to fight for every breath. "Ian!" I shout.

Ahead, I hear footsteps, and I start running. I catch a glimpse of him in the hallway ahead and call his name again, but he doesn't slow down. He doesn't even seem to hear me. I keep running until I manage to catch up to him and grab his arm.

He turns to face me. His face is pale and drawn beneath the bruises, his eyes haunted.

"I'm sorry," I whisper. The words feel limp and pathetic. "Sorry" is what you say when you borrow someone's shirt and accidentally get a stain on it. There ought to be a different word for the death of someone's only parent. But it's all I can think to say. "I'm so, so sorry."

His hand curls into a fist. "I knew her Type had started to slip. And then she vanished. But I never thought . . ." He trails off, eyes unfocused. His breathing quickens. "I need to go."

"Where are you going?"

His expression is tight and grim. "To volunteer. I'm going on this mission, whatever it takes."

My stomach turns to lead. "Ian, no. Listen to me. You're grieving. You're not thinking clearly—"

"We came here to fight, didn't we?" His eyes are wild, white around the edges. "If we're not willing to do that, what the hell is the point?"

"This won't bring her back." I grip his shoulders, willing him to understand. "You know people are going to get hurt, right? They're going to set off a bomb in the heart of a major city. There's no way they can do that without endangering innocent civilians. Is this what your mother would have wanted?"

He smiles. It's a horribly bleak, empty, un-Ian-like smile. "Guess I'll never find out." He turns away and keeps walking. I'm left standing alone, feeling small and cold.

I think about Ian's mother, her bloodstained hair and wide, empty eyes, and an ache splits me down the middle. Ian is never going to be the same. IFEN has reached into his soul and gouged a deep scar, broken something inside him. All the anger and frustration that's been building inside me over the past few days suddenly coalesces into a single burning hot point in my center. I want to break something.

Ian and Steven. The two people I care about most are both going on this mission. And I'm going to be left behind.

I can't lose both of them. I won't. I have to do something. I start walking, a fire burning a hole in my gut. I need to find Rhee.

25

In the mess hall, I find Noelle mopping the floor. "Excuse me. Do you know where Rhee is?"

She looks up, blinking. "Um . . ." She bites her thumbnail. "During her free time, she's usually in the training room."

"I'll check there. Thanks."

When I reach the training room, I ease the door open and peer in. Rhee is there, shadowboxing. For a moment, I just watch her. She whirls, kicks and punches invisible opponents with the grace of a dancer. In a single fluid movement, she draws two long knives from sheaths at her hips and thrusts them through the air at an invisible opponent. Swish-swish-swish. The blades cut through empty space, slashing the imaginary enemy to ribbons. Then she spins them through the air, catches them, and slides them back into their sheaths. I wonder how many hours she had to practice to perfect that technique.

I clear my throat.

She spins to face me, every muscle tense and alert, and I'm reminded of a deer hearing the crackle of approaching footsteps.

"Sorry. I didn't mean to startle you. I was just watching. That was really impressive."

Her brows knit together, as if she's confused by the praise. She looks away. "I should have been more on guard. I didn't notice you standing there. If you were an enemy, I'd be dead by now."

So serious. It occurs to me that I've never once seen her smile.

"Did you want to talk to me?" she asks.

"Yes." I take a deep breath, bracing myself. "That mission, the one Nicholas was talking about . . . how many people are going?"

"Six," she replies. "That's all we'll need."

"And how many have already been chosen?"

"Five."

My heartbeat quickens. Steven's already joined, I'm sure, but I might be able to save Ian. "Can I . . ." I stop and take a breath. "Can I go? I mean—I'd like to volunteer."

Her eyebrows lift a tiny bit. "You've never expressed any interest in volunteering before. What's changed?"

"I want to help. That's all."

"You're not very experienced in the field," Rhee says, "and this is a crucial mission."

"I want to prove myself."

Her gaze drills into me. I feel like she's scrutinizing my heart. "Well, your scores are excellent," she says. "Shana and Joy have already been chosen, and they're accustomed to training with you. It might be better to send you rather than someone they barely know. Are you prepared to die for the cause, if it becomes necessary?"

She asks it almost casually, like she's checking off an item on a list. But at those words, something in my chest seizes up.

From the moment I decided to reveal the truth about IFEN, I knew that I'd never be safe again. I knew there was a strong chance that, somewhere along the line, I'd end up getting killed or mindwiped. I've been prepared to die for a long time. But to die for the Blackcoats? That's another matter. Can I honestly say I'm ready for that, that I'd do it without hesitation?

For the Blackcoats, no. But to save Ian . . .

"Yes," I say.

Rhee nods once. "The mission briefing will take place in the Assembly Hall at eight o'clock. Be there." She walks out. I'm left standing alone in the training room as the full weight of my decision sinks into my bones. I might not come back from this alive.

But I have to do something. Ian's protected me and helped me so many times. Now he needs protecting too, even if he might not see it that way. He's in a state of rage and despair—he's on the edge, and he's about to fling himself off. This is the only way I can stop him.

If he finds out why I volunteered, he'll be upset, maybe even furious. But it will be worth it, if I can just keep him alive.

*　　*　　*

When I get to the Hall, a handful of volunteers are already assembled. It's strange to see the vast room mostly empty.

Shana sits on the floor with her arms crossed over her chest, and Brian—the curly-haired boy from Steven's training group—stands next to her. Joy, the short, chubby girl with the braids, is there too. She perches on the edge of the stage, swinging her legs and eating a juicy red apple. My stomach drops when I see Steven standing on the other side of the room. Even if this is what he wants now, I hate the thought of him being thrown into the fray.

"Hello," I say. My voice echoes through the stillness.

Joy waves at me. Her mouth glistens with apple juice. "Hi."

Steven turns toward me, and the color drains from his face. "Lain? What are you doing here?"

I interlace my hands behind my back, feeling suddenly, oddly shy. "I volunteered."

Shana arches an eyebrow. "Well, color me surprised. Maybe you're not completely useless after all. You're not going to piss yourself and start squealing like a scared little piggy once the actual mission starts, are you?"

I decide not to dignify that with a response.

Steven's mouth works silently for a few seconds before he finally squeezes out a single word: "Why?"

I shrug with one shoulder. "I changed my mind. I decided it's time I started participating."

Anger flashes in his eyes, but beneath that, there's a dark, growing void of fear. "Are you trying to prove some kind of point?"

My back stiffens. "No. I'm here for the same reason you are."

"You don't even believe in this war," Steven says.

"You're the one who kept telling me that it's necessary to fight back," I snap, losing patience. "Well, here I am. What's the problem? Isn't this what you wanted? Or did you just want me to agree with you?"

Brian rolls his eyes. "Can we keep the lover's quarrel out of this?"

I wince. "We're not . . ." The words die in my throat. My face burns. What *are* Steven and I? I don't even know anymore.

"You're not even qualified for this mission," Steven says, ignoring Brian's remark.

I grit my teeth. Now he's just being petty. "I'm absolutely qualified for it. My training scores are probably better than yours."

"And if you have to shoot at a real person instead of a holo? What then?"

"Enough, all of you," Rhee snaps. "Lain has made her choice. It's not your place or anyone else's to tell her whether she should or shouldn't be here."

I look at her in surprise. Rhee is the last person I expected to jump to my defense.

Steven glares at her. "I'm not—"

"One more word from either of you, and you'll be dropped from the mission."

His face flushes, and he presses his lips together.

An ache fills my chest. A part of me can't help feeling that Steven is right—I don't really belong here. *Ian is safe,* I remind myself.

There's a rustle of movement behind me. I turn . . . and freeze.

Ian stands in the doorway. "Am I late?" He smiles with one corner of his mouth. Then his gaze lands on me, and the smile falls away. The color drains from his face.

My mouth works silently for a few seconds before I find my voice. "What are you doing here? The mission is full."

Rhee strides forward. "I heard from Zebra just a few minutes ago." She touches her earpiece. "He said there'd be one more participant coming."

"I made a case to him," Ian says. He's still pale, looking dazed. "He told me he didn't need any more volunteers, but I said that I wanted more than anything to go on this mission. He made an exception for me."

"We only really need six bombs to blow up the facility," Rhee remarks. "But it couldn't hurt to have an extra, in case one of them fails."

I feel strangely empty. My volunteering was all for nothing. I couldn't save him, after all. And it's too late for me to change my mind now—not that I even want to. The two people I care about most are going. If it fails, I don't want to be left alone. I force a smile onto my face. "Welcome to the team."

"I don't understand," he whispers.

"We've already been through this," Rhee says flatly. "Lain has made the decision to join this mission, and she's staying. That's that."

Ian sways on his feet, eyes wide. He looks like he might collapse. And for a moment, I almost regret my decision to come.

But maybe if I'm there, I can help protect him . . . and Steven, too. I can't lose either of them.

Rhee walks to the base of the stage and stands, facing us. She pulls out a remote control and presses a button. The enormous wall-screen winks on, displaying a mazelike array of hallways, certain spots marked with green X's. A map. "This is the facility." She waves the remote control, manipulating a holo cursor until it hovers in the center of the screen. "This area is the database. We're going to be planting bombs in six different locations around its perimeter. We'll each carry one. We'll go in through this entrance, here." She points. "Then we'll split up, which will reduce our chances of being taken down by guards. Though, if all goes according to plan, the building will be empty. There's a station up front where the guards monitor the interior and the surrounding area by camera; we have a contact there who's supposed to slip them a sedative. Another contact will hack in and temporarily disable the security system. All we have to do is get in, plant the bombs, and get out before anyone realizes what's happened. Just like a training drill. The bombs will be detonated as soon as we're safely out of range. They're very powerful, so even if we don't all make it to the target, we should still be able to take out the database."

She makes it sound simple. Of course, if something goes wrong, we'll all be killed or captured.

Brian raises his hand.

"Yes?"

"How will we get in without attracting attention? Isn't there a fence around the building?"

"A cleaning supply truck is scheduled to arrive this morning," she says. "We'll be inside that truck." She presses another button, and different routes light up with different colors. "Each of you will be assigned a specific route. Memorize it. We'll be wearing our communication helmets, which will contain a map, but this will go a lot more smoothly if you don't have to pause and think about where you're going. Lain, you'll be the green route."

She keeps talking as I study the route—only a few turns, so there's not much chance of getting lost. I can feel Ian's and Steven's gazes on me, a pressure against my skin. Ignore them, I tell myself. Focus. I'll need all my concentration for this.

After going over the routes, one by one, Rhee deactivates the screen. "We'll leave the Citadel at 4 a.m. Go back to your rooms and get some rest. You'll need it."

I leave the room, walking quickly, not looking back. We only have time for a few hours of sleep before the mission.

Behind me, I hear footsteps and freeze.

"Lain . . ."

I turn slowly to face Ian. His expression sags with weariness. I wonder if he's told anyone that the woman in the recording was his mother, or if I'm the only one who understands the real reason he volunteered.

He opens his mouth, closes it, then starts again. "I won't try to talk you out of this. Because I know it won't work. I just wanted to say . . ." The muscles of his throat work as he swallows. He looks at me, and I see the longing in his eyes. The pain.

"What?" I whisper.

He drops his gaze and shakes his head. "I'll tell you when we get back."

Before I can respond, he turns and walks away.

I don't see Steven anywhere. Maybe he's already gone back to his room. Probably, he's still angry at me—even though, logically, he should be delighted with this turn of events. I can't leave things like this, can I? I need to say something to him.

I make my way toward the dormitory wing. I can't feel my legs; I have the sense that I'm drifting down the hallway like a ghost. I stop in front of Steven's door, and knock. "Steven?" No answer. I try again; still nothing. Where is he?

I retreat into my room and lie down, staring at the ceiling. Rhee said to get some rest. I should probably take her advice, though I know I won't be able to sleep. The details of the mission replay through my head over and over. When I close my eyes, the map hovers in bright lines against my eyelids.

Tomorrow, I will become a terrorist. We'll strike back against IFEN. We'll stain our hands with blood.

I think about all the horrible things IFEN has done to Steven, to Rhee, to Father. I think about the collars, about Somnazol, trying to make myself angry enough to blot out the fear, trying to fill my veins with rebellious fire. But the fear remains—a hard, cold center.

There's a knock on my door. Thinking it must be Steven, I sit up and call, "Come in."

The door opens. It's Rhee. In one hand, she grasps a tattered black trench coat. In the other, she holds a pistol. It's large and old, its metal dull and tarnished. "These are for you."

Slowly, I stand.

She approaches and hands me the coat. The leather is old and butter-soft against my fingers. I study the high collar, the long sleeves. There are no designs, no frills; it's a simple, functional coat, but it has its own stark beauty. Wearing this, maybe, I could *feel* like a revolutionary. Still, I don't put it on. "Have you seen Steven?" I ask instead.

She shrugs. "He's sulking. He didn't expect you to join the mission and he doesn't like the idea of you being in danger."

Of course; he made a promise to keep me safe. Though that feels like an eternity ago. Despite the emotional wall between us, he still takes that promise seriously. Is that why he's angry? "He wants to protect me," I murmur.

"It doesn't work that way," she says. "We're all soldiers, and no one's life is prioritized above the cause. I explained that to him after the briefing."

A tiny smile tugs at my lips. "Somehow, I don't think he was very receptive. He doesn't like being told what to do." My smile fades. "I thought he'd be happy about me joining."

"Just give him some time. He'll get over it."

The words should reassure me, but all I can think is that Steven and Rhee must be even closer than I imagined. She's grown to know him so well over such a short time. I swallow. "Rhee . . . is Steven . . . I mean, are you and he . . ." I can't bring myself to ask it aloud.

Rhee just stares, a small furrow in her brow. Apparently, she's not going to help me fill in the blanks.

A quiet sigh escapes me. "Never mind." I need to focus. I'm about to venture into the field of battle. Well, okay, not exactly—I'll be sneaking around in an empty building to plant a bomb, which sounds a bit less noble. Regardless, if my head is clouded with relationship drama, I'll likely end up dead. Whatever is going on between the two of them, we can sort it out once we've all gotten back alive.

I turn my attention back to the black leather coat in my hands. There's a bullet hole in the chest. I run my thumb over the small, ragged aperture. "Who wore this before me?"

"I did," Rhee says. "I outgrew it. Look." She pulls down the collar of her shirt, revealing the puckered white scar just beneath her collarbone. "I was shot during one of my first missions."

My eyes widen. "You're okay with me having this?"

"I wouldn't have given it to you if I wasn't." She hands me the pistol. "This is a Beretta. For your build, I think, something small would work better. After the mission, it will be yours to keep."

I curl my fingers around the grip. It fits neatly in my hand, but it's heavy compared to the plastic training gun. I slide it into the holster at my hip, uncomfortably conscious of its weight, and button up the coat. The buttons are silver, faded to the same tarnished, matte patina as the pistol.

She nods toward the adjoining bathroom. "Take a look at yourself."

I step inside and look at myself in the mirror. In the black coat, I look like another person, someone dangerous and wild, and I understand why the Blackcoats chose this as their symbol, their namesake. The leather whispers against my skin; it smells, very faintly, of gun smoke and blood. Perhaps it's my imagination. "It's . . ." I trail off, not sure what to say. *Beautiful* doesn't quite fit, but it's certainly something. "It's a good coat. Thank you."

"You've earned it. And you wear it well."

A flush rises into my cheeks. Everything about her makes me uneasy, yet a part of me still craves her approval. I wish I understood why. "Thank you."

She nods and starts to turn. "I'll see you tomorrow."

"Rhee—"

She stops.

"Why did you agree to let me go on this mission? I mean, you were right. I'm not very experienced."

Her sharp green eyes flick toward me. The bronze flecks catch the light. "I saw that you'd come to a decision. You wanted to demonstrate your commitment, and that's something I respect." Her gaze cuts away. "Zebra was reluctant. He doesn't want to send you into the field, because your skills are valuable to him. He'd prefer not to risk your safety. But I told him that you couldn't truly be one of us until you'd stained your hands. And once you've crossed that line, you can't ever truly go back."

God, what have I gotten myself into? I swallow, mouth dry. "And Ian?"

"Same reason, more or less. Two Mindwalkers. A valuable asset to us, but only if your hearts are committed. This will burn out your uncertainties, make you like metal purified by flame . . . assuming, of course, that you don't crack. But I don't believe you will."

"Glad to hear it," I mutter, staring at my feet.

She cups my chin, lifting it, and I tense in surprise. I see myself reflected in the centers of her clear, brilliant eyes. "I see the warrior in you. Even if you don't."

Once she's gone, I sit on the edge of the bed, staring into space. I take out my gun and hold it, feeling its heft. The power of life and death in my hands—a terrible power.

26

Green numbers glow on my wristwatch. 5:15 a.m.

I sit in the back of a truck, the pistol tucked in its holster. I'm carrying a faded black backpack, like everyone else. Next to me, Joy wriggles in her seat like a puppy. I'm not sure if it's excitement or nervousness or both. We're all huddled together in the dimly lit space, breathing quietly.

An hour ago, before we left the Citadel, Rhee handed us each a bomb—a simple black cube no larger than a softball—and said, "You activate these by pressing in the code on the top panel, four-four-nine-one. The bomb will detonate ten minutes after activation. These are a new technology, designed by Zebra himself. Extremely powerful. Needless to say, do not activate them until you're absolutely sure you're ready."

Ian gives me a nervous smile, which I return. Steven hasn't looked at me or spoken to me once since the briefing last night. He seems determined to pretend that I'm not here. I have an urge to step on his foot or start poking him in the face like a child, just to make him acknowledge me. I might do it, if silence wasn't crucial to our success.

Rhee sits very still, eyes closed, legs folded in front of her, hands resting on her knees with the palms up, as if she's meditating. Maybe she is.

The truck slows, and I hear the creak of a gate opening. A few seconds later, we pull forward. We're inside the fence. Almost there.

My heart punches my sternum. I'm very conscious of each beat. It feels like a countdown. If I die tonight, I have a finite number of them left. No. I need to stop thinking like that. We can do this. I know the layout of the facility by heart; I can see the map traced in my head when I close my eyes. The plan is perfect. As long as we all do our part, it won't fail.

My breathing echoes through the confines of the truck. It's so loud, I feel sure that everyone within a mile of us can hear it.

The truck jolts and lurches to a stop. Silence falls over us, thick and oppressive. We sit in darkness, waiting. Then the doors of the truck creak open, revealing a wide, empty parking lot surrounding a plain gray building. The truck is parked close to the back of the building, near a row of dumpsters and a pair of wide metal doors. It's still dark out, not yet dawn, though I can see a pale glow on the horizon.

Rhee climbs out of the truck and motions for us to follow. We hustle out, single file. She kicks the doors, and they swing inward, revealing a dark, empty hallway. Rhee gives us a nod, and we enter, guns drawn. Silence covers everything like a layer of dust. Dimly, I can make out nondescript gray walls and a beige-tiled floor. Earlier, Rhee told us that the security system had already been disabled. Still, this feels too easy.

Don't think. I just have to plant the bomb and get out. A map appears in glowing blue lines on the visor of my helmet, and I follow my route, breaking off from the others and veering down another, narrower hallway. The silence is deafening. There's only the dull thump-thump of my footsteps and the rattle of my heart in my chest. Fear presses against the walls of my mind, trying to overwhelm me, to paralyze me.

I pretend that I'm back in the training room, running through a simulation. Just another day at the Citadel.

The blinking dot on my visor-map moves slowly, slowly up a hallway toward the target, which is marked with a bright green X. *Almost there—*

"*Freeze!*"

Two figures in dark clothes leap in front of me, blocking the hallway. In the near-darkness, I can't make out their features, but I can see the guns in their hands.

"Don't move!" a deep voice barks.

There's no time to think. My body moves automatically as I turn and bolt in the other direction, zigzagging to make myself a more difficult target, as I learnt in training. Gunshots go off just as I round a corner. Adrenaline shoots through me, making me run faster than I thought myself capable of. They were waiting for me. *A trap.* Are the other hallways blocked off too?

More gunshots go off. I ignore them and keep running blindly. "Lain!" a voice cries out. I whip my head to one side and see Brian stumble from an adjacent hallway, his face pale and bathed in sweat, his eyes huge and twitching back and forth. "They were waiting for me," he gasps out.

"Me too."

"What do we—"

"Run." Unthinkingly, I grab his hand, and we keep running. I hear other voices shouting in the darkness—there's Joy, tears streaking her small round face, and there's Steven, grim and silent. When his eyes lock with mine, I see a flash of relief on his face.

"Have you seen Ian?" I call out.

His expression closes off. "No."

"We have to find—"

"We can't afford to wait," he says. "Keep moving. The mission's been aborted. We have to get out of here."

"I'm not leaving without him!"

"He's probably waiting for us at the exit. *Go!*" Steven grabs my arm and drags me forward.

Finally, we come to the open doors, and I stumble through.

Glaring halogen lights snap on, dazzling my eyes. I fling up my hands, shielding my face. A row of figures stands about twenty feet away, aiming guns at my face. Beyond them, red and blue lights flash. Police cars, parked in a jagged row across the huge, cracked parking lot surrounding the plain gray building. I can see more armed figures standing outside the cars. My stomach sinks. The building is completely surrounded.

"Put your hands in the air," a woman calls. When I don't move, she snaps, "*Now!*"

Then the *rat-tat-tat-tat* of a machine gun rings out, and the police fall in a row, like dominos. I spin around to see Rhee charging out of the building, calmly mowing them down.

"Run," she says. She marches forward, spraying bullets. Some of the officers return fire; some duck behind the vehicles, hiding. But none of them is fast enough. Bodies flop to the pavement like dolls. Screams slice through my ears.

"Come on!" Brian shouts. He charges, brandishing his rifle. We all follow, pouring out into the cold, dark morning, feet pounding the pavement. My body seems to be moving in slow motion through a blurry chaos of lights and yelling. Someone throws a small object, and clouds of foul-smelling orange smoke belch into the air, burning my nostrils and tear ducts. It's like breathing in poisonous nettles. Tears flood my eyes, blinding me.

More gunfire rattles. Brian goes down, his chest stained with blood. He gurgles once, then falls silent.

I'm going to die within the next ten seconds. The thought is strangely clear, strangely calm. My body keeps moving forward, feet pushing off the pavement, propelling me through the dreamy unreality of smoke and lights and gunfire. It seems like I should be petrified, but I feel disconnected from my body, my fear. It's remarkable, the mind's ways of protecting itself.

Ian is running beside me. Ian! His face is pale, cast in harsh shadow, his eyes enormous. Shana howls like a wounded animal, charging straight ahead and spraying bullets as she goes. A shot clips her shoulder. She stumbles but keeps going, plowing through clouds of smoke, and disappears.

"Lain!" Steven shouts. "Behind you!"

I spin around and find myself staring into the dark muzzle of a gun. The man at the other end is wearing mirrored shades that reflect my own terrified face back at me. "Put your hands up!" he brays. My body reacts automatically; I whip up my pistol and fire. Blood blossoms from the man's shoulder, and he staggers backward and falls to his knees. The gun slips from his fingers, and he clutches his wounded shoulder, squeezing curses between his teeth.

I shot someone. I shot someone.

The gun slips from my hands. Breathing fast, I turn and start to run. I don't even know where I'm going, just that I have to get out of here. The smoke scours my lungs, choking me. A thin stream of bile surges up my throat and into my mouth, and I double over, retching onto the pavement, then keep running. I nearly trip over a body; I look down, into wide, glassy dark eyes. Joy. Blood spreads on the pavement beneath her head. I stop, transfixed.

Minutes ago, she was running alongside me. Now she's dead. This seems like a logical fallacy, somehow, like an error that will be rectified at any moment.

Beside me, I hear a ragged sob. I snap out of my trance and spin around. Ian is on his hands and knees, his body shaking so hard, it looks like he's having a seizure. I grab his arm and pull him upright. "Come on!" I scream close to his ear. Then we're running, feet hammering the pavement, toward the fence. It's about eight feet high, chain link. We might be able to climb over—

A shot rings out, and he stumbles. I scream his name.

269

"Don't stop," he gasps. His leg is bleeding. He lurches forward another few steps, then cries out in pain and collapses.

Men in uniforms are running toward us, pistols aimed. I reach for my gun, but it isn't there. Oh God. Did I drop it? Why did I do that?

"Run!" Ian's eyes are wide, desperate. He lies on the ground, clutching his wounded leg.

Time slows. I have just a second or two to make a decision. If I run, I can escape. But they'll kill him.

Then rough hands grab me from behind and drag me away, behind an empty police car. I struggle instinctively. "Hold still!" It's Steven.

He yanks a grenade out of his backpack, pulls out the pin with his teeth, and flings it. It hits the fence and explodes with deafening thunder and blinding fire, blasting bits of chain link in every direction. A sharp bit of metal flies past me, nicking my cheek. He yanks me toward the billowing cloud of smoke, then through it, and suddenly we're in the street, surrounded by fog and looming brick buildings. Most of them look like abandoned warehouses and factories. He pulls me into an alley, behind a dumpster. His hand covers my mouth, stifling my cry.

We crouch behind the dumpster, motionless. I pant against his palm, straining my eyes upward so I can see his face. He stares straight ahead, face pale and dripping with sweat. Gunshots bark, and a woman screams. In the distance, sirens wail as more police flock to the scene.

Steven moves in a crouch, crab-like, along the wall, dragging me with him. We round a corner. Then he lurches to his feet and starts running, pulling me along. His fingers are clamped around my arm. We duck down another narrow street and run between chain link fences and lots filled with broken glass. In a tiny cement yard, a black dog strains against a chain and barks at me, pink tongue flapping.

"Steven," I pant, "we have to go back. The others—"

"We can't go back." He doesn't look at me. His pulse flutters in his throat.

"You're just going to abandon them? What about Rhee? What about Ian?"

He doesn't answer.

We keep running. I don't have a choice; his fingers are anchored into my arm like claws, and I stumble along behind him. Each breath sears my lungs. A deep stitch throbs like a knife buried in my side. When Steven slows to catch his breath, I elbow him, hard, in the side. He loosens his grip in surprise, and I pull free. "What the hell is wrong with you?" I shout.

"There was nothing we could have done!" he shouts back, eyes wild and bloodshot. Beads of sweat stand out on his forehead; a vein pulses at his temple. "We walked right into a trap. We had no chance against them. If we hadn't run, we'd be dead or captured."

"I'd rather be dead or captured than be a coward who left my friends to die!"

He flinches back, and instantly, I regret the words. Then his expression goes blank. "Hate me if you want. But I'm not going to let them get you, too."

We stand in the alley, staring at each other.

"We've got to find our way Underground." He turns and keeps walking. His rifle is gone; he must have lost it in the chaos.

I follow him. Shame burns in my gut like acid, eating a hole through my insides. Deep down, I know that Steven did the only thing he could do. But still, I hate the fact that we ran and left them behind. I think about Ian's warm smile, about Rhee handing me her coat, telling me I'd earned it. A scream builds up in my chest, and I choke it down.

Thunder breaks apart the air, and the ground vibrates beneath my feet. I stumble and fall against Steven. "What was that?" I ask, breathless.

He doesn't answer. He's staring at the sky, where a dark column of smoke rises toward the clouds. "Well," Steven says, "I guess someone managed to set off one of the bombs."

I can still see the outline of the warehouse—the column of smoke is to the left of it. The bomb wasn't detonated inside the facility, so it probably didn't damage the database. Whoever set it off must have been trying to create a diversion so the others could escape. I just hope it worked.

Another explosion rocks the air. More smoke rises, thick and black as tar, filling the sky. Even from this distance, it sears my lungs.

"Lain," Steven whispers. He sounds a little unsteady. "You see that?"

I look up, and my stomach drops. There's a huge face in the sky, projected on the clouds of smoke. At first, I don't recognize the girl staring down at the city—a girl with pale skin and large, haunted eyes, a girl with short, ragged brown hair. Then a voice echoes through the fiery dawn, amplified by unseen speakers, booming and ominous, the voice of a vengeful goddess. A small, choked sound escapes my throat.

It's me.

"We are all born with the right to freedom," says my sky-self. "But that right doesn't come automatically. It must be defended, and the moment we stop fighting for it is the moment we begin to lose it. It's not an easy choice, and never has been. It's a contract signed in blood."

I press a hand to my heart. The recording loops back and starts again. My face looms against the billowing smoke clouds, lit from behind by the blazing orange glow.

Well, Zebra promised me that everyone would hear my words. He kept that promise, all right. This will probably be on every news station. It will be seen throughout the URA and Canada. Of course, he conveniently left out the part where I urged people not to resort to violence.

A high, thin ringing fills my ears, and my vision fades around the edges. I seem to be falling into a deep hole inside myself.

And then suddenly I'm on my back, blinking up at the sky.

"Lain!" Steven's face fills my vision. He pats my cheek.

The world tilts, then reasserts itself. Did I faint? I sit up, touch the back of my head, and wince. That's going to leave a lump.

Steven's arms surround me, pulling me close. "Come on," he murmurs in my ear. "Let's get out of here."

I walk numbly, letting him guide me. The giant face in the sky has finally disappeared. Maybe the police found the projector and destroyed it.

"Look." Steven points, and I see a Z spray-painted on a manhole cover. He crouches, grabs the edge, and strains to pull it aside, but it doesn't budge. "Help me."

My body doesn't want to move. I feel like something inside me has shut off. The distant wail of sirens catches my ears. If we don't get Underground very soon, the police will find us. I pinch the soft inside of my wrist and twist, and the pain is a sharp jolt. The world shifts, and everything snaps into focus.

I crouch and grip the other side of the manhole cover. We pull. The metal disc slides to one side with a scraping grind, revealing a cement hole and iron rungs leading down into darkness. We descend into a subway tunnel. Steven hauls the manhole cover back into place and jumps down, skipping the last few rungs to land beside me. A flashlight beam cuts through the darkness. "Hey . . ." Fever-hot fingers touch my cheek. "You okay?"

How am I supposed to answer that question? "I'll survive."

The flashlight beam sweeps over a wall covered with tangles of graffiti and streaks of glistening wetness.

"Do you know which way to go?" I ask.

"Sort of."

We walk past campfires, past the huddled groups of people in makeshift blanket tents. A scruffy yellow cat sits, watching us with eerily brilliant orange eyes. Nearby, its owner—a bearded man with scars instead of eyes—plays a beat-up saxophone. The low, mournful strains fill the tunnel.

I follow Steven numbly. We're in the tunnels for a while—my sense of time is distorted, so it's difficult to say how long, but I think it's at least a few hours. We pass a cluster of dirty mattresses filled with sleeping people. In one tunnel, a giggling young couple are kissing, their hands inside each other's shirts. When they spot us, they dash away like startled rabbits, disappearing into the shadows. Just when I start to think we're going in circles, I look up, and we're standing before the towering doors of the Citadel.

Steven balls up a fist and bangs on the doors. "Hey! Let us in!" We wait, and after a minute or two, the doors creak open.

Nicholas stands there, flanked by two armed Blackcoats. His lips are set in a hard line. "So. You're all that's left."

My heart sinks. "You mean none of the others has come back?"

"Just because they haven't doesn't mean they won't," Steven says.

"Don't stand in the doorway. We're not heating the entire Underground, you know." Nicholas beckons, curling a white-gloved finger.

We enter the Citadel, and the doors swing shut behind us. An image of Ian's terrified expression fills my head, and suddenly, it hurts to breathe. He has to be alive. He *has* to. I won't allow myself to think otherwise.

"Well," Nicholas says, "we might as well get this over with now." He nods to the two armed Blackcoats. "Take her in for questioning."

I back away. "Questioning?"

The Blackcoats advance toward us.

Steven tenses. "What the hell is this?"

They don't answer. They just keep coming. Steven swings a fist at one, and the man tackles him, pinning his arms behind his back.

"Let him go!" I shout.

274

The other man pulls a hypodermic from his pocket. He grabs hold of my arm, and I struggle, panting. "Hold still," he says. "The more you cooperate, the sooner this will be over with."

There's a small, sharp sting in my neck, and blackness pounces.

27

I wake in a strange room, bound to a chair. My head throbs, and thirst claws at my throat. I swallow, and a tiny stab of pain goes through the raw flesh. It takes all my willpower just to open my eyes a crack. The world swims, blurry, and my brain is swaddled in gauze. Am I drugged?

Leather straps dig into my wrists and ankles, painfully tight. More straps run across my chest and stomach. It's mostly dark, so it's difficult to see how large the room is. Something pinches my brow and presses against the crown of my head. A helmet. A *Gate*.

Another chair stands across from me, lit by a bright, glaring overhead light. Nicholas sits in the chair, legs crossed.

"What is this?" My voice comes out a weak croak. I'm trying, unsuccessfully, not to panic. "What's going on?"

The harsh overhead glare transforms his face into a mask of light and shadows. "You're aware of what happened during the recent mission?"

I don't answer, because it's a rhetorical question. Obviously I'm aware. I was there. I wait, but he doesn't seem inclined to say anything else. "What about it?"

"All the participants have been captured, except for you and Steven. As we speak, the prisoners are locked inside Area 9. The Canadian officials are negotiating with IFEN to have them returned to the URA, where their memories will be scanned for information. After that, they will likely be mindwiped."

"No," I whisper. My eyes fill with tears, and one spills down my cheek, a warm trail.

But they're alive. I cling to that thin thread of hope. If they're alive, there's a chance of rescuing them.

"Everything was carefully arranged," Nicholas says. "The plan should have gone smoothly. So why do you suppose there were police cars waiting for you?"

Again, he waits, as if he expects me to answer. "I don't know."

"Really? You don't?" He widens his eyes in mock puzzlement.

I'm shaking now, angry and confused and terrified. I try to focus on the anger. "Is this some kind of game? How would I know?"

"Well, that's the question." He folds his long fingers in front of him, his eyes never leaving my face. "We're trying to figure out how the authorities knew what we were planning. The only thing I can think of is that someone—some very naughty person—found a way to alert them. Do you realize what this means?" He leans forward and grips my chin between a thumb and forefinger. I tense. He smiles, his eyes like crystals of blue ice.

I swallow. "Let go of me."

His grip tightens, claw-like fingers pressing deep into my flesh, into the bone. My eyes water. "Do you know what I think, Lain? I think it's you. I think the little canary had a change of heart and decided to start singing to the other side. That's what you do, isn't it? You sing and sing. You can't keep anything to yourself. It all just dribbles out of you, doesn't it?"

My head swims. The room spins around me, like I'm trapped on a carousel careening out of control. A weak sound escapes my throat.

"Now you're going to sing for me," Nicholas says. "You're going to show us the truth. Let's review some of your memories, shall we?"

Zebra must be on the other end of this Gate. He's probably observing my thoughts right now. Anger mounts inside me, despite the blinding terror. After all he's put me through, how could he do this? How could he *dare*? "No."

Nicholas narrows his eyes.

"Zebra's already rummaged through my head once. He knows I'm trustworthy. Why is he doing this? Did you talk him into it?"

He backhands me across the face, hard enough that my head rocks back and my ears ring.

I glare at him through the haze of drugs, my face stinging, and visualize a solid brick wall blocking my thoughts and memories. I'm done playing games. I've compromised my principles for them, fought for them, nearly died for them. I'm not giving them anything else.

"Show us. Show us how you betrayed us, Lain." He backhands me again, and a flashbulb goes off behind my left eye, momentarily clearing the fog. "Stop resisting."

It's a struggle to form even a single word. "No."

He rises from his chair and paces around me, a hard gleam in his eyes. He's actually drooling a little, like a rabid animal. He wipes the back of one hand across his lips. "I don't believe you." He seizes my hand and starts to bend my index finger backward. I let out a choked scream. He stops. "A little more pressure, and the bone will snap," he whispers close to my ear, like he's talking to a lover. "So what will it be?"

I clench my jaws against the pain. He bends the finger back a little farther, and my vision goes white. But still, I keep my head empty, keep the brick wall in place. They can do whatever they want to me, but I won't cooperate. I won't make it easier for them. Nicholas applies a little more pressure, and I sob once, a hoarse bleat.

"That's enough, Nicholas," Zebra's voice calls from the shadows. Nicholas releases me. He rolls forward, into the circle of light around the table, and removes his helmet. His face is drawn and ashen. "Let me speak to her alone."

Nicholas scowls and opens his mouth, but Zebra raises a hand, forestalling his protests. "Undo her restraints."

Nicholas hesitates, then unbuckles my straps.

Zebra sets his helmet on Nicholas' now-empty chair. "Go."

"You're too soft on them, you know," Nicholas says. "If you let me break a few fingers, I could get some real answers."

Zebra's slender shoulders stiffen. He turns his face toward Nicholas, eyes narrowed to a hard line. "I will decide what is too soft. Remember who found you in the gutter, half-starved, with your eyes scratched out and bleeding from a fight with some other Underground brat. Who fed you, Nicholas? Who gave you top-of-the-line artificial eyes because you kept crying about being scared of the dark?"

Nicholas' face flushes brick red. He storms out of the room, slamming the door.

Zebra and I face each other. Slowly, he reaches out, unbuckles my helmet, and pulls it off. Cool air washes over my sweat-damp scalp. "I'm sorry for this," he says. "You are correct. It was Nicholas who urged me to do this. I don't truly believe you're the one who leaked that information to the police, but I let him plant a seed of doubt in my head." He sets the helmet on the chair, next to his own.

My head throbs dully; it's a struggle to focus. "That was a nasty trick you pulled," I say. "With my face in the sky. Twisting my words."

"I never promised you that I'd play the entire message."

"Next time you promise something, I'm going to pay very close attention to your wording."

The faintest ghost of a smile twitches across his lips. "Personally,

I thought it was very effective. Very dramatic. All that fire and smoke. You were like an avenging angel."

I glare at him. "How many people died tonight? Do you even care?"

He lets out a small sigh. "Odd, how you're so torn up over the deaths the Blackcoats have caused, yet you don't feel the same level of horror over the countless deaths engineered by IFEN. And I don't just mean the experiments. You have to take Somnazol into account. How many more thousands of human lives will have to disappear before you will acknowledge the necessity of what we're doing?"

My thoughts are fuzzy, and my face throbs, and the last thing I want to do is have another debate with Zebra. "I hate Somnazol. I always have. You know that. But it isn't the same. A humane, painless drug that people take voluntarily isn't the equivalent of blowing someone up or riddling them with bullets."

He arches one slender brow. "You don't know, do you?"

I wish he'd just stop talking. Still, I can't help asking, "Know what?"

"You're aware of how Somnazol is *supposed* to work, I'm sure. The first layer induces a state of euphoria. The second renders the person unconscious. The third paralyzes all their muscles, including the heart. Or at least, that's what they say. Except the second layer of the drug—the sedative—wears off before the person is entirely dead. They wake up, paralyzed, unable to move or scream, and feel the poison burning out their insides."

A chill ripples through me. It has to be a lie. IFEN's done terrible, cruel things in the past, but they always did them for a reason, a goal—not out of sadism. "That doesn't make any sense. Why would they—"

"It wasn't deliberate. It was a miscalculation. By the time they discovered the error, it would have been costly and difficult to completely reconfigure the chemical formula . . . and of course, if they recalled the existing drug, people would know they'd made a mistake. They weren't willing to risk looking bad and losing public support. So they did nothing. They believed that no one would ever find out the truth, since those who experience the effects firsthand always die."

No. No, that's crazy. "Why should I believe you?"

"It doesn't matter whether you believe me or not. But the Blackcoats have known this for a long time, ever since hackers found the information in IFEN's private database and leaked it on the Deep Net. Classic IFEN. As long as suffering happens silently, out of sight, then to them, it's not real."

I gulp, pulse fluttering in my throat. Why does the revelation rattle me so much? After learning about IFEN's illegal experimentation and secret police, this shouldn't be surprising. But this . . . this is somehow even worse. A dozen ads spill into my head like a deck of playing cards—a calm-faced woman staring out over the words, *My life, my choice*. A soft pink sunset under the words, *When all else fails, a gentle sleep is the kindest answer*. A pink pill alongside the tagline, *Dignified, painless, humane. Ask your doctor*. I think about all those vulnerable, depressed people seeing the pretty ads and succumbing to the temptation of oblivion, swallowing the pills and closing their eyes to drift off to sleep.

I imagine those same people waking up paralyzed, helpless, their bodies on fire, spending their last moments in silent agony, unable even to scream. That would have been Steven's fate, if I hadn't reached him in time. That terrifying night is still fresh in my memory—the moment I saw him crumpled on the floor and knew what he had done.

"Now, tell me, Lain," he continues calmly. "Do you know anything about why the police were waiting for you?"

"I was there." I squeeze the words through clenched teeth. "I could have been killed. My friends could have been killed. Ian was captured. Do you really think I helped set this up?"

"That's what I'm asking."

I glare at him, my mouth loose and trembling. "No. I don't know anything."

"Do you have any idea who the traitor might be?"

My gaze jerks angrily away. "No."

"Look at me, Lain."

I don't. He cups my chin in one gloved hand, the touch almost gentle. His clear gray eyes find mine, and I can't look away. After a long moment, he nods, releases me, and leans back. One by one, he unbuckles the straps holding me to the chair.

I try to push myself to my feet, but suddenly, the exhaustion and the weight of sedatives is too much to bear. My legs are jelly, and my head is filled with cement. It takes all my effort just to hold it up. "What now?" I mutter.

"Now? We keep moving forward with the plan. We don't have much time left."

"Time before what? What plan?" My voice cracks with exhaustion. "You people keep talking about some grand plan, but no one seems to have the slightest idea what it is. I'm starting to wonder if even you know, or if you're just making things up as you go along."

"Oh, there is a plan. When the time is right, I will reveal everything."

"So what are you waiting for? Whatever you're going to do, why not just do it?"

"We need more soldiers," he says firmly. "What do you think all these rescue missions are about? The greater our numbers, the greater our chance of success when we strike."

"You're far too candid with her," Nicholas calls from outside the room. "You haven't even told me all the details, and now you're spilling your guts to one of IFEN's trained monkeys? What is it about her, anyway? Do you have a thing for girls her age?"

Zebra gives a derisive snort. "Don't be absurd."

"Then what?"

"If you're going to eavesdrop, Nicholas, you may as well come in."

After a brief pause, Nicholas enters. He's literally pouting, his lower lip pushed out like a sullen toddler's.

"Help her to her room," Zebra says. "She'll have difficulty walking."

"Wait." I swallow. "You're—you're going to rescue them, aren't you? The captives?"

Zebra's thin shoulders stiffen. "From Area 9? That's impossible."

Somewhere beneath the lethargic heaviness, anger stirs, a weak flame. "Don't you even care? They're your soldiers."

He's silent, lips tight. When I look into his eyes, I see pain there. His fingers are clenched on the arms of his wheelchair, knuckles white. "I don't have a choice," he says. "Attempting to rescue them would mean sacrificing many more lives, and the attempt would almost certainly fail."

"I say we focus on finding the dirty little mole who exposed our plan to the police." Nicholas bares his teeth in a smile. "And when I find them . . ." He raises his hands. "I will twist them." He clenches his hands into fists, breathing hard, and leans toward me. "We've worked too hard for this. Too many years, too many sacrifices. I won't let some sniveling rodent ruin it for us."

Zebra rotates his chair, turning his back to me, and waves a hand toward the door. "Escort her to her room," he tells Nicholas. "And if I find out you've laid a hand on her, you'll be the one in the timeout room. And I will leave the lights off."

Nicholas' upper lip twitches, as if he wants to snarl. But he merely bows his head and says, his voice soft and subdued, "As you wish."

Zebra rolls out of the room. Nicholas grips my arm and pulls me to my feet. My legs wobble but hold. As we walk back to the dormitory wing, he leans down and hisses in my ear, "If you tell anyone my eyes are artificial, I'll kill you."

I stare blankly. "Why would I tell anyone? Who cares?"

The sapphire blue irises flash. "I tell people this color is natural."

Good grief. "Fine. Whatever."

He whirls around and storms away, leaving me standing alone in front of the door to my room.

28

I lie down on my bed and stare at the ceiling. I feel like I should be breaking apart, but I'm just numb. Maybe it's the lingering effects of the drugs. My face still stings from Nicholas' backhanded blows, and I wonder if it will leave a mark.

There's a knock on the door. "It's unlocked."

Steven enters, his face pale. There's a hollow, haunted look in his eyes.

"Did they interrogate you too?" I ask.

"No." He frowns. "What did they do to you?"

I don't want to talk about this. I just want to lie down, wrapped in this fuzzy cocoon of non-feeling. But already, I can feel it wearing off. Sharp edges of pain poke at me through the cushion of sedatives. "Nothing much. Just asked me a few questions."

Something dangerous glints in his eyes. "Lain, did they hurt you?"

I shake my head. "I'm fine," I lie. A bitter knot in my throat swells, and I have to close my eyes to squeeze back tears. The merciful indifference of the drugs recedes like the tide, leaving the pain raw and exposed. "Our friends are in Area 9. There has to be some way we can save them."

His fingers dig into his thigh. "Rhee told me all about Area 9. No one's ever broken into it or out of it. Trying would be suicide."

The tiny flame of anger in my chest flares again, heating me from within. "This isn't like you. You never give up this easily."

He looks me in the eye. His face is pale, and the dark circles under his eyes are so pronounced, they look like bruises. "If you've got any ideas, I'm all ears."

I lower my head. More tears crowd my eyes, blurring my vision.

"I mean it," Steven says. "I want to save them as much as you do."

Think. I visualize fog rolling away—all the fear and uncertainty and confusion sweeping back, leaving only cold, hard reason. "What if Dr. Swan is willing to bargain?"

Steven gives his head a hard shake. "He's not going to release them, no matter what we do. You know that."

But Dr. Swan doesn't have them. Not yet. My mind races, clicking through the facts like a computer. Ian told me that Dr. Swan has grown obsessed with finding me. During both of his announcements, he asked me to come home. More than anything, he wants me back under his power—not only because it would send a symbolic message to the URA, but because I represent an embarrassing personal failure for him. I was his ward. He did everything in his power to control and mold me into the person he wanted me to become, and still I slipped out of his grasp. He won't be able to rest until he has me back. He would give up all five prisoners in exchange for me. I'm sure of it.

"Don't even think about it," Steven says flatly.

"About what?"

He stands up, and his shadow falls over me. "I'm not going to let you hand yourself over to IFEN."

I look away. "What if I could save them all? Wouldn't it be worth the sacrifice?"

"No, it wouldn't. You know what IFEN would do. They'd comb your mind for information about the Blackcoats, then they'd find some way to use you against us. It'd do more harm than good."

He's right, of course. It's a moot point, anyway, because there's no way Zebra would allow me to leave the Citadel. Bitterness knots my throat. "So there's nothing we can do?"

"Lain . . ." He exhales and rakes a hand through his hair. Then he shakes his head, as if dismissing whatever he was about to say. Silence stands between us like a wall. "I'm going to figure something out," he says. "I'm not giving up on them. Okay?"

"Neither am I." My fingers tighten on my knees. My gaze remains fixed grimly on the floor. "I need to think."

He hesitates, then reaches out to lay a hand on my shoulder. He lets it linger there for a moment, warm and steady. The touch is only a ghost of what once existed between us, but it's something. "Just don't do anything crazy. Okay? Promise?"

"I won't."

He gives my shoulder a brief squeeze, and his hand slips away. He stands there for another moment, and I can feel his reluctance to go. Then, quietly, he leaves the room.

I sit on the edge of the bed, numb. I don't know how the mission went so wrong, but I'm the reason the mission happened in the first place. I supplied Zebra with the information. I compromised my own principles and used my Mindwalking skills as a tool of war, and this is the result. I want to scream. There has to be *something* I can do.

From a corner of my room, I hear the faint crackle of a hidden speaker. I sit up, alarmed.

"Lain." The familiar voice emanates from nowhere and everywhere. "I need to talk to you."

I blink. "Zebra?" He sounds uncharacteristically subdued.

"Yes, it's me."

So, the room is bugged. Somehow I'm not surprised. I still can't tell exactly where the voice is coming from. "Do you have microphones in *every* room, or am I special?"

"Never mind that. We have bigger problems right now. You want to save your friends, don't you?"

My heartbeat quickens. "Yes," I whisper. "How?"

"Come to my study. It's better if we talk about this face to face."

I slide out of bed, slip on my shoes, and lay a hand against the wall panel, opening the doors. I look back and forth, but Steven is nowhere in sight. The hallways are silent and empty as I make my way toward the Gate room. By now, I've memorized the route.

I stand in front of the metal door. A few breaths pass, then the door slides open, revealing the room with the Gate at its center, just as I remember it. There must be a security camera near the door, though I don't see one. Are there hidden cameras all throughout the Citadel?

I step in, and the door whisks shut behind me. The wall opens with a grinding rumble, revealing the now familiar sight of Zebra sitting in his study. He closes the holographic screen in front of him. He must have been watching the outside hallway. Maybe this is his life—sitting in the shadows, secretly observing everything around him.

I sit in the chair across from his and dry my sweat-damp palms on my pants. "You said there's a way to save my friends?"

He rubs one gloved hand over his arm, an uncharacteristically uncertain gesture. "How much would you be willing to sacrifice?"

I hesitate, but only briefly. "I would give my life, if it was the only way."

He meets my gaze. "And what if you had to give up something more precious than your life?"

Suddenly, the room feels too cold, despite the fire crackling in the hearth. "What do you mean?"

He rubs his right thumb absently over the knuckles of his left hand. "We're in a bad position. Very bad. We may not have very much time." His voice is low, urgent. "As you know, someone leaked our plans to the police, which means there's a mole in the Citadel. By now, the enemy probably knows our location. Of course, because of international treaties, they can't simply march across the border. But they will find a way around that, no doubt. The Canadians don't want us here. If IFEN can promise to get rid of us, they'll cooperate, even if it means letting American troops into their country. Which means that our time is limited."

"What does any of this have to do with me? Or with saving the hostages?"

He leans forward. "I'm telling you the situation, so you understand what's at stake. Our only chance to stop IFEN is to learn their deepest secrets and expose them before they can destroy us. Truth is their Achilles heel. Right now, the American people's hearts are divided. Many of them don't like the status quo, but they also fear what will happen if IFEN disappears. They fear another war. They need to understand that those who rule them are not protectors, but oppressors. Then, and only then, can IFEN be truly defeated."

"Get to the point."

"As we both know, IFEN has a weapon. Something called Project Mindstormer. We're aware of its existence and its capacity for widespread damage, but we don't know what it is. The information about it is too scarce, too well guarded." His expression is grim. "I need someone who can get close to Dr. Swan, who can convince him to share top secret information. You are the only person who can do that. The only one who has a chance."

Realization settles in, and my chest turns hollow. "You want me to offer myself in exchange for the prisoners," I whisper, "to turn myself over, so I can get into IFEN headquarters as a spy and find out about Project Mindstormer."

"That's right."

I shake my head. "But that's—" My mouth works silently as I fumble for words. "Dr. Swan will just look into my head with the Gate. He'll know why I'm doing it."

"Not if you forget about this conversation afterward."

My heartbeat quickens. An unwitting spy. I wouldn't even know the real reason I was there. "If I don't remember, how will I know what information to look for? And how will I get this information to you? Once I'm inside headquarters, I'll be stuck."

Am I really thinking about doing this?

"I can implant subliminal suggestions using the Gate," Zebra says. "As for getting the information to me . . . well, there is a way, but it will involve submitting to a rather invasive neurological procedure. One which is still highly experimental. Essentially, I would give you an implant that would function as a long-distance Gate."

The muscles in my back stiffen. So he wants to do brain surgery on me, too. "And using this, you'll be able to see what I'm seeing. And record my memories as proof."

"Yes."

"And once you have the information, what then? What happens to me?"

"I'll try to arrange a rescue. But I can't promise anything. The security in IFEN headquarters is very tight."

And if he fails to rescue me, I'll be left at Dr. Swan's mercy, and he'll do everything in his considerable power to break my will. What Father feared more than death—becoming a helpless puppet, stripped of his most precious memories and turned against everything he held dear—will become my fate. It's an insane plan.

It's also the only possible way I can save Ian and the others. Once the exchange is made, there's a chance our duplicity will be discovered, but at the very least, I can get them out of Area 9. A peculiar numbness creeps over me as I weigh the options in my head. Stay here and do nothing—or offer myself as a sacrifice, freeing my friends and potentially striking a critical blow at IFEN. Of course, that's assuming the scheme works. If not . . . well, if Zebra is right, the Blackcoats' secrecy has already been compromised, so their situation can't get any worse.

From a utilitarian perspective, it's a simple ethical equation with an obvious solution. I have the potential to do so much good, at the cost of merely myself. It would be easy, if not for one thing. Steven's face flashes through my head, and pain rips down the center of my body, gutting me like a fish.

His expression is blank, his hands clasped tightly together. "So. What do you say?"

"I don't have much of a choice, do I?"

"Of course you do. I won't do this without your consent."

"It's my fault they were captured," I blurt out. My voice shakes. "I have to do whatever I can to save them. It's my obligation—"

"There is *always* a choice." He regards me through cool, metal-gray eyes. "Every day, the world tries to pull us one way or another. And most people simply go with the current. But to forsake one's power of choice is, in itself, a choice. We can't escape the burden of free will, no matter how hard we try. Even when there's a gun to your head—especially then, perhaps—one decision can change everything."

My nails dig into my palms. I close my eyes, breathe in, and open them again. "Then I choose to save them." The alternative is unthinkable.

He steeples his fingers, staring at me over the tips. "And what about Steven?" His voice is dangerously quiet. "What about the boy you love?"

Pain rips through my center again, but this time, I'm ready for it. I only flinch. "He's made his choice, too." This is his home now. Sort of a dysfunctional home, but still, it's better than nothing. "He's decided to stay here and fight. With or without me."

"I see. So you're willing to break his heart in order to save Ian."

"Not just Ian. All of them."

His eyes are sharp and clear, cutting into me. "Steven's mind is still delicate, you know. I can see that, even without going inside. I've reviewed all the data about his past. So much trauma. He's been shattered more than once, and the glue holding the pieces of him together is still weak. Your loss might be the thing that dissolves him."

Once, that may have been true. But so much has changed. Steven has changed. "That won't happen." A thought occurs to me, suddenly—that he grabbed my hand when he fled. He chose to save me, not Rhee or any of the others. I push the thought away. "He doesn't need me. They do."

One corner of his mouth twitches. "Self-sacrifice runs in the blood, hmm? Or maybe I should say self-destructiveness."

"Leave my father out of this." When did he learn about the real reason behind Father's death? When he was digging through my mind? I take a deep breath, fighting for control. "Why are you trying to talk me out of this, anyway? Isn't this what you *want* me to do?"

"I want you to understand fully what you're agreeing to. Including the sacrifices."

He could just do it to me, I realize—just summon his goons to restrain me, drug me, do his experimental procedure, and send me into IFEN as an unknowing spy. Why doesn't he?

I remember his face—pale and drawn—while he was watching Nicholas torture me. I remember his fingers clenched on the arms of his chair.

There are limits to what Zebra will do. He has no qualms about using us, but in some twisted way, he also feels responsible for his army of child soldiers. And he sincerely hates IFEN and everything it represents. He believes in the importance of choice. Even if he's willing to bend his own ethics, he must believe in them on some level, or else why would he be doing any of this? There are easier ways he could achieve power, if that's his goal. "I have to admit," I say. "I misjudged you a little."

"Oh?"

"Yes. You're sneaky, manipulative, and egomaniacal. But you're not evil."

A smile twitches across his lips. "You forgot 'brilliant and charming.'"

"Charming? I didn't notice."

He chuckles. Then the smile fades. "I am asking a lot of you, I realize."

The air feels thick between us. I'm worn out and raw and about to turn myself over to IFEN; I may never see Zebra again. I may as well ask, even if he doesn't answer. "Who are you, anyway? How did you become the leader of the Blackcoats? And why?"

He raises an eyebrow. "Why do you ask?"

"I want to know what kind of man I'm trusting to perform experimental brain surgery on me."

"Ah. Well, I suppose I owe you this much." His voice is low and pensive, as if he's speaking to himself. I wait.

He closes his eyes briefly. "All I know about my mother is that she abandoned me at a hospital as a newborn. I came into this world with part of my spinal cord protruding from a hole in my back. They had to tuck it back inside me and sew me shut, but the nerve damage was already irreversible. My earliest memories are of growing up in a state home. I was raised by individuals who saw my very existence as something tragic. An orphan and a cripple, and a Four to boot. Even when they smiled at me, I could always feel their pitying eyes crawling over my skin like roaches. When they thought I was asleep, I overheard them talking, saying it would have been kinder if I'd been euthanized as an infant. Every night, I fantasized about burning that place to the ground."

If they pitied him, they were fools. Wheelchair or no wheelchair, Zebra is not someone to let your guard down around. I have a feeling they found that out the hard way. "How did you get out?"

"I found my way onto the Deep Net using a cell phone I'd stolen from one of the staff, and I got in contact with the Blackcoats. Of course, back then, they were much more disorganized—they rarely worked together. Still, they were willing to help, if you could promise them something in return. I'd acquired some useful skills combing the Deep Net. I learnt how to make bombs from cleaning supplies."

"You started your rebel career early."

"You might say that."

"So why 'Zebra?'"

He gives me a deep, searching look. Then he begins to unbutton his shirt.

A flush rises into my cheeks. "What are you—" I fall silent.

Scars stripe his chest. Four long, horizontal scars of rough, rippled pink tissue. "I have them on my back, too," he says. "All over me, in fact. These scars were inflicted by a sadist with a taste for adolescent boys. She was a member of IFEN's board, a respected and influential figure. She managed to fool the system for years. When you're rich and powerful, you can find ways to avoid neural scans or fake them. It was easy for her to find playthings." He smiles, though there's a terrible deadness in his eyes. "Though I was young, I'd already been a Blackcoat for a few years. I was discovered and captured, and I found myself under her control." He buttons up his shirt. "After the worst few weeks of my life, my fellow Blackcoats rescued me and brought me to Canada, where I started a new life for myself. If you're clever, it's easy to make money in Canada. And I am very clever. I quickly became one of a highly secretive, underground upper class, a group of businesspeople who trade information and amass fortunes in anonymous online accounts. I have no real-world identity—not anymore. I don't need one. I'm only Zebra."

My mouth has gone dry. "The woman. What happened to her?"

"Eventually, IFEN found out what she was doing and expelled her from the Board of Directors. But she was never punished. You see, to punish her, they would have had to reveal her crimes to the public. Instead, they claimed that she retired because of her failing health. Some years back, I hired an assassin to take her out, so she will never hurt anyone again."

I stare into his cool, gray eyes. What are the scars from? A whip? A branding iron? "Zebra," I whisper. "I—"

He lifts a hand, silencing me. "No need for that. I told you my story because I want you to understand what IFEN is capable of. For weeks, that snake kept me locked in a closet so small I could barely turn around. She had a room filled with torture implements in her summer home. And when they found it, they simply brushed it all under the rug. These are the sort of people we're dealing with, and you're their enemy, now. When you walk back into their jaws, they won't show you any mercy."

I gulp. "They aren't all like her." Aaron isn't. I only explored a small corner of his mind, but still, I sensed he wasn't a bad person.

"Perhaps not. But the way they handled the incident is typical. They don't care about abstract concepts like truth or human rights."

I look at the tightness around his mouth. And suddenly, I understand why he never leaves this room.

I had a client once—a young woman with an abusive spouse who would lock her in her bedroom for days on end. She got so accustomed to being a prisoner that eventually, he didn't have to lock the door. She was too afraid to go outside.

"I could erase the memories for you, if you want," I say quietly.

He tenses. His gloved fingers are clenched on the arm of his chair. "Do you think I've never considered the possibility? If that's what I wanted, I would have found a way." A muscle in his jaw twitches. "The anger—the desire to never again be so helpless—was what fueled my ambition. It's how I clawed my way up to where I am now. I can't afford to lose that."

I lower my gaze. Of course, I already knew what his answer would be. But I had to offer. Deep down, I'm still a Mindwalker. The hunger to take away people's pain is still there. I draw myself up, squaring my shoulders. "Let's do this."

He relaxes, nodding. "Once the preparations have been made, it will be best if you leave immediately, in secrecy. If you want to say goodbye to him, I'd advise you to do it now."

I lower my gaze. I can't, of course, tell Steven that I'm planning to turn myself over to IFEN. He'd do everything in his power to stop me. But I have to say something. My legs suddenly feel as weak as water, but I need to stay strong. Just for a few minutes.

"All right."

* * *

I knock on the door to Steven's room. It slides open. He's sitting on the edge of his bed, his face drawn, his eyes shadowed with exhaustion. He gives me a wan smile. "Can't sleep?"

I shake my head and quietly enter, gaze lowered. The door whisks shut as I walk slowly to the bed and sit down next to him. My hands are balled into tight fists in my lap.

"Lain?" His voice is soft, puzzled. "What—"

"Will you hold me?" I whisper.

He wraps his arms around me. I hug him back, my cheek against his shoulder. It doesn't feel the same as before. His arms have grown stronger, corded with muscle from his training—but that's not the only thing that's changed. Even though we're pressed together, there's a gap between us, as if we're separated by a thin layer of clear plastic.

I close my eyes and try to forget everything. Just for this moment. I want to melt into him, to return to the time when it was just us against the world, when we were fugitives together. Strange, to feel nostalgic for such a frightening time. My arms tighten around him, and I try to imprint his scent deep in my mind.

Will I even remember this, once I leave the Citadel? Or will Zebra have to erase this moment, too?

I rest my cheek against his heart. "Why does everything have to be so confusing?" I whisper.

"Been asking myself that for a long time." He strokes my hair, combing his fingers through it slowly. "I'm sorry." His voice breaks. "For everything."

Tears prickle at the corners of my eyes, and I blink them away. "This isn't your fault." If anything, it's mine.

Steven's arms tighten around me. His breathing is hoarse and ragged. "I love you," he whispers. "You know that, right?"

My muscles go rigid. No. No, he can't say that now, not now. It's not fair. My throat swells shut. Why is he doing this? "Steven . . ."

"You don't have to say anything." He hides his face against my hair. "I just needed to tell you."

I close my eyes, squeezing back tears.

He touches his thumb to my chin. "Look at me. Please."

I force myself to meet his eyes, and I lose myself in their color—a tapestry of blue, gray and silver. Faded denim and mercury and the ocean on a cloudy day. His eyelashes are pale gold, almost invisible, except when they catch the light at a certain angle.

He frames my face between his hands and leans in, but I turn my head away. "I can't," I whisper. "Not now. Not when our friends are . . ." My voice breaks.

Silence stands between us. "Okay," he murmurs, and drops a soft kiss on the top of my head, instead.

"I'm sorry."

"No. I get it." He gives me a weak smile.

What's happening to Ian and Rhee right now? Are they being tortured? Are they even alive?

But that's not why I turned away. If he kisses me now, I won't be able to go through with this. I'll fall apart and I'll tell him everything. I hide my face against his chest, unable to look him in the eye. I can't afford any weakness.

I can't let him know that I'm about to betray him.

* * *

We lie down in bed, holding each other, until Steven drifts off. I close my eyes, listening to his breathing.

He'll survive; I truly believe that. He's no longer the broken boy I knew. He has comrades, friends among the Blackcoats, and once I make the exchange, he'll have Rhee. Still, this will hurt him deeply. The ache deepens and burrows into me, splitting me apart.

The worst of it is, I can't even tell him why it's necessary. I have no choice but to sneak away like a thief.

Will the plan even work? Once the exchange has taken place, once I'm a prisoner, will I really be able to discover anything about Project Mindstormer? Zebra seems convinced I can get the information out of Dr. Swan, but we're leaving so much to chance. And even if I succeed, even if I learn the truth and Zebra shows the proof to the world, who's to say that it will change anything?

That's what I'm most afraid of, I realize—that I might succeed in exposing the worst thing about our government, the darkest secret, and that no one will care.

But I have to try. Not just for Ian and Rhee and the others, but because the world *needs* to know. Whatever Project Mindstormer is, whatever IFEN is planning, it's too big and too dangerous to remain a secret.

Slowly, so slowly, I climb out of bed. I pause for just a few seconds to drink in the sight of Steven Bent one last time. His lips are parted, relaxed, but even in sleep, I can see the faint lines of tension around his eyes. They roll beneath the lids as he dreams, and his soft breathing fills the room. The longer I look at him, the more it hurts. I turn away.

As soon as I'm in the hall, the knot in my chest unwinds, and a calm sense of determination fills me. Now that my choice is made, everything seems much clearer. Steven will hate me for doing this, but in the end, it will be better for everyone.

When I return to the study, Zebra is waiting. Across from him, there's an empty chair with padded restraints on the armrests.

I place my hands on my hips. "You'll arrange the hostage exchange?"

"I'll take care of everything."

I nod. "In that case, I'm ready."

He smiles. There's a black box in his lap, about six by six inches. His hands rest atop it. "Sit down."

*　　*　　*

An engine rumbles, vibrating through the seat beneath me. I blink a few times, trying to clear the cloudiness from my eyes. There's drool on my chin—I wipe it away with a sleeve. My thoughts are a watery smear. Where am I? Why can't I think? Have I been drugged?

I'm in the backseat of a truck rumbling through a dark forest. The headlights cut a swath of light through the shadows. There's something heavy around my wrist—a thick, chunky black bracelet. In front of me, I see the back of a woman's head. Her short hair is like a shiny black helmet, slicked down with gel. "Who are you?" I ask. My lips feel thick and clumsy, like they've been anesthetized. "What's this thing on my arm?"

She casts a glance over her shoulder and purses her blood-red lips. "Try anything, and you'll find out."

"Where are we going?"

"No more questions. You belong to the Canadian government now. We don't owe you any explanations."

Confusion is slowly giving way to terror. I fumble through my memories, searching for some clue as to how I got here. I vaguely recall a conversation with Steven in his room, a sense of sadness, of loss. That's right. We were in the Citadel. We went on a mission, and it failed. Ian and Rhee and the others were captured.

The Citadel . . . where is the Citadel? I remember my time inside it, but the journey there is a blur.

My memories have been altered. By who? Zebra. My breathing quickens. It must have been him. But why?

My thoughts are closing in, strangling me. I have to get out of here. I fumble for the door handle, but I'm locked in. I pound a fist against the window of the truck.

The woman pulls a device resembling a cell phone from her pocket and stabs a button with one finger. Pain shoots up my arm like red lightning, and a choked scream bursts from my throat.

"That was the lowest setting," the woman says. "Don't make me turn it up."

The agony fades, but my arm still throbs and burns. It feels like the entire limb was immersed in fire and then doused with acid. When I look down at it, I'm faintly surprised to see that the flesh is smooth and unmarked, not stripped raw and bleeding. "Let me out, or you'll answer to the Blackcoats." My voice shakes. I don't expect the threat to have any effect, but I'm desperate enough to say anything. "They'll come for me."

"I doubt that. Your own people handed you over."

That can't be true . . . can it?

The trees thin out until we're driving across an expanse of open field under the cloudy sky. I lean back in the seat, exhausted by the pain.

Even if the Blackcoats did hand me over, they wouldn't have done it for no reason. There's only one explanation I can think of: Zebra made a hostage exchange. That means Ian and Rhee and the others are safe. I cling to that knowledge. I have no idea if I volunteered for this or if he did it against my will, but if my sacrifice has won their freedom, it's worth it.

What's going to happen to me now?

In the distance, a shadow looms through the rain. At first, it's only a collection of amorphous shapes. Then it slowly grows clearer, and I see the fence. It's concrete, topped with snarls of barbed wire, and much bigger than the border fence. And looming above it, an enormous, monolithic gray building. When I see the blocky black letters across the front, my heart sinks.

Area 9.

The massive gates swing open as we approach. Cameras perch like vultures atop the fence, peering down at us as the truck pulls into the enclosure. The gates slam shut behind us with a resounding bang. Rain hammers the muddy ground, forming puddles, as the car rolls slowly down the road, which sucks at the wheels like it's trying to pull us under. The whole place is a swamp of mud. The gray building towers over us, featureless, save for rows of tiny, cramped windows.

We drive toward a vast iron door, like the gate of some medieval castle. As the car approaches, the gate slides open with a rusty, grinding roar, then slams shut behind us, engulfing us in cool darkness. Dozens of lights snap on at once, illuminating a cavernous concrete garage.

The terror begins to ebb back into numbness as I follow the woman across the garage and through a door, into a gray hall. Gray, gray everywhere. Is it cheaper to paint everything the same color? Or is it a deliberate choice meant to suck away the prisoners' will to live?

As we walk, my surroundings fade into a haze; it's too much to absorb. I just keep moving like a robot, one leg forward, then the other. The woman walks close behind me, her thumb on the button of the remote control.

A pair of wide metal doors slides open, revealing a vast, harshly lit room with naked cement walls. I blink. The gray-tiled floor stretches over a space wider than several football fields put together. It's lined with rows of rectangular steel boxes, slightly larger than the refrigerator I had at home. My guard walks me briskly down the narrow aisle between rows, and I see that there's a number stamped on the front of each box. As I realize what I'm looking at, the sickening coldness in my stomach deepens and spreads. No—surely not. There can't be *people* in those things. They're not even large enough to be called cells. You can't just stuff people in boxes and leave them there. They'd go insane from sensory deprivation.

She stops in front of a box and opens it, revealing four blank walls and a floor scarcely wider than six feet. There's a hole in one corner, presumably for bathroom purposes.

I stand outside the tiny, coffin-like room, breathing raggedly. Then I turn and bolt. I know I won't get far, but I have to try. I haven't gone twenty feet before a huge, crushing blackness descends on me, pinning me against the floor. I'm being squeezed, flattened like gum beneath the sole of a shoe. My arm is on fire. My legs twitch and shake. Then hands seize me, drag me across the floor and shove me into the cell. The door slams shut.

A tiny, dim bulb comes on overhead, but there's no opening in the door, not even a crack, nothing to let in the outside light. I might as well be buried alive.

I sit down on the floor, which has a thin layer of padding. My own breathing echoes through the cell's confines. The walls seem to be getting closer. I know it's my imagination, but that doesn't do anything to dispel the creeping panic. The urge to scream rises inside me again, clawing at the inside of my chest. The boxes are probably soundproof. I could scream for hours, and no one would hear me. No one would care.

Ian is safe, I remind myself. Rhee is safe. Steven won't be alone. As long as they're all okay, I don't care what happens to me; I keep telling myself that. I focus on breathing, fighting back the fear that floods my head like cold, black water.

I don't know how long I spend huddled in a corner of the box, counting my heartbeats. I study the walls and see long scratches gouged into the metal, places where former prisoners tried in vain to claw their way out. I shut my eyes and think about Steven—about his scent, his wiry arms around me. I can almost hear his voice. *You can handle this, Doc. I know you can. Just keep breathing.* His hands are warm, his thin, calloused fingers gentle as they stroke my hair.

I wish there was some way to send a message to him, to tell him how much he means to me, but it's unlikely that I'll ever have the chance to speak to him again. The words will remain locked inside me forever. I close my eyes and think, *I love you.* I put all my will and heart into the thought and imagine it flying through the ceiling, up through the floor above, and into the sky. I send it winging to the Citadel and pray that it somehow reaches him.

I love you. I love you. I love you.

* * *

The door opens with a metallic *ka-chunk*, and I blink at the sudden flood of light, shielding my face with one hand. Dr. Swan stands in the doorway, wearing a bone-white suit and flanked by two armed guards.

I never thought I'd be glad to see him. Though I suspect my relief will be short-lived.

"Well," Dr. Swan says. "I must say, I was surprised to learn that you'd turned yourself in. Did you miss me?"

I don't answer. I don't want to give him the satisfaction of acknowledging him at all.

Dr. Swan breathes a small sigh.

A guard prods me with an ND, and I stand slowly. I stare straight ahead as I follow Dr. Swan out of the vast room and into a tiny elevator. The two guards crowd in with us, keeping their weapons trained on me. We glide up and up, until finally, we emerge onto the roof of the building, where a helicopter waits, propeller whirring.

For an instant, I think about running toward the edge of the roof and flinging myself off. One of the guards notices the direction of my gaze and presses an ND between my shoulders, a silent warning.

I get into the helicopter.

Dr. Swan settles into the seat beside me, shuts the door, and glances at the dull metal bracelet. "We'll leave that on for now. Just a precaution, you understand. They gave me a controller." He holds up a small silver remote, the same device my guard used to shock me. "But I'd prefer not to use it. Don't give me a reason to, and we'll be fine."

I don't answer, don't look at him. He leans over and buckles my seat belt. My skin crawls when his wrist brushes against my arm.

"Ready?" the pilot asks. He's wearing IFEN white, but I don't recognize him.

Dr. Swan nods.

The helicopter lifts into the sky. I watch the guards on the roof dwindle to tiny specks, then disappear. Area 9 becomes an oval of mottled brown and gray, then we're soaring over rippled green forest interspersed with fields. The dull roar of the engine fills my ears.

Dr. Swan interlaces his hands, watching the land far below. He's lost weight, I realize. His cheeks are hollow, his clothes loose, and his skin is paler than I remember. On his TV interviews, he managed to mostly conceal it with makeup, but this close up, it's obvious that the stress has taken its toll on him. It appears he's human, after all. "You've caused us quite a bit of trouble," he says. "We've had to clean up a lot of messes, thanks to your reckless actions. Protests, riots, terrorist attacks. Higher Types always look for an excuse to see themselves as victims of a corrupt system."

I can't hold back any longer. "Maybe because that's exactly what they are?"

His face remains expressionless. "IFEN didn't make them criminals. Violent people have always existed. Sometimes it's bad genes, sometimes a bad environment. Either way, their existence is a problem that must be dealt with. The collars have given them an unprecedented level of freedom. You'd think they would be grateful, but no."

"Grateful?" I ask, disgusted.

He shrugs. "In the pre-Republic days, those same people would have spent most of their lives in prison or institutions. You've just seen for yourself what that's like. You learnt in school about why the old system didn't work—how it just made people worse instead of rehabilitating them, how it separated parents from children and husbands from wives, perpetuated the cycles of poverty and violence. The collars at least allow people to stay in contact with the outside world. Isn't that an improvement?"

He has a bit of a point. But damned if I'm going to admit that to him. "You don't know what their lives would have been like. In the past, people were only sent to prison if they actually committed a crime."

"And it was a terrible system, one which resulted in countless, needless deaths," he replies. "We tried freedom. It didn't work. This is what we're left with. The rest of the world is gradually coming to the same conclusion. If the Blackcoats had their way, our society would be reduced to rubble within a few years."

I remember the Blackcoat thugs beating Aaron senseless, the fire and smoke of the explosion in Toronto, and a part of me wavers.

Then I think of Steven, of how hard he fought to survive against all odds, of all the prejudice and cruelty he endured. I think of his smile, the one he gives me when no one else is looking, brave and fragile at the same time. He's one of those people whose existence Dr. Swan sees as a problem. And not just him—all the Blackcoats. No matter how damaged they might be, they constantly amaze me with their resilience, their willingness to keep living, to keep fighting. "You're wrong," I say quietly.

He raises an eyebrow. "Am I?"

I don't respond. I grip the metal cuff on my wrist and wonder suddenly—what happened to Aaron? Is he still Dr. Swan's protégé, or has he been cast aside for another replacement—me, I realize. I want to ask, but I don't want to reveal the fact that I've met him. I won't volunteer any information. "What are you going to do, anyway? Mindwipe me?"

"Of course not. What would that accomplish? We need you with your mind intact—more or less."

"So you're going to probe my memories for information. Well, you can try, but I doubt you'll get anything valuable out of me. I don't remember the location of the Citadel."

"We already know where it is," Dr. Swan replies dismissively. "At this point, I doubt there's anything we could learn from your memories that we haven't already discovered."

"Then why am I here?"

"Because you're going to help us clean up the mess you created."

I look at him from the corner of my eye. "I'm not going to cooperate with you." But the words feel hollow, and my mouth is suddenly dry. By now, I've certainly been declared a Type Five, which means Dr. Swan can do whatever he wants to me. No treatment is too extreme for someone deemed a threat to the country's safety.

I start to tremble.

Dr. Swan watches me calmly. "Soon," he says, "you'll be on our side again."

29

It's dawn when the helicopter lands. From there, a car takes us to IFEN headquarters. It's been so long since I've seen it—or at least, it feels like an eternity. The sight of the familiar white building looming against the pale, lavender-gray sky stirs a strange mixture of emotions in me. Not long ago, I worked here as a Mindwalker. Now, it feels like I'm looking back on someone else's life.

As we drive closer, I see that there are people in the parking lot. Not just a few, but a small crowd, cordoned off by red velvet ropes and watched carefully by IFEN security guards wielding NDs. The crowd presses forward, straining against the ropes. As the car pulls into the lot, I notice that most of them are holding up cell phone cameras. Flashes go off here and there. My heartbeat quickens. Reporters. How did they find out that I'd been captured?

Dr. Swan swears under his breath. The car parks. "Walk quickly," he tells me. "Keep your head down."

As if I'm going to listen to him.

The driver circles around and opens the door on my side. He grips my arm, steering me out of the car, and I flinch away. For a moment, I think about making a run for it. But the driver is standing right there, holding a gun. I wouldn't get far. Maybe it would be better to be shot here and now, in front of everyone. That would certainly cause a splash.

Except I can't die—not yet. As long as there's even the slightest hope of returning to Steven, I have to stay alive.

I square my shoulders, look straight ahead, and walk toward the building.

More flashes go off. Reporters shout questions, but I can't make them out over the roar of the crowd. People are chanting, and a prickling chill washes over me as I realize that it's my name on their lips. Fists pump in the air. A homemade sign rises up above the crowd: FREE LAIN FISHER. And another: TRUTH IS NOT A CRIME! Awe touches me as I realize—most of the people gathered here aren't reporters, but protestors. They came to support me. Warm tears flood my eyes.

I raise a fist into the air, and the crowd goes into a frenzy, whooping and waving their signs. The guards form a line and push them back, brandishing their NDs.

Police cars pull into the lot, sirens wailing. A man with a bull-horn gets out of the first car and starts yelling. "This is an unlawful demonstration! All of you, get back!"

Hands shove me forward, toward the door.

The policeman keeps shouting: "Unless you have a media permit, you must leave the premises! We are authorized to use force!"

His shouts just seem to stir the crowd into a bigger frenzy. They surge forward, breaking through the red ropes. The police shove their NDs against protestors' heads, and several fall to the ground, convulsing. The crowd walks right over them. Another policeman throws a softball-sized object, and clouds of orange gas erupt. I'm nowhere near the clouds, yet my eyes start to sting and water and my nasal passages burn. And still, the crowd pushes forward.

Then Dr. Swan shoves the main doors open, drags me through, and slams the door shut. A lock clicks. The thunder of the crowd falls silent, as suddenly as if someone turned off a television. If I strain, though, I can still hear them faintly through the thick Plexiglas.

Dr. Swan straightens his collar. There's something red dripping down the side of his face. For a moment, I think it's blood, then I see the seeds. Someone must have hurled a tomato at him. A giggle bubbles up in my throat, and I don't bother to suppress it.

He glares at me, then the driver—who's standing stiffly by—as if we're somehow to blame for the indignity. He reaches into his pocket, fishes out a kerchief, and wipes away the mixture of juice and pulp. "Do you see what these people are like?" he asks. "Do you see what they're capable of?"

"Throwing fruit? Yes, truly horrifying."

His expression darkens. "Take a closer look." He points to the seething crowd outside. I can barely see what's happening anymore; it's an explosion of flashing lights and orange gas. But I glimpse blood spattering the pavement. The clouds start to clear, revealing bodies strewn across the lot—some in civilian clothes, some in uniform. I can't tell if they're unconscious or dead. The remaining protestors and police are still brawling.

"This is happening all across the country," Dr. Swan says. "Angry mobs attacking treatment centers, breaking windows, throwing rocks. Innocent bystanders are trampled by crowds. Citizens are afraid to go outside at night. This is what freedom means. This is what you've started."

"No," I say quietly, "this is what you've started."

He snorts.

"Why are you even bothering to lecture me, anyway? You're just going to Condition me until I agree with you."

He takes a deep breath, smoothes a few errant strands of hair from his face, and hands the soiled kerchief to the driver, who tucks it into his pocket. "Conditioning will be the first stage. If it's not enough, we will progress to other treatments." He starts walking.

The driver presses a gun between my shoulders. I follow Dr. Swan. "Kidnapping and brainwashing me won't help your public image, you know."

Dr. Swan walks ahead of me, hands interlaced at the small of his back. "Deprogrammed. You're about to be *deprogrammed*." He says the word as if it should be in air quotes. "When we found you, you were violent and incoherent. We discovered you'd been subjected to torture and mind-control techniques in their head-quarters, and we did what was necessary to bring you back to reality. That's what the world will hear, after this is all over. That's what you will believe."

My nails dig into my palms. A weight fills my chest, pressing against my lungs. It's a struggle to draw breath.

We reach a door. He keys in a code, and the door slides open, revealing a simple white-tiled room containing a chair and a screen. I recognize it. I've been here before, in this very room. After my father's death, I voluntarily submitted to Conditioning.

The Conditioning Unit, as it's called, resembles an MRI machine—an enormous white cylinder. The patient, usually restrained, lies on a padded table, enclosed completely by the machine, which uses magnetic pulses to stimulate or suppress different areas of the brain. For decades, it's been an effective treatment for depression, anxiety, and other psychiatric illnesses. Conditioning has fewer side effects than drugs—and, of course, it's not dependent on patient compliance—and as such, has replaced psychiatric medicines almost completely. In many ways, the treatment revolutionized the mental health industry.

Of course, there is *one* side effect—one which, IFEN quickly discovered, could be very useful. Patients are highly suggestible during treatment.

"Lie down," Dr. Swan says, nodding toward the padded table.

I lunge for the door, and rough hands grab my arms, hauling me back. There's a sharp sting in my neck, and my vision blurs.

My limbs go limp, muscles turning to overcooked spaghetti. The guards shove me down to the table and buckle the restraints. With a whir, the table slides into the cylinder.

"I'll adjust it to the strongest possible setting," Swan says. "I suspect you'll need it."

The table clicks into place, leaving me completely enclosed inside the coffin-like white tube. Soft lights glow all around me.

My struggles have stopped. The drugs are pulling me down into a fog of apathy. As I hear the hum of the machine starting, I want to scream, but I can't find the energy. I've never felt so utterly helpless. This . . . this should never be done to anyone against their will. It's inhuman. "Please." The word is a tiny whine; I hate myself for sounding that way, but I can't stop. "Don't do this."

From outside the machine, I hear Dr. Swan's muffled reply: "You're being unnecessarily dramatic. This is therapy, not torture."

Directly above my face is a screen, currently dark. A tiny star of light appears in the center of the screen, then expands out to show an image—a protest in the street. Broken glass glitters on the pavement, and people are screaming angrily, waving signs. The crowd surges forward, striking out blindly with their fists. The hum of the Conditioning machine fills my head, growing steadily louder, and a wave of weakness washes over me. I can barely feel my body. The fear and helplessness evaporate. I'm having trouble remembering why I was so afraid a moment ago.

In some distant corner of my mind, I know what's happening. The first thing Conditioning does is to suppress the brain activity responsible for someone's sense of self—the ego. The result is a disassociated state similar to that experienced with mind-altering drugs. My scalp tingles lightly, almost pleasantly, as more images move across the screen, more protestors rampage through the streets, though this footage looks grainy and old. It cuts to a shot of a building exploding. Screams.

A narrator's voice, a soft, deep baritone, overlays the screams. "The terrorist group known as the Blackcoats has struck again, leaving a deep scar on our national psyche. War has been declared by an angry and troubled minority."

Photographs of burned bodies appear, one after another. Protestors surge through the streets, mouths open in angry roars. Their faces shift and blur, contorting, until they're the faces of animals—hyena-like jaws gaping, eyes glowing yellow. Images of the dead and wounded float across a charred cityscape.

No. No. Make it stop.

And then it *does* stop, and a huge, smothering calm descends on me. The screen goes blank, then displays an image of a group of men and women sitting around a table in a sunlit room. A gentle female voice intones: "The Institute for Ethics in Neurotechnology was created by a coalition of scientists and government officials with the goal of maintaining a safe, secure country through non-violent means." The voice continues, reciting statistics about the reduction in various forms of crime since IFEN was created, as the screen displays photos of clean, orderly streets and smiling people in white lab coats. After awhile, I can't even focus on what the voice is saying. The gentle tones wash over me, sinking into me.

30

When the screen finally goes dark and the machine shuts off, I'm numb, inside and out. The table slides out with a faint whir and clicks into place.

The world is enfolded in a soft, white haze. Colors are muted. Nothing seems quite real. Slowly, the haze clears, and I find myself staring at my own left hand, idly studying the folds in the skin of my knuckles, the ragged edges of my fingernails. I wiggle my fingers. Hands are funny things. Like elongated, hairless paws with opposable thumbs.

Idly, I note the straps holding my arms down. I can't quite remember why I'm restrained.

When I look up, Dr. Swan is sitting in a chair across from me. "How do you feel?" he asks.

I blink a few times and wonder how to answer that question. My mind feels weak and wobbly—fragile, like it might break apart under a puff of air and scatter like dandelion seeds to the wind. What am I doing here? "I feel . . ." I moisten dry lips with my tongue. "Thirsty."

He holds a cup of water to my lips, and I sip. It's cool and has a faint, flat, metallic taste. "Do you know why you're here?" he asks.

I know this room. "Conditioning," I murmur. I'm here for Conditioning because . . .

Because I'm grieving for my father, and I've been depressed. A lump fills my throat. Father is dead. A tear slips from one corner of my eye and falls down my cheek.

No. Wait. That was years ago. So why—

"You've been very sick," Dr. Swan says, interrupting my thoughts.

"Sick?" I murmur.

"That's right. You ran away. Do you remember?"

That does sound familiar. But I can't recall why. I know all the information is there in my mind, but it's all scattered, disassembled. I can't connect the pieces.

"Don't think too hard," he says, smiling. "It'll come back to you. The important thing is that you're safe now. The nightmare is over. You've come home."

"Home," I murmur.

His eyes light up. "Yes, that's right." He holds the cup to my lips again. I stare into the clear water. The cup is plastic. Pale blue. Like Steven's eyes.

The thought is a lighted match tossed into my brain. The fire grows and spreads, illuminating everything.

Dr. Swan's face hovers over mine. With all my strength, I spit up at him; a white glob lands on his cheek. Dispassionately, he wipes it away and sighs.

"You can do whatever you want to me, but it won't change what's happening in this country," I say. "You can't Condition everyone. The people have woken up. They're sick of your lies, and they're going to change things."

He narrows his eyes. "And how do you expect them to do that?"

I'm still weak and fuzzy-headed, but I manage a wobbly sneer. "You're getting a little nervous over the Cognitive Rights Act, aren't you?"

"Oh. That. Would you like to see how that played out?" He rises, walks over to the other side of the room, and waves a hand over a wall sensor. A holoscreen appears, floating in front of him.

Jana Rice—the head of the National Ethical Committee—stares into the camera. Her graying blond hair is neatly trimmed, face expertly made up, manicured hands folded. "Good evening," she says in a smooth alto. "We, the representatives of the people of the United Republic of America, have reached a decision. We've sought the counsel of experts at IFEN, and of course, we have taken the public vote into consideration. Rest assured that our decision has been carefully calculated to ensure the greatest good for the greatest possible number of citizens."

I hold my breath, but I have a sinking feeling that I already know what's coming next.

"In the best interests of the United Republic and its people, we have decided not to pass the Cognitive Rights Act."

"No," I whisper aloud.

"We understand the concerns of those who support this Act," Jana continues. "But the simple fact is that, given the nation's tumultuous state, the drastic changes proposed would result in—"

Dr. Swan waves his hand, and the screen disappears. "Was there ever any doubt?" His voice is oddly gentle.

I turn my face away, staring at the opposite wall. The hollowness in my chest grows, spreading, eating me from the inside.

Dr. Swan approaches the Conditioning machine, his footsteps slow and deliberate.

"Don't put me back in there," I whisper.

"It will happen as many times as it needs to." His face is weary, lines cast in deep shadow. "I'm not cruel, Lain. I just do what needs to be done." He pushes a button, and I descend back into hell.

31

For a long time—days, it seems—I drift in and out of a dreamlike state. I'm plunging into a dark well of terror. A heartbeat later, I'm floating in a sleepy golden bliss. Then a heavy nothingness descends over me like a blanket made of lead.

It would be so easy to give in, like sinking into a warm bath. I can barely even remember why I'm resisting. I'm so tired.

When I come back to myself, I'm drenched in sweat, lying on a narrow cot in a small, dimly lit room. My body is strapped down, immobilized.

"Lain," a familiar voice whispers. "Lain, can you hear me?"

I blink a few times, struggling to focus my eyes. The pale, blurry oval above me resolves itself into a face—a young man with dark hair, glasses, and bright green eyes. It takes me a few seconds to put a name to the features. "Aaron?" I murmur, puzzled. "What are you doing here?"

He gives me a pained smile. "You recognize me. It *was* you who saved me, wasn't it?"

My breath catches. "You—you remember that?"

"No. But it wasn't hard to put the pieces together. I knew that someone erased my memories, and I knew that the Blackcoats wouldn't have been so merciful, left to their own devices. If you hadn't been there, they would have killed me." He swallows, his expression tight. "I'm sorry about this, Lain."

I squeeze my hands into fists. "If you're really sorry, then help me get out of here."

"I can't do that. You know I can't."

I turn my head away.

"I swear, if I could stop this, I would." A trace of desperation creeps into his voice. "I'm not even supposed to be talking to you. I'm here for Conditioning. Dr. Swan thinks I'm too unstable. He keeps telling me that if I want to work here, I need complete mastery of my emotions. Which means, basically, that I'm not allowed to *have* emotions." He lets out a flat laugh. "I'm starting to understand why you left. I—I don't think I can keep doing this. Still . . . I never imagined he'd go this far. I never thought he'd do this to you."

"Then you don't really know him." I roll my head back toward him. His eyes are wide, frightened, but filled with concern. "Aaron." My voice shakes. "If there's anything you can do, anything at all, I'm begging you. Help me."

He winces and bites his lower lip. "I—I might be able to help you after."

"After? After what?"

He glances over his shoulder. Footsteps echo down the hall. "I need to go," he whispers. "I'll come back later, if I can." Quickly, he slips out of the room through a door in back. The footsteps draw closer. Sweat trickles down my temple. The other door creaks open and Dr. Swan steps in.

He pulls up a chair. Slowly, as if the movement hurts, he sits. For a moment he just looks at me. He doesn't even try to disguise the raw exhaustion on his face. Deep lines stand out, carved into his cheeks and around his eyes. "Have you had enough?" he asks.

I turn my head away.

317

He breathes a small sigh. Silence fills the room like a tangible presence.

"Lain," he says. "If you keep fighting me, I will have to dig deeper. I'll have to erase the memories of everything you've been through. You realize that, don't you?"

My heartbeat quickens. Steven's face blazes in my head. Dr. Swan is going to make me forget him. I try to sit up, but of course, I can't. "So why haven't you done it yet?" I squeeze the words between gritted teeth. "It would be easier, wouldn't it?"

A brief pause. "I wanted to give you the chance to repent."

Repent? I laugh, a thick, choked sound. "You're disgusting."

He regards me with an empty expression. "Let me tell you a story."

"I'm not interested."

He continues as if I haven't spoken: "There was a woman, once. Your father loved her dearly. I don't suppose he ever told you the details." He reaches up and pulls a square of paper from his pocket. A photograph of a woman with straight black hair, warm brown skin, and large, dark, doelike eyes.

I stare.

Father *did* mention that there was someone very dear to him— someone who took her own life. All he'd ever said was that she had been kidnapped by some men who did terrible things to her, and afterward, the pain had been too much for her to bear.

"She was a Type Four," Dr. Swan says, "a deeply disturbed person. Lain was convinced he could help her. That was his weakness, you know. He wanted to fix everyone. He had a brilliant mind, but a weak and foolish heart." He tucks the photograph into his pocket.

"What does this have to do with anything?" I ask, but my voice comes out unsteady.

"He told you, I understand, that she was attacked by a group of men who hurt and violated her, and that she killed herself afterward. What he probably didn't tell you is that she took their daughter with her."

For a moment, I can't respond. "Their daughter?"

"Yes. Your father had another child, before you. Kalila—that was the woman's name—jumped off the top of a building with the infant in her arms. In the note she left behind, she said that she didn't want their child to grow up in such a cruel world. You can imagine his grief. I was the one who urged him to clone himself, so he'd have a successor . . . and a reason to live. I convinced him that he had to keep living, in order to help create a world where people like Kalila could be helped. If not for me, you wouldn't exist. In a sense, you are my child, as well."

"I'm not yours," I murmur, but there's no force behind the words. I'm aching and confused.

Is it true? Was I born just to fill the hole in Father's heart? A tear leaks from the corner of my eye, down my temple.

"There's a great deal of suffering in the world, Lain," he continues softly. "By now, you've seen that. People lash out in anger and fear, and they hurt not only themselves, but everyone around them. Believe it or not, I've suffered too. I've lost people I loved." He smiles tightly. "You're so like him. You're attracted to lost causes. Like that boy. You want to help everyone. What you fail to understand is that I'm on your side. I want to ease the suffering of the world, just as you do. Perhaps I've made mistakes. Perhaps we don't always agree on the best methods. But we are both fighting for the same goal. Understand that much, at least."

I close my eyes. I don't want to listen to him or talk to him. I just want to sleep. *Ask him about Project Mindstormer.* At the sudden thought, my eyelids fly open. *Ask him.* The words are in my own voice, inside my own head, yet they feel somehow separate from me. My brows draw together.

This is your chance! the voice—mine and yet not mine—hisses.

"Lain? Are you all right?"

I take a shaky breath. Something tells me that this is important, even if I can't remember why. "If that's true . . ." I try to swallow the dryness in my mouth. "If you really believe we're on the same side—then answer this. What is Project Mindstormer?"

His face is stone. "And where, exactly, did you hear about that?" he asks, voice dangerously soft.

My pulse thuds in my wrists. "So it *does* exist?"

"I would advise you not to put too much faith in rumors."

"Don't *lie* to me." My voice rises. "You're building a weapon, aren't you? If you're willing to use things like that, then how are you any different from the Blackcoats?" The anger burns away my fear and fatigue, giving me strength. "All these conspiracies, all these secrets. Yet you want me to believe that you have the best interests of the American people at heart?"

"Some degree of secrecy has always been necessary. Every government keeps classified information." But there's the slightest hesitation in his tone, as if he's been knocked off balance.

Keep pushing him, the voice in my head whispers. *Convince him that you want to work with him.* "I'm not asking you to tell the public. I'm asking you to tell *me*," I say. "I'm not a Blackcoat. I don't want another war. I just want a more equal world, a world where a person's worth isn't measured by Type. I want to believe that there's still goodness in IFEN, that it *can* be a force to help people instead of keeping them enslaved. But how am I supposed to believe anything you tell me if you won't even give me the truth?"

"Last time you learnt a delicate truth, you went public with it. You betrayed me."

Betrayed him. I almost laugh. Instead, I give him a pained smile. "Obviously, I can't do that now. Even if I wanted to, there's no one I can tell. And you can always erase my memories afterward if you feel like it. So please. Just tell me. I want to understand what IFEN is really about."

Another long silence.

At last, he lets out a small sigh. He pushes a wheelchair up to my bedside and unbuckles my straps. "Get into the chair."

My limbs are weak and shaky. Making a run for it isn't an option, and there's nowhere to run, anyway. But with his help, I'm able to climb into the padded seat. He secures leather straps over my wrists and ankles, but they seem redundant. If I tried to stand up, I would collapse.

I try to keep my breathing steady. *Good*, the voice in my head whispers. I wonder if this is a form of stress-induced schizophrenia.

He wheels me down a long series of white hallways. We get into a tiny, gray elevator, which goes down and down, the buttons lighting up one by one—the ground floor, then the basement, then a sub-basement, then a level marked SB2. I didn't realize there was anything below the ground level of IFEN. Just how deep does it go?

The elevator stops, and the doors slide open to reveal a cavernous white room lit from above by fluorescents. The walls are lined with steel panels covered with rows and rows of blinking green lights. I stare, unsure of what I'm seeing.

"This is Mindstormer," he says. "Not a weapon. A computer." He wheels me forward, into the room. The air is unnaturally cold, perhaps to keep this enormous machine from overheating.

"I don't understand," I say.

"Think of it as an extremely powerful Gate, one which is not limited by distance. It sends out pulses of energy that interact with the human brain. In its final form, it will be able to target specific individuals or a large group of people, all at once. The technology is still in development—still in the theoretical stage. But we are close, now. Our scientists are working around the clock, tweaking the programs and scrutinizing the logistical issues from every angle. As soon as we make that breakthrough, we'll move onto the experimental phase."

Which means they'll be using this thing on people. The machine hums softly, a low drone, more in my bones and teeth than in my ears. This whole thing feels unreal. "Interact with the human brain," I repeat slowly. "To do what?"

"Anything. As I said, it's still in development. But in the future, we may be able to, say, suppress aggressive impulses. Or even subtly influence an entire population's mood to make them more peaceable, more cooperative, more empathetic."

This has to be a lie. Something like this is not—should not be—possible. "You're talking about mind control."

"Not control," he says. "*Guidance*. We refer to the theoretical uses of this machine as 'nudges.' Subliminal suggestions. Most people won't even be aware of when they're being nudged. The human psyche, after all, is already influenced by a wide variety of external factors. Personalities are shaped by upbringings, by genes, by advertising, by the opinions of friends and family. Even a persuasive argument can do the trick. When you revealed the truth about St. Mary's, you knew it would have an impact on people's behavior. Were you controlling their minds?"

"That's not the same." My breathing has quickened. The dreamlike quality of the experience is starting to fade, replaced with growing fear and anger. "There's a difference between influencing people and taking away everyone's choices."

"This will not take away everyone's choices. Do you imagine that we would be able to monitor and control *all* people, every moment of every day? Do you think we could create a nation of zombies, or that we'd want to, for that matter? Absurd. Most individuals will go about their lives unhindered, as they always have. But we will watch the patterns. We will intervene in careful and specific ways, to avert tragedies and to guide our country along the right path."

My pulse drums in the hollow of my throat. "If you wanted to target and erase a specific memory in a specific person—you could do that, too?"

"Once the technology is perfected, yes."

So it would become even easier for them to hide unpleasant truths. "And you're not even a little bit worried about how this will impact people's basic human rights?"

"I am concerned with human welfare, not human rights. This whole business of rights causes nothing but trouble. If a car or computer is broken, you don't ask its consent to be fixed, you just fix it."

"People aren't machines." A statement like that shouldn't even be necessary. I feel like I'm trapped in some sort of silly dream.

"Of course they are," Dr. Swan replies readily. "You know it as well as I do. Nevertheless, there will be strict guidelines and protocols to prevent abuses of power. It will only be used when necessary."

"And who will decide when it's necessary?"

"You, maybe."

I look up at him in confusion.

He smiles wearily. "Your replacement, Aaron, is not working out. He's too . . . sensitive. I must admit, I still have hopes for you."

"Even after I ran away to join a terrorist organization?"

"And now you've seen what they're like. What they're capable of. Rebellion is a natural part of growing up, but I think you're coming to the end of that particular phase. I've always felt that you would be the one to take my place. Call it an instinct. If I'm correct about that, then you—as the Director—would make the final call on when to use Mindstormer. Of course the Board would give you input, but you would have the right to veto any of their suggestions."

I almost laugh. Even after everything he's done, he still thinks I'd consider working for IFEN?

But in spite of myself, I find myself thinking. If I really had that sort of power, I could make sure this machine was never abused. I could—

I slam that mental door shut. No one should have this power. It shouldn't even be an option.

Dr. Swan leans in. "You are right about one thing—the status quo can't be maintained indefinitely. Actually, the Type system was never meant to be permanent. It's an imperfect solution. But once Project Mindstormer is fully implemented, collars—and Types—will be phased out, because they will be redundant. People will be equal. Isn't that what you want, Lain? Equality?"

I shake my head frantically. "This will make things *more* unequal. A small group of people will have limitless power over everyone."

"Not limitless. As I said, there will be strict protocols—"

"Just like there are protocols about how and when to change someone's Type?" I ask bitterly.

"Nothing is perfect. But it's *better*. Just imagine the potential. We can end war, forever. For the first time in history, that is a real possibility. Of course, Mindstormer's reach is limited, but once we've established bases in other countries—well, imagine for a moment that some mad dictator gets the idea to start collecting nuclear weapons. We can put a stop to it. Easily, bloodlessly. Think about that."

And for a moment, I do think about it: a world where tragedies can be prevented without collars or Types. That's what I'm fighting for, isn't it? What the Blackcoats are fighting for? And now, Dr. Swan is telling me that it can happen. We can be equal.

Equal in slavery. Not the makers of our own future, but simply tools in IFEN's grand design, manipulated and shaped without our awareness. And that's the best possible scenario. "This isn't right," I whisper.

He lets out a small, tired sigh. "What is it you *want*, Lain? You hate the way things are. You don't want to return to the way things were. I show you a new way of dealing with problems, and you reject it. So what's your answer? What do you suggest we do?"

I don't answer. I don't have an answer. My fingers tighten on the arms of my chair.

Slowly, he turns me and wheels me out of the room, and the doors slide shut behind us. We take the elevator back up. I stare straight ahead, a knot burning in my chest.

"Well," he says. "I tried." The elevator doors slide open, and he wheels me down the hall. "You've left me with no other options, Lain. Your memories will be erased. You'll be reset back to the point before you met Steven Bent."

I clench my jaws.

Stall him, the voice in my head whispers frantically. *Convince him that you agree with him. Pump him for more information.*

I shake my head, like a horse trying to dislodge a fly. What does it matter? How will that help, when I can't tell anyone about this? I'm so tired. I just want to give up . . .

Don't you dare! the voice hisses.

I place a hand against my temple.

"Lain?" Dr. Swan's eyes narrow. "What's going on?"

"I . . . I don't know. My head feels strange."

Don't tell him about me. The voice is shifting. It no longer sounds like my own. Zebra. Somehow, he's talking to me inside my head. *You have to learn more.*

Dr. Swan grips my chin. "You're communicating with someone, aren't you?" His voice is hard and tight. "How?"

"I'm not—I don't—I don't know—"

He backhands me, hard, knocking my head back. "Tell me!"

"*I don't know!*" I scream at him. "I don't know why! I just started hearing his voice in my head, and then he—he—"

Dr. Swan grips my hair and probes at my scalp and neck with his fingertips. He presses a sore spot near the base of my skull, and I flinch. "A surgical scar," he mutters. "Almost invisible. We should have examined you more thoroughly, but I never suspected the enemy's technology was this advanced." His voice is ice. "So, you have an implant. Clever. He sends you in as a spy, watches through your eyes and listens through your ears."

An implant. That's why Zebra allowed me to turn myself over to Dr. Swan, to exchange myself for the hostages—he wanted information on Project Mindstormer. He used me.

Dr. Swan breathes in and straightens, smoothing his hair back. "We'll have to remove this device and study it. But first . . ." He takes a cell phone from his pocket, flips it open, and presses a few buttons. He holds it to his ear. After a few seconds, he says, "It's time." Just those two words. He turns off the cell phone, shoves it back into his pocket, and resumes pushing my wheelchair down the hall.

"Who was that?" I ask.

Dr. Swan doesn't answer. I grit my teeth, nails digging into my palm.

Zebra? Can you hear me? Are you there? Tell me what's going on!

I'm sorry, Lain. It's disorienting, to hear someone else's voice so clearly inside my own head. But you agreed to this, even if you don't remember now. And it worked. I'm recording your memories on a Gate, and I have the images of the Mindstormer computer and Dr. Swan's explanation of its capabilities. What they're doing is a crime against humanity, and if we tell the world, we can bring them down. Please believe me. I know what you think of me, and you're right. I'm a terrible person. But you've done a great service for the Blackcoats. No—for humankind. I'm going to get you out of that place, just like I promised. Just hold on a little longer—

Abruptly, the voice cuts off. There's a shock, a jolt that shakes me to my core. My vision goes white, and pain rips through my chest, a huge, unthinkable pain. It fills my consciousness, drowning out everything else. I gasp, clutching my chest. It burns. I open my mouth to cry out, but my throat is suddenly paralyzed, locked tight.

Zebra's voice filters through the pain, weak and broken. *Lain . . . listen to me. You have to . . .* A choked gasp cuts off the words. I can't move. My mind is slipping, scrambling to find a toehold. Every breath is a struggle against the red avalanche crushing my chest. My vision fades in and out.

Then the pain is fading. I can feel him slipping away. But his voice comes through, very faintly. *Stop Nicholas*, he whispers. *He's dangerous. You have to find . . .*

There's a snarl of white noise between my ears. "Zebra!"

The room. Tell them. Fainter and fainter still. Then, so small and weak it's almost imperceptible: *Paradise lost.*

And then he's gone. The pain is gone, too, leaving me gasping and drenched in sweat. Tears roll down my face.

Dr. Swan shows no signs of surprise or confusion. He keeps walking stiffly, pushing the chair along.

"What did you do?" I whisper. He doesn't answer. "*What did you do?*"

"You pushed me into a corner, Lain. I had no choice. You must understand; if this information leaks out before the proper time, the consequences will be disastrous."

My nails dig into my palms, almost hard enough to draw blood. I'm still shaking. Though the searing pain in my chest has faded, I feel bruised and broken, like I've been run over by a truck. "You killed him. How?"

"You ought to know by now, we have an agent inside the Citadel. Zebra has been taken care of, and the contents of his Gate will be wiped."

I remember Zebra's words: *Stop Nicholas.* I should have known. He's the only one who could have gotten close enough to do this, the only one Zebra trusted. I know, and there's nothing I can do about it, no way I can warn the others. My chest is shrinking, squeezing like a fist. "The Blackcoats will figure out what happened."

"No, they won't. It will look like Zebra died of natural causes. He was given an injection of liquid Somnazol with a needle too small to leave a noticeable mark. Certain tests would reveal the real cause of death, but the Blackcoats' medical technology is rather unsophisticated. He'll be discovered in his study, looking for all the world as though he died peacefully in his sleep."

I want to scream.

"Even if you could warn them, it wouldn't matter," Dr. Swan continues. "It's too late."

A chill skates down my spine. I twist in my chair to look at him. "What are you talking about?"

"You needn't concern yourself with that. Soon, you won't even remember them. Just as you won't remember this."

The helplessness burns, twisting inside me like a knife. "You can't hide the truth about this place forever."

He stares straight ahead. "Perhaps not. But by the time it comes out, the public will be ready to accept it. We'll make sure of that." The wheelchair rolls forward. "Soon," he says, and his voice is almost soothing, "this will all be behind you. We can start again."

*   *   *

In a white room, Dr. Swan and a nurse strap me down to a cot, numb the back of my neck with cold anesthetic jelly, and extract the implant. It resembles a glittering silver spider, or maybe a jellyfish—a transparent node filled with tightly packed circuitry, with long, hair-thin, iridescent wires trailing from one end. I watch fuzzily as Dr. Swan places it in a jar of clear liquid, and it floats, the long wires waving and undulating of their own accord. Wisps of blood—my blood—trail through the fluid.

Did I really agree to let Zebra put that inside me?

I suppose I'll never have a chance to ask him. My chest cramps at the memory of the burning, suffocating pain. So that's what it feels like to die of Somnazol. That's the so-called mercy of IFEN. Zebra didn't deserve that. No one does.

As they stitch me up, my mind races. With Nicholas still on the inside, the Blackcoats are vulnerable. Now that Zebra is gone, there's nothing to stop him. He could expose the location of the Citadel to the Canadian authorities, open the front door for them, and watch them slaughter everyone. The question is, why hasn't he already done that? Is he planning something else?

In a short while, I won't even be able to wonder. The truth is about to be stripped from my mind, and I'm powerless to stop it from happening. The questions fade as I stare at the wall dully, too drained to even be scared.

Shadows move behind me, and surgical implements clink softly together as the nurse finishes her work.

Dr. Swan and the nurse leave the room, taking the implant with them, and I'm alone, lying on my side, still strapped down.

After a few minutes, I hear the creak of wheels. The door opens, and Dr. Swan is there, along with a nurse pushing a wheelchair. "It's time," he says. He's holding a hypodermic. "Are you going to come with us quietly to the Immersion Lab, or will we have to drug you?"

My fingernails dig into the cot. They're going to take away everything. I'll forget the Blackcoats, St. Mary's. Steven. These are my last few minutes to hold onto my memories of him. I don't want to spend those moments in a drooling stupor. I close my eyes. "I'll cooperate."

"Well. It's about time."

The nurse undoes my straps, and I get into the chair. I'm dizzy and weak, and my vision keeps blurring as they wheel me down the hall, toward the Immersion Lab. A strange feeling washes over me as the doors open, and I see it: the pristine white walls, the bright lights, and the two chairs. I treated clients in this very room.

As they strap me into the chair, I think about Steven—his smile, his scent—everything I'm about to lose. This isn't happening, can't be happening. It's too cruel. Before I can stop it, a tear slips down my cheek.

Dr. Swan looks away. "When this is over, you'll feel better."

I don't want to feel better. I want to keep everything, even the pain.

Once the treatment is over, I'll be the girl I was a month ago. She'll know nothing. She'll be helpless, like a child. I feel a strange protectiveness toward her, as I might feel toward a little sister. I wish I could be there to help her, to guide her—but of course, that's impossible. I'll *be* her.

Dr. Swan sits down in the chair beside me and pulls the helmet on. The nurse is standing by, still holding the hypodermic, in case I get uncooperative.

"Go back to the first time you met him," Dr. Swan says. "Remember, the more you cooperate, the smoother this will go."

There has to be a way I can guard at least some of my memories, a way I can keep Dr. Swan from stealing everything. I remember my training exercises, the ones I used to compartmentalize my emotions. Maybe it's possible. If I lock away a few—

"Lain," he says, a chiding note in his voice.

The nurse advances toward me, hypodermic gleaming. "No." I shake my head, pulling away. "Wait."

The needle pricks my neck, and I sink into a heavy gray nothing. I'm slipping away, vanishing like water down a drain. I'm crumbling to dust beneath my fingers, falling away into a dark, bottomless void.

Focus. Remember.

Steven's smile, that wry quirk of thin lips.

I'm walking through a stone labyrinth.

Steven standing on the other side of a parking lot, hands in his pockets, bathed in the glow of a streetlight.

I come to a wooden chest. Open the chest.

His eyes.

I put this image inside and lock it away. Lock it tight.

Steven. Steven. Steven.

We're in the secret room beneath Gracie's house, his lips against mine—

Please, please, don't let me lose this. Not this.

I struggle to hold onto the memories, but they break apart and tumble into the void. I'm drifting through a place without time. A gray place. There was something I wanted to remember. What was it?

Someone's eyes. Mercury. Faded denim. Clouds reflected in the ocean. Blue.

Blue

Blue

Blue

Blue

Bl—

PART III

CHOICE

32

I'm in an empty place. Not black, but white.

Darkness is *something*. Darkness has a tangible quality. But white is absence, negation, emptiness. White is oblivion.

Slowly, very slowly, the world reforms itself.

My head is a sledgehammer. My brain feels like it's been rolled in shattered glass, dunked in lemon juice, and then unceremoniously stuffed back into my skull. Dimly, I'm aware of a mattress beneath my back.

Where am I?

I try to sit up, but my body won't listen. Voices float at the edge of my mind, filtering in and out of my awareness. "This was a mistake." Steven. Steven is talking, his tone choked, like he's fighting back tears. "We shouldn't have done it. I knew this would happen, and I didn't stop her."

"Take it easy." That's Ian. "She's just overwhelmed. Her mind needs some time to sort through it all." But he sounds scared, too. "She'll get better."

"What if she doesn't?"

"She will."

I want to tell them that I'm awake, that I can hear them, but when I try to open my mouth, nothing happens. I manage to open my eyes a crack, but the world is a soupy swamp of browns and grays. My eyes sink shut again, and Steven and Ian's voices fade into silence.

Time passes in slippery chunks. I open my eyes and find myself staring at a dilapidated, wood-walled bedroom.

Wait. Wasn't I just in IFEN headquarters?

No. That's right—I escaped. We escaped, and now we're in a safe house in the woods.

Dust motes spiral through the beams of sunlight that slant down through the hole in the ceiling, making the room appear misty and glittery. A roach crawls across the wall, tiny antennae wavering. A gigantic red-and-yellow spider, the size of a rat, dangles from the ceiling. I close my eyes, and when I open them again, it's gone.

Voices slide along the edge of my mind. Shadows, passing figures, flicker along my peripheral vision. A gentle hand touches my face, then slips away. A black orb floats over my bed, and a girl swims inside it like a mermaid, smiling down at me. Then she too vanishes.

Gradually, the inferno in my head dies down to something resembling a normal headache. The shiny mist dissolves, and the world looks normal, albeit a bit blurry, because focusing my eyes takes a monumental effort.

Slowly, I turn my head to the side. Steven is sitting by the bedside, dipping a cloth in a bowl of water. Carefully, he spreads the cool cloth across my forehead. There's a tiny furrow between his brows, like he's performing a delicate operation.

"I know you," I whisper.

He freezes. The breath hitches softly in his throat.

Slowly, I reach up and slide a palm over his cheek, feeling the prickle of pale, invisible stubble. "Hi, Steven." A weak smile tugs at my lips.

The muscles of his throat constrict as he swallows. He presses my hand to his cheek, turns his face, and kisses the center of my palm. "Hi, Doc," he whispers back.

*   *   *

I sleep for a while. When I wake up, I feel weak and shaky all over, and my body is drenched in sweat, but I sense that the worst has passed. The Lucid hangover has broken like a fever, and bright noontime sunlight shines through the dirty window and the hole in the ceiling. My stomach growls.

Slowly, I sit up. I blink a few times. The room remains stable. I spread my fingers and count them, then do a few basic math equations in my head. I silently recite the lyrics to a pop song. So far, so good. All the basic equipment is functional. No multicolored spiders or weird, floating black orbs in my field of vision.

God, what a trip. I never want to take Lucid again, if I can help it.

A pair of green eyes flickers through the tangle of memories. Aaron. He was in IFEN headquarters. He must have been the one who sent that nurse to slip me the pill. I remember talking to him while I was a captive. I remember.

I touch my temple. Yes. It's all there . . . or everything that counts, anyway. The events immediately before the modification are shrouded in fog—I recall the Conditioning sessions, the conversation with Aaron, and then things get a little confused and I can't separate reality from dreams—but I remember the Citadel, and Rhee, and Zebra, and all the other Blackcoats. And I remember Steven. I want to weep with relief. I feel the Lain I was slipping away, rapidly swallowed up by the Lain I am now, and there's a faint pang somewhere inside me as she disappears.

But I'm here.

"Steven?" I call. "Ian?"

Their footsteps thunder up the stairs, and they burst into the room, breathing hard. "Lain," Steven gasps. "Are you—"

"Better." I smile. "Do you think you could bring me something to eat? I'm starved."

Minutes later, we're all sitting on the bed, passing around a can of hash, though I end up eating most of it. I can't recall the last time I've been so ravenous. When I'm finished, I lick my fingers clean. They watch me with wide, nervous eyes. So far, they haven't spoken; it's as if they're afraid to ask me any questions, afraid that if they put even the slightest strain on me, I'll crumble to bits again. "That was good," I say. "Thank you."

Ian clears his throat. "So. Did it work?"

"Yes. It worked." I turn my gaze to Steven. He gives me a tentative, one-sided smile, and I stare into his light blue eyes. A flush creeps into my cheeks.

Ian looks down, and his expression tightens. "I'll give you a minute." He leaves the room, closing the door behind him.

Steven reaches out and lightly touches my cheek with his fingertips. "I thought I'd lost you," he whispers.

"I'm here now." I lay a hand over his. "And I swear, I'll never leave you again."

He drags me into a rough hug and buries his face against my hair, breathing in as if I'm the only source of air in the world. I hug him back, soaking in his warmth, the *realness* of him. A part of me is afraid to believe, convinced that this is an illusion that will be ripped away at any moment. But he's here. I'm here. I'm alive, holding him, feeling his arms around me, his heart against my cheek. He clings to me so tightly, it hurts my ribs, but I don't want him to let go. And I say the words I should have said before: "I love you, Steven."

"Love you too," he whispers into my hair.

He pulls back and smiles, his eyes shiny and reflective with tears, and I drink him in—the pale golden lashes, the tapestry of gray and blue in his irises, the scar on his cheek. That's new. I explore the thin, hard ridge with my fingertips, and he closes his eyes, as if savoring the touch. "How did this happen?"

"Got into a fight with Nicholas," he murmurs. "He didn't want us to rescue you. He said you were a lost cause, that it was too risky. I attacked him, and he gashed my cheek open."

Nicholas . . . The name triggers a brief flash of . . . something. What was it about Nicholas? Then it slips away. I stroke Steven's scar. "I'm sorry."

"It's nothing. That BlueGoo stuff is really amazing, you know? It heals pretty much anything."

My fingertips slide along the curve of his jaw line, feeling the prickle of fine, almost invisible stubble. I'm afraid to blink, lest he vanish while I'm not looking. "I'm sorry. I should never have left. I—"

He kisses me, cutting off the apology.

His lips are just the way I remember—cool and slightly rough, tasting faintly of the ocean. I want to breathe him in, to climb inside him and swim around in him, to meld my body with his so that nothing can ever come between us again. When we finally come up for air, I'm pleasantly dizzy. I rest my head on his shoulder, and for a while, we just hold each other.

I hate the fact that I forgot this feeling—forgot him. The idea that something so precious can be stripped away by a machine makes me want to rip apart IFEN headquarters with my bare hands. And I understand, in that moment, why Father killed himself rather than risk having his memory erased.

"Lain? You're shaking."

I press closer. "I'm all right. Just hold me."

I remember the terror and sickening helplessness, the sinking dread when I realized that Dr. Swan intended to steal my memories. And I wonder—is that how Steven felt every time he was Conditioned against his will? No wonder he despises IFEN so passionately. No wonder he's so determined to wipe them off the face of the Earth.

Until now, I don't think I ever understood that, not completely. Maybe I had to experience it for myself. Even if I've gotten my memories back—some of them, anyway—I'll never be the same. Something that used to be clean is now dirty. The hurt is difficult to pin down in words, but no less real for it. And I know, in this moment, that IFEN can't be reformed. The rot goes too deep.

I pull back, rubbing at the corners of my eyes. Steven touches the underside of my chin, tilting my face up, and studies it carefully. His expression is so serious, so intent, I smile despite the ache in my soul. I could happily spend the rest of the day in his arms, but there are too many questions. They crowd inside my skull, jostling each other, and I sift through them, trying to pluck out the most important ones.

I take a deep breath. "So. What's happening back in the Citadel? Earlier, Ian said something about not being sure whom to trust. Does that mean Zebra hasn't found the traitor yet?"

His shoulders stiffen. A strange look slips across his face.

"What's wrong?"

His lips press together in a thin line, and he turns his face away. "Zebra is dead."

Dead. I flinch. But somehow, the word doesn't shock me as much as it should. It's as though a part of me knew already. "How?"

"He was found in his study, sitting in his chair. No one really knows how it happened. There are security cameras throughout most of the Citadel, but not in Zebra's study. He was always really private. It looked like a heart attack or a stroke, but Ian and I both think it was a little fishy."

A trickle of cold runs down my spine and through my nerves. "You're saying he might have been killed."

"Yeah. That's what we think."

My mouth has gone dry. Memories scratch at a door inside my head, trying to get out. There's something important, something just out of reach, lost in the fog. I raise a trembling hand to my temple. "If he *was* killed, who did it?"

"We don't know." He opens his mouth, then looks away. When he answers, his voice is soft, like an apology. "There are a few people who suspect you."

"Me? But how would I even—I wasn't *there* when it happened!"

"Most of the Blackcoats know that you had nothing to do with it," he adds quickly. "It's just a few troublemakers."

I feel sick. But if I look at it from the Blackcoats' perspective, I can understand their suspicion. I'm a Mindwalker, a symbol of everything they hate. Living among them was hard enough before. What will it be like now that some of them suspect I'm a traitor?

"We don't *have* to go back, you know," he says.

"Then where should we go?" I ask. "What should we do? We can't stay here. Sooner or later, the authorities will come looking for us."

He nods reluctantly.

I sit on the bed, hugging my knees. "So if Zebra's gone, who's in charge of the Blackcoats now?"

"Nicholas, kind of," Steven says. "I mean, he was second-in-command, so he's the natural successor, but not everyone wants to follow him—people don't have the same respect for him that they did for Zebra—so the Blackcoats are split and arguing over everything. It's chaos."

Nicholas.

There's another flash in my head. I stiffen, clutching my shirt as a memory of suffocating pain fills my chest. My lungs constrict and burn as if filled with poison gas. I let out a ragged cry as a hot spike stabs through my head.

"What's wrong?" Steven asks, eyes wide.

Images flicker dimly. Blinking lights. White walls. A sense of dread. The memories are spinning, careening around and around. "It was him." I manage to hold my voice steady. "Nicholas. He's the murderer."

Steven's eyes widen. "Are you sure?"

"I felt Zebra die. I remember—I remember him telling me to stop Nicholas." I swallow the sourness at the back of my throat and force myself to breathe through the nausea and the stabbing pain in my head.

Steven's brows draw together. "How is that possible? You weren't there when he died."

"I was, though . . . sort of. Zebra implanted a device in my head, so he'd be able to communicate with me while I was in IFEN headquarters. We were connected at the moment of his death. I know it sounds crazy, but it's the truth. As long as Nicholas is there, all the Blackcoats are in danger. We have to warn them." He doesn't reply immediately, and a wave of despair washes over me. "You don't believe me?"

"I believe you," Steven says grimly.

"Lain?" Ian stands in the door. "I heard a shout. What—"

"Contact Jackal using that emergency cell she left us," Steven says. "Tell her to come pick us up. Now."

*   *   *

After Ian makes the call and Steven explains the situation, we wait on the rickety front steps outside the house. The trees sway and creak in a heavy wind, and a few raindrops spatter against the wood as thunder rumbles in the distance. I try to breathe through the squeezing panic in my chest.

"We need to work out a plan," Steven says. "First things first, we have to tell the other Blackcoats about this, but we have to make sure Nicholas doesn't catch on that we know."

Ian frowns. "Shouldn't we be sure, before we say anything to anyone?"

"Lain says he's the traitor," Steven replies. "That's good enough for me."

Ian opens his mouth, then closes it. "Okay. So what do we do, then?"

"As soon as we get to the Citadel, we track down Rhee or Burk," Steven says. "Someone we can trust. We make some excuse to talk to them alone. And Lain can tell them everything. If we run into Nicholas before that, we act normal. Don't let him know that Lain has her memories back." He looks me in the eye. "Right now, he doesn't know that you know, right?"

"I—I don't think so. No."

"Good. We'll keep it that way. He won't be happy about having you back, but he won't want to blow his cover, either. If he's still hanging around in the Citadel, it means there's something else he needs to accomplish, something he's planning to do."

"But what?" Ian asks. "Do you know, Lain?"

"No." I feel like I should know. But there's that patch of fog in my head, that blurry area right before the moment I woke up in IFEN headquarters with my memories gone. There's something I'm missing, some crucial piece.

"We'll find out," Steven says grimly. "Once we've told the others, we'll work out how to take Nicholas down—it shouldn't be hard, if we have help—and get some answers out of him." His eyes are hard and flat, like slate. "I'll wring the truth out of him myself, if I have to."

For a moment, I waver. What if I'm wrong? What if those flickers of knowledge are part of a dream or hallucination? What if—

No. I know what I saw.

Ian gives my shoulder a squeeze. Ever since I recovered my memories, he's been avoiding eye contact with me, but his voice is as warm and gentle as ever. "We'll get to the Citadel as fast as we can. I promise."

I manage a faint smile, but my rapid heartbeat refuses to slow. A sense of dread looms over me, and I can't shake the clinging terror—the feeling that everything is about to end.

The wind picks up, whistling. An echoing boom of thunder rolls toward us. Just as it starts to rain in earnest, cold pellets hammering the top of my head, a faded, dirty red pickup truck rumbles up the gravel driveway toward the house. The pickup stops, and Jackal opens the door, sticking her doglike head out. "Ready?" she calls.

We pile in, wet and shivering. I sit squeezed between Steven and Ian as the truck roars down the road, leaving a trail of dust. Tense silence hangs in the air as the windshield wipers swish, cutting through the downpour. Her headlights are twin yellow paths in the gloom.

"So," Jackal calls from the driver's seat. "Have you heard the latest news? Dr. Swan is dead."

"Yeah, we heard about that," Ian says.

A shudder runs through me. I'm still trying to adjust to the idea that he's gone. Of course, Jackal doesn't know that we were involved. Maybe it's better to keep it that way.

"So who's gonna take his place as Director?" she asks. "Any ideas?"

"No, not really," Ian replies. "Standard procedure is that the old Director nominates a new one. Officially, the elected reps on the National Ethical Committee have to approve the choice, but they've never gone against IFEN's decision."

"Fake democracy in action," Steven mutters.

"The URA's in an uproar," Jackal continues. "Everyone's panicking. They think it's the start of a new war. Hell, even up here, people are freaking out. They're talking about establishing curfews. Curfews, in Canada!"

My thoughts flash back to Dr. Swan's meeting with the Minister of Psychological Welfare. Is IFEN already stretching their influence into this country?

The journey to Toronto is a blur of field and forest and billboards half-seen through a gauze of rain. The city itself is a hazy glow of colors and fragile-looking, improbable skyscrapers on the horizon. As we draw nearer, Jackal leans forward, peering out the windshield. "Huh, that's weird. That wasn't here last time."

A white, peak-roofed building, no larger than a shack, stands next to the road, a security camera blinking on the roof. A metal gate bars the way. My stomach sinks. It's a checkpoint. I recognize it because there are checkpoints stationed at every road leading in and out of Aura, my home city.

We draw nearer to the gate. I can't see if there's actually anyone in the building, but there's a small security camera on the roof.

"Maybe we should turn around," Ian says.

"Fuck this crap," Jackal growls. She pulls out her pistol, rolls down the window, and fires a shot. The security camera spins off the roof.

Steven whistles, impressed.

"Uh, what about the gate?" Ian says nervously.

Jackal veers off the road, so suddenly that I clutch the seats in terror. Her tires rip through mud and grass, bumping over rocks as she drives around the gate, and the whole vehicle rattles and vibrates around me. An alarm starts beeping, but it fades quickly behind us as she swerves back onto the road and resumes driving. "Whoever built that thing didn't plan very well. Why the hell are they trying to monitor traffic, anyway? I mean, what is this, the URA?"

The question leaves a hollow feeling in my chest. I don't want to think about what this means, but I know: IFEN's already extended its reach into Canada.

33

Toronto enfolds us. It's all so strange, and yet so familiar, like remembering something I've seen in another life. In the sky, I see the giant, holographic dragon making its rounds over the city, scales gleaming red and bronze, fire spewing from its open mouth. A row of cartoon pink elephants swagger through the sky, smiling. The candy-bright glow of signs and the hard, bright squares of store windows shine through the gray haze. People are laughing in the streets, people as colorful and strange as the city around them. The city is a fever-dream of endlessly flowing pleasures. Somewhere in the distance, gunshots bark and police sirens howl. But the pedestrians go on laughing and chugging from bottles.

Jackal drops us off on a street corner.

"Thank you," Ian says. "For everything. You've helped us a lot."

She flashes white teeth in a smile. "No problem. Anything to help the cause." She drives off, leaving us alone in front of a Chinese restaurant, rain still sheeting down around us. A large, golden lucky cat smiles at us from the window, paw waving back and forth.

We enter, tracking in water. A tiny, wizened old woman stands behind the counter, peering at us with dark eyes. Steven exchanges some sort of hand signal with her—it looks like he's tracing letters or numbers in the air—and the woman nods. She smiles, showing a row of very small, very white teeth, and gestures to a door behind the counter.

We follow her down a narrow, twisting set of stairs to an underground room, where she moves aside an elaborate tapestry to reveal a rough hole in the brick wall.

"Thanks," Steven says.

She nods, her face crinkling in a smile. She hasn't said a word the entire time.

Ian fishes a flashlight out of his pack and hands it to Steven. "Ready?"

"I suppose."

We enter the tunnel, which isn't large enough to stand up in, or even crouch. Ian takes the lead, Steven the rear. The walls are rough earth, held up here and there with wooden beams, and fine grains of dirt fall down around us as we crawl, giving me the panicky sense that the roof will cave in at any moment. I try not to think about how many bugs, rats or snakes are probably squiggling and scuttling around in here. My own heartbeat is deafening.

We keep crawling through the narrow, claustrophobic space for what feels like hours. Then it opens up, and suddenly, we're standing in a wide, shadowy subway tunnel with splashes of graffiti on the walls, bright streaks of color lit up by our light against the dull brown brick.

Steven squints, pointing his flashlight in one direction, then the other. He motions for us, and we start walking. The walls magnify our footsteps. All of this feels vaguely familiar, yet distant, like a place from childhood, though I know not much time has passed since I last set foot in here. Once, I spot a pair of other people—an old man and a woman, their faces black with dirt, huddled by a foul-smelling fire. They watch us suspiciously, the whites of their eyes brilliant in the darkness.

We only have to walk for a few minutes before we find ourselves standing before a pair of looming, rusted metal doors. Steven opens a panel on the adjacent wall, revealing the pad of a biometric scanner, incongruous amid the crumbling brick. He presses a thumb to the panel, which flashes lime green, and the doors swing open, revealing the wide entrance room, the towering metal walls. We enter, and the doors thunder shut behind us.

I remember this place. A rush of images and emotions sweeps over me, and I lean against the wall.

Steven grips my arm, steadying me. "Are you—"

"Fine." My chest suddenly feels too small.

"Breathe," Ian reminds me.

I nod, resting my hands on my knees until I've caught my breath.

"Well, hello."

I freeze, feeling like I've just stepped off the edge of a cliff. Slowly, I look up to see Nicholas standing in the hallway, clad in his usual long black coat, his white hair swept back from his brow, plastered to his scalp with shiny gel. He's flanked by two muscular, armed Blackcoats—a man with a panther tattoo on his neck and a bald woman with black lipstick and spiky piercings.

My pulse thuds like a hammer, drowning out my thoughts. Nicholas narrows his eyes. For a moment, none of us moves. I'm afraid to speak, afraid to breathe. He smiles without showing teeth. "It appears the rescue mission was a success, after all. I must admit, I didn't have high hopes that you'd return, but I'm delighted to see you here."

"Well, we're glad to be back," Ian says, his tone cautiously neutral.

"Rhee and the others arrived a few days ago, but they weren't sure you'd managed to escape." Nicholas takes a step forward. His gaze locks onto me. "So, Ms. Fisher. I gather you don't remember me. Or this place."

"No."

His eyes search mine, and his facial muscles tighten. I struggle to keep my expression blank. Don't panic, I tell myself. He can't possibly know that I have my memories back.

"You must be tired," he says. "Shall I escort you to your rooms?"

"We can find our own way, thanks," Steven says.

"I insist."

There's not much else we can do. Resisting would suggest we have something to hide. Reluctantly, we follow. The two Blackcoats march at our sides, pistols glinting in the holsters at their hips.

Nicholas peers at me over one shoulder. "I'm sure you've been through quite an ordeal."

"It's been very frightening," I reply, speaking slowly. "I barely know what's going on."

"I can imagine. IFEN's brainwashing techniques are sophisticated and thorough."

"Hey," Steven calls, "this isn't the way to the dorm wing."

Nicholas stops suddenly and raises a hand, and his Blackcoat guards draw their pistols. "I hope you'll understand why I'm about to do this."

"What the hell is going on?" Ian asks.

Ice threads through my veins. The Blackcoats keep their guns trained on us.

"Zebra's death occurred around the same time that Lain vanished—which, you must admit, is a bit suspicious. We can't assume she's trustworthy until she's given a thorough interrogation. And I want to make sure you two gentlemen don't interfere." He glances at the guards. "Restrain Ms. Fisher."

This is bad. I stand, paralyzed, my mind racing in a thousand directions.

Ian flings himself in front of me, forming a barrier between me and the guards. "Wait!"

"Out of the way," the male Blackcoat growls, finger on the trigger.

Ian doesn't move. His arms remain outstretched, as if that will stop a bullet. "Lain sacrificed herself to save me and Rhee and the others," he says firmly. "She's not a traitor, and you know it."

"But she's been under the control of the enemy," Nicholas says. "We don't know what they've done to her mind. This is a necessary precaution."

"Bullshit," Steven snaps.

"Steven," I whisper, a warning in my tone. The very air feels charged with electricity, as if the smallest movement, the softest word will ignite it. Nicholas' skin is drawn tight over the bones of his face, his teeth bared. His hatred is a tangible force emanating from him like an aura. He wants us dead. Probably the only reason he hasn't given the order to fire is because acting too quickly will blow his cover.

Whatever happens, we can't let them lock us up. If we do, we'll never get out. Nicholas will make sure of that.

I take a cautious step forward, past Ian. He starts to reach out toward me, to stop me, but I push his arm down and turn toward the nearest Blackcoat—the woman with the pierced nose and eyebrows. Her eyes are dark and alert, and I see her finger twitch on the trigger. "We just want to talk to Rhee," I say. "Or Burk, whoever you can find first."

Her teeth catch on her black-painted lip, tugging, and I realize suddenly how young she is—not more than fifteen or sixteen.

"I'm in charge here," Nicholas says. "Whatever they want to say, they can say it here and now."

"Fine," Steven says. "Then I'll say it. You're the traitor. You murdered Zebra."

The guards' faces go blank with confusion. "What?" the man says.

Nicholas' expression darkens. "That's quite an accusation. Are you prepared to back it up with evidence?" Silence. "No, then?"

This is bad. This is very bad.

"Perhaps I shouldn't bother arresting you," Nicholas says. "Perhaps I should just have you shot right here."

The girl's eyes dart back and forth. "Do you really want to kill them? If we bring them in for questioning—"

Nicholas whirls toward her. "Should I question your loyalty as well?"

She takes a nervous step back.

In a blur of movement, Steven draws a pistol and aims it at Nicholas, but his hands are shaking. Sweat glistens on his temple, and I can see the pulse fluttering beneath the surface. "Let us through," he says.

"So you're threatening me now?" Nicholas tilts his head. "You've never actually made a kill, have you?" His tone is strangely conversational. Casual, almost.

A bead of sweat trickles down Steven's neck. His finger quivers on the trigger. "You don't think I'll shoot, if you make a move? Try me."

My ears are ringing. I don't know what to do, what to say. Everything is spinning out of control.

Nicholas' fingers twitch and curl, as if they want to sprout claws. Then he folds his hands in front of him and smiles suddenly, magnanimously. "Clearly, there's been some misunderstanding. We all lost our tempers. Things got a little out of hand. But this doesn't need to end in bloodshed. We're all on the same side, aren't we?"

"I doubt that," Steven mutters. He doesn't budge.

Nicholas extends an open hand toward Steven, who flinches. "Why don't you come with me? I'll take you to Rhee and Burk, and we'll all talk this out." As he speaks, his other hand moves toward something at his hip.

"*Steven!*" I scream.

The next few things happen in a blur. Nicholas pulls out a pistol. Before he can raise it, a *crack* splits the air, and he staggers backward, a bullet hole in his chest. The gun slips from his fingers and clatters to the floor. He coughs, and blood dribbles from his mouth, thick and dark as he slumps against the wall and slides down, leaving a crimson smear.

Ian takes a step back, face white. I press a hand to my mouth and choke down the scream that fills my throat. The two guards watch, jaws hanging. Steven stands rigidly, a pistol clutched in both hands, smoke trailing from the muzzle. His eyes are enormous and dazed.

Nicholas lets out a low groan. He coughs, and more blood bubbles from his lips. His eerily perfect blue eyes roll toward me, and his lips stretch into something between a grimace and a smile. "Twenty-four hours," he rasps. "You're all—" another cough—"going to die."

"What do you mean?" Ian asks. He grabs the front of Nicholas' shirt. "What's going to happen in twenty-four hours?"

Nicholas laughs, then his voice breaks off in a wet rattle, and he goes still.

The pistol trembles in Steven's hands, slips from his fingers and hits the floor.

For a few seconds, no one moves.

I've seen death before. I felt Zebra die. Yet watching the life leave someone's body, that moment when a sentient being becomes an inanimate hunk of meat, still feels so . . . unnatural. So wrong. There are times when death itself feels like a mistake.

The din of approaching footsteps breaks the silence, and I look up just in time to see Rhee and Burk striding toward us, rifles drawn. They stop.

"What the hell is going on here?" Burk asks.

The girl with the piercings slowly turns toward him. Her gun hangs limp and forgotten from her hands. "He said we're all going to die." Her voice sounds faraway. "He said it would happen in twenty-four hours."

"Who did?"

"Nicholas." Ian steps forward. "He was working with IFEN. He was the one who killed Zebra. And he tried to kill Steven, just now. Steven shot him in self-defense."

"Impossible." But Burk looks shaken. "This is absurd. You—" He points at the guards. "Restrain these three. Lock them up."

Rhee holds up a hand. "Everyone, take it easy. I'll review the security footage. In the meantime, the three of you will be confined to your rooms. You'll be questioned separately. We'll get to the bottom of this."

I have to hand it to her—she's very functional in a crisis.

"Rhee, you know we aren't traitors," Ian says.

"Just a precaution," Rhee says. "I believe you're innocent, but if you cooperate this will go much more smoothly."

Steven still hasn't spoken a word. The zombie-like way he stands there, staring at the body, worries me. I have the sense that he's drifting away. "Steven," I say quietly. He blinks twice and turns his head toward me. "Are you all right?"

"I—yeah. Fine."

Nicholas' eyes are still open, his head tilted at an odd angle. He seems to be staring at me, his mouth twisted into a loose grimace, teeth bared. I'll probably see that image in my nightmares.

"Burk, keep an eye on Steven and Ian. Lain, come with me," Rhee says, interrupting my thoughts.

I hesitate.

"They'll be fine. I promise."

Reluctantly, I follow her down the hall. My mind seems to be floating somewhere above my body. It's surreal, being back in the Citadel after everything that happened. The familiar, muffled thump of machinery emanates through the walls and floor.

"I take it you've recovered your memories," she remarks.

"Yes. Well, mostly."

Rhee simply nods.

After we've been walking a few minutes, she opens a door. When I recognize the room beyond, I take an involuntary step back. This is where Nicholas interrogated me after the failed mission. As I stare at the four blank walls surrounding the table and two chairs, my chest seems to shrink. I remember the flash of pain as he backhanded me across the face.

"You won't be harmed," Rhee says, her voice softening slightly. "I'll make sure of that. Just wait here. You'll be questioned shortly."

"All right." I hesitate. "Rhee . . . you believe me, don't you? I know there are people who believe that I'm the traitor. I'm not. I swear."

"I know."

The tightness inside me loosens. I don't know why her opinion matters so much, but it does. "Thank you."

For a moment, she just stands there, staring straight ahead, and I'm not sure if she's waiting for me to go inside or if she's forgotten about me entirely. "So. Nicholas is the one who murdered Zebra," she says finally, low and pensive. "Are you certain of that?"

"Yes. Zebra told me. Before he died. I know it sounds crazy, but he put some kind of implant in my head to communicate with me while I was in IFEN headquarters."

"I see." Still, she doesn't look at me. I remember her telling me how she owed Zebra her life, how he saved her from a rough, half-starved existence in the Underground. He meant something to her. And now he's dead.

"I'm sorry," I say.

"For what?"

"About . . . you know. What happened to him."

"Not your fault." A moment of awkward silence passes. "Go on in," she says.

I step into the room. She turns to go.

"Rhee, wait," I blurt out. She stops, and I'm left fumbling for words. I'm not even sure what I want to say to her, but I have to say something. "I—I never really thanked you."

"For what?"

"For training me. For making me stronger. I don't think I'd have survived this long, if not for you."

A tiny furrow appears between her brows. "I was doing my job. You don't need to thank me."

"I want to. Not because I feel obligated to. Because I'm grateful. Just accept it. Please?"

She hesitates . . . then gives a small nod. "You're welcome." She opens her mouth, as if she's about to say something else. Then she closes it and presses a panel on the wall. The door slides shut, and the echoes of her receding footsteps fade into silence, leaving me alone. I slump in my chair, resting my cheek against the cool surface of the tabletop.

My whole body aches like a collection of bruises, and the inside of my head is a jumbled mess. It feels like I've been through more in the past seventy-two hours than any human being should be sensibly expected to endure in a lifetime. Then again, the fact that I'm alive at all is a miracle, after all the risks I took. Some far off part of me wants to cry, but it feels like a waste of energy. Mostly, I just want to sit here, staring blankly at the wall.

Steven's face floats up behind my eyes. I see the gun quivering in his hands, the deadness in his expression. His first kill.

The door clicks open, and I sit up, jolted from my reverie. Burk wheels in a cart. Sitting atop it is my Gate. Ian walks in behind him, expression solemn. There's a nervous flutter in my stomach.

"Here's what's going to happen." Burk pulls up a chair. His habitual grim visage is a bit more severe than usual. "You're going to show us some of your memories. Your friend is here because he's currently the only person in the Citadel who knows how to use a Gate, but I'll be watching him very carefully. If either of you tries anything funny, there will be repercussions. Understand?"

I nod.

We sit, facing each other, as Ian places a helmet over my head, then dons his own. "Don't worry," he murmurs. "This'll go quickly."

All I want right now is to talk to Steven. I need to be sure he's okay. But the sooner I cooperate, the sooner this will be over with. "Go ahead."

Ian turns on the Gate, which projects a screen into the air, displaying a rotating image of my brain. Burk scowls at it as if it's some sort of technological voodoo. He pokes at the screen with a thick finger. Ian clears his throat. "Let me handle this, please."

Burk crosses his arms over his chest.

Ian touches a corner of the screen, and it goes blank. "I'm switching to visual mode now." He hands a pair of earbuds to Burk. "This will allow you to listen in, even without a helmet, while you watch the screen. Lain—pull your visor down and focus on seeing the memories clearly in your head. We'll start with the mission to blow up the database in Toronto. Go back to the beginning."

My breath comes short and fast. This isn't something I want to relive, but I pull down the dark visor, close my eyes, and bring up that moment—the rumble of the engine, the faint smell of smoke, the green numbers of a digital clock glowing through the darkness.

Ian guides me through the session, his voice soft and gentle, a path to follow through the forest of emotion. I show him the interrogation session after the failed mission, followed by my meeting with Zebra. I try to forget Burk's presence and imagine that I'm just showing this to Ian. It makes it easier, just a little. But as I move through my time in IFEN headquarters, I start to shake.

Ian places a hand on my shoulder. "It's okay. You've given us enough."

I exhale an unsteady breath and pull my helmet off. Sweat drenches my hair.

"Put that back on," Burk says. "We're not done yet."

"What more do you want?" Ian asks, anger heating his voice. "Swan tortured her. If that isn't proof that she's not working with IFEN, what is?"

"This still doesn't prove Nicholas was the traitor."

"We heard him threaten, with his dying words, that we were all going to die. And the security footage confirms it. We're wasting time here. We need to be figuring out what we're going to do about this attack."

Burk huffs and pushes himself away from the table. "Personally, I think it was a bluff. If IFEN were capable of attacking us, they would have done it already."

Maybe he's right—maybe Nicholas just threatened us out of anger. But something in my gut tells me otherwise. "IFEN already knows our location," I say quietly. "International treaties have held them back, until now, but things are changing. Jackal said there are curfews in Canada now. And we drove through a checkpoint to get here. That's IFEN's influence at work. The border won't keep them out much longer."

Burk's lips tighten. "That's quite a leap."

"Well, something is definitely happening," Ian says. "Either way, we can't afford to take his threat lightly."

"We'll be prepared." Burk stands. "There's an emergency Assembly in twenty minutes. In the meantime, go back to your room. Take a shower." He wrinkles his nose. "You could use one."

I sniff my shirt. "Well, we have been living in a cabin in the woods for the past few days," I mutter. "There was no running water."

Burk stalks out, leaving Ian and I alone.

I sigh. "He still doesn't trust me."

"Don't worry about him. He can complain all he wants, but he's not the leader here. He doesn't call the shots."

"So who is the leader?"

"Dunno if we even have one. Rhee's the closest thing, or at least, she seems to be the one whose orders everyone respects. She trusts you, and if it comes down to a conflict between her and Burk, people will side with her." His gaze searches my face. "You okay?"

"As well as can be expected, I guess."

Ian lays a warm hand against my back. At that simple, comforting gesture, my throat swells, and I nearly come undone. "I'm sorry," I whisper.

"For what?"

"For dragging you into this. All of this. If not for me, you'd probably still be home."

"The URA isn't home," he says. "Not anymore. This is where I want to be." He gives me a tiny smile.

With sudden, vivid intensity, I remember the kiss I shared with him in the forest outside the safe house. Heat rushes to my cheeks, and my fingertips stray to my face, brushing over my lips. Was that really just this morning? It feels like a lifetime ago now. God, this is all so confusing. I love Steven. I know that now. And yet what I felt for Ian in that moment is still so fresh and real in my head. "Ian . . . I . . ."

"It's all right. I understand." He looks away. "I knew what would happen, if you took the Lucid. And I—I felt it, through the Gate. The way you feel about him, and how he feels about you. I don't think I can compete with that." He lowers his head. "I'm not going to stand between you."

I reach for words and come up blank. "I'm sorry," I say again, not even sure what I'm apologizing for.

"Don't be." His voice is gentle. "I'm happy for you. I really am." Tears glint at the corners of his eyes, and he blinks them away. "Will you tell me one thing? If—if you'd never met Steven . . . if it was just you and me . . . do you think maybe you . . ."

My heart gives a small lurch. In a vivid burst, I recall the softness of his lips on mine, the gentleness of his fingertips on my face. I open my mouth, but the word sticks in my throat, because I don't know if speaking it will ease his pain or make it worse.

"Never mind." He gives me a strained smile. "You don't have to answer that."

34

Back in my room, I take a quick shower, sluicing away the sweat of the past few days, then change into fresh clothes. It feels amazingly good to be clean again. Rhee's voice emanates from the speakers, announcing the emergency Assembly.

In the Hall, Blackcoats jostle each other, murmuring together in low, puzzled voices. I can't get through the crowd, so I'm left hovering alone near the back of the crowd, standing on tiptoe to see over a forest of heads.

The noise dies out as Rhee ascends the steps to the stage and faces the room, a tall, slender figure, bathed in a reddish spotlight. She adjusts the microphone on her collar. Her face is as stony and expressionless as ever. "As I'm sure you're all aware by now, Dr. Swan is dead. He took his own life to avoid capture."

She gets right down to business. It's such a contrast from Nicholas' showier style.

"Now," Rhee continues, "his successor has been chosen. Earlier today, this appeared on the news."

She pushes a button on a remote, and the screen lights up, displaying a face I recognize. A cry leaps from my throat before I can stop it.

"Good evening," Aaron says in a firm, low voice. He's wearing a white suit, and his hair is neatly combed and parted as he stares straight into the camera. There's a slight glassiness to his green eyes, a pallor of exhaustion to his face. "My name is Aaron Freed. And as of today, with a heavy heart, I assume the position of Director."

My head spins. The last time I saw Aaron, he hardly seemed prepared to lead the most powerful organization in the URA. Does he even want this?

"Three days ago," he continues, "Dr. Swan was murdered by terrorists. These tragic circumstances have forced me to step forward. I realize that I'm young, but I've been working closely with Dr. Swan for some time now, and I will do my best to carry on his legacy. We will find and stop these terrorists, and we will use any tool at our disposal. The time for hesitation and moderation is over. We must take an unflinching stance against the violence and cruelty of those who would tear this land apart for the sake of their own selfish, radical ideology. I urge all of you, as citizens of the United Republic of America, to join me in making our country safe once again."

Those aren't his words. It's clearly Aaron on the screen, but his tone of voice, the cadence of his speech, everything is off. He's either been heavily Conditioned or coerced into reciting this message. Still, the sight of him there, in Dr. Swan's place, is powerfully unnerving.

Aaron continues: "In issues of national security, there can be no gray area, no compromise. The time has come for action against those who would destroy our way of life." There's a pause. Then he leans forward, a strange, intent look in his eyes. When he speaks again, his tone has changed. "Remember." His voice is low, urgent. "Remember what these people are capable of."

A moment's disorientation sweeps over me. It feels, suddenly, like he's speaking directly to me.

"They will use every tool at their disposal," he says with that quiet intensity. "Fear is their greatest weapon, because the ultimate battle isn't physical—it's psychological. The question is whether we will surrender, whether we will allow ourselves to be beaten down by those who seek to instill fear in our hearts. I've come to realize, in these past few days, that we cannot afford a peaceful solution. We have no alternative but to fight them."

He's not talking about fighting the Blackcoats, I realize suddenly. He's talking about IFEN, and he's trusting me—us—to understand.

"Very soon now, they will strike again," he says. "Unless we stop them. Unless we take action first. It is our only hope. And so I say to you, now—stand up. Stand tall. Strike back. *Do whatever is necessary.*" The screen winks out.

Silence hangs over the hall. Aaron is trying to warn me.

Remember, he said. Remember *what*?

"It occurred to me that no one has yet given Zebra a eulogy," Rhee says, jerking me from my thoughts. "There hasn't been time for a proper funeral. So I'll say a few words on his behalf. I warn you, I'm not much good at making speeches." She pauses. "Physically, Zebra was not a strong man. But he refused to be pitied, bullied, or broken. His mind and spirit were indomitable. He's gone, and his death, as you all know, was very sudden. But I believe that as long as we carry his memory, he is with us. He will lend us his strength, and we will honor him by staying true to ourselves, by refusing to compromise our rights and our lives." She presses a fist to her chest in salute and bows her head. The other Blackcoats do the same. I glimpse tears glinting in the eyes of a few listeners.

Rhee raises her head. "And now, more than ever, we will need that strength. Zebra often spoke of the importance of readying ourselves for war. It seems that war has come to us. We've received intelligence that IFEN is poised to attack us within the next twenty-four hours. We don't know what form this attack will take. But we can be sure that they'll try everything in their power to wipe us out."

A hush hangs over the room. The listeners stare, stunned, soaking up the message.

"We all knew that this day would arrive," she continues. "This may not be how we expected it to happen, but there's no cause for fear. This is what we've been training for and preparing for all this time. When they come, we will be ready."

The Blackcoats around me are drying their tears, straightening their shoulders, expressions turning grim and determined.

I try to ignore the tightening in my gut. Aaron's words fill my head: *Remember what these people are capable of.*

"We've already developed a plan," Rhee says. "There's only one entrance to the Citadel, and that's the main doors. We'll fill the room with traps and explosives. If IFEN tries to invade, the traps will take out a significant number of their soldiers."

IFEN will probably be anticipating something like that. And who's to say they'll even send soldiers through the main doors? They could just as easily attack us by flooding the Citadel with neurotoxins. Or sending in mini-drones and detonating them remotely. It occurs to me, as well, that they could simply starve us out. Zebra controlled everything. Now that he's dead, where will we get our food and water?

Of course, Rhee is already aware of all this. She must be. But she's trying to hide how dire our situation is, to avoid causing panic—trying to convince everyone we have a chance of winning.

"Yes, our enemy is strong," Rhee continues. "But we have always been prepared to die defending our cause, to keep fighting for our freedom, no matter the cost." Her face remains composed and still, but her eyes shine with a cool, intense fire. "Freedom is a contract signed in blood. It's the pact we've made with each other, the oath we swore when we joined the cause. And we will not forsake that oath." She raises her rifle into the air. The Blackcoats raise their fists in answer.

I bite my knuckle, hard enough to draw blood. I don't want to believe that it's hopeless. But when I look at the rifle-carrying teenaged soldiers around me and imagine them up against the technological and political might of IFEN, I feel sick.

This won't be a battle. It will be a slaughter.

* * *

Rhee announces a special training session in the simulation room to go over battle strategies, then ends the Assembly. I don't plan to attend the training session.

As the Blackcoats filter out of the room, I scan the dispersing crowd for Steven, but still, I don't see him. Did he miss the Assembly? That's unlike him. I make my way back to the dorm wing and knock on his door. "Steven? It's me."

After a few seconds, the door slides open. It whisks shut behind me after I enter. Steven's sitting on the edge of the bed, expression blank, and I'm struck suddenly by how young he looks. His fingers clutch the edge of the mattress, and his narrow shoulders are hunched, as if braced against a coming blow. Slowly, I approach and sit next to him. He doesn't look at me. His face has lost all color, save for the dark circles around his eyes.

"Are you all right?" I ask.

He stares straight ahead, his gaze unfocused. "I shouldn't have brought you back here." His voice seems to be coming from far away. "This place isn't safe."

"I don't think we'd be any safer outside."

Steven crosses his arms over his chest, gripping his biceps. His breathing sounds strange. I shift on the bed, uneasy. "I think we should talk," I say.

"About what?"

"About what happened with Nicholas."

Still, he doesn't look at me. "There's nothing to talk about. He was a traitor. Now he's dead."

"This is the first time you've killed a human being," I say. "Even if he was a horrible person, it's completely understandable to feel something."

He raises one hand, stares at it, and slowly curls the fingers into a fist. "That's the funny thing. I don't. I'm not angry, I'm not sad, I'm not guilty, I'm not happy about it. I'm not even relieved. It's like—" He knocks the fist against his chest. "Wake up in there. You know?"

I examine the glassy, unfocused sheen on his eyes, and a chill trickles down my spine. "I think you're in a disassociated state. You've detached yourself from your emotions."

"Yeah?" A smile ticks at the corners of his lips, as if the thought amuses him.

"Numbing yourself might help you function, for now, but it's dangerous in the long run."

"Believe me, I know all about that. I used to numb myself all the time. Remember those little white pills?" He lets out a flat, humorless chuckle. "I'm okay."

"You're not okay, Steven."

He snorts. "Thanks for the vote of confidence, Doc. Really helps bolster my already wonderful self-esteem."

"Hiding behind sarcasm doesn't help."

"Sarcasm's my default setting. Also, in case you forgot, we've got one day before the shit hits the fan. Everyone in the Citadel is in danger. Shouldn't we be talking about that instead of dissecting my feelings?"

"Don't you dare start pushing me away again," I say, sharper than I intend to. "We've been through too much."

He tenses. For an instant, something flickers in his expression, then his gaze jerks away.

I soften my tone. "Please."

His lips tremble, a movement so slight it's almost imperceptible. Then he presses them together into a hard line. "I'm not
pushing you away, Lain. I just—I can't afford to get bogged down
in all my mental crap. If I do, I won't be able to move. Later, after
we deal with this situation, we'll talk about this. Not now."

What I'm afraid to say aloud is that there might not be an after.
I bite my lower lip.

"Did Rhee say anything about a battle plan?" he asks.

"She said there'd be a training session right after the Assembly."

He stands. "Then I'm going."

"Do you honestly think we have a chance?" I blurt out.

His back stiffens.

"You know the Blackcoats can't win against the URA's military.
This is mass suicide. We need to be making plans to evacuate, to
escape before they—"

He faces me. "Evacuate to where? The Underground? How
long do you think we'd survive? You just said it yourself—it's no
safer outside. We've got to fight. It's the only option we have." He
stops, dragging in a heavy breath. "No matter what happens, I will
protect you. I swear."

Before I can say another word, he turns sharply and walks
out. The door slides shut behind him with a metallic whish, like
a guillotine.

"Damn it," I whisper. I follow him out of the room, but he's
already disappeared. I slump against the nearest wall and press
my forehead to the cool metal.

It wasn't supposed to be like this. Steven and I have finally
been reunited, even after all Dr. Swan's efforts to rip him out of my
mind. We're supposed to be together now. Everything is supposed
to be all right. Instead, he's getting ready to die in a hopeless battle.

The death-frozen faces of Brian and Joy flash through my head,
and my pulse speeds again. No. I won't watch anyone else die. There
has to be a way out of this. I shut my eyes, focusing my thoughts,

gathering all the available data and laying it out in my head like an array of spreadsheets.

Still, there's that maddening foggy spot in my memories. If I concentrate, I can see flickers and fragments of something within, but I can't make sense of it. It's like sifting through a handful of puzzle pieces, trying to figure out what kind of picture they'd make if I had them all.

Something sparks, and I straighten, heart pounding. *Paradise lost.* Zebra's last words, whispered to me through the neural link. The title of an epic poem. He has that book in his study. It must mean *something.* Maybe it's connected to his plan. Maybe this is the thing that will save us.

I start walking quickly toward Zebra's study. Then I round the corner and nearly run into Burk.

He smiles, a hard, unpleasant expression. "There you are." He grabs my arm and marches me down the hall, like a parent dragging his disobedient child to her punishment.

I struggle, but his grip is iron. "What is this?"

"Maybe Rhee has foolishly decided to trust you, but I don't. I've decided to take matters into my own hands." He opens a door, revealing an empty, closet-sized room with plain metal walls, and throws me in. The door slams shut, sealing me in darkness. In an instant, I realize where I am—the timeout room.

"Burk!" I pound my fists against the door. "Let me out!"

A slot in the door opens, and he peers in. "You're going to stay in there, where you can't cause any trouble," he says.

"How long?" I ask, frantic.

"Until I decide to let you out. Nothing personal, but we can't afford to take risks."

No, no, no. He can't do this to me, not now. "Wait! You don't understand! I have to go to Zebra's study. He left me a clue. It's some kind of code, and I need to figure it out before IFEN attacks us." The words spill out of me in a rush.

He snorts.

"I swear, I'm telling the truth."

"I very much doubt that," he says. "I'll send someone to bring you your dinner later. Oh, and don't bother screaming. The walls are soundproof." The slot closes. Darkness and silence engulf me.

I keep shouting his name, pounding my fists against the door until they ache, but of course, there's no response. My legs crumble beneath me, and I sit, leaning back against the door, exhausted. I shut my eyes and press the heels of my hands against my lids.

The Citadel is about to be attacked, and there's nothing I can do. I'm stuck in here, helpless. Sooner or later, someone will notice I'm missing and come looking for me. But by then, it might be too late.

Because there's nothing else to do, I pace the tiny room. The darkness feels close, tangible, like it's shrinking around me. In a flash, I'm transported back to my time in Area 9, and I have to concentrate on breathing to dispel the weight pressing on my lungs. Back and forth, back and forth I pace, counting my steps.

How do prisoners go to the bathroom in here? Am I just expected to hold it? The thought occurs to me at random. It hardly matters now; maybe it's just my mind trying to stave off the encroaching panic.

I'm not sure how much time has passed when a dull, metallic clank breaks the silence, and the slot on the door slides open again. I leap to my feet. "Hello?" I call, breathless.

A pair of dark eyes appears in the slot. "I'm here to give you your food. I'm just going to push it through here."

Shana. My heart sinks. "Does this mean you think I'm a traitor, too?"

"I'm just following orders."

I doubt I'll have much luck convincing her to let me out. But I have to try. I take a deep breath and lower my voice. "Shana, listen.

I don't know what Burk told you, but I'm not dangerous and I'm not brainwashed, and I need to get out of here. Now."

Her eyes narrow. "Why?"

"You heard Rhee's announcement at the Assembly. IFEN is going to attack us very soon. There might be something I can do, but I need to get to Zebra's study. I think there's a message he left for me."

"A message," she repeats.

"Yes. I think it might be connected to something that can help us."

"And why should I believe you?"

"I can't prove anything. I'm asking you to trust me." I keep my hands pressed to the door, staring frantically into her eyes. "I know you don't like me. But please believe me when I say that I want to save the Blackcoats. At least, I want to try. But I can't do that from inside here."

There's a long pause. "You realize that if Burk finds out, it'll be my ass in the timeout room. Hell, he might just shoot me. He's gotten a little twitchy since Zebra died."

"I noticed. But in less than a day, that won't matter, because if we don't do something, this place will be rubble, and we'll all be dead."

"That's assuming this attack is even gonna happen."

"It will. And unless we figure something out, they will wipe us off the face of the Earth. Please, Shana. I'm begging you."

There's a pause. "Say that again."

"I'm begging you," I repeat, my frustration mounting.

The slot closes, leaving me in total darkness once more. My heart plummets. I should have known better, I think. Why would she want to put herself on the line for me?

Then the door opens, and she's standing there, arms crossed over her chest, a cellophane-wrapped tray sitting near her feet. "You won't have much time," she says. "An hour or two, maybe.

Sooner or later he'll check on you and realize you're not here. And I can't help you with whatever you're planning to do in Zebra's study. Burk will get suspicious if I don't report back to him."

"I understand." I jog down the hall, then stop, peering over one shoulder. "Shana? Thank you."

She looks away. "Just get out of here before I change my mind."

I stride forward, fighting the urge to break into a run. Running will attract attention. My pulse drums in my neck and wrists as I make my way toward Zebra's study. The silence magnifies and doubles my footsteps. The metal corridors are eerily empty, like a labyrinthine tomb. Everyone must be in training.

Behind me, I hear what might be a footstep, and I spin around. The hall is unoccupied. I exhale, annoyed at my own jumpiness. No one is following me.

When I arrive, the door is unlocked; it slides open automatically at my approach. The back wall is open, revealing Zebra's empty study. I brace myself and step inside.

His wheelchair sits in the center of the room. Someone has placed a single lily on the seat. It's a little wilted around the edges. I wonder what the Blackcoats did with his body—if they simply cremated him, or if he's buried somewhere in the Citadel, sealed inside a vault. Maybe that's what he would have wanted, to be a part of this place forever. Or maybe not. He spent so much of his life trapped in this room, afraid to venture into the outside world. He was both king and prisoner here. If his spirit still exists somewhere, I hope it's flying free. Freedom meant so much to him.

I shake the thoughts off, walk across the room to the bookshelf and run my fingers over the titles, and there it is, just where I remember it: Milton's epic poem, *Paradise Lost*. I slide it out. Then I bundle up all my hurt and confusion and fear and misery, stuff them all into a box in the corner of my head, and lock it up tight, focusing all my attention on the object in my hands. *Take in every detail.* I trace the letters of the title. They're gold and faintly indented, pressed into the leather, which is dark brown. The first page is blank save for the title and author, centered, in blocky black type.

I flip through the pages, examining each one with a forensic analyst's eye. The paper is so old; it feels like it might crumble apart under my fingertips.

What was Zebra trying to tell me? What if it's nothing at all? What if he started hallucinating in his last moments?

No. I don't believe that. He wouldn't waste his last words on something meaningless.

Desperate, I hold the open book up to the lamp and flip through again, hoping the light will reveal some secret, but there's no hidden writing, no messages scribbled in the margins in invisible ink. If there's a clue buried in here, I'm too exhausted to see it. The words keep blurring and shifting around on the page.

Maybe there's something in the room itself. I put the book down and check under the desk, in the corners and under the bookshelves. Nothing. My desperation is growing. It won't be long until Burk figures out I've slipped my prison cell, and if he gets his hands on me again, my chance will disappear forever.

The fireplace is empty and dark. I crouch in front of it and run my fingers over the stones of the mantle. I reach over the burned-out logs and ashes, to the cement wall in back, and feel around until my fingertips encounter a rough edge. I pick at it, pry it open, and a square piece slides away to reveal a keypad, the numbers glowing a soft, ghostly green. *Yes!*

A code. I need a code.

I punch in a few random strings of numbers, just to see what happens. Predictably, nothing does. The code must be hidden in the book.

I sit down and open *Paradise Lost*. Because I don't know what else to do, I start speed-reading, hoping something will jump out at me.

Even in my frantic state, it's hard not to appreciate the beauty of Milton's poetry. The words have a power undimmed by the centuries. But what always stuck with me most strongly was the character of Lucifer. In Milton's hands, he's a tragic, complex figure, poisoned by hatred, yet crafty and determined. His struggle is ultimately, inevitably futile. No one can win against God, after all—the rebellion is doomed from the start. Yet he keeps fighting, driven by some dark inner fire.

Then a particular verse leaps out at me: *The mind is its own place, and in itself can make a Heav'n of Hell, a Hell of Heav'n.* The quote sounds familiar. My pulse speeds. Zebra spoke those words to me once—I can't remember the exact circumstances, but I recall his voice reciting them. Could it be? Is this what I was meant to find? But that would mean he intended the code specifically for me. Is that possible?

I try replacing each letter with a corresponding number and key it in. When that doesn't work, I reverse the order of the numbers, then try a basic Caesar's cipher. Still nothing. Maybe something simpler, then? Like the book and verse. I type in 1, then 254. When the keypad doesn't respond, I add the page number.

Finally, something clicks.

A low, grinding rattle fills the room as unseen gears turn. The entire fireplace slides down into the floor like a giant block in a three-dimensional puzzle, disappearing with a dry snick of stone on metal, revealing an empty rectangle. A doorway. Inside, a sloped cement corridor leads steeply downward, into darkness.

35

For a moment, I just stand there, my breath rapid and fluttering. Fear nails my feet to the floor. I have the inexplicable sense that something terrible awaits me down there, and I wonder if I really want to find out what it is. But of course I'm going down.

Slowly, I pry my feet off the floor and descend. My steps reverberate through the silence, which is so profound it seems to have a tangible weight. At the end of the narrow corridor is another door, an ordinary wooden one, just barely visible in the light filtering down from the room above. When I turn the knob, it clicks open, revealing a room the size of a standard basement. The walls are bare cement, and there are dead screens everywhere—ancient, boxy-looking monitors with glass faces and masses of wires trailing from the back. Other machines line the wall, things I don't recognize—gray boxes covered with blinking lights.

I take a small, careful step forward. Abruptly, all the screens wink on. I let out a startled shriek. My heart trips in my chest. Holding my breath, I take a cautious step forward and examine the screens. Each one displays grainy security footage of a building. In the center screen, I recognize a familiar, towering shape against the skyline—the silver pyramid of IFEN headquarters. My eyes widen.

The buildings are all treatment facilities. At the bottom of the screen, the name of each is listed, along with the city of its location. Realization sinks in—these are the facilities that house IFEN's databases.

I take another step forward, staring at the console under the row of screens. Jutting out from the central panel is a large, dark lever. It resembles a joystick I once saw on an ancient videogame controller in a museum—a column fashioned from dull, black metal, with a semi-translucent red orb at the end. Slowly, I reach toward it.

Abruptly, a purple bat appears in a flurry of sparkles and hovers in front of me, wings flapping—Zebra's holoavatar. "Hello!" a little voice chirps.

I take a startled step back. It takes me a few seconds to remember her name. "Delilah? What are you doing here?"

"Voice identification confirms that you're Lain Fisher. I will answer any questions you have."

So Zebra programmed her to respond to me, specifically. Why? Did he suspect something was going to happen to him? "This . . . place. What is it?"

She flies in a circle around the room. "This is the culmination of all my master's plans. Hundreds of bombs have been secretly planted in various IFEN facilities. They're well hidden. Some of them are inside the walls, or buried within the very foundations." Her cheerful tone never wavers. "These buildings contain the databases for the National Registry of Mental Health. In other words, the backbone of the Type system."

A thin line of cold runs down my spine. Am I misunderstanding? Is she really saying what I think she's saying?

"And this lever," I whisper, "what is it for?"

"When you pull the lever, all the bombs will be simultaneously detonated."

I'd wondered, before, what a few hundred kids with guns could do against IFEN. But in a situation like that, maybe a few hundred *would* be enough to shift the balance of power. They could march in and seize control while everyone was still scrambling to figure out what had happened.

So this is what it's all been building up to. This is why the Citadel exists, why Zebra was training an army here. All the rescue missions were merely to swell his ranks for the coming invasion. Everything the Blackcoats have done up until now has been just a prelude to the real show. "Why didn't Zebra tell anyone about this? If he had the ability to blow up IFEN at any point, then why didn't he do it?"

"I'm sorry. I don't have that information in my databank."

Suddenly, it's a struggle to draw breath. This must be what Nicholas was searching for, why he was still in the Citadel. He knew it existed, even if he didn't know how to find it, and he wanted to make sure those bombs were never set off. This is the answer to everything. Yet now, I find myself terrified to touch the lever. People would undoubtedly be injured or killed by the explosions— innocent civilians as well as IFEN personnel—but that's not the worst of it. This would plunge the Blackcoats and IFEN into a new civil war. The conflict could spread into Canada, or even further. More violence, more fear, more misery.

Maybe that's why Zebra couldn't bring himself to set off the bombs, despite his hatred for IFEN. This wouldn't just wipe out the Type system. It would destroy the URA. And there's a good chance that Aaron would be killed, as well, if he happened to be in IFEN headquarters when the bombs went off.

Aaron himself told me that I had to fight back. Or was that just my imagination?

Remember, he said. *Remember what these people are capable of.* He knew something about IFEN. Of course he couldn't tell me outright. But maybe the information is already locked in my head, and I just can't reach it.

"Delilah . . . did Zebra tell you anything else about this plan? Anything at all?"

"I've told you all I know, I'm afraid. My master was a very secretive man."

Was. So, she understands—in her limited holoavatar way—that Zebra is dead.

"Is there anything else you wish to know?" Delilah asks. "If not, I'll deactivate myself permanently. Since my master is gone, I no longer have a reason to exist."

Is that how Zebra programmed her—to self-destruct once she outlived her usefulness to him? It seems so cruel. "Is that what you want?"

"Yes," Delilah replies calmly. She smiles, showing tiny, sharp teeth. Her eyes glow a soft yellow. "That is what I wish. I would be greatly relieved if you would grant me permission."

A lump rises unexpectedly into my throat. Practically speaking, I should probably keep Delilah around, just in case, but I doubt there's anything more she can tell me. And if this is truly her desire, it seems unfair to deny her that much. "Go ahead."

"Thank you, Lain Fisher." She spreads her wings, tilts her head back, and fades into the air. A few purple sparkles remain, floating in emptiness, then they twinkle out as well, like a firework melting into the sky, leaving me alone with the row of screens.

I stand motionless, lost in a mental haze. Why do these choices keep finding their way to me? No one should have this kind of power.

I start to reach out, then stop, fingertips quivering a few inches from the lever. My arm drops to my side. I can't do this, not now. I need time. I need to think—

Behind me, there's a rustle of movement. I spin around, and Steven is there, staring at me with an unreadable expression. "Steven," I blurt out. Did he follow me? "I—I thought you were in training." My heart bangs in my chest. "How much did you hear?"

"Enough." He slowly approaches the row of screens in back. He studies the lever, then turns to me. "So. All we have to do is pull this."

My mouth is dry. I swallow. "Let's just stop and think about this for a minute."

"There's nothing to think about." His voice is a low monotone, like someone under hypnosis. His eyes are fixed on me, but they don't seem to see me.

I struggle to keep my voice calm. "We need to tell Rhee and the others before we do anything. We can *use* this. We can bargain with IFEN."

"They won't bargain with terrorists."

"You don't know that."

He looks through me, his face a mask.

"Listen to me," I say, my tone low and urgent. "If we set off those bombs, the URA will tear itself apart. The death toll will be astronomical."

He doesn't respond.

I search his eyes with mine. I feel like I'm casting ropes down into a deep hole, waiting for the tug that tells me someone is still alive at the bottom. "Do you even hear me?"

"I hear you." He turns his face away. "There's no other way, Lain. Back home, people who try to fight back or escape the country are being slaughtered, and it'll keep happening until we do something. The Cognitive Rights Act failed. IFEN stopped it dead in its tracks. As long as they exist, there's no chance. None."

My mind races. I can't just stand back and let him do it—I can't. "If we're willing to kill innocent people to get what we want, how are we any better than Dr. Swan?"

He flinches. The muscles in his face tighten, and I wish immediately that I hadn't said that. I don't really believe that it's the same. But it's too late to take the words back.

He lets out a flat, harsh laugh. "Maybe you're right. Maybe it makes me as bad as them. But I don't care. If I have to become a mass-murderer to stop them, then that's what I'll do." I see his expression closing down, see him retreating from me again. When he speaks again, his voice is soft, almost gentle. "After this, if you never want to see me again . . . I don't blame you."

Steven reaches for the lever.

He seems to be moving in slow motion. Terror blazes through me—and in an instant, I understand what a selfish person I am. Because the thought looming inside me at this moment is not that countless people will get hurt or killed, but that if Steven pulls this lever, I'll never get him back. This will transform him into someone else, and I'll lose him forever. I've already lost him once. I won't let it happen again.

I tackle him from behind and drag him back, away from the control panel. He freezes up for a moment, stunned, then starts to struggle. "Let go!" he growls.

But I don't let go.

He thrashes harder, and I tighten my grip, pinning his arms to his sides. I'm stronger now than I was. He lurches to one side, then the other, and my shoulder bangs against the wall, and still, I won't let go. We stagger across the room and crash into one of the control panels. Sparks leap and crackle. Steven loses his balance and topples to the floor, taking me with him. I land on top of him. He tries to get up, but I grab his wrists and pin him to the floor. My sweat drips down onto his face. Cords of muscle in his neck stand out as he struggles, bucking, his eyes rolling and flashing white like a panicked horse's.

Finally, he manages to wrench his wrists free and shoves me off. I sprawl across the floor. The back of my head bounces off the wall, and stars explode across my retinas. The breath has been knocked out of me, and for a long, terrifying moment, all I can do is lie on the floor with my mouth open like a beached fish, unable to breathe. Then the air whooshes back into my lungs. My head throbs dully.

Steven stands over me, panting. As he stares, his expression slowly clears. "Lain," he whispers.

Slowly, I sit up, and dizziness rolls over me. I touch the back of my head, and my fingers come away stained with blood.

Steven's eyes are wide, dazed. "You're hurt." Slowly dawning horror fills his expression. "I hurt you." His legs crumple under him, and he falls to his knees. I crawl toward him, and he flinches back. "No. Don't—don't come any closer." He huddles in a ball, hands covering his face. "I'm not safe. I'm a monster. I'm—"

I grab his wrists, pull his hands away from his face, and glare at him. "Stop that nonsense. Stop it right now." My voice comes out rough, almost angry. My head still pulses, but the dizziness has passed.

"You're bleeding. Your head—"

"Forget my head. I need you to promise me that you are not going to pull that lever."

He looks at me with wild, bloodshot eyes. "Don't you get it?" his voice breaks. "If I don't do this, we'll all die. You'll die. If I can't keep you safe, then what the hell is any of it for?"

My heart seizes up.

He pulls back, rocking on his heels, and gathers his fists at the sides of his head. "You never would've come to this place, if not for me. And now IFEN is going to attack us, and I'm scared that I won't be able to save you, I won't be able to do anything. If I pull that lever, it'll all disappear. I know you'll hate me, but I can live with that, as long as you're okay."

"Don't be ridiculous." I reach out to lay a hand on his cheek, feeling the bristle of stubble against my palm. His breath catches. "I've fought too hard and risked too much to lose you now," I whisper. "*We've* fought too hard."

He blinks, his eyes bewildered and shiny with tears. "Lose me? What—"

"Just promise me. Promise me you won't pull it." I won't let him take on this burden. Not for my sake.

His Adam's apple jerks up and down. He squeezes his eyes shut. "I promise."

I exhale the pent-up tension in my chest and sit back, feeling weak and shaky. "IFEN will bargain with us, once they learn about this," I say. "You'll see." And if they don't—well, I'll think of something else.

Rhee's voice echoes in my head: *Sometimes there are only two paths, and they're both ugly.*

I push the voice away. If there are only two paths, then I'll blaze a new trail. I'll find a way to save us all without killing anyone.

"I'm sorry," Steven whispers. He huddles on the floor, head bowed.

"Don't be." I pick myself up off the floor, then offer a hand to him. He blinks at it. "Come on," I say.

He takes my hand, and I help him up. The dazed, haunted look doesn't quite leave his eyes as we walk up the stairs, out of the study and down the hall. "We should take you to the med wing," he says. "Have them look at that bump on your head."

"I'm fine. It doesn't hurt." Well, that's a lie—the back of my head is throbbing. But it's the least of my concerns.

He stops suddenly.

"Steven?"

He touches my hair, and his fingers come away stained with blood. Slowly, he curls his hand into a fist. He looks like he's about to be sick. "Sometimes, I wonder if those doctors knew what they were doing when they put a collar on me."

"Am I really hearing this?" I face him, planting my hands on my hips. "You're the one who convinced me the system is wrong. We gave up everything to come here and fight IFEN. Now you're questioning your ideals? Because of this little bump on my head?"

"I hurt you, Lain. Don't act like that's not a big deal." His voice is soft, but his gaze is intense, unwavering.

I exhale a frustrated breath and rake a hand through my hair, pushing it out of my face. "It was an accident."

His jaw tightens. "I spent my childhood being afraid of the people who were supposed to be taking care of me. I don't ever want to be the guy making someone else feel that way."

"You won't be," I reply firmly.

"Are you sure about that? You studied this stuff in shrink school. You know how it goes. Kids who've been hurt grow up and hurt other people. It's like a virus that keeps getting passed on."

This might not be the best time for this conversation, but I won't stand by and let him say things like that about himself. "Statistics are just statistics. They're not fate."

"And yet I *did* become a killer."

I open my mouth, but suddenly, I can't find words. After a beat, I say, "That was completely justified. Nicholas would have killed us."

"I know. That's what I keep telling myself. But I keep seeing that moment, when he . . ." His eyes slide out of focus again. "Earlier, after we talked in my room, I said I was gonna go to training, but then I saw them shooting those holos in the simulation room, and I—I couldn't do it. I kept remembering how much I enjoyed it before, and then thinking about Nicholas, and . . . I couldn't stand the thought that maybe that's who I am." He gulps. "I'm afraid," he whispers. "I'm afraid there's something inside me that wants to hurt people. And that one day, it'll hurt you. *Really* hurt you."

The throbbing in my head has subsided to a dull ache. "There's no 'it,'" I reply quietly. "There's just you. Your past doesn't define you. Your choices do. If you really *were* a cold-blooded killer, then you wouldn't feel this way. You're ripping yourself up inside over the death of a man you have every reason to hate. Because you're a gentle person."

"Gentle," he says incredulously. "That's what you think?"

"You try to hide it. But I know." I stop, taking a breath. "If you had pulled that lever, it would've destroyed you. And I couldn't bear that."

"You . . ." He lapses into stunned silence. "That's why you stopped me?"

I turn away, suddenly self-conscious. My cheeks burn. "We'd better go. People are probably wondering where we are."

We keep walking.

"You really believe that?" he asks.

"Hmm?"

"That people can choose to be who they are."

"Of course. Don't you?"

He walks with his hands in his pockets, shoulders hunched. "Sometimes. But sometimes I remember those days before I met you, when I'd wake up feeling like I'd been run over by a steamroller, like I was glued to the sheets. And I'd hear people on TV shows saying things like 'happiness is a decision' and 'you can do anything you put your mind to,' and I'd think to myself, what a crock of shit. When you're in that place, the idea of free will starts to seem like a sick joke." He looks at me from the corner of his eye. "You know what I mean. You've been there too."

I do know what he means. All too well. The memory of that dark time after Father's death is still clear in my head. The pain was a living thing, a parasite eating me from the inside out, and the knowledge that I was so helpless in the face of my own emotions just made it worse. *What doesn't kill you makes you stronger . . .* Such a ridiculous statement. Pain humbles you, breaks you, carves away pieces of you, and leaves you as weak and fragile as a paper husk.

And yet . . .

"We both made the choice to keep living. Didn't we?"

"I had help," he points out.

"Even so. There may be some things beyond our control, but

I believe we're more than just puppets controlled by our brain chemistry."

"And if we're not? What then?"

"Then we might as well go on living as if we *do* have choices. Because if we don't, then nothing matters anyway, and we're just here to eat and defecate and die."

A smile twitches at the corner of his mouth. "That should be on one of those motivational posters. Over a picture of an ocean sunset."

I smile back, just a little. And I find myself thinking, suddenly, about the first time we met. He had no one and nothing, and he reached out and asked me—a complete stranger—to enter his mind, plunge her hands into the clay of his essence, and rework him into something else. I can't imagine the sort of courage it took. "I believe in you, Steven. I think you've already chosen the sort of person you want to be. And he's wonderful."

His mouth opens. Fresh tears shine on his eyes, and his throat muscles flutter. He lets out a rough chuckle. "Gotta question your taste in men, Doc."

I stop, place my hands against his chest, and kiss him. His breath hitches. He tenses briefly, then relaxes, lips parting, and I feel his skin growing warmer. His stubble scrapes against my skin as he deepens the kiss.

It would be so easy to lose myself in him. But there's a decision to make, and we can't put it off. I pull back, breathing hard.

His eyes close, and I see him struggling for control. "So what now?"

"We need to tell the others," I reply, breathless. "About the lever." There's the problem of Burk, but once he learns about this, hopefully his suspicions about me will fall by the wayside.

"And if they want to pull it?" Steven asks.

I hadn't thought that far ahead. Come to think of it, the other Blackcoats almost certainly will want to pull it. Why wouldn't they?

Their entire goal is to destroy the Type system. I shake my head, pushing the thoughts away. There's no way I can keep something like this a secret—not with the Citadel in imminent danger. "I'll talk them out of it. I believe there are other ways. This gives us an unprecedented amount of leverage—no pun intended."

"That was a pun?"

"I'm just saying, IFEN has to take us seriously now. They have no choice but to bargain." And if they refuse . . .

No. I won't let myself consider that. They will listen to us.

The halls are silent, spookily still as we walk along, the ghost of our footsteps trailing behind us. I suppose everyone is still in training.

Steven stops suddenly. His eyes lose focus, and he raises a hand to his chest, as if feeling his own heartbeat.

I stop beside him. "What's wrong?" Come to think of it, my heart is racing as well, and I'm not sure why. I look down at my hands. They're trembling slightly.

"You feel it too?" he asks quietly.

I gulp. "What is it?"

"Dunno." He curls his hands into fists. "Something bad."

I close my eyes, focusing on the feeling. It's difficult to put into words, but the more I think about it, the more nauseous I feel. There's a sense of danger in the very air. It's like looking at the sky and seeing clear blue, but knowing, somehow, that a storm is on its way. Clammy sweat dampens my palms. I want to get away . . . but get away from what? "Let's just keep going," I murmur.

The ever-present electric lights hum overhead, but aside from that, I can't hear anything out of the ordinary. Everything looks normal. Yet the hovering anxiety remains. It's as if fears tucked away in a corner of my mind are suddenly growing larger, expanding, crowding out my thoughts. My breathing quickens.

"This isn't me, right?" Steven says.

"No. It's not you."

"Because it feels like a panic attack is about to hit, but if it's both of us—"

"Something is wrong. Something bigger." Slowly, I lift one shaking hand to my temple. The walls waver around me, blurring and tilting.

A dull boom shakes the world, and the floor vibrates beneath my feet, making me stumble. "What was that?" I ask, breathless.

"Sounds like an explosion."

The main entrance. Without thinking, I start to run.

Steven runs after me. "Lain, wait!"

When we reach the entrance room, I stagger to a halt, panting. The door's been blown open. The edge is singed black, still smoking, but there's no one there—which means whoever blew open the door is already inside the Citadel. My thoughts whirl. This can't be happening. It hasn't even been twenty-four hours. We were supposed to have more time!

And then the alarm goes off. It blares, filling the halls with sound and flashing lights. Burk's voice emanates from the hall speakers: "We are under attack! Repeat, we are under—" His voice cuts off in a choked scream. The alarm falls silent.

36

Steven and I look at each other, wide-eyed. "Shit," he mutters.

I nod in agreement.

We turn and run back into the hallway. And suddenly, there's chaos all around us—people bursting out of doors, shouting, footsteps thundering through the corridors, Blackcoats everywhere. They cock their rifles as they run past me, coats flapping behind them. Voices roar around me, filling my ears.

"Battle stations, everyone!" a man yells. "This is not a drill! Repeat, this is not a drill!"

I look around wildly, but I can't see anyone who might be an enemy. Where are they?

The crowd thickens, stampeding through the hall. I've lost sight of Steven. I cry his name. Someone bumps into me, and I lose my balance, falling against the wall. My eyes dart frantically back and forth.

Where is he?

I call for him again, but the din swallows up my voice. I push through the crowd, my own breath echoing through my ears. It's like trying to swim against rapids. Bodies buffet me from side to side. The ominous feeling inside me is still building, swelling.

Where's Rhee? Where's Ian? What do I do? I'm not even carrying a gun. Why is it so hard to focus? My thoughts are spinning around wildly, colliding and breaking apart like agitated molecules.

I lean against the nearest wall and press a hand against my chest, fighting for breath. Whatever was happening to Steven and I a few minutes ago, it's still there, and it's getting worse.

The room blurs and tilts, darkening, like something seen through tinted glass. For an instant, everything seems to be rushing toward me, and I can't breathe, can't move. Then a black wave descends.

It's not fear or even terror. That's too mild a word. I open up my mouth to scream, but nothing comes out. This is worse than the grief I felt when Father died, worse than the skin-crawling horrors of St. Mary's, worse than being captive in IFEN headquarters, knowing the memory of Steven was about to be ripped away from me. My mouth is frozen open, silent. I can't breathe, can't think. My legs give out, and I fall to my knees. The world won't focus. The hallway has transformed into a carnival mirror, a hellish parody of itself.

In an instant, the wall in my mind breaks. The memories come rushing back—the white walls, the blinking lights and rows of switches, the unnaturally cool air under IFEN headquarters—and all at once, I understand what's going on.

This is it. This is Mindstormer.

Dr. Swan claimed the technology wasn't fully developed yet—not developed enough, perhaps, for the sort of subtle social control and thought manipulation that he envisioned. But enough to bombard us with waves of raw animal fear.

All around, Blackcoats drop to the floor, clutching their heads. Moans and screams mingle with the constant blare of the alarm. The flashing lights blind me. But suddenly, it all seems far away and muted, like I'm in a dream. I'm falling into a dark abyss inside myself.

I lurch to my feet and start to run. My body seems to be moving in slow motion, like the very air has thickened, resisting me. Every instinct inside me screams *escape*, but there's nothing to escape from, nowhere to go. Everything is my enemy—the walls, the floor, my own heart pumping in my chest.

I try to scream Steven's name, but only a strangled whimper emerges. There's something around my neck, squeezing.

I nearly trip over a Blackcoat, a young man curled into a fetal position on the floor. He's bitten his tongue, and blood spills from his mouth; his body twitches and shivers in spasms. I stumble backward. He doesn't look up, doesn't acknowledge me—he's whining under his breath, small, frightened, animal sounds.

The shadows on the wall stretch toward me like grasping black fingers, like tentacles. There's a knife-hilt sticking from a sheath at the man's hip. I yank it out and slash at the shadow-tentacles, but they keep coming, lashing and coiling around me. My skin burns where they touch. I rip free, turn around and bolt in the other direction, still clutching the knife. My vision keeps blurring, and the walls pulse and wriggle as if covered by thousands of insects. I pass another Blackcoat, a young woman crumpled against the wall, her face pale, staring blindly into space as she claws at her own neck, leaving bloody runnels in her flesh. Ahead, I spot a flash of green hair. Shana. She's sprawled across the floor, gaze pointed at the ceiling, her eyes two empty holes, her mouth a black O.

Shots ring out.

I turn a bend, looking around wildly. The hallway is smeared with blood. It drips from the walls and pools on the floor. Dead bodies—more Blackcoats—lie sprawled like discarded toys. Dead. I still haven't so much as glimpsed the enemy, yet they're among us—an invisible, poisonous smoke, killing at will.

My throat squeezes shut. I keep running blindly. The world is shrinking around me, the air pressing against me. A wave of dizziness slams me down, and I black out. When the darkness lifts, my cheek is pressed against the cool metal of the floor, and a voice is saying, "Lain. Lain, what happened to you?"

It's Rhee. We're alone in the hallway. She helps me to sit up, propping my back against the wall.

I try to speak, but all that emerges from my mouth is a weak croak. How can she even stand? Whatever's happening, it's not affecting her. I blink, struggling against the fog of terror. The world tilts and distorts around me. Her face slowly comes into focus. Her eyes are clear and intent. "Say something if you understand me."

I whimper.

She slaps my cheek, and the pain momentarily blasts the fear from my head. She frames my face between her hands, anchoring it. "Listen to me," she says quietly. "Whatever you're experiencing right now, it's not real. Move through it. Past it. Do you understand?"

Tears blur my vision.

She grips my shoulder tightly. "They taught you how to compartmentalize your emotions, didn't they? All Mindwalkers know how. Do it now. Think."

I manage a tiny nod. It's hard to think about anything with the black wave roaring through my head, gripping my body like physical pain. *It's not real.* I repeat the words over and over to myself. My thoughts keep splintering into pieces. The walls are moving toward me. They're alive, pulsing with malicious intent. I moan.

Then there are footsteps coming toward us. Heavy boots, slow, deliberate thuds. Rhee tenses, releases me, and draws her rifle from the holster on her back.

A group of uniformed men and women turn the corner. They aren't IFEN soldiers. It's difficult to focus my eyes, but I'm certain of that much. Their uniforms are not white, but dark gray, with helmets that cover their entire faces and armbands bearing a strange, red insignia: a human face divided in half by a lightning bolt. They're all armed with enormous assault rifles.

I feel like I'm having a nightmare. Images are distorted and blurred, sounds echoed—yet I can see and hear everything. I just can't move.

"Who are you?" Rhee asks.

The newcomers look at each other through their dark-tinted faceplates. Then the one in front takes off his helmet, revealing the face of a dark-haired young man with a scar over his left eye. He smiles. "We're soldiers," he says, and I recognize his voice—he's the one who made the announcement telling us to surrender or die. "Modified soldiers. Like you."

Her expression goes blank. Uncertainty flickers in her eyes, and she takes a step back. "What?" she whispers.

"You *are* one of us, aren't you? You must be, if you can still stand. No ordinary person can endure the Mindstorm." He smiles. There's a strange quality to his blue eyes. They're bright and alert, yet somehow empty.

"She must be a survivor from the first wave," a woman's voice says from within a helmet. "She's imperfect. Her modification was not complete."

The man stretches out a gloved hand toward her. "Come with us. They can make you perfect. Have you ever felt like there's an empty space inside you? Something missing? That's merely an echo, a phantom pain. We can make that go away."

Rhee doesn't move. "You can't be real," she says flatly. Her eyes are wide, unfocused. "The—the experiments were abandoned. I'm the last one."

"The first set of experiments was abandoned," he corrects her. "Because the technology was still undeveloped."

She's breathing fast. Her hands tremble slightly on the gun. It's the only time I've ever seen her on the verge of losing control. "I thought I was alone," she whispers.

"You're not alone." He holds her gaze. A cool fire burns in his dark blue eyes. "You don't really want to stay with them, do you?

Look at these creatures." He gives me a disdainful glance. "They're ruled by blind animal fear and pain. It drives everything they do. Their very identities are constructed around the desire to avoid it. All you have to do is excite the neurons in their amygdala, and they're reduced to helpless, quivering bundles. But we—we have slipped our chains." He takes a step forward, hand still outstretched. "Come with us. We'll kill the rest of these rats, then go home. You'll like it there. They'll give you everything you'll ever need."

Slowly, she lowers her gun.

My cheek is pressed against the hard, cool wall. I stare helplessly through the fog of terror, unable to move or speak. *Help me*, I think.

She doesn't look at me as she walks forward, toward them.

"That's right," the man says gently. "Come home—"

Abruptly, she whips her gun up and starts firing. Thunder fills the air. Blood spreads in a wet patch on the man's chest. He blinks, an expression of mild surprise on his face, and falls backward. The others reach for their guns, but not fast enough. Blood spatters the walls, and two more soldiers go down. A bullet grazes Rhee's arm, but she doesn't stop, doesn't even slow.

More soldiers appear, filling the hall. She charges, bullets spraying. Rhee's body jerks from the impact as a bullet hits her, then another. Still, she keeps going, and unstoppable juggernaut. The soldiers keep coming, and she keeps killing them.

Time seems to stretch around me, so she's moving in slow motion. When she runs out of bullets, she discards her gun and pulls two long, serrated knives from the sheaths at her hips, then she rushes forward again toward the third wave of soldiers. Corpses litter the hallway like leaves. Six of them, seven of them, eight, a dozen. Her clothes are drenched with blood, and she's still fighting—spinning, thrusting, kicking, stabbing. A dance of death.

She's incredible.

When it's over, she's the last one standing. Blood drenches the hallway; it smears the floor and drips from the walls. She exhales, shoulders slumping, and sheaths her knives. Her legs crumple beneath her, and she collapses.

For a few seconds, I don't move. Somehow, miraculously, I'm unhurt, weak and shaky but whole. She protected me. Tears slide warmly down my face. Then my gaze focuses on the motionless form in front of me.

I crawl forward. "Rhee . . ."

Wet, raspy breathing echoes through the silence. She blinks at me a few times. Blood soaks her clothes and hair and stains her skin. So much blood. Already, her eyes are starting to cloud over, and I know—with a cold, sinking feeling—that there's no chance of saving her. I reach for her hand and clasp it. Her fingers are slick, wet and warm. "Hold on," I whisper. "I—I'll find help."

She gives her head a small shake. "It's all right." A smile twitches at the corners of her bloodstained lips. "I'm not afraid." Her voice is growing fainter, but her gaze is fixed on me.

Tears mist my vision. I stroke her bloodstained hair, smoothing it back from her face. I don't know what else to do.

She whispers a word, so faint I can't make it out.

"What?" I lean closer, turning my head so my ear is close to her lips. Her breath rasps, weak and wet.

"Live. You have to live." Her voice is fading, falling away. "You . . ." She lets out a small sigh.

I pull back. "Rhee?"

She blinks one more time. Then her eyes go still.

I used to think that Rhee's eyes were always empty. But I was wrong. As I see them turn truly blank, I realize how much was there before, how much I never saw. Tears drip from my face and onto hers. I remain where I am, sitting by Rhee's side and clutching her hand. The black cloud of terror hangs over me, but anger burns through it.

They killed her. IFEN killed her.

Death cries echo through the hallways. There are other soldiers here, and the Blackcoats, paralyzed by terror, are helpless to fight back. If I don't do something, stop this somehow, they'll all be killed.

I think about IFEN headquarters, about the huge computers lining the walls in the secret room underground. And I know what I have to do.

Breathing hard, shaking, I push myself to my feet. I try to pick up one of the soldier's guns, but it's so large and bulky I can barely lift it. I let it fall. The knife is still lying on the floor—it doubles and triples in my spotty vision, then shrinks back into a single object. With trembling fingers, I pick it up. It's something.

I start to walk. It takes all my strength, every ounce of my focus. One foot in front of the other. Waves of terror slam into me, trying to push me back down. Pain rips through my spine, splitting my back down the center, and I stumble, fingers clenching on the knife handle. *Not real.* The searing pain flays me open. My knees quiver and give out, and I retch. A thin, hot stream of bile splatters onto the floor.

Pressure squeezes my temples until it seems my skull will burst open like a pinched grape. But worse than the agony is the huge, deadening weight of fear bearing down on me, a relentless pressure. My fingers clench on the knife.

If I can just fight the fear . . . if I can distract myself, somehow . . .

With a cry, I slash my own palm open. The pain is blinding and bright and *real*, and it cuts through the black haze like a flash of lightning. The knife clatters to the floor. The haze clears from my head as blood flows freely from my palm, forming a shiny red puddle.

I've cut myself deeper than I intended to, opening not just my palm, but part of my wrist—a flap of skin hangs loose, and blood runs in thick dark streams from a severed vein. The sight makes me momentarily dizzy, but it's something to focus on. I squeeze my hand into a bloody fist and force my muscles to keep moving.

*　　*　　*

The room in Zebra's study is just as I remember it—the rows of screens, the panels of blinking lights, and the huge lever jutting out from the central panel. With blood still streaming from my mangled hand, I lurch forward and reach out to grasp the lever. At the last instant, I freeze, fingertips trembling in midair.

If I pull this, it will destroy Project Mindstormer, and we'll all be saved. Simple as that. So why am I still hesitating?

Because it isn't that simple. If IFEN is wiped out in an instant, the URA will be plunged into anarchy. More war. More death. More fear and hate, and the cycle will continue. I'll be a murderer. I'll be the person who single-handedly destroyed the United Republic of America.

Yet if I don't pull that lever, Steven will die, Ian will die. All the Blackcoats will die, and their deaths will be for nothing.

My fingers are stiff. I force them to unbend and curl them slowly around the plastic column. I struggle to think, to breathe through the crushing pressure in my chest.

Zebra's voice echoes in my head: *We are fighting for something more important than life itself.*

And what is that?

Our souls.

My ears ring faintly. The world has gone slightly foggy. I've lost too much blood; I can feel myself slipping down a steep incline toward unconsciousness. I only have a few seconds left before I'm too weak to stand. And in that moment, I make my choice.

I'm not a rebel or a fighter, but I can do this much. I can shoulder the sin.

I pull, but the lever won't budge. A ragged sob escapes my throat. I'm not strong enough.

And then there's a hand over mine, covering mine, and I look up into Steven's pale blue eyes. He's pale, his face drawn, his breathing ragged and whistling through his throat, but he's standing. He smiles at me, muscles tight with pain. "We'll do it together." His voice is soft, gentle and steady.

My throat swells up, so I can't speak, but I hold his gaze with mine and give a tiny nod. "Together," I manage to whisper.

"On the count of three."

My pulse drums in my wrists and throat. "One."

His fingers tighten on mine. "Two."

"Three."

We pull. There's a brief resistance; then the lever snaps down and clicks into position. For a few seconds, the room is utterly silent, utterly still.

There's a mechanical *fwoomp*, like a dozen machines starting up at once. A low hum fills the air, growing louder. I stare at the grainy gray footage on the screens as one by one, the buildings explode, white blossoms of flame opening, debris shooting outward. Windows shatter. Smoke pours into the skies. A dull, vibrating roar emanates from the speakers. There's a thin, inhuman scream inside my head, cutting through my brain like a bright wire. And then it falls silent. The black cloud lifts.

All at once, it's over.

Dizziness washes over me, and spots chase each other across my vision as I slump against the console. I press my hand against my shirt, trying to staunch the flow of blood, and it soaks through in a dark, wet, spreading patch.

Steven's eyes widen. "Shit." He pulls off his own shirt and wraps it around my wrist. "Hold on. Just hold on."

I open my mouth to reply, but nothing comes out. *So tired.* I close my eyes. The blood is everywhere. Surely, a person can't lose so much of it and live. On the edge of my consciousness, far away, I hear him calling my name, but I can't find the strength to respond. I'm already sliding into the abyss. And all I can think is, *Thank you,* because if I have to die, this is exactly where I want it to happen—with Steven.

37

I open my eyes, mildly surprised to find myself still in the world of the living.

I'm on a narrow cot in a small room. There's a stainless-steel sink in one corner, and a row of cabinets, and a table lined with bottles and surgical implements, which probably means I'm in the med wing. My right hand throbs, a dull, steady, red pain. I try to sit up, then sink back down as vertigo crashes over me.

"Hey," says a familiar voice. Steven sits in a chair at the foot of the bed. He gives me a faint, wan smile. "Don't try to move too much. You're still weak."

With my left hand, I rub my aching head. Vaguely, I remember the battle. I remember stumbling to the secret room beneath Zebra's study and setting off the bombs. But none of it feels quite real. I might even believe it was a nightmare, if not for the pain in my hand.

Steven is alive and safe. I cling to that.

I don't want to ask any questions, because I'm afraid of the answers. I want to lie here, not thinking. But I know that the longer I wait, the harder it will be. "Is everyone all right?"

"Relatively speaking. People are pretty traumatized. Half the

Blackcoats are sedated right now, because they kept having panic attacks even after it was over, and the few who aren't completely freaking out are keeping an eye on everyone else. I dunno why I'm okay. Maybe I'm just so used to trauma that I've developed calluses on my brain."

A thought sparks, and my heartbeat quickens. "Ian—"

"He's fine."

I breathe out in relief. But the feeling is short-lived. "And Rhee?" I have to ask, though I already know the answer.

"She's gone." His voice wavers. He clears his throat. "Burk, too. There were other casualties—we're still trying to figure out how many we have left. But we're lucky to be here at all."

"And the soldiers?" I whisper. "The ones from IFEN?"

"All dead. Once that—that thing stopped happening, we were able to fight back." He hesitates. "Lain . . . do you know what it was?"

I close my eyes. "They called it the Mindstorm. Project Mindstormer. It . . . it's something IFEN created. I saw it when I was in their headquarters." It takes an effort to form words. "Dr. Swan told me it was a computer capable of influencing the human brain, even from a distance. But I didn't know it was capable of . . . this."

Steven's expression hardens. "IFEN must have decided to take it for a test run."

A bitter taste fills my mouth. Dr. Swan said that Mindstormer would only be used for peaceful purposes. To prevent violence, not inflict it. Maybe he really believed that. He should have known better.

I can see why IFEN kept this weapon a secret. Something like this should not exist. But a part of me has to admire the cleverness of their strategy. Use a long-distance mind-control device to para-lyze your enemies with fear, then send in fear-immune soldiers to pick them off at their leisure. Unlike a chemical weapon or a bomb, it's easy to contain the damage, at least in theory. They could use the weapon to wipe out pockets of resistance at no risk to themselves, and without endangering the lives of civilians.

Rhee's bloodstained face flashes through my head, derailing the thought. A shudder grips me, and I meet Steven's gaze. His eyes glisten with tears. "I'm sorry," he whispers.

An ache squeezes my chest. *Rhee.* I start to reach out my right hand, to take Steven's, and then I see—I no longer have a right hand. Just a bandaged stump.

Steven lowers his gaze. "I tied a tourniquet around your arm to stop the bleeding. It kept you alive, but it cut off the blood flow completely. They couldn't save the hand."

I stare stupidly at the stump, as if my hand might rematerialize at any second.

"But it's okay," he adds quickly. "They have amazing prosthetics in Canada, right? They can get you a new one, and it'll be just as good as the old."

My arm flops weakly to my side. My right hand burns and throbs. "I can still feel it," I say. My voice sounds distant, faint.

I remember the soldier talking about phantom pain. Of course. Just because something's no longer there doesn't mean it can't hurt.

I close my eyes and imagine curling the fingers of my non-existent hand into a fist. It feels so real, even if it's just a memory. They must have pumped me full of drugs while I was asleep; otherwise, I'm sure the pain would be a lot worse.

Steven touches my cheek. I open my eyes. "I'm sorry," he says again.

I manage a weak smile. "It's just a hand. I have a spare. See?" I hold up the left one.

For a few minutes, we just look at each other. His eyes are glossy and reflective with tears, his face pale, smudged with a bit of blood on one cheek from I don't know where, and his hair is in disarray. I start to raise my right hand, to touch his cheek, and the bandaged stump looms in my vision again. It took me all of ten seconds to forget, and the sight surprises me anew. I start to laugh. I can't help it.

He blinks. "Lain?"

My arm falls to my side, and I keep laughing, though it starts to sound like crying after a while. Tears roll down my face. Steven hugs me close, and I cling to him.

He smoothes my hair, whispering into my ear that everything is all right, everything is going to be okay. I cry against his chest, soaking his shirt, until I've heaved the last sob out of my chest, and I'm left feeling light and empty, like I might float away. "Are you going to tell them?" I whisper.

"What?"

"That we're the ones who pulled the lever?"

He pauses. "Do you want me to tell them?"

Maybe I should be proud of what we did. We saved the Blackcoats, after all. But when I think about those buildings exploding, my chest feels empty. In the end, we couldn't fix things with words or ideas. Our only option was to blow it all up, along with the people inside. I hate that we live in a world where violence is so effective. "Up to you," I whisper.

He opens his mouth, then closes it again and simply nods.

*   *   *

The next morning, the Blackcoats assemble in the Hall. They all move in small, shuffling, careful steps, eyes huge and haunted. More than a few are clinging to each other shamelessly, like children lost in the woods. The Mindstorm has rubbed all the sharp edges off them, torn their armor apart, and reduced them to a bunch of shivering kittens.

Less than half our original number remains, though maybe some of the injured are still in the med wing. I scan the group for familiar faces, wondering how many have survived; I spot Shana, though I can't see Noelle anywhere. And there's Ian, bruised and shaken but otherwise none the worse for wear. I find my way over to him, interlace my fingers with his, and clutch his hand. We don't talk, just stand side by side, staring straight ahead. There are no words.

Steven climbs onto the stage. His face is drawn and ashen, but he looks remarkably collected, all things considered. "By now, you probably all know what happened. This was an attack by IFEN. They used some kind of new secret weapon—Mindstorm—to screw around with our brains and sent in their soldiers to exterminate us."

I have to hand it to him—he has a way of getting to the point.

"Rhee took down most of those soldiers, at the cost of her own life." His voice grows a little husky, and he clears his throat. "She was able to buy enough time for us to fight back. We're safe now. IFEN headquarters—along with the Mindstorm weapons—has been destroyed. As it turns out, IFEN made a big mistake in attacking us."

He pulls a remote control from his pocket and presses a button. The screen flicks on behind him, displaying images of chaos and destruction in Toronto. The streets are filled with abandoned vehicles. Stores have been broken into and vandalized, and shattered glass litters the sidewalks. A few people wander around with wide-open eyes and mouths, as if they're still not sure who they are or what's happening.

"Apparently, the weapon didn't just affect us, but the whole city," Steven says. "Dozens of civilians flung themselves off of bridges or out of buildings. Needless to say, Canada's not the biggest fan of IFEN right now. The Prime Minister just made an announcement declaring that the URA has violated the international treaty against weapons of warfare and must now be considered an enemy. Several other countries have offered their support of this decision." He pauses. "What this means, basically, is that IFEN—and, by default, the URA's government—is on the

United Nation's shit list. And that means the world is on our side now. Kind of. They're not calling us terrorists anymore. They're calling us a resistance force."

Stunned silence fills the room as the assembled Blackcoats absorb this new information.

I stare at the images on the screen—ambulances wailing through the streets, shots of traumatized people in hospital beds. When IFEN's new Director decided to use Project Mindstormer against us, he probably didn't realize that the weapon would affect all of Toronto. Or maybe he did, and he was so desperate to wipe us out, he didn't care. Either way, the Canadians won't soon forgive this.

If I had pulled that lever sooner, when I first discovered it, none of this would have happened. Rhee would still be alive. Those innocent civilians in Toronto would still be alive. Because I hesitated, they're not.

*   *   *

Over the next few days, I watch the chaos unfold on the giant screen in the Assembly Hall. Now that the National Registry of Mental Health has been obliterated, the URA is in a panicked frenzy. The footage they show—fire, smashed windows, people looting and rioting in the streets—looks like a pre-war documentary.

I haven't seen Aaron since that last announcement. I wonder if he's even still alive.

The Blackcoats in the URA come out of hiding and swarm the streets. There are battles—vicious shootouts between Blackcoats and police, snipers picking people off from windows. In Oceana, one of the five great cities, the Blackcoats seize control, drive out the IFEN sympathizers, and erect a crude government of their own, consisting mostly of militias and common law courts. The media coverage shows them marching in lockstep and adds scary music, just in case we didn't get the message that these are dangerous people.

Meanwhile, IFEN is desperately scrambling to re-establish control. With the computer system wiped out, collars are temporarily disabled, so the government has resorted to imprisoning thousands of people in hastily erected internment camps, with the promise that they'll be freed once the emergency has passed. Blackcoats immediately start attacking the camps and freeing the prisoners, most of whom join their ranks.

It's all-out war.

Steven makes another announcement proposing a new plan: gather up all the supplies we can carry, steal a few cargo trucks, and head for the border, then use the tunnels to get back into the URA and join up with the Blackcoats in Oceana. Join the fight. The plan is met with thunderous applause.

The air has shifted. For the first time since Zebra's death, there's a sense of anticipation, of hope. But it came at a heavy price.

38

"What the hell are you moping about?"

The voice jolts me from my reverie, and I look up, blinking. I'm sitting in the hallway, back pressed against the wall, knees drawn up to my chest. Shana stands before me, hands on her hips.

"I'm not moping. I'm just . . ." I stop myself and cast an annoyed glance at her. "Why do you care, anyway?"

"Because this is our last night in the Citadel. The rest of us are having a party in the mess hall and you're sitting here staring at your stupid hand-stump. Your glassy-eyed face is pissing me off. You look like a dead trout."

I've barely spoken to anyone except Steven over the past few days, but now, something in me snaps. "People are dying in droves, if you didn't notice. Am I supposed to be happy?"

She rolls her eyes. "In case you forgot, this is what we *wanted*. For the first time, there's a chance that our side actually might win. So yes, you *should* be happy. You should be dancing the fucking can-can."

I stare at her in disbelief. "Haven't you seen the footage of what's happening down there in the URA? It's hell."

She snorts. "The URA has been hell for a long time now. Maybe not for your kind, but for the rest of us, this is the first ray of real hope we've had in years. Yeah, people are dying, and that sucks, but has there ever been a war where innocent people didn't die? We have the chance to create a world that's actually worth living in, a world that's not complete and utter shit. And you're sitting around here stewing. What the hell is wrong with you?"

I look away. Of course, she doesn't know that Steven and I are responsible for setting off the bombs. Most of the Blackcoats assume the explosions were something programmed by Zebra before his death.

And then a thought occurs. Is Shana actually trying to comfort me?

"Look, if you want to sit here and marinate in misery, that's your business. I'm just saying. People keep asking where you are." A pause. "Steven's there, too. Remember him? Your Pookie? God knows what he sees in you, but he's annoying as hell when you're not around. He acts like some mopey, lovesick puppy."

"He does?"

"You didn't know this? You're even thicker than I thought."

Warmth rises into my cheeks. Steven's been withdrawn and quiet over the past few days, even when we're alone, and I know he's feeling the effects of this as much as I am. He's probably not in the mood to celebrate either, but still, he came to the party. The least I can do is be there at his side. Slowly, I push myself to my feet. "Fine. I'll come."

"Try to contain your excitement."

I follow her down the hall. My mind seems to be floating somewhere outside my body. From ahead, I can hear the sound of laughter and voices raised in song. An old song, one I haven't heard outside of historical documentaries: "From every mountainside, let freedom ring!"

Someone shouts, "Here's to the new American Revolution!"

Whoops and applause.

"I'm not going to say thank you, you know," Shana says.

"For what?"

"I never asked you to save me, that time. So if you're waiting around for that—"

"What, the hostage exchange? I wasn't expecting any thanks."

She stomps along, hands shoved in her pockets. "You probably did it just so you could feel smug and superior afterward."

Is it my imagination, or are things different between us now? Her verbal abuse seems less abusive, more like an inside joke, of sorts. "You're right," I say, very seriously. "I did."

She blinks, caught off guard. Then a tiny smile tugs at one corner of her mouth. It's fleeting, but it's something.

"Shana, can I ask you a question?"

"It better not be some self-righteous philosophical shit."

"No. About your holomask. What kind of rodent are you supposed to be?"

She gives me an utterly scandalized look. "I'm not a *rodent*. I'm a honey badger. They're the meanest animals that ever lived. They'll take on a lion. They eat poisonous snakes and bees. If you mess with one, they'll bite your fucking face off. And don't you forget it."

I turn my face aside to hide a smile. "I won't."

We keep walking. In the mess hall, the Blackcoats have broken into a rousing chorus of "The Star-Spangled Banner," another song I haven't heard outside of the occasional history lesson. "*And the rockets' red glare, the bombs bursting in air . . .*" A song about war. Maybe that's why it always struck me as a little bit sad—but still beautiful, somehow. War is always ugly and brutal, yet there *are* things worth fighting and dying for. Worth killing for.

IFEN has always taught us that human history, with its numerous conflicts, is largely a product of mental illness. But maybe they see human nature itself as fundamentally ill. On some unconscious level, I always accepted that—the idea that all our problems could be framed in terms of symptoms and brain scans.

Except that's not how true understanding works. To understand someone, you have to throw away your delusions of objectivity and immerse yourself in their world, to see through their eyes and feel through their skin, even when their actions horrify you. It's not an easy thing for anyone to do. I'm still not comfortable with the Blackcoats—not entirely—but I feel like I *get* them now, at least a little.

A knot in the core of my chest loosens. For the first time since I pulled that lever, I start to feel like maybe I didn't make a mistake. Maybe this will all work out for the better.

Even so, there's a dead spot deep inside me, a small pocket of emptiness. It will probably always be there. What I did can never be erased. I will carry it inside me for the rest of my life.

When we reach the mess hall, talk and laughter envelops me. Three tables have been pushed together in the middle of the room. A ring of candles flickers atop it, and a huge, three-tiered cake sits in the center, slathered with white frosting and dotted with plump strawberries. There's a plate of eclairs, too, and a huge bowl of chocolate pudding topped with mounds of fluffy whipped cream. The spread is ridiculously lavish, especially considering that our food supplies are finite, but I suppose the occasion calls for it. Ian is passing out slices of cake on plastic plates. He's smiling, which catches me off guard. After the Mindstormer attack, I'd privately wondered if any of us would ever smile again.

Shana grabs a plate and starts shoveling cake into her mouth, dismissing me. I spot Steven sitting at the end of the table, and all other thoughts fall away. He stares into space, a plastic cup of golden liquid in one hand, an untouched slice of cake sitting on a plate in front of him. His hair is mussed, his cheeks flushed. I wave. His gaze connects with mine.

I approach. A few hands slap my back in greeting, but I ignore them, my gaze fixed on Steven. The candlelight reflects in his eyes and on his hair. "You came," he says, almost shyly.

"Of course I did. I wasn't about to miss the fun."

Someone passes me a half-filled cup—whiskey, from the smell. I open my mouth, intending to politely turn it down, then stop. Oh, why not? How often do I get to celebrate the dawn of a new era? I tip my head back and take a swig. The whiskey burns my throat, and I cough and splutter.

Steven sits up straighter, alarm flashing across his face. "Lain, are you—"

"Fine," I gasp. Do people really *like* this stuff? My eyes are watering, but I smile and raise my cup high into the air. "To America!"

"*To America!*" everyone thunders back. They break into another rousing verse of "The Star-Spangled Banner." Only half the people singing seem to know the lyrics, and the others are faking it, but no one seems to mind. They stand with their arms slung around each other and their cups upraised, swaying to the melody.

I sit next to Steven and take another swig from my cup. I'm prepared for it this time, so I don't cough. The taste is still foul, but I like the way it feels in my stomach, warm and tingly. Like fire spreading through my middle, making me glow.

The flush in his face brightens as he gazes at me. "You're so pretty," he whispers.

"You're drunk," I whisper back.

He gives me a lopsided smile. "You should take advantage of me."

I let out a small, breathless laugh. He *does* look adorable like this, with his cheeks pink and his eyes all sparkly and heavy-lidded from the whiskey. I reach up, take his face between my hands, and kiss him full on the lips. The crowd cheers and wolf-whistles. I ignore them and keep kissing Steven, slowly and thoroughly. I pull back, breathless, to tuck a curl of hair behind his ear. My hand brushes against his dark coat, which is open, revealing the T-shirt beneath. I slide a hand over his chest and feel his heart beating under my palm. "Have I ever told you how handsome you look in this coat?"

His heartbeat quickens. His eyes take on a smoky glint. "Do I?"

"Practically edible." I lean in and nip his ear. The whiskey's made me bolder than usual. I should probably be careful with that stuff.

For a few minutes, we take turns feeding each other bites of cake, which is sticky-sweet and filled with strawberry cream. Steven gets a bit of frosting on the tip of his nose, and I wipe it off with a finger, then lick it clean.

He turns his head and places his lips against my ear. "Let's get out of here."

We slip out of the mess hall. It's not difficult—the crowd's attention has already shifted away from us, though a few more wolf-whistles follow us out, making me blush. As we step into the hallway, Steven stumbles, and I hook an arm around him. He leans against me, his head lolling on my shoulder. We keep walking, and his feet seem to go in every direction. "You are very drunk," I say.

"'M fine. Jusht—just need a second." He slumps against the wall, hiccups, and clamps a hand over his mouth.

"I think you need to lie down."

I help him back to his room and ease him into bed. I start to pull the covers over him, but he catches my wrist and brings my hand to his lips. He kisses each of my fingertips, then the center of my palm, then nuzzles into my hand like a cat. "Stay with me," he whispers. He slips his arms around my waist, looking up at me with those soft, hungry eyes. His lips are still damp from whiskey and kissing, slightly redder than usual. He looks so beautiful, and at the same time, so lost.

I take off my shoes and lie down in bed next to him. "I'll stay."

He relaxes against me, eyes slipping shut. He pulls me closer, but then he just presses his face against my neck, hiding there.

"What happens when all this is over?" he asks quietly. His slur has disappeared, and I wonder if he was pretending to be drunker than he is. Maybe he just wanted an excuse to get away from the party.

"The war, you mean?"

"Everything."

I swallow. Gently, I touch the soft, warm skin at the nape of his neck, where his hair is a little longer and curls just slightly. "I don't know. But we'll figure something out."

"Yeah. We made it this far." His hand rests against the small of my back, and his eyes move in little flickers, lingering on each of my features in turn, as if he's trying to burn me into his memory.

I lean my head against his shoulder, breathing in his scent. Rain and smoke and the ocean. Steven. How could I ever have forgotten this? Even now, the memories are in fragments, and I have trouble putting it all in order, but I remember enough to know that he's part of me. He always will be.

We stretch out in his bed, arms around each other. Our bodies are pressed together, so close that I can feel every movement. He brushes a hand along the curve of my neck. In the dim light, I can just make out his features. "You remember the day we met?" he asks. "In the parking lot, outside the school. You were wearing that white winter coat. Your hair was in pigtails, and I remember thinking . . . *God, seriously? Pigtails?*"

"What's wrong with pigtails?"

He laughs. "Nothing. Nothing at all." He rests his cheek against my hair. "All around us, everything was rainy and dirty-looking, but you were so clean, like none of it touched you. It made me . . . I dunno. Angry, almost. That you were here in this shitty school when you could be anywhere you wanted to be. Like you'd come there just to show off how clean and perfect you were. But then I really looked at you, at your eyes. And I saw . . ." He sighs. "Sorry. I'm no good at this stuff."

I prop my cheek against one fist. "I thought you were doing fine."

He drops his gaze, smiling.

"Go on," I say. "You looked at my eyes and you saw?"

"I saw—I dunno. A surprising lack of bullshit, I guess."

"So romantic."

He lets out another short laugh. "I mean, you had that wide-open face and those big eyes, and you were just so . . . nice. But not weak. You called me on my crap, and you were so sharp, and you had this crazy power over me. Not just because you were a Mindwalker. Because you were you. And it scares the hell out of me, but I wouldn't trade it for anything."

"I wish you had told me all this before."

His smile fades, his eyes moving in small flickers as they search my face. "I never have the right words when I need them. I don't know how to make things sound . . . true. Even when they are. I tried to tell you that I wasn't in love with Rhee, but I don't think you believed me."

Yes—I remember that now. He spent so much time talking with her, sitting with her. It hurt me. "Then why . . ."

"Because she and I were alike. She was the way I used to be, I mean, before I met you. She shut herself off from everyone. I wanted to help her. I thought—I thought that I could be like you. That I could save someone."

"But you seemed . . ." My voice wavers a little, despite my efforts. "When you were fighting side by side, you seemed to click. And not just her. You seemed to fit in with the Blackcoats. It was like you didn't need me anymore. And I should have been happy about that, maybe. But I wasn't."

He shrugs. "Sure, I agree with the Blackcoats about a lot of stuff. Maybe too much. At first, it was great to be around people who were just as pissed off about everything as I was, but after a while, it got old. If you let that kind of anger consume you, it burns you out fast." He stares at the ceiling. "Rhee and I, we both

411

need—needed—something to fight for. We both had these empty spaces inside. We couldn't fill each other. I wanted to explain that to you, but I didn't know how. And when I finally did, you were gone."

My pulse drums in my throat. "What am I to you?" I whisper.

"After all this, do you really not know?"

"Tell me."

For a long moment, he's silent. His Adam's apple bobs up and down. "When you got your memories taken away, I knew it would've been better for you to leave you in IFEN headquarters, because as long as you didn't know anything, you were safe. But I couldn't. I'm that selfish. You're the only reason I even bother to keep breathing, and if they take you away, none of it means anything. Without you, the whole world is bullshit." He meets my gaze. "You're everything."

For a moment, I can't breathe.

He brushes a few strands of hair from my face. "It's not fair to you. I know that. You never asked to be the glue holding me together." He lets out a small, choked laugh. "Who the hell would want that?"

"I do," I whisper.

His breath catches. He rests his forehead against my shoulder. "Maybe that's just because I infected you. I knew the first time we met that I was going to get you dirty. Make you sick, like me."

"You aren't sick."

He smiles, eyes filled with pain. "You really believe that?"

I give a small shrug. "Maybe we're all sick."

"Not you."

Abruptly, mind flashes back to the initiation, to Zebra's hand moving under my skin, touching my heart. My secret. A knot fills my throat.

Zebra's dead now, so I'll never get the chance to ask what he saw, but maybe deep down, I've known all along and just didn't want to deal with it. After everything that's happened—after

I essentially blew up the URA's government—it doesn't seem like quite as big a deal. But it still takes an effort to speak the words. "I always told myself that I wanted to become a Mindwalker so I could help people. So I could make the world a better place. But it's not like that." I can't look him in the eye. Heat swarms my chest; there's a squeezing pressure around my lungs.

"What do you mean?" A hint of unease creeps into his tone.

"You asked me once what my drug was, and I told you that it was this. Saving people."

"Well, yeah, you do have kind of a Messiah complex going on. So?"

"It's not that noble." My voice is tiny, barely audible. "It's not that I need to feel like a hero. It's not even self-destructiveness. I'm an emotional vampire. I feed on trauma. I don't help people. I use them. I eat their pain and darkness, because it's what I need."

There's a long pause. I count my heartbeats in the silence.

"Damn," he mutters. "And here I thought I was the regional champion of self-hatred." In the dimness, I can't make out his expression. "Who made you believe this about yourself?"

I turn my face away. "I'm not looking for reassurance. I'm telling you the truth. I'm not what you think, I'm not good—"

"If you're not a good person, then I don't know what the hell a good person is," he says firmly. "You don't have to be perfect. God knows I'm not."

My heartbeat quickens. I close my eyes, feeling the warmth of his breath against my skin.

"If this is something that really bothers you, we can talk about it more, but I want you to know now—whatever secrets you've got, whatever you have inside you that you think is ugly or weird or whatever, I can handle it. Hell, it can't possibly be worse than what you've already seen inside me."

"Are you sure about that?" I whisper.

"Yeah. I'm sure. I want *all* of you, not just the parts that are easy to deal with. I mean, have you not noticed the fact that I'm completely, pathetically, head-over-heels in love with you?"

I try to swallow the tightness in my throat. Maybe he's right. We have something good together. Perhaps this guilt is just the stubborn voice of my Mindwalker training trying to ruin it for me, to pick it apart and frame it as an unhealthy codependence. The way I feel about him does seem too intense to be normal, at times. But who decides where that line is drawn? Can't we just let feelings be feelings, without analyzing where they come from or what they mean? Isn't it enough, sometimes, just to love someone? Or am I still rationalizing?

Even if I am, I don't care.

"I've missed you so much." I gently, carefully touch his face, like he's made of glass or crystal, something precious and delicate. "I hated feeling like we were always apart."

Pain flickers through his eyes. "I'm sorry. I shouldn't have—"

I touch his lips, silencing him.

And then his lips are pressed against mine.

The kiss is cautious at first, experimental; I move my lips against his, seeing what feels right. He tastes clean and warm, and slowly, I start to lose myself in kissing him, and a pleasant vertigo creeps over me. It's like immersion—that warm tingle, starting in my scalp, then slowly spreading through my body. Every nerve is awake. When he pulls back for air, I'm flushed and straining to catch my breath, and my lips are swollen and pleasantly raw.

He looks into my eyes. His calloused thumb touches the corner of my mouth, then feathers across my lower lip. The touch sends an electric current through me. "I still don't know how I got so lucky," he whispers.

His thumb glides across my lower lip again. Does he have any idea how distracting that is? I lick my lower lip, tasting the faint hint of salt left behind by his skin. My eyes have adjusted to the dim light, and I can see one side of his face—the curve of his cheek, the short, pale fringe of his lashes, the shine of his eye. "You're beautiful, you know."

"That's my line."

I rest a hand against the side of his face. His palm slides over my shoulder, down my side, to my hip, as if he's memorizing the shape of me. My hands slips into his hair. "Steven?"

"Yeah?"

"I'm scared."

"Me too," he whispers. "It's okay, though. That's how you know you're alive."

Then his lips meet mine, and for a while, we lose ourselves in each other, exploring each other's bodies in small, careful touches. I can feel the connection between us, like a cord running from his chest into mine, snugly encircling my heart. My fingers wander through the cornsilk forest of his hair, feeling the tiny, rippled, familiar scar on his scalp. His lips touch my neck. "I love you so much. You know that?"

After what I did—*we* did—I have no right to be happy. I know that, and I can feel the weight of the dead like cement in my bones. I'll carry it for the rest of my life. But for now, there's no IFEN, no URA, no Blackcoats. There's only Steven, me, us. "I know," I whisper.

39

We leave the Citadel at dawn and head south.

Stealing the trucks wasn't difficult; with the city still reeling from the aftermath of Mindstormer and the police trying desperately to control a terrified populace, no one tried to stop us. We just hopped the fence around a factory and hotwired a half-dozen vehicles.

I sit in the cargo bed, squeezed in between Steven and Ian, our breaths echoing through the silence. We drive through the night. Once we reach the fence, Steven locates a tunnel, and we file through, emerging into the woods on the other side of the border. Dawn frosts the horizon with pale light, and a crow caws, three harsh, rusty notes. We stumble through the woods, lugging overstuffed supply packs.

Apparently, we're in Upstate New York, just a day's walk from Oceana. By late afternoon, we can see it in the distance—a collection of sharp-edged black skyscrapers, cutting clean silhouettes against the pink blaze of clouds. The city is surrounded by a towering cement wall. As we draw nearer, a gate swings open and a platoon of dusty trucks glides toward us. They're filled with men and women in camouflage vests and pants, all carrying huge rifles.

I clutch Steven's hand, my heartbeat drumming in my finger-tips as the trucks rumble to a stop about thirty feet ahead. The Blackcoats—our Blackcoats—huddle together in a tight knot. A tall, bronze-skinned woman hops out of the truck in front and strides toward us. Her hair is short and bushy, her eyes a pale violet-gray. "Who is the leader?" she calls out in a clear voice.

To my surprise, Ian steps forward. "Sorry, our leaders are all dead. You'll have to talk to me."

She looks him up and down and smiles, showing a row of very white teeth and an unexpected dimple. Then she sticks out a hand. "I'm General Guthry of the North American Alliance. That's what we're calling ourselves now. Pleased to meet you."

Ian hesitates briefly, then shakes her hand.

"You'll be safe here," she says. "Come on. You look like you could use some rest."

We all pile into the trucks. Guthry barks an order, and we head back toward the city. I suppose I should feel something—relief? Nervousness? But I'm just too tired. I sit next to Steven, my head on his shoulder. He slips an arm around me, and I stare at the skyscrapers in the distance, watching them grow larger and closer. It's hard to focus; my vision has gone fuzzy with fatigue. Faintly, I can hear Ian talking to Guthry in the front of the truck, filling her in on our situation.

"What do you think we'll do once we get there?" I murmur.

"I don't know. Just stay here until the war is over, maybe." He looks around at the huddled, hollow-eyed Blackcoats. "I don't think they'll want to keep fighting."

What will happen, I wonder, if their offer to let us stay is conditional upon our willingness to fight? We'll deal with that problem when we get there, I suppose. "What about you?" I ask. "Do you want to keep fighting?"

For a minute, he doesn't respond. He strokes my hair, his fingers warm and gentle. "I never want to touch a gun again," he replies.

Maybe the words should surprise me, but they don't, all things considered.

My eyelids drift shut. I doze, lulled by the rumble of the truck and by Steven's heartbeat. I don't know what will happen to us now, but then, no one ever knows what the future will bring.

We're alive. We're together. And there's one thing I'm certain of—no matter what happens, I'm never going to leave his side again.

EPILOGUE

I open my eyes and stare at my bedroom. Sunlight filters in through the pink curtains, illuminating the familiar walls, the desk, the row of stuffed animals on the shelf.

It's still strange, sometimes, to wake up in my old room in the house I once shared with Father. As if none of it ever happened. I'm fortunate that this place even survived the war; many parts of Aura had to be rebuilt. When I first returned, most of the appliances had been looted and the food in the pantry was gone, but aside from some gouges in the wall and a few scrawls of graffiti, the house itself was untouched. There are mornings when the war feels like a dream. But if I want proof that it was real, all I have to do is glance at my right hand.

Slowly, I clench and flex the artificial fingers. It responds exactly like the old one. The doctors told me that they could make it look like a real one, too—the most advanced prosthetics are indistinguishable from real limbs—but I chose a jet-black model with red stripes running along the fingers. I didn't want to pretend.

For a few minutes, I watch the dust motes spiral in the sunlight. "Chloe," I say.

She appears at the foot of my bed in a flurry of sparkles. "Good morning, Lain! What can I do for you?"

She's not exactly the way she was before—occasionally, I'll notice small differences in her responses and personality—but she's pretty close. Since Dr. Swan destroyed the original, I had her programming reconstructed. "What time is it?"

"One thirty in the afternoon."

I wince. I really should start setting an alarm. "Could you send a message to Steven's phone? Tell him that I'll meet him in the Underwater Café after his training."

"Certainly."

Slowly, I slide out of bed and get dressed.

It's been three years since Steven and I fled to Oceana with the other Blackcoats, two years since the war ended. The tide turned quickly once Canada lent its support to the rebels. The Canadian government offered a fast track to citizenship for any refugee who joined the military, and their ranks swelled. IFEN—weakened and fragmented—was quickly overwhelmed, and a provisional government was formed by the North American Alliance. All that feels like such a long time ago, now. Another life, almost.

"Don't forget your medication," Chloe chirps.

I roll my eyes. "I never forget them." I head into the bathroom and open the medicine cabinet. The amber bottles stand in a row—the one on the left is for anxiety, the next one over is an antidepressant, the third is a mood stabilizer, and the fourth . . . honestly, I've forgotten what that one does. The fifth is vitamin D, because I don't get enough sunlight these days. I open the bottles one by one and shake the appropriate dosages into my palm.

The nightmares and panic attacks began shortly after we returned to the URA. That dead spot deep inside my chest—the one that settled in after I pulled the lever and blew up IFEN—slowly grew into a vast void. A voice in my head kept whispering, *What right do you have to be happy, after what you did?* I knew that such thinking didn't do any good, and I tried to fight it, to cling to the knowledge of everything we accomplished. But still, the darkness crept through me, poisoning my thoughts. I spent so many nights crying or lost in a numb haze of depression, until finally, Steven convinced me to seek treatment.

Psychopharmaceuticals aren't as effective as Conditioning, but I've decided I'm never going back into a Conditioning unit as long as I live. I've resigned myself to the fact that I'll probably be taking this cocktail of drugs for the rest of my life. Oh, well. There are worse things than swallowing a few pills every day.

"You should go outside today!" Chloe calls cheerfully from the bedroom. "You'll be glad you did!"

I sigh. Sometimes, I wish I hadn't programmed so many reminders and pep talks into her. "I'll take a walk after breakfast." There's a place I want to visit, anyway.

I eat a slice of cold leftover pizza, then shrug into my black leather coat—it's the one Rhee gave me back in the Citadel, the one with the bullet hole—and leave the house. The day is bright and breezy, the sky a warm, innocent blue dotted with clouds. Birds sing in the trees. Sunny days annoy me; they feel sardonic, somehow, like the weather is mocking me. I want rain. Or at least some dark clouds.

I walk with my hands shoved into my pockets and my gaze downcast. My hair has grown out, and it hangs around my face in a loose, unkempt curtain, shielding me from the view of passers-by. My feet carry me to the mono station, and I take the train downtown.

The city of Aura is the same as ever, at least superficially. Oh, there's some damage from the war, a few crumbled buildings, but the worst of it has been repaired, the glass and ashes swept up, the bloodstains scrubbed away. Video advertisements still dance across the sides of skyscrapers. No more Somnazol ads, though. Here and there, screens display propaganda for the North American Alliance, and it's not uncommon to see Alliance militias patrolling the streets. But by and large, life goes on.

From the corner of my eye, I glimpse a familiar face, and I halt. Aaron Freed—Dr. Swan's former protégé, the boy I interrogated in the Citadel—smiles from a video poster, dressed up in an expensive suit and tie. He's put on a little weight since I last saw him. *Need help? You're not alone! PhrenTech is a privately owned mental health service. We offer free, anonymous counseling sessions and a legal guarantee that your medical data will be deleted after treatment. Learn more online.* A Net address scrolls across the bottom.

Funny, I never pegged Aaron as an entrepreneur, but he's done pretty well for himself. The void left by IFEN is now filled by dozens of small clinics offering pills, cognitive therapy, Conditioning, and even Mindwalking. The downside is that they're not very well regulated. They run the gamut from highly professional and impeccably ethical (always more expensive) to shady fly-by-night operations offering cheap, shoddy services to desperate people. There was a case last year of someone getting brain damage from a sloppy neural modification. That company went out of business pretty quickly, but the hapless patient still can't control the left side of his body.

I keep walking until I come to a park, an expanse of green amid concrete and metal. A low stone wall surrounds the rectangle of grass, which is larger than a football field.

It's still hard to believe, sometimes, that this is where IFEN headquarters stood. What was once a prominent and easily recognizable part of Aura's skyline is now an empty gap. There was talk, for a while, of erecting another building in its place, but the new government decided against it.

A marble sign near the front reads ELIZABETH BRANDEN MEMORIAL PARK—named after Steven's friend, Lizzie. Beneath the words are listed the full names of all the children who died in the St. Mary's experiments. There are others, too, below them. Hundreds of tiny names, some living, some dead, all people who suffered at the hands of IFEN, victims who remained unrecognized before now. Rhee's name is there, lost among the others.

Standing before me, rising from the center of the neatly mown expanse of grass, is a work of abstract art—a huge, glittering silver ring with a gap near the top, as if it were forcibly pried open. Closer examination reveals that it's actually fashioned out of thousands of discarded collars. The sunlight strikes it, making it glow like a beacon. On a silver plaque set into the base of the statue are inscribed the words: *Thou shalt not be a victim, thou shalt not be a perpetrator, but, above all, thou shalt not be a bystander.* It's a quote from a long-dead historian named Yehuda Bauer, referring to another dark time in human history.

I sit on the sun-warmed grass and stare at the words.

The public still doesn't know that Steven and I were the ones who triggered the bombs that wiped out IFEN. There's been endless speculation and investigation, but it remains one of those great unsolved mysteries for the ages. Reporters have approached me—my friends, too—but we've refused to speak about our time with the Blackcoats. We all want to be left alone, to heal in private, not to be the focus of a media circus.

I'm a hypocrite, I know. After all, I'm the one who exposed the truth about St. Mary's, and here I am, hiding my own sins from public scrutiny. But if there's one thing I can say for myself, it's this—I wasn't a bystander. When I had the choice to act, to strike a blow against the system, I acted. I can't regret that, no matter the cost. But I can't shed the guilt, either.

"Hey . . . are you Lain Fisher?"

I look up. A girl, a few years younger than me, stands there looking at me curiously. She's dressed in a school uniform, and she wears her hair in pigtails, the way I used to.

I pick myself up, brush the loose bits of grass from the seat of my jeans, and reply, "I'm nobody." Before she can respond, I turn and walk out of the park. I feel her gaze on my back, and panic builds in my chest, pressing against my lungs. I hurry down the street until I'm out of sight, then lean against a rough brick wall. I count my breaths, keeping my mind blank, and the rope around my lungs loosens.

I've gotten good at staving off the panic attacks. Sometimes, I think that's the only thing I've accomplished in the past three years. I start walking again, keeping my head down, and catch a glimpse of my reflection in a window. My hair is a mess, my skin too pale, and there are purplish bags under my eyes. I'm wearing old jeans and a faded, oversized T-shirt with a stain near the hem. I'm amazed that girl even recognized me.

At some point, I'll have to start doing something with my life aside from merely surviving each day and giving myself a meta-phorical gold star every time I make it through another twenty-four hours without having an emotional meltdown. I should probably at least finish high school and take a few college courses so I can get a decent job. I'm not going back to Mindwalking. I refuse to touch anyone's mind with these bloodstained hands. I'll be a dental hygienist or something. Wouldn't that surprise everyone. Lain Fisher, the girl who exposed IFEN's dark deeds to the world and fled to Canada to join the rebellion, cleaning people's teeth.

But even if I did get a job, I'm pretty sure it would just feel like going through the motions. The government gave me a good-sized chunk of money in recompense for all the hardship I've been through—a PR stunt, mainly, but still appreciated. Numerous other survivors, including Ian and Steven, received compensation as well. I don't *need* to work. But now I fill my days with long, aimless walks and painting.

I make my way toward the Underwater Café and seat myself at an empty booth, where I drink cup after cup of chai and absent-mindedly read through emails on my cell phone. There's one from Ian: a picture of him holding up his new puppy, a Shiba Inu with large, quizzical brown eyes. *I think he looks like you*, says the message.

A faint smile touches my lips. Ian's doing well, it seems. He has a minor position in the new government. During the war, he stepped up and made some tactical suggestions that earned him a lot of points with the higher-ups. We still have lunch together sometimes, but there's a distance between us now, unspoken but unmistakable. He doesn't know what I did. I could never bring myself to tell him.

I scroll down. There's another message from earlier in the day, also from Ian: *Are you ever going to show me your paintings?*

I send a reply: *They're pretty ugly.*

A response comes almost immediately: *I bet you're better than you think.*

I actually *have* gotten pretty good, but it's not about my skill level. The paintings are ugly because they represent what's in my mind—amorphous swirls of red and gray forming screaming faces, angry, jagged black lines slashed in a chaotic frenzy, buildings exploding into orange blossoms. Scenes of fire, of death. I keep them locked in the secret room that once held my Gate, which I now use as my studio.

I started painting soon after the war. When the depression set in, I saw a psychiatrist, who recommended a hobby as an outlet. At first, I did it grudgingly, but as time went on I found myself spending hours each day in my studio, losing myself in the thick swirls of paint.

"Have I ever told you that you look good in black?"

I look up to see Steven leaning against the booth, arms crossed over his chest. A faint smile tugs at my lips. "Have I ever told you that you look good in white?"

He glances down at himself. "I still feel weird wearing the robe. Like I'm dressed up as a monk for Halloween, or something." He makes a face, tugs at the collar of his Mindwalker's robe and sits across from me. "I seriously think more people would join this program if the outfits were cooler."

I let out a tiny laugh. I'm surprised that I can still laugh, after everything. Some days, I'm surprised that I'm still breathing. "If a Mindwalker can't handle looking a little unfashionable, they're probably not tough enough for the job."

"*Touché.*"

I tuck my phone into my pocket. "So, how's your training coming along?"

"It's . . . hard." He exhales a careful, controlled breath. "But I'm holding together." A smile quirks at one corner of his mouth. "I've had a lot of practice dealing with bad memories."

Still, I can see the toll it's taking on him, the lines around his eyes and mouth. I know, firsthand, how brutal the immersion sessions can be. I still remember the shock I felt when Steven announced that he wanted to be a Mindwalker. Given the horrors that IFEN put him through, it seemed like the absolute last thing he should want to do with his life.

Or maybe it's not so surprising. After all, it was a Mindwalker who accepted him when no one else would. And he's not working for IFEN, since it doesn't exist anymore; he's with a company called Healing Springs. One of the better places, definitely.

Of course, something like this wouldn't have been possible for Steven under the old order. He would have been ineligible for the job because of his Type. Now, everyone gets a fresh start. People who previously would have been barred from becoming doctors, lawyers or politicians suddenly have the chance to pursue their dreams. Most people had their collars removed after IFEN's computers were bombed, rendering the technology ineffective—and now, people can only be collared after committing a violent crime. The collar is removed after a certain number of years, unless they commit another crime in the interim. No one wanted to go back to the old system of prisons, so this was the compromise. It's not perfect, but it's an improvement.

"I wonder what Rhee would think of all this," I murmur.

Steven places a hand over mine.

Though I can sense pressure, heat and cold with my artificial hand, it's not quite the same as the original. The computerized nerves, however sophisticated, are only an imitation. I can feel the shape of his fingers, but not the texture of his skin.

A lump swells in my throat, and I choke it down. "It's strange. While she was alive, I never felt close to her, except for that moment at the end. I mean . . . she was always so distant, like she didn't need anyone. I think I was jealous of her, more than anything, because I thought she was stronger than me. But now that she's gone . . ." I don't have to finish the sentence, because I know Steven feels the same way. Not a day goes by when I don't think about her, at least for a moment or two.

He wraps his fingers around my wrist, pulls my right hand to his mouth, and kisses the artificial knuckles. The sensors register pressure and warmth. "We're alive," he says. "That counts for something, right?"

"Yes. It does."

As long as you have a purpose, you can keep living, no matter what horrors you've endured. That's what the Blackcoats have taught me—what Rhee taught me.

What is my purpose, now?

"Hey," Steven says, "I'm starved. Want to order something?"

"Maybe a tuna sandwich."

Right now, I decide, my purpose is to have a good lunch, and then to finish the painting I started yesterday—a blood-red sunrise over a forest of naked white trees.

Keep living. Keep moving forward into the future, step by step, toward the hazy silhouette of a better tomorrow. It's all we can do.

It's all anyone can do.

*   *   *

That night, we lie together under the covers. We've been living together for almost a year now, though his schedule is so busy that I often have the house to myself for long stretches of time. His warm, naked skin is pressed to my back, his leg hooked over my waist, his breath soft on my neck.

"Will you marry me?" he asks, his lips moving against my cheek.

My breath catches. It's not the first time he's asked, but I've never been able to answer. I don't know what holds me back. True, we're still young, but we've both learnt how short and fragile life is. And I can't imagine spending my life with anyone other than Steven.

I can feel his disappointment at my silence.

I look around my room—our room, since he sleeps here too. It hasn't changed much since I was thirteen. In some ways, despite everything I've been through, I still feel stuck at that age. Maybe I never really got over Father's death. My artificial hand clenches into a fist.

There've been times when I've thought about asking Steven to erase it all. All the struggles, all the pain. But that would mean forgetting him as well, and that's unacceptable.

"I'm not well enough yet," I say. It's what I said last time too. "Right now, I'm not living, I'm just surviving. You've got enough problems of your own. I don't want to saddle you with mine, too. Before I make that sort of commitment, I want to be totally healed."

He breathes a small sigh. "No one is ever totally healed, Lain. Do you think I am?"

"You're doing better than me." It comes out sounding like an accusation. "I'm not—" I swallow the words *good enough*. "I'm not ready. I have to focus on myself right now. On getting better."

There's a long silence. "It's your choice," he says at last.

I wonder how many years I'll continue giving him that line. And I know it's stupid, because we're already living like a married couple. It's just a matter of signing a piece of paper, yet somehow,

I can't take that final step. I can't chain him to me. I can already see our future. He'll become a pillar of the community, respected by all, and I'll be the crazy wife hiding out in the basement with her crazy paintings and having conversations with her holo-cat. I'll be the one people whisper about at parties, shaking their heads sadly. *Such a shame . . . but she's so lucky to have someone so selfless to take care of her.* That's not what I want us to become.

And then I wonder, suddenly, if that was how Steven felt back when he was the crazy one. Was that why he spent so much time pushing me away? Because he didn't want to become my obligation?

When will we learn?

"Steven . . ." I stop and take a breath. "Yes."

His muscles stiffen against me. His heartbeat speeds. "You mean . . ."

"Yes. What the hell. Let's get married. If you've decided you want to spend the rest of your life with a certified lunatic, then who am I to deny—"

He presses his lips against mine and kisses me deeply and thoroughly, as if we're kissing for the first time. We come up for air, gasping and flushed, and then kiss some more.

Later, we lie together, bathed in cooling sweat and floating in a sweet daze. Steven's hands move through my hair, and I smile. For the moment, at least, it's good to be alive. I think that maybe I want to start showing my paintings to people. Or at least one or two of the best ones.

This is how healing happens—bit by bit, in moments so small and ordinary, you almost don't notice them. It happens every time you wake up and decide to stay alive for another day.

Maybe we never get better, not completely. But we keep healing.